the Sins of the Father

Annie Whitehead

Published in 2021 by FeedARead.com Publishing

A CIP catalogue record for this title is available from the British Library.

7th Century
Britain

PICTS

DALRIADA

STRATHCLYDE

LOTHIAN

BERNICIA

RHEGED

MAN

DEIRA

ANGLESEY

ELMET

PECSÆTE

GWYNEDD   WRECONSÆTE

LINDSEY

POWYS

MERCIA

MAGONSÆTE

MIDDLE
ANGLES

EAST
ANGLES

AROSÆTE

GWENT

HWICCE

CHILTERNSÆTE

EAST
SAXONS

WEST SAXONS

KENT

0   20   40   80 KM

Royal Houses Family Tree

Mercia

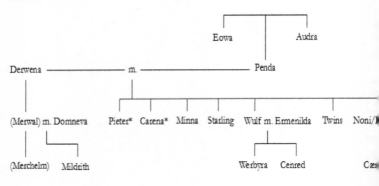

Northumbria

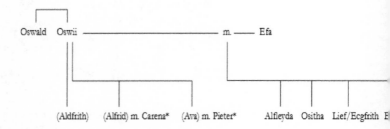

( ) = by a previous partner

Real historical names in Author's Notes

Chapter One

Mercia AD658

The attackers moved softly and swiftly, holding only small hand knives. Stepping over the withy-hurdle fencing, glad to be standing up after hiding all day, they made their way to the great hall, sidling along, staying close to the low eaves. In the gloom, one of them did not see a discarded willow basket. It clattered with the kick, disgorging its contents of what sounded like small metal items, perhaps keys, spoons, or brooches. They all stood still.

Nothing stirred, no animals cried, and they moved on, steps taken even more cautiously now. The leader stopped at the corner of the building, peering round. The gabled entrance prevented his view of the door but there were two guards seated on a long bench to the side of it. He ducked back and held up two fingers to his waiting band. He gestured that one of them should double back and come at the gabled doorway from the other direction, and they waited. Across the yard, moths were flitting in and out of the night-flowering white campion. The faint sound of oxen in the shippen sent low rumbles through the night air. For a moment, all was calm.

An owl-like cry: a signal that the other man was now positioned on the other side. The leader and his second slipped round the edge of the building, coming up behind the guards and stemming any alarm calls by slitting their throats. They held the bodies as they slumped, letting go only when they hit the earth. Silence was still imperative.

The rest of the warband came from the side of the building, and they gathered in front of the door. With all those inside asleep on the benches, it was a work of moments to send them all to permanent slumber. The hearth fire had been banked, and in the soft glow of its remaining light, the bodies resembled shadows. Wiping his blade on his sleeve, the second looked to the leader. "What now?"

The leader cast a glance at the hall full of dead men, who never saw their assailants, who were not given a chance to fetch their weapons. "Now," he said, "we go and get the youngling."

Powys, Wales

He had thought he would be safe. Last night Sikke had told him that ale made a man sleep heavily, so Noni had drunk enough to fill his bladder three times over. He'd staggered to his bed but had not been drunk enough to need carrying, and therein maybe lay the fault, for the nightmare came back.

Sometimes Noni knew he was dreaming, but at other times it felt all too real. He could feel his nails digging into his palms as he made impotent fists. He saw every swish of the woman's cloak as she made her way towards the big man who was standing with a sword in his hand. A little boy was with her, and he looked up at her as if uncertain. She nodded, gestured that he should go to the man, and then she seemed to change her mind, for she bent down low and hugged him into the folds of her cloak. The boy responded, putting his small arms around her waist. She straightened, pushed the boy gently ahead of her, and then stepped forward again. The big man shoved the boy none too gently into the grasp of a guard. He raised his sword. The patterned blade glinted in the torchlight, then the weapon sliced through the air. Noni screamed and felt the press of strong fingers gripping his shoulder and dragging him away so that he lost his balance and half-ran, half-stumbled.

In his dream, the scene always faded here to black and he awoke, drenched in sweat and crying, mumbling the same word that had tumbled from his mouth that night three years ago. "Mother."

Sikke was by his bedside. "You are safe, little Lord."

Noni sat up and wiped his face with his hand. "I saw it again."

"Yes. I heard you call out." Sikke sat down, cross-legged as he always did, on the floor beside Noni's bed, back straight, big shoulders relaxed, speaking only when required. The Frisian had been a calming presence for so long now that Noni couldn't remember a time when he wasn't there. He'd served Noni's mother, and before that his father's cousin. He was not yet grey-haired but must be as old as the mountains themselves. Over his linen shirt, Sikke had on his otter fur jerkin, and Noni could not recall a single occasion when the big man hadn't worn it, although these days it was looking a little moth-eaten.

A candle had already been lit but placed on the table on the far side of the room, where it gave only a comforting glow. Sikke knew not to shine a light upon Noni's face, for the close brightness often scared him, making the shadows darker beyond the flame.

Noni lay back, thinking that he at least ought to attempt to recapture his sleep. Morning was still some distance away, for there were no chinks of light creeping through the edges of the shutters, and the hall, only the other side of the wooden partition, was almost silent, save for the occasional grunt or snore of sleeping men. Noni's chest tightened, and a light pain travelled up towards his mouth, arriving as an ale-flavoured belch. "I shall not heed you next time you try to ply me with drink."

7

Sikke's mouth twitched. "No, little Lord."

"Will you stay until daybreak?"

"If I am needed."

Noni opened his mouth to respond, then closed it again. He had been but a child when they first sought refuge in the lands of the Welsh, but now having seen his fourteenth summer, he was straddling the chasm between boyhood and manhood. How could he be a man yet still be frightened of the dark?

Sikke had been the one gripping his shoulder that night, pulling him to safety. Noni thought that Sikke's brother had been there too, and Noni had never seen him again. He had been only small when his mother was killed, too young to fight, and others had laid down their lives for him. Three years in hiding, reminded of his status as a member of the ruling Iclinga tribe of Mercia, and yet with no sense of living like a lord, much less the son of a king, made him humble and left him ever wondering why men should wish to serve him so.

He closed his eyes, hoping that if he breathed calmly his mind would begin to drift. He waited for the moment when thoughts became less lucid, to be replaced by dreamlike images, but was distracted by what sounded like hoofbeats. He shifted in his bed, turning onto his side, assuming that the noise was the rush of his blood pumping into his ears and that it would cease to be so noticeable if he jammed one ear hard against the pillow. But the noise did not go away, growing louder until it blended with raised voices, both from inside the hall and out. Dogs began to bark, he heard the rush of running footsteps on the hall floor and, as he sat up, he saw the flicker of lights licking the edges of the shutters.

Sikke had already unsheathed his knife and was standing by the door, one ear pressed against it. He put his free hand to his mouth, signalling Noni to be silent, then opened the door and edged his way carefully into the hall.

Now Noni's heart really was pounding, as if it wanted to jump up and out of his mouth. His clothes were strewn across the room, tunic on the wooden chest, breeches on the floor, leg bindings in a knot beside them, but his belt was nowhere to be seen and he had no weapon to hand. He tried to think where he had left his knife the previous evening after Sikke had been teaching him to whittle, belatedly realising that he had left it in the hall, embedded in the table when he'd vented his frustration at not being able to carve like his teacher. All that stood between him and the attackers was Sikke. He waited.

The noise continued but did not sound like armed combat. Voices were no longer raised, but reduced to a low rumble, punctuated every so often by a shout and then, after a short while, by laughter. Noni got out of bed, gathering up his clothes and dressing, before venturing towards the door. He put out a tentative hand and nearly had it bent backwards when the door flew open.

Breathing heavily, the stranger glanced once around the room and then said, "Lord Ethelred?"

Noni had not been called that name in a long time, if at all. He was the ninth of his mother's children, hence the nickname, and Sikke only ever called him his little Lord. He nodded.

"Good," said the stranger. "Your brother Wulf has overthrown the Northumbrians who claimed our land for themselves. He is now king and bade us fetch you." The man sank down on one knee and bowed his head. "Lord, allow us to escort you home to Mercia."

They rode out not long after dawn, when the breeze was still chilly enough to drain the blood from fingertips and the horses' breath showed cloudy in the air. Noni was glad of the sheep's wool stuffed into the bottom of his shoes.

Edbert, for that was the stranger's name, rode at the head of the group with Sikke, as always, alongside Noni. They had changed location often in the last three years and he'd got used to life on the move but, as they said farewell to their latest hosts, Noni had taken sad leave of his friend Rhiryd, who was younger than him but had provided much-needed companionship as well as helping to improve Noni's Welsh. It might have surprised the Northumbrians, who'd no doubt searched for them, that the fugitives were so close to the border; only a day's ride would see them, Sikke told him that morning, overnighting at Noni's eldest brother Merwal's house at Hereford.

Merwal was, in fact, his much older half-brother and Noni had seen little of him in the years leading up to his exile. His stomach fluttered at the thought of seeing Merwal again, but Edbert slowed his horse and, once Noni came alongside him, said, "Lord Merwal is not here; he has ridden to join the king."

Keen though he was to be reunited with his kin, part of Noni was relieved that he would have another night to gather his thoughts and feelings. More than one of his elder siblings had left home when he was still small. He remembered some more than others and did not know yet what had become of any of them after he and his mother had fled.

The little boy who had been with them that night was the son of Oswii of Northumbria, who had waged war on Penda, Noni's father, even after having given over his son to the Mercians as a surety for keeping the peace. Penda responded by riding north, leading a mighty army from all the southern kingdoms opposed to Oswii's aggression, but had lost at the battle of Winwæd. Noni's mother had gone to return the heir of Northumbria, believing, wrongly, that a man's love for his child would see her go free.

As he dismounted and prepared to go inside, Noni took a

deep breath. His mother's last moments were still clear in his mind, yet with so many blank spaces where other memories should be, and so many unanswered questions, freedom felt almost more intimidating than exile.

Merwal's hall was more richly decorated than some of the places he'd called home in recent months. The floor was lined with wood, rather than packed earth, and carvings laced around all the upright columns and snaked across the supporting beams. The interweaving animal motifs were brightly painted, and huge embroidered hangings lined all the walls. The fire gave a welcoming glow and Noni stopped in front of it, sniffing to ascertain the fragrance given off by the flames.

"It is from our apple trees. The small sour ones."

Noni turned at the sound of the female voice and saw a woman whom he thought was Merwal's wife. The keys and small relic box hanging from her belt announced her status. "Efi?"

The woman smiled and put a finger to her necklace of shell beads, something else which was somehow familiar. "Efi," she repeated. "Your kin's name for me. I have not heard it in a long while." She stepped forward, her kirtle making a soft swishing sound but her slippers noiseless on the floorboards. She took his hands in hers and kissed his cheek. She smelled of herb water, a scent which he could not name but which evoked something from the past. "You will be told this many times in the coming few weeks, but I shall say it first. You have grown up, little Noni. Praise God that you are returned to us."

Noni had received little in the way of religious instruction, but he nodded. "I never thought to see any of my kin again." The last word was uneven in pitch and tone, but whether this was emotion choking him, or the now frequent cracking of his voice, he could not be sure. He tried to think of the last time he had seen his half-brother's wife and he

11

cast a glance around the hall.

She released his hands. "You are looking for the children."

Noni nodded.

"This is the first of the bad tidings you will hear. My dear little son was taken from us last year, before he had even seen his fifth summer." She shook her head. "No, say naught, for you will bring on yet more of my tears."

Noni swallowed hard. He would not cry; if this woman could be strong in the face of grief, then so could he.

"I still have my little Mildrith whom you must meet and," she patted her stomach, "soon she will have a brother or sister. My stepson is also well, and you will see him when you arrive at Wulf's hall."

He remembered her stepson, his nephew Merchelm, who was close to him in age. As little boys, they had both called her Efi. Perhaps, he thought now, it was not proper, for he was no longer a child, and she was the daughter of a king of Kent. "Lady, what name are you really known by?"

With her hand at his elbow, directing him to the dais beyond the central hearth, she said, "I was known as the Domne Eafe, which became Efi in your young speech, but most folk call me Domneva." She stopped and hugged him, and he mused that it was his first real touch from another person in three years that was anything more meaningful than a friendly slap on the back. "Ah, it is good to see you," she said into his shoulder. Releasing him from her embrace, she bade him sit in the carved chair on the dais. "Merwal will not mind," she said, and gestured to a servant to bring them some ale.

Edbert, having overseen the stabling of the horses, came to join them and as he gave his report to Domneva, who was keen to know how things were in the Welsh settlements over the border, Noni stared out at the hall, and tried to bring forth some long-forgotten details. He knew Merwal to be dark-haired, but was he really tall, or did he simply seem

12

so to a small boy? He could not hear the older man's voice in his head, and when Domneva laughed at something Edbert said and she shifted in her seat, the scent of herb water wafted Noni's way. Was it perhaps familiar because his mother wore the same scent in her hair? If this hall here at Hereford felt full of departed spirits, what would his old home of Tamworth feel like? Much was recognisable but also strange, as though he lived in two worlds.

As if hearing his thoughts, Edbert asked him, "What do you recall?"

Noni suppressed a shudder. He saw it all so often in his dreams that he did not like to think about it when awake. "My mother was killed. By King Oswii." He brought his drink to his lips, feeling the dribble of ale where his hand had shaken too much to hold the cup steady.

Edbert nodded. "We thought as much when she did not return to Tamworth." His voice wavered. "She was a good woman." He paused, took a deep breath, and said, "Do you remember any more of that night?"

"I am not sure." He knew what had happened, but his remembrances were bits of frayed cloth, stitched together with pieces of knowledge supplied by Sikke. "My brother Pieter came home after the battle at the River Winwæd and told my mother that Father was dead."

"Yes, Lord. The Northumbrians had used treachery to persuade some of your father's friends to leave the field the night before the fight. Oswii's own nephew had turned against him, but he too ran away at the last hour."

Was he there, when Pieter broke the news, or had Sikke told him that part? It was the same with all his earlier experiences, he realised. The night his mother was taken from him had cast a black shroud across his mind, so that looking past it into his childhood was often impossible. He could shake some details free, but others remained hidden. "After we heard that all was lost, my mother took the boy

13

back to Oswii and hoped that he would spare our lives in return. I watched him raise his sword when Mother walked towards him. Sikke says he dragged me away."

Domneva laid a comforting hand on his arm. "Poor love, to have witnessed such wrongdoing. Small wonder if you cannot bring it all to mind."

The gesture made him tearful, and he blinked a few times before focusing once more on his recollections. Something stirred in his mind. "There were others there. My sisters the twins, and...Where did Wulf go? He rode out with us, but he was not there when..."

"He hid with Welsh friends, much as you did, young Lord. It was deemed safer that you keep apart. Had you both been found, there would have been none left to wear the Mercian king-helm."

"I understand." Merwal was already sub-king here in the lands of the Magonsæte and Pieter was sub-king of the Middle Angles. Noni knew, for Sikke had often-times reminded him, that the Mercian heartlands were centred around Tamworth, and in the Trent Valley, but many smaller tribes and kingdoms allied themselves to its banner, retaining some independence but swearing oaths of loyalty to the Mercian over-kings. Sometimes, they had none to lead them, and this was how Merwal and Pieter got their king-helms. Wulf was the next in line for the Mercian king-seat and, should he die childless, Noni would succeed him. The loneliness of exile had at least been for a sound reason.

Noni was fairly sure he'd been a witness when Pieter was baptised and married Ava of Northumbria, and waved them off when the newlyweds left for Middle Anglia, but had he been told about that afterwards? And had his parents argued at the wedding, about his eldest sister? Why could he not catch these memories and hold them? He thought again about the upcoming reunion, and his stomach lurched. "Are all my brothers at Tamworth?"

14

Out of the corner of his eye he thought he saw Domneva shaking her head, and Edbert coughed. "Best we wait until we are back at King Wulfhere's hall before we speak more of the tidings of your kin. He will wish to tell you himself where everyone is."

Wulfhere. The use of his brother's full name jarred as much as hearing his own. Wulfhere had been nicknamed Wulf because two of their sisters had been too young to say his given name. Discomfited by Edbert's reluctance to tell him about the rest of his family, Noni held out his cup when Domneva lifted the jug. Perhaps the ale-haze would dull the clamour of his thoughts and keep him safe in a drunken world until he could find out more.

It was the time of year when food supplies were sparse, the long winter months having drawn to a close and the stores being depleted, while the new year's food was still growing. Domneva's table was not heaped high, but there was smoked hard cheese, unleavened bread, and fresh fish caught from the river. As the folk came into the hall at the end of the day's labours, the noise increased and Noni fell to watching them as they moved between the tables, the many voices speaking in the Mercian tongue sounding odd to his ears after his years away.

Most of the folk here were fairer-haired than the Welsh with whom he'd been living, but a young girl, perhaps a year or so younger than him, came in with some others of Domneva's waiting-women, and her hair was so dark as to be almost black. It was hard to discern in the dim light of the hall, but her eyes looked to be a deep shade of brown. She looked across at the head table, dipped a bow to Lady Domneva, and gave Noni a shy smile.

Three further days of riding and two friendly halls gave Noni more time to reflect on his changed circumstances. There had been a warm welcoming hearth everywhere he'd

15

lived in the last three years and this was no different but, with every overnight stay, every mile ridden, the sense that his life was about to change grew stronger.

As they rode through the gates of the settlement at Tamworth, his vision blurred. Yes, there were tears in his eyes, but they were only part of the problem. Too many images swirled around him: of his parents, his siblings, childhood friends; of chasing chickens, throwing stones in the river, and trying to catch fish by dipping hands in the chilly water. The yew tree where he thought his parents had worshipped appeared smaller, but of course, he had grown. Beside it, a group of men digging post holes stood up and leaned on their shovels as the riders went by. "New chapel, Wulf's orders," Edbert said.

They dismounted in front of the hall and Noni had the urge to walk round to the back of the building, where he thought he might find a separate bower. He saw himself as a tiny child, running to find his mother in that dwelling house, and he was sure that if he went there, he would see a carved portico in front of a big oak door, and a red and black raven banner flapping in the breeze. As he handed the reins to a stable-hand he said, "There were some big trees nearby?"

Edbert turned and waved a hand towards the gate. "The other side of yonder field. Your father left gifts for Thunor there. Beyond them lies the moot mound, although they met for moots in the hall once Penda had it made bigger."

Noni looked at the building again, squinting, as if by squeezing his eyes he might bring up the sight of his father, overseeing the work on the extension to the hall.

And then, standing in the open doorway of that very building, Merwal and Wulfhere were solid, not half-remembered, not shadows. Merwal, an adult before Noni was born, looked no different, except perhaps for some grey flecks in his beard. Wulf had grown, though he was lithe and wiry, not built as though hewn from a lump of rock, like

16

Sikke. Neither man moved; they were staring at him intently and he realised that they were less sure of what they were seeing, for he was the one who had changed the most.

As Noni and his group approached, it was as if something snapped. The past broke away, and the three brothers were jumping up and down, clasping each other in bear hugs, slapping each other on the back and crying through their laughter.

"Look at you, little Brother; I can barely see over the top of your head now!"

"I can scarce believe that you and he are now both grown men."

"If you saw the grey in your own beard, you would believe that time has indeed passed, old man!" And with that, Wulf stepped back, still beaming, showing one of his dog teeth jutting forward slightly, and appraised Noni anew. "You have the look of our mother about you. Merwal, what think you; is it the eyes?"

Merwal, stroking his beard now as if to hide the afore-mentioned grey, nodded. "Aye, the same shape, but browner in hue. And your hair! You were a white-haired bairn but this," he flicked a hand at Noni's hair, "this may yet become as dark as Father's. You have the same little line in the chin that he did, too."

"Well, when he's man enough to grow a beard, he can hide it, no?" With that, Wulf flung his arm about Noni's shoulders and walked him into the hall, ducking at the doorway. Another flash of the past: had their father had to do that too? To the child, Penda had been a tall man, but perhaps he'd also stood higher than most grown-ups.

Inside, a young man smiled, waiting to be introduced. Noni looked at him, then at Merwal, and held up his hand in greeting. "Merchelm?"

"Aye," said Merwal, "my eldest. He is your nephew, but whenever you met as bairns you played together, more like

17

brothers."

Noni was swept along by Wulf, but he managed to say over his shoulder, "We will speak later," and was rewarded with a nod and a smile.

In truth, aside from the different shape, this hall looked similar to those where he'd been a guest for the last few years, and there was little inside to poke Noni's memory awake as the three brothers walked its length. Only when they got to the dais at the far end did he manage to dredge up a picture, nay, a feeling. He walked over to the big carved chair and got to his knees. At such a height, he recollected being just able to reach up and run his finger along the carved indents on the arm of the king-stool, tracing the curling serpent tails that intertwined along the whole length of the chair arm. Thus he had idled away the time while listening to the rumble of a man's voice, his father's, presumably. Overwhelmed, he stood up and stepped back. This was Wulf's chair now.

Wulf, though, did not take his seat. Taking his younger brother's elbow, he indicated that they should move to the back of the hall where, despite the enlarged space, there was little furniture and less light. Away from the others, and in the quiet corner, Wulf unknowingly repeated Edbert's earlier words. "What do you recall?"

"That I was with Mother and the twins, and that Sikke pulled me away but that his brother died. I know what happened to Mother, but the twins?"

Wulf put his hand to the back of Noni's head and pulled gently on his neck until their foreheads were touching. "I cannot find them. I have men out searching and I swear to you I will not give up hope."

The twins were not their only sisters. "And Minna and Starling? I know Mother thought they would be safe, wed to thegns who had not marched with Father."

Wulf let go of him and leaned back against the wall, one

leg bent with his foot against the upright plank. "She was wrong. They were both widowed. Minna has gone with her daughter to Medeshamstede there to run the abbey which Pieter ordered to be built. I pray that the twins are living likewise, somewhere. Starling has grey hairs now."

"Grey hairs?" Ethelred wiggled his fingers, reckoning. Starling, named so because of her black hair, was surely less than a handful of years older than Wulf. "Where is she?"

"She is here and asked that she be sent for, once you have heard everything."

Noni had not been so young, or away so long, that he had forgotten how many older siblings he had. His eldest sister, Carena, was presumed safe in the north, having long ago married Alfrid, the son of King Oswii of Northumbria, and moved to live there. That left one unaccounted for: his other brother, Pieter. "What is it that no one seems to have the balls to tell me?"

Wulf kicked away from the wall and laid a hand on Noni's shoulder. "Pieter is dead; this much you have gathered. It is the manner of it that is so painful."

Fear swirled cold through Noni, replacing the warm blood in his veins. What was so terrible that must be told to him here, away from the hearth, with only family and loyal companions nearby?

"Pieter was killed less than a year after the battle."

Noni lowered his head. "I thought as much."

"But none of us would have guessed how it happened. It was Ava."

"What was Ava?"

"She murdered him."

The floor turned soft, as if melting from the heat of the fire. Noni began to sway, and sweat trickled at first warm, then icy, down between his shoulder blades. Ava, daughter of Oswii, who'd sworn she wanted naught to do with her father after he abandoned her and her brother. Ava, who fell

19

in love with Pieter, a man then so besotted that he became a Christian in order to wed her. How could she have done such a thing? "Why?"

"We do not know. I only learned of it myself last Yuletide. Oswii's men were all over Mercia, until we rose up. One of them must have brought word from him that he wanted Pieter dead. I can only think that it was meant to serve as a warning. Come, Brother, let's sit down and drink in remembrance of our lost ones."

On wobbly legs, Noni followed. To Wulf's back, he murmured, "How?" but when Wulf turned, and asked him to repeat his question, Noni shook his head. "Naught." He'd realised that he did not want to know. His shaky limbs were weakened further when he thought back to his conversation in Merwal's hall. Pieter had surely been killed because he had Penda's blood, and the debt owed to those who'd kept Wulf and Noni safe from harm was beyond any payment.

They took their seats, Wulf in the carved king-stool, Merwal and Noni on either side of him. Edbert was on Noni's other side, and Sikke was sitting on the lower tables with the rest of the young warriors who had risen up and overthrown the Northumbrians. Noni was gradually learning who they were, and had especially noticed Immin, introduced as the son of Lothar, his father's most loyal hearth-thegn, who'd been with Noni and his mother that fateful night. Noni leaned in to ask Wulf, "Lothar died?"

Wulf continued smiling out at the gathering, but he said, "He did. Immin stayed behind, not yet old enough to fight and was able, when the time came, to lead the uprising, along with Edbert and, you see over there?"

Noni's gaze followed the direction of his brother's pointing finger to a man he'd seen earlier, standing arms folded near the doorway when Wulf and Merwal had come out to greet the arrivals from Wales.

"That is Heaferth of the Arosæte. His brother was wed to our Aunt Audra. You used to play with her little boy. He was but a few years younger than you."

"Is he, is she, are they..."

Wulf still did not turn, but said, tonelessly, as if he had spoken the words too many times already, "Gone. I know not how. Some have it that the Northumbrians found and killed them, some that her man rode to fight the West Saxons after Audra died, still blaming them for her sad life. We never found the lad."

Noni only dimly remembered his aunt Audra. She was the lady who had a long stripe of white hair, and he knew from tales told by others that she had fallen in love with Cynwal of the West Saxons and that he had put her aside to wed a Christian. Penda had chased him down and forced him out of his lands and into hiding in the kingdom of the East Angles. Noni locked gazes with Heaferth for a heartbeat and saw the bitterness born of violent loss in the other man's deep-set eyes.

Wulf had made sure that the feast was the best possible, given the time of year, to show that he was a lord worth following. Flatbreads, the last of the preserved nuts and the shoots of stored root vegetables, fish caught from the nearby river, and plenty of ale, all made for a fine meal. Noni for one never minded such fare, for it was a reminder that winter was over, that soon the grass would be long enough to feed the animals, and there would be fresh meat, milk, and soft cheeses. All those gathered in the hall raised their cups to the new king, and after the meal the leading men of Mercia stepped forward to swear oaths of fealty to him. Heaferth of the Arosæte spoke with a passion that seemed to burn in him, and Noni understood that this man had scores aplenty to settle.

Heaferth, Edbert and Immin were called forward again, to receive gold arm rings from Wulf in thanks for their part in leading the uprising. Wulf's voice had rung out commandingly, but it faltered and broke when he called the next man, Penwal of the Middle Angles. This man, with red hair and beard, stepped forward, eyes brimming with tears. He opened his mouth, but Wulf shook his head, silencing him. They both took a moment, and then Wulf presented him with his gift of gold. As Penwal went back to his place, Merwal leaned across Wulf's empty chair and explained. "He was there, when Pieter was killed. When he heard the shouting he ran to help, but whoever planned the foul deed with Ava whisked her away before anyone could stop them, and slew Emmett who had shouted the warning." When Noni shook his head, he continued, "You were too young to recall, but Emmett was the horse-thegn who went with Pieter when he left to rule the Middle Angles. He was steadfast to the end."

With the tables cleared, and the gift-giving complete, it was time for the scop to speak of the bravery of those who had overthrown the Northumbrians. All those present were bonded together by their lord king, by the need to help each other to stay alive, but it was the storytelling which really brought them close and gave them their shared memories. As the scop wove his tale, a young woman slipped into the hall and Edbert stood to give up his seat for her. She slid into the place next to Noni and immediately rested her head on his shoulder, before turning and sobbing into his neck, crying a wet patch onto his tunic. He was not sure how to respond, so he waited.

After a while, she lifted her head, wiped her cheeks, and said, "I never thought to see you again. And in truth, I will never see that sweet child again, for here you are, a man grown."

Her dark hair was greying in places, just as Wulf had said. "Starling?"

She smiled. Yes, the name stuck, even if I'm no longer so

black-haired. We have lived through much."

"So many dead. I did not know."

She put a hand up to silence him. "How could you? And for our part, we did not know whether you were alive or dead, until we had word from Rhiryd's father in Wales that you were his guests."

"You know of Rhiryd? How?"

"When we sent out for tidings, we heard of a young man who had made friends with Rhiryd the lame boy, and had made his Frisian hearth-thegn carry Rhiryd on his shoulders. Who else could it be but you and Sikke?"

Noni felt like he had been force-fed butter and then been spun round three times. It was all too much to take in, and now he yearned anew for the little friend with the withered leg whom he'd had to leave behind.

The scop had finished, the whooping and cheering and foot stamping had faded away, and Wulf was addressing the gathering. In formal wording, he thanked his loyal hearth-thegns, the men of Mercia and those of the tribe lands, and pledged that he would always lead, listen, and provide. Then he turned to face his brothers and sister and said, "We are the children, yet we are grown now. There will be a reckoning."

The drinking would continue until well into the night. In this, the Mercians were no different from the Welsh. Bewildered still, Noni sat back in his chair and looked again at all those whom he knew he would encounter time and again. Heaferth, with his clear hatred of all West Saxons and Northumbrians, Immin and Edbert who, along with Heaferth, had freed them all, Penwal of the Middle Angles, and Merchelm, the nephew who had been a friend, and who was now smiling at him again across the hall. Seated next to him though was Sikke, his hand by his mouth, pushing the ends of his moustache between his lips and chewing on them. He was not drinking and now Noni came to think on it, he had not eaten much either. This man, along with his brother, had served the Iclingas since before half of Noni's brothers and sisters were born. It must have cut him deeply to learn of Pieter's death. Perhaps he sensed the scrutiny, for he looked up. Noni raised an eyebrow in query and was answered with a sorry shake of the big Frisian's head. And then it was clear: even though he had protected Noni for the last three years, he still felt that he had failed in his promise to keep the children of Penda safe from harm.

Wulf however was in joyous mood. They had drunk to the memory of lost kin, and to all the dead Mercians, for almost everyone in the hall had lost a loved one and they had all suffered. Tears had been wept. Now though, Wulf was talking loudly to Merwal. "I need a Kentish bride, but she must be as lovely as yours."

Merwal laughed. "There is not a woman who walks God's earth who is as lovely as Domneva."

Wulf chuckled and took another swig of ale. "True, true."

Noni smiled. Lovely was an apt word, for she was radiant. He had felt naught but soothed while in her presence, and he longed to see her again.

Merwal said, "Domneva does, however, have a cousin who is as yet unwed, but I cannot speak for her nature." He leaned across in front of Wulf and said to Noni, "I am sorry though; it is only the one cousin who is unwed."

Wulf cuffed him playfully round the head and pushed him back into his seat. "Noni may not be the bed-wetting child we knew, but he is not yet man enough to think of taking a wife!"

Noni tipped his head in acknowledgement of the fact, but he said nothing. For, when his thoughts had taken him to Domneva and her welcoming home, they had let him linger at Hereford a while, to recall the dark-eyed girl who had smiled at him there.

Springtime at Bamburgh was usually a happy time and it was her favourite of all their residences; she liked it when they spent prolonged periods here. The sun's rays glinted on the water and the views out to Holy Island were clear. Efa enjoyed the freedom of movement that came with the passing of winter and always looked forward to the point where, travelling across her husband's vast lands, they came to the fortress on the rocks, the timber hall offering a warm welcome in the centre of hard stone boundary walls. Today, though, the atmosphere in the hall was far from cheery. Oswii was stomping across the floor, slopping ale as he went, and every so often stopping midway to spit out fresh loud invective. Efa knew better than to interrupt and pretended close interest in her needlework, but her patience was thinning with each traverse of the room. "Perhaps you might like to sit down?"

"Sit? I should not even be standing. I should be on my horse riding south to kill those bastards. Aye, and with my bare hands. How dare they? I took my sight from those stinking-arsed Mercians for a heartbeat and look what they did. I should hang them all from a tree like they did to my brother."

"It was their father who did that, and long before most of his brood was even born. Be still. Even the mighty king of Northumbria cannot look two ways at once."

He stopped pacing then, and threw himself into the nearest chair, his whole body seemingly made heavier by his frustration. "I had thought, when I made my nephew king of the Picts, that my northern border would be safe."

Efa, knowing that he was too preoccupied to notice, dared a little sarcasm. "How ungrateful of him to die."

He sat forward and slapped the table board, making her jump and propelling her needle into her finger. "Indeed!

25

And so I've had to trouble myself with a ride north, give them a new king, and meanwhile those scheming Mercians have killed my men and taken their kingdom back. I have had to send warbands and raiding parties into Wales. Too little, too late, but at least the Welsh will now be sorry for helping the Mercians."

Efa sucked at her finger and put her embroidery down. "Your blood will boil and stop your heart if you do not calm yourself. Can you really blame the Mercians for wishing to rule themselves? It is no wonder that the whole family hates you. You slew their father in battle and as for what you did to their poor mother…"

Oswii waggled a finger at her. "Enough, Woman. Watch your tongue or I might do the same to you."

"You would not dare!"

Muttering darkly, "Do not tempt me," he picked up his empty ale cup, hurled it across the room and stalked off, pausing only to growl at the young woman who stood aside for him in the doorway.

Efa set aside her needlework altogether and sighed. The truth was that she rarely tempted her husband at all these days, in any manner. Time was when they would have furious rows followed by vigorous activity in bed. So much had changed in the three short years since Oswii had defeated Penda of the Mercians. As promised, their youngest daughter, Alfleyda, had been given to the Church, in thanks to God for the victory. She was safe in the care of Efa's kinswoman, Hild, but Whitby Abbey was a long way away and Efa missed them both. The celebration babe, conceived on the night Oswii returned from the battle, had died in infancy. Their remaining daughter, Ositha, was a living and therefore constant reminder to Oswii that his special babe had perished and Ositha was growing up sullen and resentful. Efa hadn't the heart to tell her that he was that way with all his children.

And then there was Ecgfrith, her little Lief as he'd been known, who had been a hostage in the Mercian court and had returned to Northumbria a changed child. He'd been back home for more years than he'd been away, but he knew his father had endangered his life by going to battle while the Mercians held his child, and it must have upset him, although Derwena – Penda's Welsh name for his wife – had looked after Ecgfrith like one of her own.

Efa had been grateful for the messages that were sent; even though the Mercian king and queen were hostile to Northumbria, Derwena knew that a mother would worry about her son and made sure Efa received tidings telling her of Ecgfrith's health and progress. Efa guessed that her boy had memories of Derwena's warm embraces, of playing happily alongside her children, but Penda had been a thorn in Oswii's side. She caught Ecgfrith sometimes, staring wistfully out to sea, no doubt struggling to reconcile his feelings of love for a woman who had not been his mother, but the wife of an enemy.

The young woman who had narrowly escaped being barrelled out of the doorway by Oswii, now stepped into the room. If ever evidence was required to show how badly Oswii treated his children, then folk would need look no further. Ava, daughter of the British princess whom Oswii had wed in exile, was only two years younger than Lady Efa. Until two years ago, the women had never met. Ava had journeyed with her brother, Alfrid, from the kingdom of Rheged to Mercia, where they had both fallen in love with children of Penda's. Now Ava's husband, Pieter, was dead and she had fled to a place she'd never called home, to live with a father who'd shown not a morsel of care for her. She haunted the great hall and settlement at Bamburgh, eyes sunken in blue-tinged skin, cheeks hollow, and veil pulled tightly over every strand of hair. She slid into a chair, shuffling back as if she might blend into the furniture and not be seen.

Elwyn, Oswii's henchman and lifelong friend, strode into the hall. "That way," Efa gestured, knowing that he was looking for his king. Elwyn nodded his thanks, but also glanced at Ava and his expression puzzled Efa, for it was a conspiratorial wink. Ava looked down at her hands, and Efa wondered, remembering.

Years ago, her kinsman had set himself up as king in Deira, the southern kingdom of Northumbria, and was lured into a trap and murdered, on Oswii's order and by Elwyn's hand. Elwyn had also been responsible for the death of a Pictish king, whose demise allowed Oswii's nephew to be given the king-seat of the Picts. Then there was the mysterious death of Oswii's sister-by-law. Rumours had occasionally whirled around the great fortress that it had been no simple accident. If Elwyn had helped Ava to kill, it would be no great surprise.

The clear spring breeze blew salty and tangy from the sea and as his father stepped outside the hall Ecgfrith watched as it pushed Oswii's hair into his eyes. The king batted at it angrily and swore. Men and women were busy in the yard, some patting fresh daub onto the walls of the buildings, others moving from the bake house to the hall with the first of the day's cooked loaves. Luckily for them they knew better than to catch their king's eye, and they went about their business with gazes cast down. Ecgfrith, standing by the stone chapel, watched him, close enough to hear, but being wise enough to stay out of sight.

"Elwyn!" His father bellowed, but there was no need, for Elwyn had anticipated being summoned and was already outside and making his way hurriedly to the spot by the wall where his king was waiting. "Lord?"

"I am beleaguered; by troublesome Picts to the north and the Mercians, whom I thought were bested, have risen up

28

while my back was turned. Even the death of Pieter, son of Penda, was not enough of a warning to them. Why have I been forsaken?"

It was a question, but Elwyn knew better than to answer, and stood in silence. Ecgfrith nodded to a passing thegn and then turned his attention back to his father's rant.

"I gave my daughter to the Church, as I swore to do if I won the fight against Penda. I made another child after that, but the runt was too weak to live. My wife is cold to me now and thinks me a cursed man." He swiped at his hair again. "She was ever the shrew, berating me for what she calls my ungodly ways, but she always had a way of bringing me round to her way of thinking, eh?" He bumped his elbow against Elwyn's ribs.

"Yes, Lord. You and she have often taken your troubles to bed and made them disappear there."

Oswii chuckled. "Aye, she has a sharp tongue but the rest of her was ever soft enough, and willing, be it for making children or simply for my need to release."

Ecgfrith looked down at his shoes and kicked at a clod of mud, made loose and circular by a hoof. He was not especially close to his mother, but it still occasionally made his skin prickle to hear her spoken of in such a way. Each time he heard it though, it became less shocking.

Oswii had not finished. "These days she's as doleful as a fisherman who's lost his day's catch, and my cock seldom awakes even when she is unclothed. She had her uses, though, with blood from Deira in her veins."

"Yes, Lord, and Kentish blood, which is good, too."

Ecgfrith often thought this last was the most important point for his father. His mother's Deiran blood had lessened that kingdom's dislike of Oswii when he claimed the whole of Northumbria but Kent, though not mighty in terms of warriors, or even in land, was the seat of Christianity and had trading links over the sea. Every king felt raised up by wedding a woman from there. Oswii didn't like the fact that they worshipped in the Roman way, but he needed the respectability of the union with the southern kingdom. It was pitiful, really.

His father was still protesting and appeared not to have heard Elwyn's last point. "But now that my boy Alfrid holds Deira for me and I sit snug on the king-stool, what use can she serve, if she cannot make my cock rise any more? Kentish you say…"

Ah, so he had heard the final part. Ecgfrith tried to move away when he saw his father look round, but he was too late. "Boy! Come here!"

As he approached, his father continued talking to Elwyn. "Look at him. Like a pup with feet too big yet for its body. His mother coddles him, you know, since we got him back. How old are you now, Boy?"

"I've lived thirteen summers." His voice changed from boy to man and back again even in that short sentence. He looked out across the water to Holy Island, and wondered, not for the first time, if the monks there could hear it when his father was shouting.

"Hmm. Elwyn?"

"Yes Lord?"

"Find me a Kentish princess."

"Another one, Lord? Lady Efa might have something to say about that."

Oswii lifted his arm and made to cuff the man round the head. "Not for me, you addle-headed arse-wit. For him."

Elwyn looked at the ground.

Oswii's patience, never much thicker than a strand of twine, was probably ready to snap. "What?"

"That is why I was coming to find you, Lord. Word has come that Wulfhere of Mercia is to wed Ermenilda of Kent. There are no more Kentish princesses to be had."

This time Oswii did not hold back, but slapped Elwyn

round the ear. "Then find another one from somewhere else. And if you can't, then be sure to hurl yourself from this wall onto those rocks, ere I push you myself."

Ecgfrith stared at his father's back as the older man stomped off. Like Elwyn, he was used to Oswii's outbursts, and was not cowed by his shouting. No, it was not fear that he felt, but something more bitter. A man who claimed to be overlord of all the kingdoms yet could not keep the Picts and Mercians in their place, nor a willing woman in his bed, invoked not fear, or respect, but merely scorn.

Chapter Two

The monk's voice was pleasant to listen to. Too pleasant, in fact, and Noni found that it resonated at the same pitch as the bees investigating the flowers which lined the small sward outside Merwal's hall. The sun was kissing his cheeks and nose and though he tried to concentrate on his lessons, his mind kept taking him to much less holy places.

As soon as the worst of the winter weather was over, he'd made a point of travelling to Hereford whenever he could, and his visits had lasted longer and longer. This time, he'd been at his half-brother's hall for more than a fortnight and was in no hurry to leave. Merchelm was supposed to be learning the liturgy and the word of the gospel with him, but more often than not suddenly found jobs to do in the stables whenever Father Cedda arrived. It was one of the few times of day when the two were not together, for they had bonded strongly.

There was much to like about having company his own age again, after leaving Rhiryd behind, but Merchelm was no scholar, and horses and swords would always appeal more than anything Cedda had to say. Heaferth, who now rode with Noni as his hearth-thegn, had also made himself scarce and Immin had not accompanied them at all this time, having announced that Hereford was dull, with more priests and sheep than comely women.

Noni had laughed but he was still drawn to the quiet settlement, and in particular the serenity of his sister-by-law. He wished to find the peace that enfolded her so completely, so he tried to be attentive to the words of her priest. Today though, with the summer heat and the calm before harvest began, he was drowsy and all he could think about was Arianwen: the back of her neck when her long plait was pulled forward over her shoulder, the shape of her hips when she hefted a basket and it pulled her kirtle tight, the slenderness of her fingers when she reached out to place something on the tables.

And, as if his thoughts had summoned her, she walked by. He sat up, and she dipped her head in acknowledgement of his silly grin. "Lord Ethelred."

He opened his mouth to say, "Call me Noni, everyone does," but as usual his tongue curled itself into a knot and, in any case, he recalled their conversation earlier in the year. *I cannot. It is your kin's name for you and even if it were not, I should not be so bold. You are a lord; more, you are an atheling, and I am no one.*

That was only partly true. He was next in line to wear the king-helm should it slip, for whatever reason, from Wulf's head. Plans, however, were in place for Wulf to wed, his bride would be arriving in Mercia any day now, and there was no reason to think that he and his new Kentish wife would not have children. And Arianwen was not no one.

However, she had given him something to think about and he decided that perhaps, with Mercia back in rightful ownership, and his brother about to be a wedded man, it was time for the youngest of Penda's brood to grow up too. Henceforth, Noni was no more, and Ethelred would be a man. A devout, Christian man. Soon. Today he was in pursuit of less lofty ideals. He sprang to his feet and with a perfunctory, "Sorry, Father Cedda," skipped alongside Arianwen and offered to carry her basket. This time, he was rewarded not only with a nod, but with a blushing smile.

He ran his fingers along the embroidered cuff of his tunic sleeve and said, "You know I might never be king? My brother is young and set to wed…"

"What are you saying?"

"I am saying that yes, I am Lord Ethelred, but that does not mean I am any more worthy to walk alongside you than the next man."

She smiled, which made his chest feel like it was melting, just as it had when she'd smiled at him the very first night in Domneva's hall, and then she turned to look behind her. "I see no other man, sadly. Thus I shall have to walk with you, shan't I?"

He was not swift enough to think of a witty reply, so he had to think of some other way to keep her interest. He reached to take her basket of kindling from her. She hesitated.

"It would not be…"

"Seemly? Nevertheless, I shall carry it." He swung the basket onto the arm furthest from her, realising that it was not heavy, and he was not the rescuer he had hoped to be. As they walked, his free arm occasionally brushed hers. He noted that she did not move away, and he was sure at one point that her arm deliberately pressed into his. His heart thumped. He lifted his face to the sun, savoured the warmth again, and thanked God that the dark days were truly behind him.

Arianwen went to the cook house, and he continued towards the heart of the settlement. In the hall, servants were preparing for the impending visit to Tamworth, hurrying towards the doorway, carrying boxes and leather bags through from the curtained sleeping area behind the dais. Domneva's steward was barking orders and yet everything was going smoothly. The steward's voice was raised but only so that everyone could hear, and his tone was far from sharp. Ethelred's grin stayed fixed; every time he walked into this hall it felt like he'd come home.

On a cushioned seat next to the hearth, Domneva was

sitting with a thin cloak draped over her, nursing her daughter, born last Yuletide. Ethelred dipped his head in question, and she nodded, patting the space next to her with her free hand. He deposited the basket on the floor and sat down.

She said, "You look carefree indeed."

He flicked hair from his eyes. "I was merely thinking that this place feels like home to me."

"I should think you must feel at home all the time now, be it here or at Tamworth. It is only right that you should feel thus, for you are back in Mercia."

"Yes, but…" How could he say that a sense of home was dependant on her presence? He had barely begun to examine his feelings towards this woman, to think about whether she gave him the thing that was ripped so cruelly from him: a mother's love. He was saved from answering by Arianwen's return. She picked up her basket of kindling and began to stack the contents in neat piles by the hearth.

Domneva leaned towards him and said softly, "There is your reason, I think."

Ethelred said nothing, and sat as still as he could, hoping that Domneva would not turn. His ear tips were burning, and he knew she would see that they were bright red.

She patted his arm. "Arianwen is Merwal's ward. Her father was a Welsh leader who lost his wife. We are blessed that she is a skilled healing woman. What matters it if she is also lovely to look upon? I cannot think why Father Cedda has such a hard task keeping your attention during lessons."

Ethelred turned, mouth open to offer profuse and heartfelt apologies, but closed it when he saw Domneva's shoulders shaking gently with mirth.

The day dawned bright and clear, for which they all gave thanks. The chapel had been newly daubed and lime-washed; it needn't have been, for it had rarely been used in their parents' day, and then only by itinerant priests, but the sons and daughters of Penda and Derwena had all embraced the new faith, and it was important to show Wulf's bride that Mercian Christianity was as strong as Kent's. Kent had been the first kingdom to convert, and the contingent from the southeast needed to be impressed.

A wooden canopy had been erected above the chapel door, and ribbons, threaded through it, flapped gently in the breeze. Sweet-smelling blossom covered the stone floor, and beeswax candles gave a soft yellow glow, throwing dancing shadows on the walls, even though outside the sun was now at its highest. Father Cedda had arrived at Tamworth the previous evening to perform the ceremony.

Ethelred, standing next to Domneva, looked at his brother in admiration. Wulf was wearing a coat of dark grey, trimmed with a contrasting lighter shade and edged with tablet-woven embroidery, three-coloured bands of threads dyed with woad, madder and dyer's broom to give delicate shades of blue, red and green. On his belt was a garnet-set flint purse, though Ethelred thought it unlikely that there was any of the usual birch bark tinder inside; this purse was ceremonial. Wulf's cloak, dyed with madder and woad to give a deep, dark red, would probably be removed as soon as the ceremony was over, for the day was shaping up to be hot. The cloak was pinned with an ornate brooch, a great disc of gold, with filigree in a coil, and on any other day it would have been impressive.

His bride, Ermenilda of Kent, was dressed as finely as he was. Her kirtle was a rich deep red, and the delicate veil on her fair hair was fastened with tiny pins which caught the light, glinting like stars in the night sky. Around her neck a string of shell beads, so favoured by the Kentish folk, was outshone by her brooch, which must have been as long as a man's thumb from one side to the other. It was round, like Wulf's, but there the similarity ended. Yes, there were coils of filigree, but between each coil there were circles inlaid with blue glass, white shell, pearl, and garnet. Domneva sometimes wore a brooch such as this and Ethelred concluded that this was a style much favoured in Kent. He, though, after admiring the dazzling sight of his new sister-by-law, had eyes only for Arianwen who, as waiting-woman to Domneva, was standing alongside Penwal of Middle Anglia's wife, Tette, who had been appointed as a hand-woman for Lady Ermenilda.

Arianwen was dressed less brightly, although her blue kirtle shone as if it might have some gold thread woven into it, and her dark hair was only visible at the front, for her veil covered the rest of her head, but her pins did not glitter. Nevertheless, to him she was the most beautiful woman in the chapel and when she glanced sideways at him and twitched a smile, it was like the sun had come in with her and now warmed him from the inside.

After she had looked away, Ethelred took a moment to study the guests who had travelled with Ermenilda from her own land. Ermenilda's parents, the king and queen of Kent, had brought their young son, Ecbert. The opportunity had been taken for a kin-gathering, and Domneva's immediate family were there too: her father, who was the king of Kent's brother, and her younger brothers, Æthelred and Æthelberht.

There had been much weeping and rejoicing when the Kentish party had arrived the previous evening but now Ethelred detected tension. It was nothing overt, but Domneva's family made sure to stand on one side of the chapel, while Ermenilda's parents and brother stood on the other. Little Ecbert cast the odd scowl in the direction of his two male cousins and occasionally even poked his tongue out at them, then looked up at his own mother, who ruffled his hair.

As if she sensed Ethelred's curiosity, Domneva spoke softly from the corner of her mouth. "My father was overlooked for the kingship but has always been content with the order of things. Ecbert however takes a keen delight in goading my brothers, reminding them of their lesser status. He is young, but already aware of his worth."

Ethelred accepted her statement, if nothing else because a lengthy conversation, even whispered, would have been distracting to the congregation, but it was the closest he'd ever heard her come to uttering unkind words, and he couldn't help wondering why the son of a crowned king, and thus almost certain to succeed to the throne, would waste his time needling his male kinfolk if he felt utterly secure. Perhaps the king had less right to wear the king-helm than Domneva's father, and they all knew it? He looked from Domneva to her brothers and back again. With all but the front of her hair hidden by her veil, and their youth still holding back their masculine features, it was hard to tell the three faces apart.

The wedding party emerged from the chapel and made their way to the hall, while the ceremonial horn blew across the settlement to call all the folk to the feast. Having left the holy building in reverent silence, folk began conversing until by the time they reached the great hall, the chatter was loud, and the happy laughter rang out across the yard. Ethelred glanced at Father Cedda and saw the priest frown. Following his gaze Ethelred realised what a contrast there was between the painted holy images on the chapel walls and the animal carvings around the doorway of the hall, a reminder of its previous pagan residents.

Wulf and Ermenilda walked hand in hand, and every so

often their heads tilted together as if they were in private conversation. Ethelred smiled at his brother's contentment but was also shot with a bolt of emptiness and he looked across at Arianwen, walking some distance away from the royal group. She would not let him be sad though, and flashed him a brilliant smile, which sent entirely different sensations rushing through him.

They all took their seats, ahead of Wulf and Ermenilda, who waited outside, and Ethelred turned to speak to the man sitting next to him but closed his mouth. Until everyone settled down, he would not waste his voice by shouting. The wave of noise slowly rolled away, and the newlyweds entered the hall. Everyone stood up again, waiting until they reached their seats on the dais. Ermenilda remained standing after everyone had sat down again, and poured the first drink for Wulf, signalling her position as Lady of the hall. Once that ceremonial task had been performed, servants stepped forward to place jugs of wine on all the tables, and Wulf stood up and gave a short blessing in thanks for the food, plentiful now that they no longer had to send any of it north in tribute.

After the blessing, Ermenilda gave a short speech to greet her guests, ending with "I thank thee." After she'd taken her seat, the noise rose again like a beast awakened from sleep, and Ethelred downed what he hoped would be the first of many cups of wine.

Little Mildrith, seated near her mother, Domneva, and too young for wine, held on to an ale cup with both hands and tipped it to her mouth, moments later making a face and puffing out her chubby cheeks. Ethelred smiled and made a similar grimace, pretending that he, too, disliked ale.

On all the tables, folk began breaking bread made from the finest-ground flour and servants brought in plates of roasted meat, from the specially fattened bullocks. Men shouted out to Wulf, offering congratulations and advice on what to do once he and his bride were alone, and Wulf shot back with arrow-swift barbs. "I know what to do; I learned it all from your wife!" and when the ladies gave less crude words of welcome, he smiled and said, "How could my Lady Ermenilda not feel at home here in Mercia, where all the women are pretty?"

The table for the main wedding party, set up on the dais, gave a slightly elevated view of the rest of the room and it was clear to Ethelred that Starling had done her job well. Until the wedding ceremony she had been the highest-ranking female at Tamworth, and she had overseen the arrangements with a skilful and diplomatic eye. Kentish nobles were seated next to Mercians, with no groups isolated. Swords and shields had been hung haphazardly on the wall, so that all were mixed, a symbol of the joining of the two royal houses but also an impediment to quick access to weaponry should a fight break out.

Not that there should be any danger of that, on such a happy day, for Ethelred was sure he'd not misread the signs when watching his brother and the bride walking between the chapel and the hall. Now the two of them were engaged in close conversation, Wulf breaking off only when necessary to answer voiced congratulations. Ermenilda smiled at the words he directed to her and answered him not as a shy bride, but as a woman genuinely interested in getting to know her new husband. It augured well.

The Kentish queen was seated next to Ethelred, but was speaking to Merwal on her other side. "My beloved sister Audrey had wished to be here, but she has been called north and has a long and arduous ride to make ready for."

Ethelred just made out his half-brother's answer. "She will be sad to have missed such a great day."

As the queen turned back to concentrate on her plate, she muttered, "Indeed."

The most accomplished scop in all of Mercia had been

summoned for the occasion and was now thrumming his fingers on the side of his wooden lyre, no doubt limbering up for his performance. It would be entertainment on a grand scale, for the party from Kent had also brought a renowned scop. Tumblers and glee-men were waiting outside until the scops had finished their solemn songs in praise of kings present and previous, and the riddles had been delivered and guessed at. Ethelred had stolen a few moments the previous day to watch them practising their jumping and dancing skills and had asked that, when the glee-men struck up happy tunes for the dancing to begin, they play one tune especially, one he'd heard at Rhiryd's house. When the Welsh melody rang out, he would stand up and ask Arianwen to dance with him.

Smiling at the thought, he was slow to become aware that voices were rising on the table next to his. It was not the volume which caused concern, but the tone. Ethelred checked his cup. It had been refilled but was not empty again; it was unlikely that the men now arguing had taken more than two cups of wine, so the disagreement was unlikely to have been stoked solely by drink. He looked over and realised that those caught up in the argument included Domneva's brothers, their young cousin Ecbert, and his man, who was burlier even than Sikke.

Ethelred could not make out the words at first, but they were angry enough to be accompanied by pointing fingers, and fists thumping on tables, and intervention was necessary.

Wulf, staring intently at his bride, was in no mood or position to deal with the situation and so Ethelred, sitting nearer the end of the main table anyway, slid out of his seat and made his way to stand in front of the group. As he edged around the crowded hall, he caught a glimpse of Domneva, sitting at the opposite table and watching, her face impassive. Surely concerned, she was remaining calm,

41

doing naught to draw more attention to the drama and bring shame to her kin, or to spoil Wulf's day.

Taking his cue from her dignified response, Ethelred pulled his lips into a big smile and said, "My lords, is everything to your liking?" He noticed, with relief and gratitude, that Merchelm had also left his seat and was now standing behind the group, his back to the wall but not so close to it that he could not move forward quickly if needed.

One of Domneva's brothers – they looked so alike he could not be sure whether it was Æthelred or Æthelberht – put his hand on his brother's forearm. "All is well, Lord Ethelred. It was, how shall we say, a lively differing of thoughts on the merits of, erm, taking first turn in a game of Merels and whether it would be fair to let young Ecbert take more turns than the older youths. No doubt later on we shall have the chance to prove it, one way or the other."

Ethelred thought grimly that it would be a long time yet before the tables were cleared and the night given over to board games, by which time a lad this young ought to be in bed. What had the fight really been about? He directed his response to Ecbert. "And you, my lord, are you content to wait until the boards are brought out?"

A flicker of confusion on the boy's face confirmed the suspicion that the argument had been naught to do with gaming strategy, but he recovered his composure quickly enough and said ungraciously, "I'll wait. All things come in time."

Merchelm tapped a servant on the shoulder and bent to have a quiet word with him. As he and Ethelred moved back to take their places, he said, "I ordered that the three of them have their drinks watered for the rest of the day and that Sikke keep an eye on Ecbert's man."

Ethelred patted him heartily on the back, grateful for his quick thinking. Before he took his seat once more, he looked out over the noisy hall. He nodded and smiled at

Domneva, who bowed her head, and he sat back. Despite the comforting smell of sweat and ale that signified he was in the hall surrounded by friends and allies, he craved peace, and had to grip the arms of his chair while fighting an overwhelming urge to flee the hall and ride at speed to Hereford, where all would be even quieter than usual. He glanced again at Wulf, who was whispering in his bride's ear while she smiled and giggled in response.

And why would she not be taken with Wulf? The king was full of life, had an easy way with men and women alike, while Ethelred went red to the tips of his ears just thinking of or gazing at Arianwen. Wulf sat in the king-seat as if it had been carved for him, yet Ethelred had needed Merchelm's help to calm the men from Kent. He offered up a prayer that his brother might live until his beard turned not only grey but white, and that he be blessed with an army of sons. Ethelred was not ready or fit to be a king.

Bamburgh AD660: Spring

"Well Boy, what do you think?"

What did he think? Audrey was ten years older than him, at least. And her looks weren't helped by her expression, which signalled to all that she was as happy to be in Northumbria as a pig was to be in the slaughterhouse. Her garments were made from the finest cloth, but were devoid of all embellishment, the neckline and cuffs showing no embroidery. She wore no jewellery except for one heavy necklace of gold, a collar with small pieces of shining yellow and a single drop pendant, also made of the precious metal. "She doesn't look much like a king's daughter."

Oswii scratched his nose and shifted his weight from one foot to the other. "Granted, she's not from Kent, but her sister is wed to the Kentish king, so it's near enough."

Ecgfrith understood that many folk were scared of his

43

father, for good reason, but he liked naught better than pushing Oswii until he lost his temper. He wanted specifics. "Remind me again; who is she?"

"Damn you, Boy. You know fine well; you wish merely to have me say it out loud. She is the daughter of Ænna of East Anglia."

"The king whom Penda left in ragged bloody bits, splattered up and down?"

His father ignored that. "She's rich. Got lots of land from her first husband."

"And he was? Ah, do not say it again. I recall your words the first time. 'A nobody from a small tribe who live in the marshes', was it not?"

"Don't test me, Boy; you should not listen behind closed doors. She was the best we could get. It's true, she might have a few years on you, but she'll breed. And she's still southern."

"But not Kentish. Not like the Mercians' wives."

Oswii was no longer listening but had turned to watch as his own wife embraced the priest who would be conducting the wedding ceremony. "That looks like... Oh Christ, that's all we need."

Efa had not seen Wilfrid in a long time. He'd presented himself at her household when he was little more than a boy and she had commended him to the monastery on Holy Island. His gifts had been recognised and he went from there to Canterbury and then, praise God, to Rome. Now he was back, and her heart felt light knowing that he would preside over the wedding ceremony.

Her husband was scowling at her, and she had to suppress a smile. Sometimes, she had a sense of things happening as if they had before, like a dream coming true, and she was certain that Oswii was sensing something similar. She remembered her arrival on these bleak shores sixteen years

44

ago and being reunited with her kinswoman Hild. Oswii had found himself surrounded by religious folk who worshipped in the Roman way. The smile worked its way free as she recollected his devastated reaction when discovering that she observed Lent at a different time from him. Now that Wilfrid was back, Oswii would feel outnumbered again.

Her husband strode towards her, grabbed her elbow, and led her away from Wilfrid. "What is he doing here? You already have a chaplain."

She patted his arm with her free hand. "I do. And Romanus is a great comfort to me. I thought that Wilfrid could take the abbacy of the new house in Ripon?"

"Christ, woman. Must you always be asking so much of me? Was building that church not enough for you?"

Efa wondered about that little word 'enough'. Oswii had built a new church at her behest, but only to atone for the murder of her kinsman, the king of Deira. "Think about it thus, my dear. Would you rather Wilfrid went south to Ripon, or stayed here?"

Out of the corner of her eye she saw his cheek rippling as his jaw muscles tensed. He uttered a sound which was akin to the start of a cough. "You'll be punishing me for that little matter until the day one of us dies, won't you, my sweetling? Ripon it is then." He shouted over his shoulder to Ecgfrith. "Watch out Boy, they'll shrink your balls if you let them."

Making their way into the chapel were two people whose sombre expressions made Ecgfrith's gleeful in comparison. Efa was not blood-kin to either of them and yet her heart ached for them both: Alfrid, Oswii's son by the princess of the British kingdom of Rheged, and Alfrid's wife, Carena, eldest daughter of Penda of Mercia.

Efa thought of the day not so many years ago when Alfrid came north looking for a father and a kingdom. Efa had warned him then that if he was hoping for a father's love he

45

would be disappointed. He had been given a kingdom, but at no little cost, for he had lined up with his father on the battlefield where Penda lost his life; thus he had been part of the army which killed his wife's father. His reward had been the sub-kingdom of Deira, and since then he'd rarely come to Bamburgh, no doubt spending his time making peace with himself and his wife.

These days this tall young man walked with a slight stoop as if the cares of his conscience were too heavy to bear. He was beset by guilt for his part in the battle, and Efa could only wonder how Carena was able to forgive him, though she clearly had, for they walked hand in hand. Their love was strong, but had been sorely tested.

And now, before Efa could intervene, they were walking directly towards the young woman who was hovering in the shadow of the chapel doorway. Ava, Alfrid's sister, wife of Pieter, whom she'd murdered. Ava and Alfrid had sought refuge at Penda's hall when their mother died. There they'd stayed, and something more than friendship developed between Pieter and Ava. Not long afterwards, Alfrid had asked to wed Carena and though it was said that it broke her mother's heart, Carena moved with Alfrid to Northumbria. Ava had stayed in Mercia with Pieter, until his untimely death, and Alfrid and Carena had not been back to Bamburgh since her arrival.

Efa took a step forward, trying to wriggle free from Oswii's grip, but she gave up, realising she was too late. Carena had spotted Ava, and Ava was now cowering in the chapel porchway, her back against the wall and with no means of escape.

"We trusted you! We took you into our home and my brother gave you naught but love. Naught!"

"Come away, Dearling. This does no good." Alfrid tugged her sleeve.

"Why does she still live? My father and brother are dead,

my kin scattered…"

Efa could bear it no more; Carena's grief was so raw, so painful, it must feel like she had eaten shards of broken glass which now pierced her insides every time she breathed in. She pushed forward and stood between the two young women. "Alfrid, dear, take your wife inside. Ava, come with me."

As she drew Ava away from the throng and delivered her into the capable hands of her servants, Efa cast a glance at her husband. He had watched the whole scene with an expression of indifference. How could he not see that his scheming had wreaked so much pain upon not only the Mercian family, but his own, ripping them to shreds? Perhaps he did see, but simply did not care.

The ceremony was an understated but holy occasion and Wilfrid spoke eloquently. Efa had hoped to speak to him during the feast, but he was seated some distance away from the head table.

Ava had not returned for any food, and Efa wondered what they were to do with this fragile wight who was a reminder to all at Bamburgh of things best forgotten. Carena sat quietly by Alfrid's side throughout the meal, face pale and scarcely a morsel passing her lips, but at least Ava would not upset her further with her presence.

Efa was cross with herself for not forestalling the meeting; Ava should have been kept away from the festivities, but was it right to lock the girl away? Efa was not convinced that the guilt was entirely Ava's, but she'd yet to find out the truth of the matter. Patting Alfrid's arm in a request for him to sit back, she said to Carena, "I am so sorry, my dear. In truth, I had not thought to see you here."

"Forgive me, Lady Efa, but given the choice, I would not set foot in Bamburgh while your husband is here. I came only to support my husband."

Meanwhile Alfrid, never ebullient, ate his meal in sullen silence. Encountering his sister must have shaken him up, too, but it wasn't long before he had other things to worry about.

Oswii, seemingly tired of staring at Audrey, the latest addition to the family, now leaned across Efa to speak to Alfrid. "As soon as this is over, I want you to carry on north and go to the kingdom of the Picts. I need you to watch over things there. I don't trust them."

Alfrid did not look up. "I don't speak their tongue."

"You speak the tongue of your mother."

"She was from Rheged. It is not the same."

"You went there once before to do my bidding. What stays your hand this time?"

Alfrid cleared his throat and said, "As to that, it has been on my mind to go on a pilgrimage to Rome, and I wished to ask you…"

"No, I forbid it. I need you to ride north." Oswii turned to the other side and spoke to his youngest son, the bridegroom. "See how my children test me? Do not let me down, Boy. If my wife weren't past it, I'd get me some more sons to be sure of leaving my kingdom in safe hands."

Surprised by Oswii's short memory about their recently resumed physical relations, Efa did not immediately register the insult to her own person, nor put her husband right, instead feeling the tension in Alfrid's arm. She leaned in to make sure he and he alone heard her words. "I am sorry. I told you years ago that my husband does not see the worth of his own kindred. I wish I had been wrong, and I am heartsore for you."

She was rewarded with the tiniest of smiles, but when she turned to give a look of support to her own son, she found Ecgfrith's expression fixed, his stare focused not on her or his father, but somewhere out in the middle of the hall.

He'd listened to every word his father had said. In fact, the old man shouted so loudly that it was impossible not to hear. Ecgfrith wasn't being unduly sensitive, being very much aware that Oswii was indiscriminate with his targets and most people with even the slightest blood tie to the king had been insulted at some point that day. Still, it was the expectation of failure that rankled. *Do not let me down, Boy.* If his father could, he would get more sons, he'd said, as if knowing that Ecgfrith would fall short. So accustomed was he to responding to the shout of 'Boy!' that he was not sure his father even knew his name.

The old man was just that, though: old. His belly was too round for a mail shirt and he'd surely not the stamina for the battlefield these days. He must be beginning to realise what an irrelevance he'd become. Was that why he was always in a sour mood? Ecgfrith hated the Mercians, but he couldn't help recalling that even feasts were better affairs there than here. Was it tradition that the Northumbrians didn't feast as extravagantly, or was it that his father was too bored and weary even to bother?

Ecgfrith looked across the chamber at his bride, who was sitting on the bed, her arms folded across her chest, her plain robe covering every inch of her apart from her feet, neck, head, and hands. Her mouth was closed in a grim line, and he suspected that rather than bracing herself for the ordeal of this bedding, she'd already determined that it would not happen.

Undeterred, he took a step towards her, expecting her to shy away. Which was fine, because that way she'd end up more comfortably on the bed. She did not move. Not a flinch.

He'd thrown off his tunic and undershirt as soon as they'd walked into the bower, and now he kicked off his shoes, undid his leg bindings and slipped off his breeches, and put one knee next to her. Placing the other knee on the bed, he straddled her upright form, noting with satisfaction that his cock was in her face. Still she did not move, or even turn her head to one side. He grabbed her shoulders and pushed her until she was lying on her back, then stood up again at the end of the bed and tugged at the hem of her gown. She did not raise her arms, but kept them clamped to her sides, so he left the garment ruckled up around her waist.

At fifteen, he hadn't had huge amounts of experience but, even allowing for the fact that the girls who lived in and around Bamburgh and showed themselves willing enough to bed an atheling, were perhaps more practised than this royal lady, he still reckoned that his bride should be participating a little more. He lay down on top of her and tried to move her feet apart with his own foot. God but her legs were strong. His cock went limp and, instead of getting more excited by what those thighs might be able to grip, he found himself thinking that she'd be able comfortably to ride without a saddle all the way home to East Anglia when he put her aside in the morning.

But when daylight broke, and Ecgfrith went to find his father, the reaction was instant and dismissive. "You're not sending her back, Boy, she's here to stay."

Ecgfrith flexed his fingers, attempting to prevent them curling into fists. Should they come to blows, he had no doubt that he would best his father. Like an old stag during the rut, Oswii's antlers might be large, but he'd not the strength required to fend off challengers. "You know she follows the Roman ways? She'll be observing Lent while we feast at Easter."

Oswii laughed. "Christ's toes, yes, another one! At least she'll be company for your mother. Ha! You're plagued, like me." He wandered off towards the stables, still chuckling.

Ecgfrith walked over to the wall and stared out across the sea. He was not like his father. He would never be that. It was true that they were both beset by sour-faced women

50

who would not see reason, but there it ended.

His thoughts turned then briefly to his mother, who was in truth not cold enough towards him, smothering him with love and unable to refuse him any request. Memories blew up on the sea breeze of a gentle foster mother, who'd cared for him like one of her own, but he knew that his recall was false, and he ignored it. There was no room for sentiment in his life.

No, he was not like Oswii, though he was his father's son and his destiny was to wear the mantle of kingship, but he would be far, far more than that puffed up bag of wind had ever been. He would finish what Oswii started. Tenfold.

Ositha was woken early by the sun streaming through the window. It wasn't only that; she wriggled around under the covers and realised that the bed was wet. Flinging the sheet back she shifted a little and found the source of her discomfort. A patch of red, still warm. She would need to alert the servants to change her bedding and then seek out her mother to tell her that she was now, as of this day, a woman. She'd only seen twelve summers, and to anyone who might look upon her she would still appear to be a child; no hips or breasts to speak of. Not that anyone did ever look at her. Ositha was invisible. Ever since her father's famed victory over the Mercian pagan king, and the 'celebration' baby who did not live, she had felt like a child who dwelt in a shadow.

The light of their father's love shone on all his other children: Alfrid, given the kingdom of Deira; Ecgfrith, wed to a wealthy southern princess; even Ositha's younger sister, Alfleyda, deemed so special that she was given over to God who, in return, gave her father success on the battlefield and brought about Penda's death. Ositha was, she knew, neither needed nor especially wanted, until or unless some southern king or atheling came seeking an alliance.

51

So it had been a revelation to her when Ava arrived at the fortress, was met by their father who clapped her on the shoulder as if she had done something wonderful enough to earn Oswii's admiration, but then retreated, willingly, into the dark corners of Bamburgh. Ositha was intrigued; why would a daughter of Oswii's shun his love? Now, though, it did not matter. Ositha had her first bleed and was a highly valuable commodity, being the only daughter of the royal house of Bamburgh who could still be married. Now, her father would notice her.

She got out of bed with care, walking round the sleeping form of her serving-woman, snoring at the foot of Ositha's bed, and searched through the big wooden chest under the window light for the cloths that her mother had given her last year. Self-conscious, sure that everyone would know what had happened to her, she also pulled out her heaviest winter cloak and put it on, letting it swing loosely behind her in case the cloths let her down and betrayed her new status to a watching world. Luckily, few people apart from the servants should have stirred at this hour.

Her mother's chamber was empty though, so Ositha went outside to see if, unlikely as it was, the queen had slept in the king's room last night. Out in the yard, there was more activity than she'd expected. Her half-brother Alfrid was gathering his Deiran retinue, and her mother was there too, ready to wave him off. Ositha kept to the wall, not exactly hiding, but knowing that unless she moved, she would not be noticed.

Alfrid's wife was preparing to leave, but with a small escort. Alfrid called out to the man at the head of the group. "Aneurin, as soon as you have my wife safe back in York, leave a guard posted and bring all other men to meet me on the Dùn Èideann road." He brought his horse round to stand in front of the entrance to the great hall, where Efa stepped forward. "Farewell then. I shall not pass by this way on my journey back south. I will send a word-bearer to the king with any tidings."

Efa put her hand to her mouth and waved her fingers in his direction, as if sending a kiss. "He is still your father. Can you no longer bear to name him as such?"

Alfrid turned his horse round and looked back over his shoulder to answer her. "Not any more. I will do his bidding only because I must, but any candle of hope no longer burns."

"When you return, go by way of Ripon then. Speak to Wilfrid. If naught else, he will calm your spirit."

Ositha waited until all the horses and carts had clattered and trundled through the gate, and then took a step forward to speak to her mother. A heavy hand on her shoulder stopped her in mid stride, and whoever had grabbed her spoke with hot breath close to her ear. "What have I caught; a little spider watching for a fly? Or a bat, listening for one?

As she sensed her father straightening back up, and felt his grip relax, Ositha said, "I listen. No one sees me, even when I walk in plain sight, but I hear things."

The king came to stand in front of her, arms folded and an amused expression lifting his mouth and making his moustaches twitch. "And what have you heard, my little bat?"

At last, a chance to be noticed, to be of use. First Ava, and now Alfrid, had spurned their father's love. Perhaps it was time for the light of his gaze to shine warmly on Ositha. "I heard that the king might not have the love and loyalty of all those whom he rewards so handsomely."

"You think the eyes I have sent north will not watch the Picts closely for me?"

"No, Father," she replied, emphasising their kinship, "but I do think you should beware when those eyes return to Deira, for they go by way of Ripon."

Oswii scratched his chin and then ran his hand down the

length of his greying beard in a contemplative combing action. "Alfrid and the upstart Wilfrid, hmm? Well, little Bat, I think you should keep to the shadows, but not when I am near. When I am near, you must come and talk to me. I, too, can listen, and shall always welcome what you might have to say to me."

Ositha dropped into a reverent bow and went to find her mother. As she did so, she turned her face to the early morning sun. Today was the day she had become a woman, but not only that, she had truly found her place at her father's court. He wished her to be his eyes and ears, his little Bat. But as she approached her mother, she was asked to wait for a moment. Efa took Oswii aside and they had the briefest of conversations, during which the queen took the king's hand and placed it on her belly, and the king kissed his wife and picked her up, swinging her round before planting another kiss on her brow.

Chapter Three

The aged warrior straightened his spine, standing tall, and banged his axe and shield together. His head went back and he roared, a sound which seemed to have come up through the earth, entering his boots and gathering energy as it rose from his massive chest. He set off running towards his adversary, steps heavy, as if they would shake the very ground.

The young man standing in his way held his shield up, raised his axe and waited, feet apart, balancing him, keeping him steady. As the angry mass barrelled towards him, his knees wobbled and at the last moment he ducked and rolled, coming to land on the grass. In a moment, he was up on his feet and behind his attacker, holding his axe, ready to strike.

The older man took a while to come to a stop and when he did, he turned, walked up to the youngster, and grunted. "A fine trick, but it will only serve you once."

His young opponent beamed. "Once might be all I need." His audience laughed. Immin and Heaferth were by the fence, and Ethelred and Arianwen had witnessed the exchange from the grassy bank to the side of the hall. Merchelm responded to their applause by standing up and giving a deep bow. "See, I still have my axe and shield in my hands."

Sikke growled, a low grumbling which rang with a note of grudging approval. "Young Lord," he said to Ethelred, "It is your turn."

Ethelred was distracted by movement behind Sikke but did his best to keep a serious expression on his face. "Must I? I do not know how to roll and still keep hold of my shield like that."

"All the more reason."

"Besides, it is too nice a day, and I would rather…" He glanced sideways at Arianwen.

"One day you might be a king, and even if not, your learning of weapon-craft thus far has been lacking, so yes, you must. And you," he turned around as Merchelm attempted to grab him from behind, disarming the youth with one seemingly effortless flick of the wrist, "if you plan to be the eyes behind our lord's back, you must learn to move silently."

Merchelm grinned, rubbing his arm. "It was worth a try, was it not?"

Perhaps it was the years spent in hiding, rarely stepping outside, but Ethelred always felt at peace when the sun was shining. Arianwen was sitting so close to him that all he had to do was move his hand an inch and his fingers would cover hers. He sighed and hauled his reluctant body upright. "If it must be. But keep one thing in mind: Merchelm here will be a king too, and there is no doubt about that."

His friend acknowledged the statement, nodding and holding his head proud. For him, though, the situation was indeed different. Ethelred was the brother of a young king who had a daughter already, whom he and Ermenilda had named Werbyra, and would no doubt beget sons in the fullness of time. Merchelm was the eldest son of a king, and would undoubtedly succeed, but upon the death of a much-loved father. Ethelred saw the flash of sadness, and sought to lighten the mood again. "I misspoke. I should have said under-king."

Merchelm took the gift of levity and lunged at his friend, laughing. "I think my first act as under-king will be to gather my men and overthrow the king of Mercia!"

Ethelred hunkered down in a squat behind Arianwen.

"Ah, the mighty king of Mercia would hide behind a woman, would he?"

"This woman? Oh yes! My father was always friendly with the Welsh, and I aim to follow his habits."

Sikke put his hands up in a gesture of exasperation and admitted defeat. "Go then, spend your day as idle younglings. There may not be many more such carefree days. Immin and Heaferth can fight me. Two against one seems fair."

Immin affected a look of terror and said, "Lord Ethelred, speak a few words over our dead bodies later, will you?"

Laughing, Ethelred and Arianwen stood up, joined Merchelm, and they headed to the river, Ethelred in the middle, with an arm over each of his companions' shoulders. Thus entwined, they bumped and slipped as they tried to walk in step, until Merchelm broke away and ran ahead. Ethelred grabbed Arianwen's hand, pleased beyond reckoning that he was now brave enough to do so, and they followed, until they all arrived, panting, at the riverbank.

While Merchelm took off his boots and waded in to see if he could catch them some fish, Ethelred lay back on the soft bank and closed his eyes, feeling the sun warm his cheeks. He had thought Hereford to be the perfect home and hearth but Wenlock, a much smaller settlement, brought him a contentment he had not thought possible. The hall was less grand than Hereford's, though both were homelier than Tamworth. Tamworth, indeed, had a scarcely warm hearth since Wulf and Ermenilda had decided to make their home at Stone, where Ermenilda had given birth to their daughter. Similarly, Domneva had wished to move to a smaller residence, and it was here at Wenlock that she would have her next child, who currently was no more than a gentle rounding in her belly. Of course, where Domneva and Merwal went, so too did Arianwen, and Ethelred had not needed much prompting to follow her here. Was it that straightforward; was home simply wherever his Welsh beauty could be found?

He sensed movement and opened his eyes to see her picking some yellow-red flowers and putting them into her leather pouch. "For healing," she told him when she noticed his scrutiny. "Little Mildrith's skin is tasty for the gnats, it seems. When these are dried, she can rub them on the bites."

"I feel idle indeed," he said, sitting up on his elbows. "I was thinking only of how good it feels to lie under the sun, and you shame me by always thinking of others."

She closed the pouch but left it in her lap instead of returning it to the soft woven hemp girdle at her waist. She adjusted the girdle, tugging on the metal strap end, setting the spindle whorls and her little comb jangling. She shifted slightly, out of his reach, so that she could look at him. "I look around to see what might be of use later. And I think you do the same. It is one of the things I..." The sudden bloom on her cheeks could not be explained merely by the warmth of the sun. "I admire how deeply you think. Too many men rush like hounds in the hunt. There is naught wrong with being idle when you can. Life is about seeing what is in front of your eyes, and acting upon it. No more, no less."

"But..."

She put a finger to his mouth. "You must be carefree about being carefree, or else where is any peace to be found?"

He lay down, hands under his head. "What of change? What if I wished life to stay like this, here and now?"

"Ah well," she said, lying down beside him, so close that her hip touched his and made him aware of her body heat, "that cannot be. As Sikke said, one day you might be called

58

to wear the king-helm and you will have to do things you'd rather not. Meanwhile, make the most of your days."

He was thrilled and uncomfortable in equal measure at being so near to her and it was affecting his ability to think. When he spoke, his voice squeaked a little. "Do you never have any worries?"

"Oh yes, but I do not summon them. Let worries come and be dealt with when they do. But until then? No." She stood up, and he felt suddenly cold.

By the time he'd sat up, and saw her herb-pouch lying on the ground, she was in the water with Merchelm, her dress hitched up and tucked in her girdle. She waded towards Merchelm and began splashing him. Merchelm turned his back, attempting to deflect the water, and called out for help.

Ethelred, laughing, watched them for a while, but refused to come to his friend's aid. He wished only to look at Arianwen's smiling face, her dark eyes blinking swiftly as she squinted against the sprays of water, and the sound of her laugh, turning into the occasional shriek when Merchelm got his revenge by splashing her too.

The weeks went by and the weather remained benign. Frothy white blossom appeared on the blackthorn and, in the woods behind the settlement, catkins of hazel and willow began to adorn the branches while coughwort flowers danced yellow in the warm breeze. Ethelred and Merchelm, along with Immin and Heaferth, spent their mornings with Sikke and others of Merwal's guard, honing their fighting skills. At seventeen, Ethelred was now nearly the age that Wulf had been when he became king, Merchelm just a year younger. They both knew their childhood was well and truly behind them; they were warriors now.

One morning when Ethelred was getting washed and dressed he discovered that his undershirt was indeed a little snug. He had not grown taller but he now had the body of a fighting man and even a couple of downy hairs in the centre of his chest. He looked at Merchelm as he threw water over his head and upper body and noted that his friend, too, had the body of a grown man, albeit of more wiry frame. Sighing, Ethelred conceded that he would never best his friend in a running race.

He finished dressing and felt again to make sure that the amethyst necklace was safely tucked away in the leather pouch on his belt. Only a few days ago the ringing of a hand bell had alerted them to the arrival of a band of itinerant craftsmen, come to barter for new tools and treated hides. One of them, though, was a gemstone worker, and had shown Ethelred the string of delicate beads and accepted a purse of cut garnets in payment, which could be reworked. The purse had been in Ethelred's possession for years, though he'd no idea how he came by it.

After breaking their fast with bread and cheese, Ethelred and Merchelm made their way to the yard where a few of the men were already waiting, slicing the air with their swords, swinging axes, or thrusting spears into sacks of straw. Boasts about whether hazel or ash were better for spear handles soon took a lewd turn. "Harder is not always best." "No, indeed, it is better if it lasts longer."

The smoke from the smithy wafted on the gentle breeze and the sound of song came from the wattle-fenced retting pit, where several folk, including Arianwen, were working on the flax stems which had been soaked there before being dried, pounding them with mallets to remove the outer surface to get to the fibre within which could then be spun.

A servant came running to inform the men that Sikke had been taken ill. There was no reason why weapon training could not go ahead as usual, but Ethelred was concerned for his old friend and went to find him.

"It is naught," the Frisian assured him, holding his

60

stomach. "Lady Domneva warned me not to eat too many of the eels last night and I paid her no heed. Now, you see, I am paying the debt for my greed."

"Shall I call Arianwen to care for you?"

Sikke shook his head and answered swiftly. "There is no need, little Lord. The Frisian woman, Gesina, who works in the cook house, is looking after my needs."

Immin would have had a witty response, but all Ethelred could do was nod. He was at least reassured that Sikke was in no immediate danger.

Ethelred re-joined the men for the morning's session but he and Merchelm took off as soon as they could, going to Arianwen and trying to persuade her, with much bending of knee and high-pitched begging, to abandon her tasks for the rest of the day. She had in her hand her scutching knife which she was now using to remove the loosened outer layer of the flax stems, before handing them to the women who would heckle, using tools with long iron teeth to clean and separate the fibres before spinning. It was hot work, and she had her sleeves pushed back and her small workaday head-cloth was round her neck.

Valiantly, she resisted their pleading for some time, ignoring them whilst she concentrated on the flax, working up and down with her knife against a wooden board. "Not until this batch is done. I cannot be idle like young lords."

They waited, not patiently, and when she eventually put down her knife, the three of them set off together towards the woods. Ethelred knew that if he turned, he would see Heaferth some distance behind them, always following when he was able, always loyal.

The trees had begun to unfurl their new leaves and soon the woods would be darker as the canopy closed over the woodland floor, but for now there were still a few flowers and the faint smell of woodruff in the air. From somewhere came the plaintive cry of a buzzard. "The mouse hawks always sound so sad," Arianwen said. "Oh, look, bittersweet grows here, but it's still in blossom. I'll come back when the berries arrive."

"The berries kill. I recall at least that much from my childhood."

She smiled. "Yes, all children learn it, but small doses of the sap from them can be good for the blood and help to ease bruising."

Ethelred stole a sideward glance at her. Arianwen had lost some of the roundness in her face, no longer straddling two worlds but firmly in that of a grown woman. The sun was darkening her skin, especially her nose, cheeks, and forearms where she pushed up her sleeves while working. During their time alone, they'd done little more than hold hands, and indulge in the odd chaste kiss. His feelings went deeper than his actions suggested, but he was hoping that the necklace would say what he could not.

Merchelm, earning Ethelred's eternal gratitude, walked ahead, leaving the two of them to walk together for a while. Arianwen began singing, not the rhythmic song of earlier which she and her friends had sung in time to the pounding of the mallets, but a sweet melody which sounded like a cradle song.

"Peis Dinogat e vreith vreith.
 O grwyn balaot ban wreith.
 Chwit chwit chwidogeith.
 Gochanwn gochenyn wyth geith
"Pan elei dy dat ty e helya
Llath ar y ysgwyd llory eny llaw
Ef gelwi gwn gogyhwch
Giff gaff dhaly dhaly dhwc dhwc."

Her sweet voice soothed him, as if he were the bairn being rocked. The song stirred something else too though, and he wondered if it was a lullaby that Ava might also have known and perhaps sung to him at Tamworth in her British tongue when he was a small child.

He said, "The coat of Dinogat was spotted and speckled, and made from the skin of the pine? He wore a wooden coat?"

Arianwen chuckled. "Your Welsh is not as good as you think. His shift was made from the pelts of martens. The song is sung for little ones to help them to sleep and tells of Dinogat's father, a fearsome hunter. I sing it to Lady Domneva's babes. They too will be able to understand our tongue when they are grown up."

It was, so often, the way they learned other languages, from the songs sung by the women who rocked their cradles. Perhaps, then, Ava had indeed sung it to him many years ago. It was as if Arianwen had somehow unwittingly brought him a piece of his childhood and given him yet another reason to love her. Her hand was swinging gently by her side, and he dipped his knee to lower his height and grabbed her fingers. "Cariad," he began.

She laughed. "Ah, so you know Welsh words of love, at least."

They stopped on the path. He gazed down at her, while she tried to distract him by looking away, pretending interest in the bittersweet, but her cheeks were flushed. She had spoken of love even while he was thinking it and now all he wanted to do was to kiss her. He reached with his free hand and found the small of her back, exerting gentle pressure to persuade her closer. He bent his head to reach her mouth and she looked up at him, her smile gone, and with a look in her eyes that he hoped reflected his own desires. In a moment he would offer her the necklace as a token of his love.

"Ethelred!" His heart, already hammering, leaped in his chest. Merchelm, who had been ahead by some distance, was retracing his steps and, as he cleared the line of trees immediately in front of them, he sank to his knees.

Arianwen spoke it at the same time that Ethelred noticed it: the damp stain darkening his tunic, spreading out from his side. "Ethelred, he's hurt." She broke from his embrace and ran to help their friend. "What? Where?" she said as she pulled her head-cloth from her neck.

"Knife. In my side."

She inspected the injury and began folding the cloth. "Ethelred, I'll need you to press this and hold it tight for me."

Ethelred stepped forward and then stopped, one foot still in mid-air.

"Come, I need your help," she said, without looking up. "I need to find red nettle to help bind the wound."

"I think not, Lovely. You'll be coming with me." The man had sprung from the side of the path without sound or warning.

Arianwen's hands stopped moving. The woodland was silent save for the noise of buzzing flies and the scratching of grasshoppers and crickets in the undergrowth. She stood up awkwardly and Ethelred knew that she could feel the man's blade pressing the back of her neck.

No learned scop or wizened warrior was needed to explain the situation. Merchelm had come upon an outlaw, a man living with no lord, cast out probably for committing a crime and not paying the compensation. There had been a tussle and the outlaw had caught Merchelm's flank with his hand knife. And it was no more than a lucky catch, for Merchelm's chest was rising and falling in even rhythm and it was clear that he was in only a small amount of pain. What was less clear was how either of them could disarm the outlaw without risking Arianwen's life. She did not even have her scutching knife in her pouch for he remembered her putting it down by the retting pit fence.

"No swift moves, if you please," the man said.

He might not have realised it but complying with his

wishes gave the young friends some thinking time. Merchelm looked at Ethelred, glanced sideward at their assailant, and then silently puffed out his cheeks as if to blow his lips and make a farting sound. It was the same face that he made behind Sikke's back when he thought the Frisian could not detect his presence. Ethelred gave the tiniest of nods and awaited the signal.

Merchelm raised one leg until he was on one bended knee, feigning discomfort which the move might ease. Then, with a nod at Ethelred, he launched himself upright and onto the outlaw's back as, simultaneously, Ethelred shot forward to push the man back and away from Arianwen. She had the swiftness of mind to roll to the side and as soon as she was away from the scuffle she stood up and moved to a safe distance, stopping only to gather up the outlaw's fallen knife.

It was over in a heartbeat and Ethelred now had the man in a choke hold, his free hand pinning the outlaw's weapon hand high up behind his back. Arianwen came forward with the knife and pointed it at the thief's chest. "No swift moves, if you please," she repeated back to him.

Heaferth came running up, out of breath and muttering. Ethelred put a hand on his shoulder and dismissed his apologies. "No, you have not let us down, do not even think it. I am ever glad to know that you rarely let me out of your sight."

But Heaferth was adamant. "I was lacking in my care of you. I will never let you down again."

They marched the outlaw back to the settlement and handed him over to Merwal's men. His fate was out of their hands, but an assault on two athelings and the ward of the king would probably cost him his life. Merchelm was sent straightaway to give himself over to Father Cedda's ministrations and Arianwen was enfolded in Domneva's concerned embrace, and bundled off to the Lady's private

65

bedchamber, all the while protesting that she was none the worse for her ordeal, imploring that word be sent to Cedda to be sure to make the red nettle poultice, and still unaware of the amethyst necklace.

It was only then that Ethelred noticed the increased activity in the yard. The stables were noisier than usual, and the smith had both his sons working hard in the forge with him. Folk were dashing in and out of the bake house and the steward was more animated than usual, waving his arms at retreating backs, calling out afterthoughts of instructions. A particularly strangely marked horse with a white blaze on the side of its head, familiar bronze decorations on the bridle and embossing on the saddle, was being led round the perimeter fence by one of the horse-thegns, as if a concern of lameness had been voiced. Ethelred knew that horse. "Our brother is here," he said, in statement rather than question.

Merwal answered him, nevertheless. "He is indeed. Come within; he wishes to speak to you."

Fatherhood certainly suited Wulf. His smile stretched wide as soon as he saw Ethelred and he leaped down from his seat on the dais to envelop his younger brother in the tightest of bear hugs. He practically danced back to his chair.

Ethelred sat where he was bidden and nodded his thanks to the young girl who poured his drink, while he listened to his brother, his king.

"My borders are safe, the marches secure. The Welsh have more love for us than for the Northern bastard who sent for more tribute but two summers ago. I have proven that I can father an atheling, given time, and meanwhile I have a brother who is a man grown and a skilled fighter, if I can believe what Sikke tells me. I have come to fetch you, for the fruit is ripe for plucking."

"Fruit?" Ethelred's stomach wobbled as any hopes he'd

harboured of Wulf living to old age sailed out of his heart, taking with them his dreams of a peaceful life with Arianwen.

"I am not yet strong enough to take Oswii on, but there are scores to settle in the south and I will skin two hares with one knife, ridding myself of a foe and binding the other kingdoms to me. I am marching on the West Saxons, and I want you and the Magonsæte with me."

Ethelred twirled his cup gently but did not drink. There was no need to ask when they were leaving, for the grass had already grown tall enough to feed the horses and the best time for a campaign was now. He glanced at the open doorway where the late afternoon sun was sending speck-filled rays into the gloomy interior. His heart yearned for naught more than further sunny days spent with Merchelm and Arianwen, for he scarcely understood what any fight with the West Saxons could achieve and all he really craved was a little stillness, but this day had taught him two things: he was ready, more than ready, to join a hearth-troop, and that he would kill for love.

There had been no time to say farewell. The troops who had accompanied Wulf from Stone assembled shortly after dawn. Wulf himself was ready to lead them out not long after, and Ethelred and Merchelm and their own thegns were left scrambling to gather their weapons and the personal items they'd brought from Tamworth: their clothes, blankets, combs and spare shoes. Sikke was still not well enough to accompany them and when Ethelred had a few moments while Merwal took his leave of Domneva, the choice was between seeking out Arianwen, or paying respects to the Frisian who had been as a father to him during their years of wandering. Duty took him to the bower where he found Sikke, sitting up, but still looking pale.

"So, you are off to war, little Lord."

"Yes. Although I am not wholly sure why."

Sikke sipped from his cup and grimaced. No doubt some potion mixed for him by Arianwen. "And Merchelm goes with you?"

"He does."

The old warrior nodded his approval. "And your dearling; have you taken your leave?"

Ethelred coughed. "There is no time." Besides, he had not told her, in the end, how he felt about her and since he might never come back, it was perhaps as well. Better that there was no understanding, no hint of a promise that could not be kept.

As he walked back outside, he thought that he saw her, standing some distance off, by one of the storage huts, but he did not dare turn and look. Bad enough that he felt his heart might break, but he would not risk hers too.

Wulf was already on his horse. "Ready?"

"Aye." Ethelred coughed and tried again. It had been a while since his voice had betrayed him, the high-pitched catch reminding him how recently he had emerged fully from boyhood. In his man's register, he managed to say, "To Tamworth now?" They would need to ride east and gather the rest of the Mercian forces before they headed any further south.

Wulf confirmed it, turning his horse and heading for the gate. "To Tamworth."

After two days' rest at Tamworth, they rode out again, now at the head of a much bigger host, with men arriving all the time, answering the call to arms. Penwal brought his Middle Angles, and men came too from the lands of the Wreconsæte in the northwest and the Chilternsæte in the southeast, and even from Elmet, the British kingdom which had been overrun by the Northumbrians. They moved slowly, with foot soldiers and loaded supply carts dictating the pace. The hot summer had kept the roads dry, but not baked so hard that any ruts would impede the cart wheels or cause marching men to turn an ankle. Ethelred, as befitted his rank, rode alongside Wulf and with them were Merwal and Merchelm, and the three leading thegns, Edbert, Immin, and Heaferth, his Arosæte contingent riding with the Magonsæte. Ethelred glanced at his brother, noting how Wulf's jaw was moving as if he was grinding his teeth. "How far south will we ride?"

"Until we find the bastard Cynwal."

"I heard of no raids by the West Saxons into Mercia. I had thought those days were behind us."

Wulf's jaw twitched again. "Those days will never be behind us. Cynwal was driven from his kingdom by our father."

"Yes, and he has shown no aggression since."

"Ah, but he is back. He recovered his king-helm, after Winwæd, with the help of Oswii. He will dance to Northumbrian tunes, bark when Oswii whistles, and we are not safe with him in the south. I cannot fully throw off the northern yoke until the south is bound to me."

Ethelred said, "Doesn't that mean doing to them what Oswii does to you?"

"Oh, I will do far more than that."

"Did our father not punish Cynwal enough, taking his king-helm from him and sending him snivelling into East Anglia? He would not dare to come at us now, surely?"

Wulf shifted in his saddle and batted away a fly. "He was no threat while he was hiding in the east, and it would have been better for him had he stayed there, but I cannot let him have his kingdom back. I must end what Father began." He paused, setting his face into a kinder expression. "You were so young. You do not recall what it was like for Aunt Audra when Cynwal put her aside and sent her home."

69

There was little Ethelred could say in reply. He wondered how much Wulf, being only four years older, truly remembered, and whether he'd even been born when their Aunt Audra came home. Still, Wulf was his king and if he thought there were debts to be paid, who was Ethelred to gainsay him?

They stopped in the late afternoon to camp overnight at a small settlement which Ethelred was told had been used by their father sometimes when he rode to the southern edge of Mercian lands. The thegn who owned the hall was the last of the Chilternsæte to join them and was expecting them, but did not have enough stabling available, even for the royals and nobles. A hasty meal was served and Merchelm and Merwal chose to take their food and join the rest of the Magonsæte in the tents beyond the settlement defences.

"Brother," Wulf called out as they walked off.

Merwal turned.

"Will you come back later? There are things to be said."

"I'll bide with my men. When your guest arrives, speak to him. If he agrees, then all is well. I shall only need to know if he does not."

Ethelred was intrigued. Who were they waiting for? His knowledge of the land of his birth was shaky but if they were on the southern tip, in the lands of the Chilternsæte, then there was only one other kingdom left to join them.

His thoughts were confirmed when Immin walked in and announced, "King Enfrith of the Hwicce."

The guest and his entourage walked up to the dais, filling what had already been a room seemingly at capacity. The air was warm, and the men were sitting and standing so closely that Ethelred could smell the breath of the man next to him.

King Enfrith was of middling years, perhaps of a similar age to Merwal, but he was shorter, more compact, and with brawnier limbs. He stood now in front of Wulf, and there

70

was a shuffling up on the dais as leading Mercians hastily vacated their seats or shifted along until there was space next to Wulf. Enfrith took his seat beside him and Wulf beckoned Ethelred to sit on his other side.

Wulf said, "Enfrith of the Hwicce, you are welcome."

Enfrith waited while the lady of the hall poured him a drink, and then replied, less formally, "I think I know why you sent for me."

His blunt response was met with a smile from the king of Mercia. Wulf said, "Then let us go to the heart of things. In my father's day, your lands were overrun and ruled by Cyngil of the West Saxons. My father fought them and came home with Cyngil's son Cynwal as hostage, only to free him at the urging of my aunt who then wed him."

Ethelred could not see Enfrith's expression, but he heard the irritation in his voice. "Yes, yes, all who no longer have cradle marks on their arse know what happened then, and after. He put her aside, your father hunted him down, and he went to cower in the godforsaken bog that is East Anglia."

This raised a laugh among all those sitting near enough to hear. Ethelred had never been to the east, but even he knew a man was as likely to catch a marsh fever there as an enemy arrow.

Wulf smiled too, but then he sat up straight and stared at his guest, reminding Ethelred of the trained polecats in Domneva's sheds, who did the same when about to pounce on the mice. "But did you also know that he is back? And that he has gifted three thousand hides of land at Ashdown to his kinsman, Cuthred?"

The brief silence, the small hesitation, told Ethelred that this was indeed news to Enfrith. And where had Wulf heard it? His brother was a shrewd king indeed if, while busy wedding and bedding his wife, he had thought to send Mercian watchers into the territory of the West Saxons.

71

Wulf picked some dirt from under his thumbnail. "And do you wish to have Cynwal so strong that he might, once again, come after Hwiccian lands?"

Enfrith appeared to have recovered his speech, but not his wits. "Why would he?"

Wulf inspected the rest of his nails, holding his hands out in front of him and then, apparently satisfied, placed them on the table. "A fast rider could be from Ashdown to your heartland in Gloucester in two days. A warband in not many more. Leaving his kinsman ruling in Ashdown leaves Cynwal free to wander elsewhere. There is, so I am told, a third kinsman, who has also been gifted lands. If Cynwal is strong enough to leave his kingdom in the hands of others, he might also feel strong enough to move north. And he would reach your lands first."

Enfrith said, "And do you know where Cynwal is now?"

"I do not. If he has any sense, he will know that I am coming for him."

"But you do not intend to do that, Brother." Ethelred might not know much about the art of war, but he understood what Wulf was suggesting. "We are to ride on Ashdown, fight Cuthred, leave them weakened and…"

Wulf smiled. "And if it draws Cynwal to us, so much the better. If not, I'll leave Ashdown and the land around it smouldering and black, and I'll keep searching. So, King Enfrith, are you with us?"

"What do you offer?"

Ethelred was surprised at that, because the other tribes had come willingly enough without promises, but he realised then that the lands of the Hwicce were crucial in forming a barrier between the West Saxons and the Mercian heartlands, and might look to the south for friendship instead of Mercia. It was his first lesson in statecraft and he sighed, realising that he still had much to learn.

Meanwhile, the king of Mercia turned in his chair so that

all Ethelred could see was his shoulder and the back of his head. "I offer freedom in Hwiccian lands, which I had hoped might be enough, but I see it is not. Therefore, I hope this is to your liking." Whatever was said next, Ethelred could not hear it, so softly was it spoken into King Enfrith's ear.

"We are in West Saxon lands now."

Ethelred wondered, stupidly probably, how Wulf knew. Of course, kings had ways of knowing things, and Ethelred again experienced the almost ever-present doubt that he would ever be competent to rule. He pointed to the horizon. "What is that?"

Immin answered him. "The ridgeway." We will not ride up there or we will be seen for miles around. Edbert sent men out three days ago to seek out Cuthred's lair. Once they are back, we can plan whether to attack his fortress or draw him out in open battle."

"If I were Cuthred, and I knew that we were coming, I would go there." Ethelred pointed up the hill.

Wulf and Immin followed his gaze to the ancient hillfort, with what looked like a new wooden palisade around it. "Brother, you are right."

Ethelred tried to hide his surprise. "And we will never get up there without being seen. I think we should wait until dark and send a man up there to torch it. Draw them out, if they are there."

His companions exchanged glances of approval, and Wulf reached out of his saddle to slap his younger brother on the shoulder. "Is my king-helm safe upon my head? Immin, let's find somewhere safe to camp and then bring me your best men. I have a task for you."

Ethelred could not help smiling. Pride was a sin, Father Cedda had told him, but surely God would forgive him? Perhaps it was God who had heard his doubts and sent him

73

proof that he could, indeed, think like an atheling? But then the questioning voice murmured in his head: had Wulf already thought it all through and was simply humouring him?

The chalky soil of the down lands would make pitching camp difficult, and Wulf decided that they should dispense with the tents altogether. With orders to find shelter under the carts or scrubby trees, the men took what rest they could, but most stayed awake that night, for rumours had rippled through the ranks like a breeze through woodland treetops, that something was planned.

Ethelred gratefully took the bowl of broth handed to him as the sun sank, but he knew he would not sleep, even though nothing would happen until the moments just before dawn. This was not the weapons practice yard, and Sikke was not here, pretending to be his foe. The enemy was real, and many, and Ethelred wondered if any other Mercians, sitting in the gloaming where fear on faces could not be seen, also had the sensation that, at any moment, they would shit their breeches. He put the bowl down on the ground and prayed.

Thankfully, the summer night was short. Ethelred must have nodded off, against his expectations, for he only belatedly became aware of a stirring in the camp: whispers, grunted responses, and then the sound of running feet. Around him, men began to emerge from their resting places and those who had them put on mail coats and attempted to buckle their sword belts quietly. A dull clatter, thankfully a wooden sound which did not reverberate, was followed by a curse. A stack of shields had evidently been disturbed.

Edbert's men had not returned. There was no knowing whether any West Saxons were up in the hillfort for no smoke had been seen rising from it; anyone up there would have had a cold night. If the place was empty, then their search for Cuthred would continue. If not, there would be a battle. Ethelred stood up and vomited.

The sky lightened. It was not the sun's rays which lit up the pre-dawn, however, but a fire. Immin's men had completed their mission. The Mercians stood and watched, waiting to see how many men came running down from the height of the ridgeway. Ethelred counted only three, figures running fast and scrambling down the hillside. Then, none. There must have been no more than a token guard up there. As dawn broke and the flames licked higher, the Mercian ranks began to stand down, ready to put down their weapons, take off their helms, and try to snatch some sleep.

"Wait." Ethelred blinked, and stared at the conflagration. More men appeared, running not down the hill, but almost in circles, like disturbed ants. They were men who were confused, roused from slumber by flames, weapons grabbed hastily and sheathed and shouldered, and waiting for instructions. "Will they come, now?"

Wulf was at his side. "Not yet. When the sun is fully up, when they've had time to wipe the sleep dust from their eyes and work out what has happened. Now, we must move out into the open, choose a place to stand and raise our shield wall."

A voice called out from behind them. "You might have waited for us." Edbert's words were indignant, but his tone was not. He drew level with them, while his men went off immediately in search of food.

Wulf greeted him with a pat on the shoulder. "Ah, and there was I thinking you would miss the fight."

His deputy grinned. "Never. We rode out for some way, but there is no sign of Cynwal or Cuthred beyond the ridge. If one or both are not up there, then we have some riding still to do to find them."

Ethelred, who'd been staring up at the hillfort, dared a question. "If we raise a shield wall, and they come down the hill at us, will they not break our wall?"

"Yes, if we do not move to better ground. Edbert?"

"I have the spot. My men saw it on the way back here."

Wulf patted him on the shoulder. "Show me."

It was almost impossible to see anywhere other than straight ahead. Packed behind the shield wall, Ethelred was jammed up against the men to either side of him, while behind him was a second, reinforcing wall. Not only was this his first pitched battle but it was the first time he had been away from Merchelm, who was somewhere further down the line with his father and the rest of the Magonsæte. The sounds and smells clashed with the gentle yellow sunlight which bathed the unfamiliar, dusty landscape. Men were fidgeting, their voices rumbling without projecting discernible conversation. Banners slapped in the breeze which also carried the odour of sweat, flatulence and yes, maybe shit, too. There was no shame in being frightened. Ethelred understood this now.

There were rules, too, evidently, for there had been no mass slaughter in the dark while Cuthred's men were sleeping. Wulf had allowed them time to regroup and to find the Mercians who were calling them out to fight. In a manner that honoured their father's reputation, Wulf was continuing his campaign in a similarly fair way. This might be war, and no doubt it would be bloody and brutal, but Wulf had given the West Saxons a fighting chance.

Whether they had taken full advantage of it was debateable. Their line was ragged as they advanced. The men were marching too far apart effectively to pull back quickly into a shield wall. Next to Ethelred, Wulf muttered. "This is the best they can do? Cynwal has put too much faith in his kinsman. This will not take long."

He was right; this was not an army. Even Ethelred with his limited experience could see that the men advancing towards them were only those who manned the garrison.

Cuthred might not even be among them. They must have thought there was no threat from Mercia or they would have posted guards on their borders, or at the very least lit a beacon to send for help.

Edbert had picked the perfect site. The Mercians stood atop a slope, their flanks protected by gorse thickets. As the West Saxons approached, edging their way up the hillside, they had the morning sun in their eyes and could not dodge the javelins being hurled at them from behind the Mercian wall. Ethelred stood with one foot slightly in front of the other, balanced over both legs, braced and ready for the impact.

The line of West Saxons hit the shield wall, the thud of multiple linden shields coming together sent the whole line reverberating, and Ethelred almost let go of his shield. Now they must hold, not let the West Saxons push them back or, worse, begin to spin the line round. Anyone who was in arm's reach was poked back with a spear thrust and if anyone in the wall stabbed with his weapon, the man to the side of him kept the shields close together, protecting him.

Now that the enemy was so close the heat and stench were intense. The sound was ear-splitting, mixing cries, shouts, and the clunk of metal on wood, the song of metal upon metal. The Mercians need not have reinforced their wall for they must have outnumbered the West Saxons by at least two to one. In the end it was almost too easy. The West Saxons, pushing uphill and against a larger force, tired quickly. They could not break the wall and when, exhausted, they relaxed the pressure, the Mercian flanks came round to encircle them.

Ethelred knew that not all fights would be so straightforward. Nevertheless, he sent a silent prayer heavenward in thanks for the relative simplicity of this one, and that he had come through it unscathed. Wulf really needn't have planned this fight so intricately. It was well that he had not let these men burn in the night, but it was clear that the whole day's only purpose was to make a point, and he had certainly done that. Now, all that remained was to decide what to do with the prisoners.

Wulf stepped from the now ragged shield wall and walked towards the surrounded and defeated West Saxons. "Which of you is Cuthred?"

Ethelred had already marked out the man whom he thought was Cynwal's kinsman, for he wore a helm and his sword, glinting in the sunshine, flashed the distinctive swirls that betrayed it as being pattern-welded, a blend of twisted iron rods which made a superior blade, but Wulf needed formal identification. Would Wulf expect Cuthred to travel with them, or would this high-status prisoner be sent under armed guard back to Stone?

Wulf stepped forward and eyed Cuthred up and down, then walked back towards the Mercians. Such hazy memories as Ethelred had of his early childhood before his exile were mainly suffused with warmth. The children of Penda grew up wrapped in love and were happy. Any images he had of his brothers showed them looking down on him from their greater height and smiling at him. Neither then, nor in the years since their reunion, had he ever seen such a look of contempt on Wulf's features. Seeing it jolted his heart and made it beat faster, just when it had calmed down after the fighting. His fingers tightened around his shield strap and his sword. His mouth was dry, and not just because of the recent effort in the wall.

Wulf reached his men and nodded to Edbert. Edbert stepped forward, walked up to the vanquished West Saxon leader, reached up and drew his knife across Cuthred's throat. The dying man's face registered only surprise and in the shocked silence which followed, Ethelred thought he heard the sound of Cuthred's life blood splashing on the ground. Ethelred's throat burned as bile came from

78

somewhere deep in his guts and he was convinced he was about to spew once more.

As if aware of his shock, Wulf said, "It had to be done."

One day you might be called to wear the king-helm and you will have to do things you'd rather not. Surely this was not what Arianwen had in mind when she'd spoken those soft words to him, what felt like a lifetime ago?

The West Saxons stirred as if from a heavy slumber. Those of the elite who carried swords pulled them once more from their scabbards and the singing was of metal on metal and no longer of axe upon linden wood. Shield walls were no longer a consideration as one-to-one, sometimes one-to-two or more, combat began. A West Saxon charged towards Ethelred and he put his shield up to defend himself, absorbing the impact along his shield arm and stabbing with his sword in his other hand. He'd made contact and it took a moment for him to pull his weapon free, just in time to swipe at a man coming at him from the left. Soaked in sweat, Ethelred worried that his blade would slip from his hand. Another man lunged at him, sword high, aiming to slash down on Ethelred's neck. Ethelred parried, deflecting the blow with an upward push of his shield which left his body vulnerable. The man pushed Ethelred hard in the stomach with his shield boss and Ethelred staggered backwards, slipping on the blood-wet ground. He was down on one knee with no hope of defending himself unless with a lucky thrust that could pierce his adversary's thigh or groin. The West Saxon's sword came down hard on Ethelred's shield again and he wobbled. He commended his spirit to the Lord and prepared to die.

The wet ground squelched with the impact of the dead weight landing heavily. The body lay with legs twisted, blood bubbling gently from the exposed area of neck twixt helm and mail coat. The eyes were open, staring heavenward and, in this slaughter-field, would remain so until someone came to claim and tend the body. If they came at all.

"Here." A hand, bloodied, gestured with beckoning fingers.

Ethelred took it, stood up, and pulled Merchelm to him with his free arm. "Thank you, my friend." Merchelm had used his trick of surprise to come up from behind, and make his foe turn and find himself off-balanced.

Merchelm grunted and patted him on the back. "It would be nice not to be known as the man who fights from behind another's back. But it serves well enough!" With that, he ran off, leaving Ethelred to gather his wits.

He scrabbled around for his sword, but there was no urgent need. The field was quiet now bar the cries of the wounded and dying. Wulf had a man at sword point, and Ethelred flinched, expecting his brother to run his captive through. He stepped forward as if to beg him not to, though he knew the words would not leave his lips. This army was Wulf's to command. He, Ethelred, was Wulf's to command. He waited; what was one more death to witness after so many?

But King Wulfhere of Mercia said, with rasping voice, "Go. I grant you your life. Take my words to your king. Tell Cynwal what you have seen here and tell him what awaits him."

The man ran, stumbling in his haste. Sword still in hand, Wulf wiped blood and sweat from his chin as he walked towards his brother. "Now," he said, "now he knows I'm coming for him."

By day, they marched. At night, they pitched their tents and ate the food gathered from the settlements they passed by. They had been away from home only a matter of weeks, but supplies were low and they, like any warband on the move, were compelled to demand food from those who lived along their marching route. Thus they made no attempt to

80

conceal their presence and Ethelred had a constant prickle at the back of his neck that made him want to turn round and see if Cynwal was on their trail. He did not materialise.

There was always drinking and gaming, but often Ethelred would finish his meal, nod at Merchelm, and, with the summer nights so warm and light they would leave the others and walk the camp, just the two of them.

"You miss her."

"I do." There was no point in lying, for Arianwen was never far from his thoughts, and when he got home there were things which must be said.

Merchelm hailed one of his thegns who was sharpening his sword with a whetstone, and then continued the conversation. "One day I might know how that feels."

Ethelred stopped for a moment. It had not occurred to him that, at only a year younger than himself, his nephew was of an age where he, too, should have had a woman to call 'dearling' by now. He, though, more certainly than Ethelred, would be a king one day and perhaps would have less say in who his bride might be.

The next day as the march resumed, still with thoughts of home, Ethelred sought out Wulf to ask how much further south he intended to take the Mercians. Only another few weeks would see the harvest and the men would be keen to go back and oversee the gathering in of the crops. The terrain had changed, and ahead there was a forest which looked as if it covered the rest of the land to the sea, it was so vast. "Are we going in there?"

"Not if Immin found… Ah, it seems that he did."

A group of around thirty men emerged from the forest, Immin among them. At their head was a man dressed in a deep red wrap-over coat and riding a horse with a richly decorated bridle. Whoever he was, he was high-ranking.

Swift as ever at reading his brother's thoughts, Wulf said, "Behold, Athelwal, the king of the South Saxons." Ethelred must have been staring like a landed fish, for Wulf continued, "A mile into our ride this morning we crossed from Cynwal's lands. Now we take the fight..."

"To the South Saxons? They look as if they ride to speak with you, not to fight."

Wulf said, "Indeed. I have an offer for King Athelwal. I feel sure that after he has heard it, he will ride south with us."

Ethelred could not quite believe that there was anywhere further south. Any schooling that he'd received had been at the hands of the Welsh monks whom he and Sikke had encountered during their wanderings, and although he had been taught about the kingdoms and where they lay, he had always believed that the South Saxons ruled a land that ended at the sea. Where were they going? And what was it that Wulf would offer to persuade Athelwal to ride with them? At least he wasn't going to deal with him as he had done Cuthred, and for that, God be praised.

For once, the heat of the midday sun was not a welcome presence. Its reflection seemed to bounce from every piece of metal. Ethelred was sweating, and he felt sick. The shade of those trees looked enticing now, rather than foreboding. Sadly, no such respite was offered. Wulf and the king of the South Saxons went off together, with only their personal guards in attendance and, shortly afterwards, the southerners accompanied the Mercians on their journey, showing them where to camp that night.

Over the next few days the army, already augmented with King Enfrith's Hwiccians, swelled further with arrivals from Athelwal's kingdom, as his thegns brought their fighting men to join the allied force. Wulf did not divulge any details of his conversation with King Athelwal and Ethelred thought it prudent not to ask. Instead, he rode with Heaferth and Immin and asked how it was that Wulf knew so much about what was happening in the other kingdoms.

Heaferth said, "Our fathers served yours. Penda was a great one for speaking to many of the tribe leaders and asking what they knew. Immin's father, Lothar, was hearth-thegn to yours. He rode many miles with, and for, your father. When the time came for us to rise up again, we put that knowledge to good use and now keep watchers in as many kingdoms as we can." And, as if still ruing the attack on Merchelm by the outlaw, he added, "But I am not a watcher. I will bide with you at all times."

Immin, a man of few words and none wasted, said, "We're back in Cynwal's lands, now. There may be a scuffle or two."

Learning to appreciate the grim humour of the campaign life, Ethelred smiled at the understatement.

Yet it was accurate. As they passed through the southernmost parts of Cynwal's territory, Wulf showed a new side. A few groups of belligerent West Saxons were swiftly dealt with and occupying patrols were left to guard strategic areas, but on the whole the Mercian army moved through the southern reaches and left nary a sign, beyond taking food supplies, that they had been there.

Ethelred was still struggling to reconcile the situation with the bloodletting at Ashdown when he detected a strange smell in the air. The landscape was flatter and the sounds around him had changed, too. The birds wheeling overhead made odd, crying noises, and the wind was noticeably stronger. They'd been following the path of a river which had taken them through the lands of the folk known as the Meonwara and now that river had widened and opened out into an expanse of water that had no far bank.

Ethelred turned to Heaferth, who explained. "A wider river, not yet the sea, but we cannot cross here; we need to move along the shoreline a little."

"Cross? What do you mean, cross? Why are we...We have reached the very edge of the land. What need is there to go further?"

Heaferth rubbed his forefinger back and forth across the bottom of his nose, either scratching an itch or trying to block out the salty smell. "There is an island over there which sends tribute to Cynwal. Our lord would have it known that Mercian hands reach to the southernmost tip of Cynwal's lands."

Ethelred knew he had suffered a lack of learning during his childhood but how, he wondered, would tribute – cattle and the like – get from the island? Indeed, how were they themselves to cross? When they got to the hithe and he saw the boats and was told they must leave the horses behind, his question about cattle was answered. All other queries became less than urgent, for after little more than a heartbeat into the voyage, he began vomiting over the side of the boat.

On an overcast day, at a place called Chichester, they stood by the river. A week earlier, they had assembled to witness as Athelwal of the South Saxons, dressed in white, had the baptismal filet of cloth wrapped around his head by Wulf's priest and was received into the Church. Now, it was time for the chrisom-loosening. Wulf had stood sponsor for the new sub-king; Athelwal's lands were now subject to Mercian rule, and in return he had been given the land of the Meonwara and the island to the south. As Ethelred stood and watched the ceremony, he could also see in his mind's eye how carefully it had all been planned. King Enfrith of the Hwicce had sent for his daughter and now they were all to witness her marriage to Athelwal. Small wonder, then, that the lands of the Meon Valley had been tenderly crossed. Small wonder, too, why King Enfrith was wooed by Wulf. Now the Mercian king had lordship over the South Saxons who in turn were bound by marriage alliance to the Hwicce. Cynwal was surrounded.

The bride, however, looked less than happy. She was a slight woman, with wide eyes and a turned-up nose. Her eyebrows were so fair they were almost white. She shook a little and her voice quivered as she made her vows, and Ethelred wondered how her husband, a grizzled warlord, would treat her.

Memories came, of his parents shouting at one another. Ethelred had been young, and the discord upset him. For him to recall the occasion must mean it was unusual for them to have cross words. He could see himself, as a small boy, asking one of his sisters what the trouble was, and he could hear her saying it was something to do with Mother being wroth with Father for letting Carena wed Alfrid.

His mind might be playing tricks about their arguing; perhaps it was only about the details, of Carena going so far away, because he knew for certain that Carena, like his Aunt Audra, had wed for love. And Wulf had reminded him only recently how their father had chased Cynwal far and wide because of his mistreatment of Audra. Wasn't there also a tale about Penda's cousin, who wed Edwin of Northumbria, again for love, but was put aside, thus stirring Penda's ire?

Three Mercian princesses then, all wed outside Mercia, but all by their own choice. This young Hwiccian bride looked to have had no say in her own wedding and Ethelred was not sure how truly Wulf was walking in their father's footmarks if he was selling a bride. Was he not behaving, and making other kings behave, like the ones Penda had despised? Ethelred reached into the leather pouch hanging from his belt and ran his thumb over the cool amethysts lying there.

He kept his thoughts to himself while he witnessed the wedding, but as they made their way to Athelwal's hall, he caught the expression on Merwal's face. His half-brother's lips were pinched, as if there was a bad taste in his mouth, too. At the feast, Ethelred drained his ale cup every time it was refilled, but somehow did not manage to wash the bitterness away. He did, however, wake the next morning with a whole host of tiny carpenters in his head, banging nails into his skull.

He vaguely recalled Wulf's announcement the previous evening that Edbert's raiding party had won a skirmish and killed another of Cynwal's kin. With two of the West Saxon king's close kin now dead, and with the South Saxons beholden to Mercia and overseeing the lands of the Meonwara and the island beyond, surely the south was secure? The East Anglians had not sent out so much as one watcher the whole time the Mercians had been in the south, so he assumed they had been thoroughly bested by Penda and would neither threaten Mercia nor go running to Northumbria for alliance or protection. When the command came for the Mercians to ride out, Ethelred worried for a moment that they were, after all, going east, but to his great relief, it was a signal for them to go home.

Chapter Four

Tamworth, AD661: Autumn

Riders had been sent ahead to inform Ermenilda that the men were on their way home to Tamworth and she and her daughter, little Werbyra, were standing outside the hall waiting for them. Smoke rising from the cook house told of cheeses made with the last of the year's milk being smoked for the winter stores, and men were scaling ladders to add fruit to the high lofts in the barns. There were sheaves of harvested barley stacked outside the long wall of one of the barns, and two men were reducing the stacks and taking them into the granary. Wulf's army had dwindled similarly as men had gone home to help with the harvest, but the king was delayed by gift-giving ceremonies, so he and his hearth-troop had not got to Tamworth in time, and most of the work was done.

Ermenilda looked calm, as if it were any other autumn day, as if they had not themselves recently arrived from their hall at Stone. Only those who understood what it took to run a settlement would realise that Ermenilda's steward had been scrambling round like a chased chicken in order to make sure that this illusion was convincing. Extra loaves would already be in the ovens and no doubt there were still carts laden with supplies from Stone being unloaded behind the hall. Tamworth was no longer Wulf's main residence, but a stranger would never have guessed. Kings were wont to move between residences and the stewards were practised at ensuring that the musty smell was removed from unused halls and knew to bring food to supplement the stores.

Wulf leaped down from his horse and scooped Ermenilda

into a hug before kneeling down and remaking his acquaintance with his daughter, who hid shyly behind her mother's skirts. Domneva and her daughters had made the journey from Wenlock, too, and were smiling, waiting.

It had been a crisp, sunny morning and now that the sun was as high as it would get for the time of year, it brought welcome warmth. The coming night would be cold though, for there was not even a wisp of cloud. Ethelred dismounted, handing his reins to a waiting stable-hand, and greeted his sister-by-law with a kiss on the cheek, before Merwal pushed him gently away. "That's my wife, Lad," he chuckled, before picking her up and spinning her in his embrace. Once he'd set her down, Merchelm stepped forward, kissing his stepmother on the forehead.

"I swear you have grown some more since you rode out," Domneva said. Answering Ethelred's enquiring glance she added, "She is not here, I am sorry."

"She did not ride with you? She bides at Wenlock?"

Domneva shook her head.

"Hereford then?"

Another shake of the head. "Arianwen's sister was taken ill, and she has gone back to their brother's lands to tend her." She patted his forearm.

Anything else which might have been said was left as thoughts, for Merwal said, "Show me the bairn," and dragged Domneva away.

Ethelred stared after them, feeling lost and alone.

"Do not be sad. You still have me to speak to."

He turned round to see his sister beaming at him. "Starling! Ah, now my heart is..." Even as he stepped forward to embrace her, his sight was robbed by gentle fingers coming from behind and covering his eyes.

"Now your heart is what, little Brother?"

Released, he turned again, to see a woman who looked so like Starling, except with fairer hair, that even had he not immediately recognised her, there would be no doubt. Pushing the words past a lump in his throat, he said, "Minna! Is it really you? Now my heart is truly healed. How did you know to come?"

"When Wulf sent riders out everywhere to tell us you were all coming home, Penwal came to Medeshamstede. Since the abbey harvest is in, I thought I could take my leave for a while. And as abbess, I have none there to gainsay me, though I have left my sweet daughter this time and cannot be away for long. We brothers and sisters are nearly all of us together again. Ah, little Noni, look at you; a man grown!"

She linked her arm through his, Starling took his other arm and, with his sisters thus flanking him, Ethelred walked into the hall, answering as many as he could of Minna's rapid questions, his disappointment about Arianwen temporarily allayed by this God-given reunion, and the wonder that Minna's daughter, barely more than a babe at the time of Winwæd, had now seen nine summers. It was a shame, though, that she had not come with her mother.

There were other absences. As soon as they had taken their seats and the ale was poured, they drank to the men killed in the recent fighting, and to kin now lost to them, or unable to come home; to their father, their mother, to Pieter, their twin sisters, and Carena, far away in the north.

The feast was a triumph and Ethelred raised his cup to Ermenilda whose household had achieved so much in a short space of time. There was plenty of fresh summer cheese left to eat, and along with the last of the cuts from the grass-fed cows there was boiled chicken, a meat not normally a feast food but which was a pleasant change for the road-weary among the gathering. It was too early for some of the nuts which were even now still ripening, but along with the sorrel sauce there were fruit sauces to help with the digestion of the fattier meats. Around him, Ethelred's siblings talked at each other, round each other

89

and over each other and it was almost as if each, in his or her own way, was afraid that should silence fall, they would remember that they were feasting in their dead parents' hall.

Wulf was attentive to Ermenilda, nuzzling her neck, caring not who saw them. He was also in a mischievous mood, and Ethelred could not help but laugh when Wulf puffed out his cheeks and sank his head into his neck, producing an extra chin.

Starling said, "What is he doing?"

"He is mocking the scop of the South Saxons who does, it is true to say, have his fair share of cheese and ale, and then a lot of other folks' shares as well."

"And who is he pretending to be now?"

Ethelred didn't know, but often in the latter part of the campaign he had spent more time with Merchelm and Merwal than with Wulf and his companions. Wulf was a man transformed. In between the gentle mocking of distinctive men whom he'd encountered on their travels, he was laughing so much that occasionally he had to reach up and wipe tears from both eyes.

Starling turned to Minna and said, "Do you remember the times when Father used to…"

And Ethelred learned that their father, with the same impish playfulness, was wont to impersonate the Welsh bard who came sometimes to perform at his hall and who had an unfortunate waddling gait.

Minna said, "Were you there the time Father tried to leap with head over heels like the glee-men did? And fell flat on his backside?"

Merchelm leaned over and said, "I did not know that about your father. I cannot even properly see him in my mind's eye."

And why would he? Merchelm had only seen ten summers when Penda was killed, and most of those had been lived in Merwal's hall, not Penda's. Indeed, he and Ethelred had only really become friends since the return from Wales.

As the tone in the hall took a more sombre note and the gift-giving began, Ethelred watched Wulf calling forth his warriors in order that he might reward them with arm rings and weaponry. It had not been Ethelred's fight, but Wulf's. It was not his vengeance quest, but Wulf's. Ethelred's bond with his kin had not been broken after Winwæd, because it had barely fully formed. The siblings gathered here were so much older than him that he shared few of their recollections, meanwhile his bond with Merchelm grew ever tighter. And with that thought, his heart ached anew for the one other person who knew his and Merchelm's lives, the one person who had shared those long summers before he and Merchelm had to grow up, and who was part of the life that he could recall.

Arianwen was not to be found at the bottom of his ale cup, this he knew, but some kind of comfort waited there nevertheless, and as warrior after warrior stepped forward for his reward, Ethelred toasted them heartily. Wulf matched him, sip for sip, cup for cup, but each empty cup put a bigger grin on Wulf's face, whereas Ethelred felt his spirits sinking with every mouthful.

He awoke the next day with a thick head, a heavy heart, and a belly that gurgled and sloshed like the waves under the boat that had taken them to the island in the summer. He sat up, and instantly regretted it. Sometimes, the day after weapon training, or battle, his arms and legs cried out in pain at having been overworked. This morning his eyeballs felt as if they were doing the same. Even a slight glance to the side was agony and staring straight ahead only made the far wall of his chamber move as it would if viewed from the reflection in a puddle.

He lay back down and closed his eyes. Last night the dream had come again, but it was different. He saw his mother less clearly, and instead of waking when the scene went terrifyingly black, he'd felt a sensation of sinking between warm layers of nest feathers when he returned from his wanderings, and now, awake, he thought of the odd empty feeling that last night's gathering had invoked.

"Sikke, I saw it all again last night while I was sleeping," he said. "But this time it…"

He was answered with a grunt. "Yes, Lord, but it is morning now. All is well."

"All is well," Ethelred repeated. He sat up, far too quickly. "Sikke! You are really here!"

The old Frisian turned over on his mattress and propped himself up on one elbow. "Yes, Lord. Why would I not be?"

"I did not see you last night. I thought, but was afraid to ask…"

"I was ill when you left; I was not dying. I was uh, somewhere else last night, or I would have come to see you."

"Somewhere else?"

Sikke was older than the black hills that rose in Wales beyond Hereford, and most of his face was covered by beard and moustaches, but even through all the lines, creases, and hair, it was clear that his cheeks had reddened. "Gesina rode with me when we came here with Lady Domneva and I went to see that she was, erm, settled in her bower."

Gesina, Ethelred now recalled, was the Frisian lady of Domneva's who had been tending Sikke through his illness. Ethelred began to chuckle, but the laugh wasn't the only thing which rose to his throat. He shot off the bed, flung open the shutter, and spewed half of the previous night's ale on the ground outside.

He could hear Sikke moving around and when his gut finally came out of spasm, he turned, wiping his mouth, and saw that his clothes were laid out on the bed. "Dress, Lord.

The king wishes us in the hall."

As they crossed the yard, Ethelred gauged by the activity of the working day how much of the morning he had slept away. He grinned; for Sikke also still to have been abed so late suggested that the Frisian hadn't had much sleep the night before. Clearly, he and Gesina had more in common than their land of birth.

Ethelred sobered up fully when he saw the group assembled on the dais. Wulf was in his full kingly raiment, wearing the same coat as for his wedding day, and Ermenilda had the huge Kentish brooch pinned to her dress. Behind the dais and to the sides of the hall, Wulf's personal hearth-troops stood with their backs straight and their hands placed loosely in front of their belts, and all wore sombre expressions.

Minna was dressed as befitted an abbess, her robes neat and tidy, her veil pinned just so, and a heavy garnet-set cross hanging from her neck on a thick gold chain. Starling was there, too, looking as care-worn as when Ethelred had first been reunited with her, after the uprising. She had not looked so sad last evening; her eyes had sparkled, and her laugh had risen high above the noise of others when the talk had turned to recollections of their father's antics. Was she as hungover as her baby brother? It seemed unlikely.

Although it still hurt to move his eyeballs, Ethelred glanced at the man seated at Wulf's side. He looked to be of similar age to the Mercian king and, indeed, he was clothed in garments almost as fine as Wulf's. Though his coat had no embroidery at the cuffs or collar it was a rich hue of green, and he wore a gold brooch similar to the Mercian king's, with twists of gold filigree coiled into a spiral. Even though he was sitting down, Ethelred knew he would not be wearing a sword, for weapons were not worn in the hall. Shame, for often a man's status could be determined by the rich jewels on his sword pommel. Who was he? And why

93

was he here?

A hand brushed his, and he turned to see Domneva standing next to him, with Merwal on her other side. Nothing Domneva did was ever selfish, or a coincidence. If she was alerting him to their supportive presence, then there was a need.

Wulf stood up. "We are all gathered now; good. Let us move then to the chapel. Father Cedda?"

Why to the chapel? Ethelred caught Wulf's sleeve as he walked by. "Brother?"

Wulf stopped and half-turned. "Ah, yes. I need to speak with you, after. We must make plans for our ride north."

Ethelred tried to shake the ale-blur from his brain. "North? Wha… After?"

His elder brother smiled. "Next time take a little more food with your ale, hmm? Were you not awake when I spoke last night of how Frithuwald here would be among us and would…"?

"Frith… Who?"

"Frithuwald of Surrey. Here to take our Starling as his wife. The last little bit of the south not yet in our hands, now will be." As he spoke, he held out his hand, palm up, and then closed his fingers into an upturned fist.

Father Cedda offered his arm and Starling laid her hand upon it. Did she stumble because she got her footing wrong stepping down from the dais, or because her legs felt weak? Ethelred did not remember her first husband, but he knew that she had wed for love, even though he had not been a king, or an atheling, but simply a good man. Perhaps Frithuwald was, too, but they none of them had been given a chance to find out. How had he got here so soon? Yet more of Wulf's riders must have been sent out, probably before the Mercians had even left Cynwal's lands, a thought which made Ethelred feel ill again.

The ceremony was mercifully short. There would be a

feast later, but Ethelred doubted he would drink, for several reasons. In any case, Wulf had need of him. As the witnesses, bride, and her new husband went back to the hall, the king of the Mercians and his atheling went for a walk down to the river, passing clusters of flowering autumn crocus and hedgerows full of hips, and sloes and haws turning from green to red. They sat down on the bank, upstream of the water mill. Ethelred sensed, rather than saw, himself running near here as a small child, but the memory remained like gossamer and would not solidify.

"I cannot bide here too long; my guests are waiting. But I wished to speak to you."

Ethelred could not help himself. "She did not wish to wed."

To his surprise, Wulf merely shrugged. "But wed she must. You know it is the way, no matter how we might wish it otherwise. If our lands were ever overrun again, she would be…"

"Being wed brought her no peace last time; her husband was slain even though he was a thegn with no claim to the king-seat. Should she not have been asked for her thoughts?"

Wulf reached out and plucked a blade of grass. He ran his nail down the centre and spoke as if to himself. "No wait, that was not how we did it." He plucked another, holding them together and then blowing on them. A strange noise came out, a cross between a fart and a very badly played flute. "We did this when we were little."

Again, the picture wouldn't form fully, but Ethelred knew that if he were to copy his brother, those blades of grass would tickle his lips.

Wulf discarded his makeshift instrument. "Noni, I did what I had to, to keep our lands safe."

"Mother would not have liked it. Another of her daughters going away, and this time not even for love."

"Mother is not here."

And with that, there was silence. They were brothers, they were close friends, and they would willingly die for one another, but each carried his own thoughts about their mother, and they would always be too raw to share.

After a moment, Wulf coughed. "I am not as cruel as you think. Frithuwald brings tidings, that the twins might be at abbeys in Bicester and Aylesbury, which both lie on the road to Frithuwald's lands at Chertsey. He has given me his word that they will make stops at both houses so that Starling can see if our sisters are there."

Ethelred swallowed to try to relieve the tight ball of emotion. "Then we truly will all be together."

"No, we will never all be together, because the Northumbrians killed our parents and our brother. They must be made to pay. Now I need to ride north. Will you come with me?"

"Northumbria? We are not ready, we are not strong enough, surely, to..."

"I'm not a madman. I do not mean to march up to Oswii's door and rap upon it. But with no need to worry what is happening behind my back in the south, I thought I might see about freeing Lindsey from the bastard's grip, too."

"Lindsey borders Oswii's lands, this much I know. You might not be rapping upon his door, but if you goad such a hound as he, he will turn and bite."

"He is an old man now, and his whelp is not yet a man."

"Whelp? You mean Lief?" Ethelred remembered some of the time when the boy had been a hostage at Penda's court, perhaps because, being younglings, they had spent time together away from the grown-ups. The lad had been rather sullen, and guarded, but it was no surprise, for he had been taken from his kin and housed with his father's enemy's children.

"Ecgfrith, yes."

"He is the same age as me, give or take a summer. Are you saying that I too am callow?"

Wulf threw a playful punch at his arm. "Not at all. You have proven your weapon skills, but then, you have ridden and fought alongside the best."

Ethelred laughed, making a play of rubbing his arm, but he still felt uncomfortable about the ease with which Wulf had bartered away their sister. "What of your dear wife; would you leave Ermenilda again, so soon?"

Wulf scratched his nose. "Well, I might bide a while, see if I can't get another child on her. It is hardly a chore, I can tell you that."

"You like each other. It is plain to see. Would you not, though, wait to see if she bears a son before you ride north? It would be such a blessing." And Ethelred would no longer be the only atheling. A burden would be lifted.

Wulf shifted his position and made a fuss of selecting another blade of grass to turn into a flute. "It matters not. I know that I can... I know that we are able to spawn." He stood up and patted Ethelred's shoulder. "Think on it; in any case, I would not go until after the winter, when the grass is long enough again."

He left, running at an easy pace, a warrior in his prime. Was Wulf the image of their father? He was as dark as the shadowy man who sometimes came into Ethelred's memories, but beyond that, there was no way to compare.

He stood up, checked the back of his tunic for grass stains, and made his way up to the hall. His half-brother was emerging from a separate building where Domneva and her youngest children were staying. "Merwal!"

The older man put up a hand in greeting and wandered over to meet him. "Domneva is resting. The babe kept her up for most of the dark hours." He looked closely at Ethelred's face. "From what I see here, she is not the only

97

one who did not sleep well last night. Was it simply too much ale, or is something else troubling you?"

"Do you have time before the feast?"

"I can always make time for you, little Brother. Come, walk with me."

They went over to the practice yard, passing groups of men tossing bundles of coppiced hazel from carts. Women walked by with baskets of apples and one shouted, "You can throw me like that if you're strong enough!"

Leaning on the yard fence, Merwal said, "Tell me. It is not the ale-regret that saddens you, and I sense it is not the lack of a little Welsh lass either."

Although, her absence was not helping. Ethelred said, "I wish I knew more about our father. Is Wulf like him?"

"He was not my father."

"Oh, I did not mean to…"

Merwal laid a reassuring hand on his arm. "No, no, I know you did not. What I was going to say was that he was not my father, but it tells you all you need to know about him that he raised me as his own. Never once was I made to feel less than the rest of you; I was the first of us older ones to be given a kingdom of my own. You should also know that never a man lived who loved a woman more than Penda loved our mother."

"But he was a fighter? A man of iron?"

"Yes, he was. And he had a temper like a bear, but he only went to battle when it mattered to him. He never started a fight out of boredom. Your uncle goaded him for years before Penda bloodied his nose. Mother watched; it was the first time she'd met Penda's brother, too. Other than that, and he was poked sore before he did it, Penda only fought when his kinswomen were mistreated, or when other kings tried to take our lands."

"He did what he had to do?"

"Always. Yet there was another side to him too, and I

could tell you of many times where he bounced like a pup. He had life-gladness enough for two men and his giddiness was like elf shot that caught all in its way. Life was never dull, not with him and our mother around."

"So Wulf is the acorn who fell nearest the tree? I see both the iron will and the thirst for righting wrongs, but I also see him laughing and light-hearted. Does he look like him?"

Merwal said, "It is so sad, that what happened to you that night has forced so much of the past from your mind. Penda's hair was darker, more like mine. Some used to say that he must have had Welsh blood, and not his named father's, but none would dare cast a slur on his mother, so I think it was not true. Wulf has the same nose, and the height, but Penda was more lithe, with longer legs. Like you."

"I am not like him. I brood too much, and if you wish to see fleetness of foot and life-gladness, look to your own son. Merchelm never stops smiling and has always been the swifter runner of the two of us."

The horn blew for the feast to begin, and they made their way back to the hall. As they walked, Merwal said, "You do have something of your father in you. You call it brooding, but I call it thinking. You will always choose the right path, for you have a sense of what's right and what's fair, and that makes you your father's son."

Ethelred answered with a murmur of agreement, but he was unsure. A sense of what was right and fair would see him riding north with Wulf, surely? And as for the acorn falling near the tree, did that not mean growing up in its shadow? Was this what drove Wulf on? Was Wulf, too, frightened of not measuring up; was he just as haunted, in his own way?

As they approached the hall, Wulf was standing in the doorway talking to Edbert, Penwal and Immin. Merwal waved in acknowledgement and said to Ethelred, "You know, in one way you are naught like your father. He and his brother hated each other."

Ethelred laughed and it brought him out of his gloom.

"Oh, and another thing: I told you that our mother met your uncle for the first time after Penda had bloodied his nose, but did I tell you how your father met Mother?"

"I do not think anyone has."

"As a young man he was unsure of his role, not being the king's eldest son, and so he would take to riding off on his own. It was on one of those rides that he met the woman he would love for the rest of his life." He leaned into Ethelred, their upper arms bumping together. "So go to her; it is what your father would have done."

Chapter Five

Powys AD662: Early Spring

Despite the encouragement, he did not make his journey west until after Yuletide and the winter snow. The reunion celebrations had gone on for a while, help was needed with the storage and preservation of food after the harvest, and Ethelred also wanted to spend as much time as he could in weapon training. Sikke had to all intents and purposes hung up his axe and shield. No one knew how old he was, and it would be a brave man indeed who ventured the question, but all respected his right to live out his twilight years in peace and comfort. Ethelred, having lost his tutor, needed to learn as much as he could before the next campaign.

Work and weather were not the only reasons for his delay. He doubted that he would ever make a swift decision about anything, pondering all possible outcomes before taking action. So he had thought long and hard, even after his talk with Merwal, before setting out. The trouble was, he'd considered everything in terms of whether he would be letting Wulf down, or failing to do his duty as atheling. Only now, after they'd crossed into Welsh lands, did he consider that Arianwen, or her brother, or his hearth-troops, might not welcome him.

They were riding through a small wood. The light came dappled through the bare branches and occasionally Ethelred had to squint as the sun, though strengthening as the year progressed, still sat low above the earth. The path opened up a little and Heaferth brought his horse alongside. "Immin says he has found a good place to overnight, not far

101

ahead."

Ethelred looked up. They had perhaps two hours of daylight left. "Yes, have him show us the way. We will make an early halt today and get a good fire going." Prolonging their arrival suddenly felt like a good idea.

When they stopped, a few miles beyond the woodland, in the shelter of a small rocky overhang, Heaferth organised the camp, sent men out to hunt and forage, and came to sit by his lord. "It must feel odd to be back."

Ethelred had pushed any memories of his time in Wales to the back of his head. He had hoped to replace them with new ones, of Arianwen and time spent with her. Now his stomach was clenched with the fear that he would arrive, be turned away, and be back on the road to Mercia before any of his men could even have a piss.

The next day, when the sun was as high as it would climb before beginning to sink once more, their small band arrived on Llywarch's lands. They knew this because three men approached them and put themselves in a line directly in front of the Mercians.

Heaferth leaned over and said, "What did he say?"

The middle of the three horsemen had spoken quickly, but Ethelred had caught most of the words. "He asks who we are and what we are about." To the Welshman he said, falteringly, that he was Ethelred, atheling of Mercia and friend of Arianwen, and that he wished to pay his respects to her brother, Lord Llywarch. He told Heaferth, "These men are part of the Teulu, the hearth-troops, but it's really their word for kin."

"They are Arianwen's brothers also?" Heaferth's raised eyebrows indicated either fear, or respect. Perhaps both; these men were burly and bear-like.

"They might be, or they might be as you and Immin are to me, and Edbert and Penwal are to Wulf. Either way they will be loyal to her brother, and it is up to them whether we get any further."

The men of the Teulu spoke among themselves, mentioning their word for English, Saesneg, several times. One leaned over to see round Ethelred and Heaferth to count the number of men riding behind them. Not needing all of the fingers on his second hand to reckon, he beckoned them to proceed.

It was no surprise to Ethelred that Arianwen's brother had a hall that was more circular in shape than Wulf's great halls. Other than this, the scene would be familiar to Heaferth and Immin, with smoke rising from the forge, and men and women going about their business, but the land around the settlement was not given over to the growing of crops so much as it was in Mercia and the loud lowing and bleating demonstrated that cattle and sheep were plentiful in these parts.

The three men of the Teulu dismounted and as Ethelred followed suit, the man who'd spoken to him earlier said, "Bleddyn ydw i," and went inside.

Heaferth shook his head.

"His name is Blethin," Ethelred explained, sounding it out in English. He looked around and, at ground level and without the confidence afforded by being on horseback, felt even more foolish. Why had he come all this way? What would he say to these big bears of men; that he loved Arianwen and had simply taken a three-day ride out to greet her and see how she fared? They would laugh in his face.

The noise of voices rumbled from the main building and the doors opened on squeaky hinges. And then she was there, standing in front of him, exactly as he remembered her: the dark eyes, and the wide smile that lifted her cheeks. "Lord Ethelred! Bleddyn told me and I could not believe it."

She was grinning, and at him alone. That wide-open smile sent its warmth straight to his heart, leaving a melted mess inside his chest. She was pleased to see him. Naught else

103

mattered.

She turned round and chattered in Welsh and at high speed to waiting servants, and then touched Ethelred's elbow and applied the gentlest pressure. He took the hint and moved off to one side with her.

Her smile had fallen away, and her tone changed. "Is all well with Lady Domneva and the girls? I cannot come back now, if that's why you are here. My sister was with child and the bairn was born dead. She has not been well since then."

Now he felt more than foolish. It had been selfish to come and in all his deliberations not once had he considered her situation. "Forgive me. I…" Why would the right words not come?

She barely moved and yet somehow his hand was now in hers. "Do you think the time has come for us to speak our minds?"

Still his tongue was a big knot and would not let the words through. He shook his head.

"Well then," she said, "I shall speak for us both. My heart sings to see you here. And I fear it would stop beating if you rode away. So come, Cariad, and meet my brother."

The hall was as welcoming as any and the fire was lively in the hearth. The chatter died down as Ethelred and Arianwen walked to the centre of the room, but he detected curiosity rather than hostility, with most turning back to their drinks and conversations before the couple had passed by. A man dressed richly, but with a harp propped against his carved wooden chair, stood up as Arianwen dragged Ethelred by the hand towards him. Her hurried message had found its intended recipient for he said, "Lord Ethelred. Welcome to my house."

Ethelred had initially taken him for the scop, or bard as he would be known here, and was puzzled.

Arianwen squeezed Ethelred's hand. "This is my brother, Llywarch." She whispered, "Here in Wales the king or lord keeps charge of the harp, not the bard. The bard will play at the gwyledd, the feast."

Ethelred, wondering when he would stop feeling like an oaf, paused a moment, trying to find a confident voice. "Lord Llywarch, I thank you for your greeting. I have brought but a few men with me, here are Heaferth and Immin, my hearth-thegns, and I had not planned to bide here long. I merely wished…"

Llywarch smiled and his grin was identical to Arianwen's. "I can see very well what you wished. And for that welcome, you will need not my blessing, but my sister's." He laughed and beckoned a servant. "Mead for our guests." He gestured for Ethelred and Arianwen to join him on the dais and for room to be found for the rest of the Mercians on another table, and the general hum in the room grew louder as the members of the Teulu also resumed their conversations. So often in his life, Ethelred had felt that his memory played him false, but of the Welsh hospitality, it had not lied. To a man and woman, they had accepted his presence and that of his hearth-troops merely because Arianwen called him a friend. They were all content to take her word that he was no threat.

Not quite all, perhaps. As he held the mead cup to his lips he caught, in the side of his vision, a black-haired man with long beard and moustaches, who was wearing a large garnet-set ring on his forefinger. He was staring at Ethelred with brows drawn together and low, his mouth in a thin pinched line. Ethelred averted his gaze completely, feeling the embarrassment of being caught staring, even though the man had been doing the same. He turned to Arianwen. "How is your sister? Is she here?"

"She keeps to herself these days. Drink, rest, get to know us here and then I will take you to meet Heledd."

Ethelred feasted well on fat mutton, and bread baked not in ovens but made from oats and cooked in long-handled pans held over embers scraped from the centre of the hearth fire. He had eaten similar at the house of Rhiryd's father. The cheese was saltier than he was used to, and Arianwen explained that here they used a brine bath method when making cheese, which differed from the Mercian way. The mead, at least, was familiar, though potent.

One drink had become several and it was dark when they stepped outside. Ethelred shook his head, but the woolly feeling stayed put. "I should look in on the horses and find somewhere for the men to sleep."

"It is all taken care of. Llywarch sent orders even before I took you to meet him." She linked her arm through his. "Merchelm is not with you. How is he?"

"He fares well. You know Merchelm, never sad."

"Heledd, too, was always lively, but since she lost the bairn…"

"Her man?"

She leaned in so that their arms touched, bumping as they walked. "He died after a fall from his horse at the end of last summer. He did not even know that she was carrying his child." She had brought him to a bower some distance from the main building and a small light flickered within. Someone was standing outside and as they drew nearer, Ethelred recognised him as Bleddyn, whom he'd met earlier. "Bleddyn has never really left her side since then," she said quietly. "He is a good man."

Ethelred was about to say that all of the Teulu appeared so, but then he remembered the man who'd glared at him. "Who is the black-haired man with the great garnet ring?"

Her tone was airy, dismissive. "Oh, that's Dyfrig. Pay no heed to him."

They greeted Bleddyn, who stepped aside to let them enter, and Ethelred tried to shake the question from his mind: why did Arianwen immediately try to curb his worries about the man called Dyfrig, when he hadn't as yet expressed any?

The Lady Heledd stood up when they went inside. She was a taller, fairer version of Arianwen, with the same nose which broadened at the tip and the full lips which had no distinct bow. Her eyebrows were the same shape as her sister's, high and wide, but there the similarity ended for the candlelight did her no favours, accentuating dark shadows under her eyes, and her hair, uncovered, was straggly and uncombed. She moved a helpless hand to her head and then smoothed her kirtle, in a futile attempt to mend her unkempt appearance.

Arianwen stepped forward and took her hands. Letting one go, she turned slightly to the side and made the introductions. "This is Lord Ethelred of Mercia. Lord Ethelred, this is my sister, Heledd ferch Cadfan."

Heledd bobbed her head and bade them sit. "We should have something to drink, shouldn't we?"

Ethelred, feeling uncomfortable and too much of an intruder, said quickly, "No, no. Your brother was more than generous with his mead, and I have had a bellyful already, though I thank you kindly."

He sat for a short time while the two women spoke of people who'd been in the hall, Arianwen providing details of who'd said what to whom, switching back and forth between their own tongue and his, so as not to leave him utterly bewildered. Her chatter provoked little response from Heledd, who merely smiled politely and before long Arianwen leaned over and patted her sister's knee. "We will leave you to rest." As they stood up, she said, "You know he's still there?"

Heledd nodded. "Bleddyn has been good to me. I know not why."

Her sister replied, "And yet I think you do. He will not speak of it though. He has set himself to keep you safe and see to your every need. Whether one day you begin to share

107

his feelings matters not. He does all this out of the purest love."

They left the bower, nodding to the man of whom they'd just spoken. Ethelred bade him "Nos da" and he in turn said goodnight in English. Ethelred said to Arianwen, "When I met him earlier, I did not mark him as a man in love. He looked to me like a warrior who lives in the saddle."

She laughed softly. "He has been in love with her almost their whole lives. He never said, but I knew. Now he watches over her and maybe one day she will come to love him too. We all grew up together; me, her, Bleddyn and... Ah, here we are. This is where you are to sleep. I hope all is to your liking. Shall we ride out tomorrow?" She reached up and kissed his cheek.

She left him then, and he stepped inside to be greeted by the gentle sound of Heaferth's snoring and an aroma of banked fire and mead-induced fart. He sat down on the bed and put a hand up to his cheek, feeling the place where she'd left the kiss. It was more than she'd have given a friend, less than she would offer a lover. And what was it about the man called Dyfrig that she was not telling him?

The morning sun brought another mild day and Arianwen was knocking on the bower door before Ethelred, Heaferth and Immin were awake. She called from outside "Shake the sleep off, do! It is a wonderful day and too lovely to miss through slumber."

Ethelred grabbed his breeches, pulled them on and, one shoe on and the other in his hand, pushed open the door to see her shadowed outline framed in the doorway, the rising sun behind her. "I must, er..." Hopping inelegantly, he put his other shoe on and looked about for a latrine. He spied one, used it, and, spotting a water trough, he went to douse his face and upper body. Lord in Heaven but the water was cold. He ran shivering back to the bower, donned his tunic and snatched up his cloak, slinging it over his shoulders while he saw to his leg bindings.

Arianwen feigned impatience. "Will this take all day; shall I call for candles to light our moonlight ride?"

His stomach rumbled. "May I eat a little first?"

She patted her leather bag. "No need, I have bread and smoked cheese in here."

Her smile suggested that she was as happy in his company as he was in hers. His stomach stopped complaining of emptiness and lurched a little as if filling up with happiness instead. He grabbed her hand. "Come then, why are you tarrying?"

Laughing, they ran to the stables. She conducted a conversation with the stable-hand in a flurry of Welsh which Ethelred could not follow, but before long two horses were brought out, one his own and one, he presumed, Arianwen's. He had never seen her ride but always assumed she could. What he had not expected was for her to ride so quickly that he had a task to keep up with her. She led him to a grove of trees on a hillock, with views of the surrounding country. It was not dissimilar to his own lands, but the mountains, visible from Hereford, were much bigger now that they were nearer.

They sat beneath an oak which was already sporting its delicate catkins, and she opened her bag, handing him the bread and cheese.

"Any mead?"

"Was that not enough?" she teased. "Must I think of everything?"

She handed him a leather bottle full of the sweet drink and he laughed. "It seems so. Thank you."

It was perfect. She was perfect. If he prayed hard enough, might God allow him to bide here forever? She spoke, and caught him with a mouthful of bread. "Mmm?"

"I asked what you think of, that makes you sad."

He chewed, which gave him time to think and, after swallowing the mouthful, he said, "You. I think of you." Even the admission made his heart beat faster.

"When you are away from me, you mean?"

"And when you are near."

She looked at him then, frowning. "Whatever can you mean? Oh, I see."

"You do?"

She shuffled closer, took his hand and held it against her face, then sat with it in her grip and in her lap. "Do you love me?"

Blood flooded his face, burning his cheeks and ears. "I do."

"You are an atheling, and I am the daughter of a Welsh lord. Folk would bless our wedding. So, if you are sad, there must be another reason."

It was as if she heard his every thought. "I do not wish to be atheling. I do not think I wish to be king. I wish I could bide here forever."

"Ah, Love; what is it?" She wriggled closer still, until their bodies were touching and her head was against his chest.

He told her, then, of the things he had seen when they went into the land of the West Saxons: of the fighting, the bloodshed, and especially of Wulf's treatment of Cynwal's kinsmen; of the fire in Wulf's eyes, stoked by the blood feud; his fears that he was not worthy of being called his father's son.

When he had finished telling his tale, she remained silent for a while. Then she said, "It is not something that I would have wished to see, much less be part of, but is this not what men do? Is this not what kings must do? It is the life you were born into, and you cannot alter that, but perhaps you would not have to be that kind of king, if there were a better way?"

All of it was told now, and his words had floated off into

110

the air. He felt almost empty, and light, as if he might float away too, freed from the burden weighing him down. His hand went to the leather pouch which still contained the amethysts, but there was one thing left to tell, and to make an oath to her now, when he might soon be dead... He sighed.

"There is more. You must fight again, soon?"

"I should ride north and lend aid to my brother in Lindsey when he goes, yes."

"But not today."

Unfamiliar bravery prompted him and he kissed the top of her head, breathing in the scent of mint herb water in her hair. "No, not today." He might pay for this moment with a year's fighting but now, here, he felt a peace he'd never known.

She sprang up, pulling him with her. "Come then, let us not waste the day. Follow me!"

Leaving the horses tethered in the grove, they ran down the side of the hillock and she led him into a more densely wooded area. There was cuckoo spit aplenty covering the foliage, and masses of tightly curled fern fronds on the woodland floor, ready to unfurl any day. At times he had to crouch to avoid overhanging branches and occasionally he let out a yelp when nettles slashed his lower legs. Arianwen, smaller, avoided the branches which threatened to blind him, but how did she escape the nettle stings? When she finally stopped and allowed him to catch his breath, he asked her.

"Oh, I get stung, but if you leave the stings and do not touch them, the pain eases much more swiftly."

Caught in the act of rubbing his shin, he stood up, shamed. "I knew that," he blustered. "It was an itch."

"Of course. And at this time of year the nettles are only small anyway." She sucked on her lower lip, clearly attempting not to laugh. He stood up and stared at her, until

111

she said, "What?"

"I wonder how you take it all, from a nettle sting to your sister's sadness, and yet keep a smile?"

"Why would I not? My lot is not a bad one; I have food in my belly, most days, and more than some, and enough blankets for my bed." She looked up at him, and the smile slipped away. "And, for now, I have you. I will grab every little moment of this time." She pounced, throwing herself into his startled embrace and hugging him, and then released her grip and stepped back. "We are here."

"What? Where?"

She bent down and lifted a low-hanging branch that Ethelred had not even noticed among all the other budding foliage. "In a few more weeks it will be fully hidden. When the branches are bare in the winter, it can be seen by all. But not now."

He stooped and peered beyond the lifted branch. Tucked into the low hillside was a little dug out hiding hole, a wooden frame holding the entrance from collapse. Inside, blankets spread on the ground were held down with what looked like carefully selected stones and there was a pile of kindling, too.

"Heledd, Llywarch and I used to come here when we were little. Our mother and father knew about it, but they never said. They would send for us, but their man would come within hearing and then speak loudly, as if he did not know we were near." She took his hand and pulled. "I would share it with you."

He shook his head. "We are not children now. I should not; it was your hiding place."

"No," she said, "I mean I would share it with you, now, as we are. You might never be mine, but I have you here this day, and I wish to hold this day forever."

To make new memories. What a gift she was offering, and that it was not entirely selfless made it even sweeter. She

112

wanted him as much as he wanted her and the knowledge flooded his body, warming his blood. They were indeed not children, so they had to crawl to fit into the space. Once inside he lowered the branch to hide them from the world. As they lay down, Arianwen reached up and touched his face, looking intently into his eyes. He held her gaze for what felt like a lifetime, then bent to kiss her sweet mouth.

It was the first time, but it was not the last. No more was said though about their becoming man and wife, and Ethelred was not sure when he would have the courage to speak of it again, so he kept the necklace for the time being. They rode out often and, although Ethelred frequently had a sense that someone was following them, whoever it was kept a discreet distance. He wondered if the swarthy man Dyfrig, who disliked him, presumably for being a Saesneg interloper, was stalking them for some reason.

It was only when, returning to the stables after an early morning ride, he heard Heaferth coming in shortly afterwards, that Ethelred began to get a notion of what was afoot. "You're out early." He smiled as Heaferth wiped the sweat from his brow.

Heaferth handed his reins to the stable-boy. "I, er, needed to see, that is Lord Llywarch asked me to..." He stopped floundering and chuckled. "You have caught me in your net. I would not seek to know what it is you do when you ride out, but..."

Ethelred, enjoying watching him squirm, affected a serious tone. "But what? What is your worry?"

"You are my lord, and it is up to me to keep you safe. Immin's mind is elsewhere. As I say, you are my lord and Arianwen is, well, we all care for her so." He finished in a rush. "So I ride behind you in case you ever come to harm."

That Heaferth loved his homeland and served his lord without question was no secret, but this admission of his love for his lord's chosen woman was endearing, and something of a surprise. Still smiling, Ethelred made his way from the stables to the hall, only to find himself in company once more.

Llywarch fell into step alongside him, gesturing that they should move to the side of the building instead of going in. "You have been here a while now."

Ah, so that was it. He had been here longer than the acceptable period during which a welcome was guaranteed. "You are right," he said, his thoughts immediately turning to what would be a heart-wrenching farewell if Arianwen chose to stay here when he left. "I will gather my men as soon as…"

"No, my friend. That is not what I meant." Llywarch paused, and the only sound was the cattle lowing. "That. It should be louder. Some of our cows have been stolen. Bad enough that we have to send so many to that turd in Northumbria, but now some outlaws from west of here are stealing what we have left."

Ethelred suspected he knew what was coming, and waited for Llywarch to continue.

"Not easy to take off with stolen cows, but they slew my herdsmen so we had no warning that they'd taken the beasts. We are gathering a warband to go and get them back, and to avenge the deaths and make it clear to these cynrhon, that is maggots, that it would be best for them to keep away from my land and herds. Will you ride with us?"

The warm reception and hospitality he had received would have made refusal awkward, but that was irrelevant, for the friendship meant that he did not need to consider for a moment. "We shall be glad to ride alongside you."

Llywarch slapped him on the shoulder. "Diolch! Now, might I suggest that you go and tell my sister. Perhaps wear your mail coat and helm when you do."

He found her in the bake house, already at work. One woman was raking out the ovens, clearing the ashes ready for baking loaves, while another was preparing dishes which would then be cooked slowly using the residual heat after the bread was baked. Arianwen was sifting flour. "For old Branwen," she said. "I sift it finely for, though she does not say it, I think her teeth ache and I slip her some betony for her sore mouth."

Ethelred stepped forward and had to lower his head to avoid the birch twigs that had been dipped in liquid yeast and hung up to dry.

"I'll be taking those to the brew house shortly. Pass me them; I need to put them in water to soak off the yeast. And a little to leaven the batter for Branwen. I'll make little cakes for her that are easy to chew."

He put the nearest of the bunches of twigs on the table, slid his arms round her waist, ignoring the looks of surprised amusement from the others, and kissed her behind her ear. "I would spend some time with you."

She laughed softly. "Should I give you a sieve then?"

He nuzzled her neck and held her closer. "You know what I mean."

Placing the sieve on top of the wooden bowl, she wriggled round in his embrace until she was facing him. He relaxed his hold a little and she put her head up to look him in the eye. She was not smiling now. "Tell me."

"Not here." He led her by the hand, holding it tightly as they walked across the yard, through the gate and into the woodland beyond. He sat down on the ground beside the small brook which ran between two tree lines, and pulled her onto his lap, holding her there and stroking her back while he told her of Llywarch's plans.

She sighed. "Men. Always finding something to fight about. Although, it is not fair that they take our cattle when we have so little food as it is. Worse, they are murderers."

115

She wriggled on his lap and took his face in her hands. "Swear to me you will not get hurt."

"I will do my best." He kissed her. "But I cannot swear."

Arianwen looked around, but they were alone. Ethelred wondered if Heaferth had followed them but somehow he doubted it. She said, "Since you will not promise that you will come back alive, I had better make the most of you while you are still whole."

When his body was as one with hers, naught else mattered. Now though, in contrast to the reality of her soft skin and warm breath, his mind filled with harsher images of hard cold iron and dead bodies. Afterwards, with her lying close, he said, "Be my wife."

She snuggled closer and draped one leg over his. "When you come home. Not until then."

Her response was sensible, but she had paused before replying. Was there some hesitancy beyond the practical considerations? He let it pass. She loved him, and that was all that mattered for now. That, and coming back to her. In the warmth of the afternoon sun, he drifted off to sleep, smiling, determined to enjoy what might be the last moment of peace that he would know.

The trees were in full leaf now, and with the canopy above them closed in, the flowers on the woodland floor had finished their display of colour, fading for lack of light. Ethelred and his men followed the Welsh, from the broadleaf woodland deep into an area of beechwood where the denser foliage made the ride darker still. There was little birdsong here and a pungent smell of fox. Ethelred looked frequently to both sides of the path, sensing that here would be an ideal place for those whom they were seeking to launch a surprise attack. He caught movement and shifted in the saddle, but it was a family of young stoats darting around in play. He relaxed, but hoped that they would soon be in more open ground.

Sunlight began to penetrate the woodland and up ahead he saw a break in the trees, where the beeches thinned out and the sight of hawthorn blossom suggested that they were moving into meadow. Llywarch hung back, letting most of the others overtake him, until Ethelred came level. "My friend, when we catch up with the thieves, it will be like Hell brought above ground. We will be yelling in our own tongue. I doubt that your men, or even you, will understand it all."

Ethelred nodded. "You have a plan?" Best they discussed it beforehand. Things might go awry in a battle, but he should at least know what was on Llywarch's mind.

The Welshman nodded. "I do. Once we are out of the woods, we will stop for something to eat and I will tell..." He turned his head at the sound of a call from further along the line. "What is it?"

One of his band came riding back and said in Welsh, "The bridge is down."

Llywarch cursed and said in English, "Forget the plan. As you might have gathered, the bridge was part of it."

They sat at the edge of the meadow in a huddle, Ethelred wrinkling his nose when the odour of the hawthorn hit his nostrils. The blossom near his home always smelled sweeter and he thought he might ask Arianwen if there was more than one type. He smiled; here she was again, never far from his thoughts.

The band of Welshmen did not, fortunately, include the hostile Dyfrig, and those who had accompanied their lord on the ride were accepting enough that they spoke more slowly when conversing in their own language. Where necessary, Ethelred translated for his own men. "They say the cattle thieves have knocked down the bridge, which means we cannot follow them much further. They are thinking about turning back."

Llywarch said, "Now that the bridge is gone, we shall have to ride many miles south to the next crossing, and my guess is that they will be lying in wait for us there."

Ethelred thought for a moment, recalling his crossing from the lands of the Meonwara to the island in the far south. "How did they get the cattle over? Was the bridge wide and strong enough for livestock?"

The Welshman said, "Strong yes, wide no. Horses must go one by one, and so would cows. That would have taken far too long, so they must have swum them across."

"The nearest bridge; is it down or upstream?"

"It is downstream, miles further on where the river widens out and builds up strength. Why?"

Ethelred looked around and then said, "What if we went back into the woods? If they have watchers set, they will think you are going home. Go upstream for some miles, and swim across. It will not be too deep or too wild for the horses, and then we can come round behind them."

Llywarch sat, his head nodding slightly to left and right, as he weighed up the suggestion. He sat forward, slapped Ethelred on the shoulder and said, "You are right!" He tapped Ethelred's temple. "You, my friend, are a fine thinker." He stood up, issued a stream of instructions in Welsh, and they mounted up and turned back into the beechwood.

Heaferth drew level with Ethelred on the narrow path through the trees. "You will not have Lord Merchelm at your back, but you will have me." Immin, riding close behind him, echoed his words. "Aye, Lord, we will keep you safe."

Ethelred, though grateful, felt unworthy. He had done little, if anything, to earn such love; it should be directed at Wulf, who had proved himself a leader and a provider. If this ruse to cross further upstream and surprise the outlaws did not work, he would surely forfeit that devotion and rightly so.

They turned and left the beechwood, following the water course for some time until Llywarch declared that they had found a suitable place to cross. He thought that only in the very middle would the horses have to swim, but the men on their backs would get a soaking regardless.

Submerged up to his thighs and then suddenly his waist, Ethelred breathed in sharply as the cold hit his vitals and it took a great deal of willpower not to piss himself. His clothes hung like lead on his shivering frame, but his horse was sure-footed, did not stumble and so, unlike some of the others less fortunate, he was not pitched headlong into the water. Once across, all they could do was pray that the sun stayed high and hurried the drying process along. As it began to dip towards the horizon, they were all still damp, but they came within sight of the stolen cattle and saw, beyond the beasts chewing in the field, the men responsible for their theft.

The thieves, a small band of eight, were all waiting by the bridge. They had not left any of their group to watch the cattle, so the Welsh and their friends were able to get close without being seen. They left their horses and some moved quietly on foot, sliding between the shields provided by the black-bodied cows, edging closer to the river bank. Behind them, the others were positioning themselves to begin herding the animals slowly away.

The outlaws were relaxed, talking and laughing amongst themselves, apparently confident that they would spot their pursuers long before they came to the bridge. They would have been taken completely by surprise, except that the cattle, having been droved so far and now content to graze, objected to being moved. The first few lows and bellows were ignored, but as the indignant noises increased, the thieves stopped their chatter and turned round to discern the cause of the disturbance.

Luckily most of Llywarch's band were nearly clear of the beasts and were able to charge towards the robbers. They had not entirely lost the advantage of stealth and they outnumbered their quarry. The fight was short, but brutal, with the English having little to do. As one of the enemy bounced off Llywarch's shield towards them, Heaferth stepped forward, caught him, and dispatched him with a swift stab of his knife. Turning to grin at Ethelred he said, "Useful, these Welshmen, in a fight." It took only moments and none of the thieves was left alive.

It took far longer to get the cattle back to where they belonged. With the sinking sun, they lost the daylight, and had to sleep with the beasts where they were. At daybreak, the long trek back to Llywarch's steading began. They knew that the cattle had swum the river once, but would they do it again?

Most did, but a few began to panic, and Ethelred, nearest to them, waded in to help persuade them across. He was on foot and, as he sloshed forward, the river bed fell away and he lost his footing. Sinking under the water, he floundered, unable to see. Memories of being similarly submerged flooded into his mind, and he kicked with all his strength in an effort to get to air. A sharp pain travelled up his leg as if it were on fire. Paddling furiously, he managed to get his head above water and drag himself back to the bank. Immin stepped forward to help him out of the river, and he flung himself onto the ground.

Immin bent down to inspect him. "Head and leg. I think one of those beasts gave you a kicking and stood on you too. Do you think you can ride?"

Shivering, Ethelred propped himself up on one elbow and looked down at his leg, feeling blood dribble down his face as he did so. There was a red puddle of liquid under his calf and he was not sure how much was blood, and how much was water. He sat up further, his head throbbing. He reached down and felt a piece of sharp riverbed stone jutting out from his lower leg, just to the side of his shin bone. Despite being soaking wet, he began to sweat at the thought of having to pull it out and decided that rather than risk making it worse, he would leave it there until the extent of the injury could be assessed. Immin produced a torn fragment of cloth from somewhere, Ethelred surmised it was probably his undershirt sleeve, and tied it tightly above Ethelred's knee to stem the bleeding.

"Help me onto my horse, then," Ethelred told him, "and I will do my best." He was not looking forward to getting back in the water, but there was no choice. He could only hope that the wound was superficial and that he would not lose too much blood before they got back.

In fact, he was barely still conscious when they arrived and had to be helped from his horse and propped up between two men as they dragged him inside. He heard snatches of conversation, of Llywarch telling someone of their victory, the response, "So the English will leave now?" and Llywarch's reply that, "They will not. Not until Lord Ethelred can ride again," followed by a curse.

One day, he would tell her the truth. On that day, he would admit that his head had long since stopped spinning, that his eyes no longer ached, and the frequent urge to spew had gone. Today though, he was enjoying her ministrations far too much to confess that he was fit and well again. A few weeks' sickness and plenty of rest in bed had seen him right, but she did not need to know, not for a while.

Arianwen took the cloth from his brow and rinsed it in the water bowl, before wringing it out and twisting a corner. She dabbed at the edges of the wound on his temple, tugging the scab. He winced more than was necessary, and she said, not for the first time, "It is better to pull the scabs off while they are soft. The scarring will not be so bad."

"You are good to worry but I do not mind so much about scars."

She grinned. "Then spare a thought for those, like me, who have to look at you." Her tongue-tip went to the corner of her mouth as she continued dabbing. Then she said quietly, "You were not so pretty to begin with."

He thought about feigning hurt feelings, but there was something about the way she was looking at him that banished further attempts to deceive. He put a hand out to still hers, and took the cloth from her, flinging it to the side of the bed. He pulled her gently to him and kissed her.

"You should rest, you know," she said, breaking away.

Abandoning his pretence, he said, "I am rested; all I need now is to build my strength back up, and I have an idea how to do that." He caught her shoulders, and half-sat up, pushing her down onto the bed and hovering above her, supported by his elbows.

"My lord," she protested unconvincingly, "in your sick bed? Whatever will folk think?"

He laughed. "I do not care. Soon enough, I shall have to get up and go home. I would make the most of this time while I can." He lowered his head to kiss her again and then cursed as someone rapped loudly on the door frame. Arianwen slid from under him and went to see who was standing there.

Looking beyond her shoulder, Ethelred could see the side of Dyfrig's head. The man spoke in low tones and fast Welsh and then walked off.

Arianwen came back into the room and sat on the edge of the bed. "I am sorry, but it seems Heledd has gone wandering. Bleddyn has set out after her, but Dyfrig thinks it a good idea for me to be there when she is found. He will go with me for safety's sake."

Ethelred was sorry that Heledd was still troubled and causing concern, but he did not like to think of Arianwen

122

going off with Dyfrig. "That man does not like me."

She laughed, too loudly. "He does not know you, that is all. Oh, I nearly forgot. While you were still in your deep sleep, I made you this." She reached into the bag hanging at her belt, pressed something into his hand, and left the bower.

After she had gone, he opened his hand. Lying there was a piece of embroidery, a band of tablet-weave with woollen stitching, too short to be sewn round a hem, a neck-opening, or even a sleeve. Intricately threaded into the coloured bands of red, green and gold, there was a recurring pattern, which at first he thought was an abstract design. When he looked more closely, he saw that the symbol was made up of the letters N and A, representing her name and his kin's pet name for him. He ran his thumb over the thread, tracing the interlocking stitches, and made up his mind. He would get out of bed, he would strengthen his weakened leg, and he would wed his Welsh love and take her home with him.

His plan did not come to fruition. The giddy spells had all but abated, but his leg had been badly damaged, the muscle having been torn and an infection setting in on the journey back, and it took him many more weeks before he was fully able to bear weight on it. He was still limping when the harvest was brought in.

The annual fall began and the trees started to undress, sending their discarded leaves twirling to the ground. Cold winds blew and Ethelred wore his cloak most days when they went out. He and his men helped out around the steading, for they had long ago overstayed the period of traditional welcome. Llywarch was in no hurry to see them go, and so Ethelred, Heaferth, Immin and the others accompanied the Teulu on hunts, helped to repair buildings before the worst of the winter weather came in, and even

123

assisted in the hazel coppices, avoiding areas of the forest where the deer were rutting and repairing the fences to stop those deer, and the cattle and sheep, from eating the young shoots in the spring.

Arianwen encouraged Heledd to spend time in the hall and allowed her short walks on her own. Wherever she walked within the settlement, Bleddyn was never far away. On one occasion, Ethelred walked around the side of the hall to find the two of them together, looking at a lapwing circling overhead, and Heledd was smiling. She looked even more like her sister then, and her cheeks glowed, proof of her restored health and a hint that there might be some happiness in her life again. Ethelred smiled too, genuinely pleased to see her thus recovered, but also at the thought that perhaps Arianwen might come back to Mercia soon.

Llywarch always smiled and waved when he saw Ethelred. This morning, though, he sought out the Mercian and, dancing like a child with a full bladder, he grabbed Ethelred by the arm. "Come, come, I have tidings and I know you will wish to hear them."

Intrigued, Ethelred followed him into the hall.

Llywarch said, "Do you read? No, I mean do you read Welsh? One thing to speak it, another altogether to see it written down." He rushed on, not waiting for an answer. "Here it is, in plain ink which cannot lie. Rhiryd sends greetings!"

Ethelred was slack-jawed for a heartbeat. His childhood friend was alive and had not forgotten him. "What? How? Is he nearby; can I ride to meet him?"

Llywarch beckoned for drinks and, while they were being poured, he said, "No, sadly. This," he slapped the vellum with the back of his free hand, "came to me because I wished for tidings regarding the fighting in the north." He paused to take a sip of mead. "A long tale for the bards, but to keep it short, when I had word sent to my uncle's cousin,

124

I mentioned that you were here as my guest. Oh, so sorry, yes, my uncle's cousin is fighting his nephew's brother-by-law and..." He took another slurp of mead. "What can I say? If we Welsh have no English to fight, we make merry fighting our own kind, as you will have gathered by now. Where was I? Oh, yes, Rhiryd is kin to my uncle through his other cousin and he went off with his Teulu, not to fight, with his leg being twisted as it is, but as their bard. He heard that you were here, and sent greetings."

Finally, the Welshman came to a stop. Ethelred thought that perhaps he'd made more of the tale than need be, but then Llywarch leaned forward, the smile gone. "There is more, here. I will not bore you nor make you blush, but Rhiryd lets it be known that you were a loyal friend to him, and more. Why did you not say that you once saved his life?"

Ethelred stared into his mead cup, while his ear tips pulsed and he knew they were reddening. "It was naught. Anyone would have done the same."

Llywarch said, "Perhaps. Yet it was not anyone, but you, who went into the river and pulled him out when the bridge gave way."

It was not a day that Ethelred wished to recall. Stubbornly, the memory had often refused to shift from his mind to make way for others, but he was sure reliving it was worse for Rhiryd.

"And it makes it all the more remarkable that you were willing to swim the river with my cattle. Not only are you a thinker, but you are fearless too."

Ethelred's natural response was to deny it, but he knew it would be pointless.

He did not need to speak, for Llywarch was talking again. "This is what I think. Here, we have been under the yoke of the Northumbrians every bit as much as the Mercians have. Your father was ever a friend to Wales, and up in Gwynedd he is fondly remembered. Rhiryd now sings songs about you there, and I have seen what kind of man you are with my own eyes. We are tired of sending the best of our cattle and crops to Oswii." He clasped Ethelred's wrist. "All I am saying is, when the time comes, you need only bellow, and we will be there."

Ethelred drained his cup. It was no surprise that Llywarch and his folk wished to be free of Northumbrian interference, but it was a shock to find himself being spoken to as if he were king, and not Wulf.

That afternoon, after he and Immin had paused from cutting timbers to take a bite to eat and a cup of mead, Ethelred found himself alone when Immin went off to speak to a woman who, he said, had given him feelings which he'd blush to tell his mother about. Ethelred went for a walk, to find some quiet away from the work sheds. Here, they did not make linen from flax, only spun wool from fleeces, and the carding of the sheep wool was conducted inside. The women sang as they worked and, contained within the building, the sound was somehow louder to the bystander. He walked beyond the weaving sheds too, where the clacking of the loom weights seemed to thump against his head. As he rounded the corner, he saw Arianwen by a barn, talking to someone. Dyfrig. The man with the strange garnet finger ring was pointing that bejewelled finger at her. Ethelred's own hand curled into a fist, but he stood still, close enough to hear, not close enough to disturb.

Arianwen did not flinch even though the jabbing finger must have been intimidating. "It is my home. Lord Merwal and Lady Domneva have been as mother and father to me."

"This is your home! You would leave your sister when she needs you? When your own mother and father died it was only right that you were sent away. Your father was always an ally of the Magonsæte."

She spread her arms wide. "Well then. You understand."

126

"No! You were a child then. Now you are a woman grown. This is your brother's hall; these are your brother's lands. There will always be a place for you. And if…"

Dyfrig's anger appeared to melt away and he bent his head low, talking quietly now into Arianwen's ear. Ethelred could hear no more, and he turned and went back to the timber pile. Immin returned not long after and, if he thought that his lord's wood-chopping that afternoon was rather aggressive, he had the sense not to ask questions.

When he met Arianwen in the evening, Ethelred tried to ask his own questions, without revealing what he had heard. Walking with her to the hall, he said, "The nights come earlier now. It will be full winter soon. Do you have Bloodmonth here?" Oh, that was clumsy. Of course they would slaughter the animals in the few weeks before Yule. Welsh folk had to eat over the winter too, but if she thought his question foolish, she did not say so.

"We do. The men here will do it, though. We have no need of a slaughterman. I, however, always welcome help crushing the bones to get the marrow out for cooking and for my salves. Why do you ask?"

They were nearly at the hall. He stopped and pretended to re-tie his leg binding. Standing up straight again, he said, "I will not lie; if you have roasted pig at Hallowmas I would not wish to miss that feast, but if I were to bide much longer after that, I would be here for the winter. I'd rather not ride on frozen roads."

Arianwen had no chance to reply, for Dyfrig appeared as if from nowhere. "Did not your father ride to fight Oswii in Bloodmonth? Ah, yes, but that did not go well for him, did it? Little wonder his weakest son would fain ride only in fair weather." He walked on, not even bothering to look at either of them.

It was a brutal swipe. Ethelred was at a loss. "What did he…Why?"

127

She took his hand and dragged him away from the main route to the hall, and away from others who were now beginning to make their way into the building. "I should have told you when you first rode here. Dyfrig has always had feelings for me. He sees you as a threat. Pay him no mind. Now, what were you saying?"

He still felt there was more to the tale, but his main question must be asked. "I have to think about whether to go home before the winter sets in fully, or bide here until the weather gets better. And so I need to know if you plan to come home." He could not help but look over to where Dyfrig had been just moments before.

"Would you wish to spend all winter here? Would it make parting worse?"

He shook his head. "Why must we part? Unless you mean to live here and never return to Mercia." Had saying it out loud been a mistake? Had he now put the thought in her head?

She reached up and stroked his upper arm. "No. Heledd is much better and I think that before long Bleddyn will get his reward for his steadfastness and gentle wooing. There is a better life on its way for her."

"What keeps you here then?" His heart was beating far too fast. It made him feel like the ground was moving under his feet.

She paused a moment longer than suited his comfort before she answered, but when she did, it was decisive. "Naught. Indeed, if we spend too much longer here then it might be harder for me to leave." Her tone went dull. "Others might get too used to it."

And he, too, might get overly settled here. The welcome at Llywarch's hearth, the days spent with the Teulu, stolen moments lying as man and wife with Arianwen in the little dug-out hillside, the soft kisses and the discreet hand holding, had made him forget. To overwinter in this beguiling place would be to lose all sense of himself and his duty. "You will come, then. Tomorrow?"

A cry went up, from inside the hall.

"Son of a whore!"

"Maybe, but my arse is prettier than your mother's face!"

The two men throwing the insults tumbled outside, aiming drunken punches and falling over their own feet. Yet more, eager to spectate, filed outside, yelling, jeering, and encouraging.

"I must get Heledd out of there," Arianwen said, and ran off.

"Bleddyn will look after her," he called out, but his words were lost in the night air.

Ethelred, Heaferth and Immin spent the evening with the other Mercian men, sitting round a brazier outside, cloaks up to keep off the light rain. Tempers were raised, and it would not have taken much for the Welsh to turn on their guests, so it was better for them to remain in the open. Ethelred was acutely aware that he had kept his men from their families too long while he recovered from his injuries, and the incident in the hall confirmed his decision that it was time to go home.

He was up not long after dawn, noting how long the sun was taking these days to get up into the morning sky. The weather remained calm, holding the woodsmoke hanging in the stillness and, even if it turned, they would make good progress this day and be well on the way before they got caught in any changes.

He loitered near Arianwen's bower, not wishing to knock in case she was still abed, but as the daylight lifted the dark completely and shortened his shadow, there was still no noise suggesting movement within. He strolled over to the hall, but aside from a few of the Teulu nursing sore heads and picking at chunks of bread, it was empty.

There was no sign of her in the weaving sheds, nor, as far as he could see, was she on the outer edge of the woodland, and those who were watching over the pigs fattening on the acorns had not seen her. She liked to go into the woods and gather mushrooms and hazelnuts, and the morning was crisp and fresh, the ground hard underfoot. She would be tempted, if nothing else, by the chance to kick through the fallen bounty under the trees.

The season had turned sharply during the last week and the woodland floor was covered with red, gold, and brown leaves which emitted a loamy smell as he trod through them, disturbing the residue of moisture trapped there. He blew on his hands and rubbed them, then set off deeper into the woods to find her. If she had not already gathered her belongings together, she would be in a rush to be ready to leave with him and the men.

He got as far as their secret place without catching her up. Lifting up the branch that served as its doorway, he could see at a glance that she was not there, and had not been since they'd last lain there together. Straightening, he let the branch swing down, sidestepped back down to the path and looked around. Where was she?

Ethelred retraced his steps, going more slowly and looking first to one side of the path and then the other, but he heard only the occasional squeak of a shrew and the rustle of other small animals running away from the vibration of his footsteps. Emerging from the treeline, he looked up to see Dyfrig walking towards him.

The two men had hardly exchanged words in the whole time that Ethelred had been Llywarch's guest. Ethelred wasn't about to change that now, not on the day he was leaving anyway, but the Welshman clearly had other ideas. He opened his mouth but Ethelred decided to cut him off. "Keep any words you might have. I am on my way to seek out Llywarch, thank him and to take my leave. You will be glad to know that we are leaving this morning."

He made to walk on, but Dyfrig put a hand on his arm. "A shame you cannot say farewell to Arianwen."

Ethelred shook off his grip, and made a point of brushing his sleeve as if dirt had been left there. "I have no need to do so. She is coming with me."

"You think so?"

"Lady Heledd is much stronger now."

Dyfrig lifted his hand, inspecting that jewelled ring. "Indeed. There is to be a wedding."

"I am glad. Bleddyn will be a fine husband for her, and I hope that in time they will be blessed with healthy bairns. Arianwen and I will come back for the wedding if we are able."

Dyfrig lowered his hand, resting it on his belt buckle. "You know, surely, that we four grew up together? What on God's good green earth makes you think that I speak of Heledd and Bleddyn?"

Ethelred opened his mouth to dismiss the insinuation, then closed it again. She had not answered his question, had not actually said that she wanted to go back to Mercia with him. And what of all those moments when he'd felt there was something she wasn't telling him, about Dyfrig and his place in her life? Had Ethelred's heart been like a harp for her, to pull on its strings only when she needed entertainment?

He stood for a moment to steady his breathing and then nodded at Dyfrig. "I wish you well. And now I must find Lord Llywarch and thank him. Let us always hope that we and the Welsh remain friends and never have to meet on the battlefield." It was a miserable and impotent threat, but it was the best he could manage. He was in too much of a hurry to get back, say his farewells, and be on the road and some miles away before his heart shattered.

Chapter Six

Lindsey AD663: Early Spring

If he'd thought the wind cold in Wales, then this fierce force
of nature should have a new name, for it whipped across
from the eastern shore and was as chill as iron, slicing his
cheeks and slapping his hair across his brow. His eyes
watered constantly, and he could barely move his fingers.
Not for the first time, he wondered why they and the
Northumbrians had fought so often to keep a foothold in
this godforsaken place.

It was clear, though, that the people who lived in Lindsey
would rather rule themselves and be part of the Mercian
federation than be ruled by Oswii and send tribute to him.
Ethelred had gleaned this from the local thegn, Winta, who
had been their guide through the unfamiliar landscape. To
many, Oswii's elder brother Oswald, whom Penda had slain,
was a saint. To those in Lindsey, however, he was a
merciless invader who had put the local inhabitants under
his yoke. Wulf had encountered more assistance than
resistance on his campaign to retake the lands, but it had
been a long, scrappy campaign and now, half a day's ride
from Lincoln, Ethelred took himself out of the wind and
went to sit in a grove atop a small rise, while he awaited
word from his brother as to whether he was needed here,
elsewhere, or at all.

While he waited for Winta and Immin to return, he sat
with his back to a tree and looked down on the flat ground
beyond. Heaferth was nearby, as always, and this time so
was Merchelm. Ethelred recalled their conversation.

I will not ask you to come; this is not your fight.

I am not coming to fight. I am coming because I can see by one look that you are sad beyond reckoning. You will need me nearby.

And that was when the tears had fallen.

Now, both Merchelm and Heaferth kept a respectful distance, understanding that Ethelred still needed time alone. He was truly heartsore, and his chest ached to carry the wounded thing which kept beating despite the puncture. He tried not to think of her, he really did, but images of the way her eyes crinkled when she smiled, the sound of her joyous laugh, the scent of mint in her hair and the warmth of her soft hand in his, invaded his sleep night after night, destroying him anew. He shrugged his cloak tighter and cursed the wind that found its way even amongst the trees. God grant they were not still here in the winter, for he could not bear to think of this same wind whipping snow across his face.

God. He was no doubt displeased with this member of His flock, who had so far done naught to discharge his duty to his people, nor served his Lord in any meaningful way. Ethelred thought of the lessons of Father Cedda and felt his despair flooding through him. He had stood by while Wulf executed Cuthred. He had spent time in Wales lying with Arianwen who was not even, and now never would be, his wife. He let go of the edges of his cloak and put his hands together, bending his neck to bow his head as he spoke directly to God.

Halfway through his prayers he felt compelled to look up. The wind had dropped, the sun had made a brief appearance, and the land below the rise was bathed in a glow that tinged the grass yellow. Ethelred glanced over at Heaferth and Merchelm, but they appeared not to have noticed and were still in a huddle, crouched low to keep out of the wind. Yes, the wind was blowing again now. Had he dreamed it all?

When Winta returned, Ethelred asked him about the land

below them. "Is it firm? Not marshy?"

Winta combed his beard with his fingers. "How do you mean?"

"Could it be built upon?"

"Aye, I dare say, but why would you wish to?"

Ethelred shrugged. "I was wondering, that is all." How could he say that he thought God wished him to build an abbey on that very spot? The man would think him mad. And perhaps he would be right. "What word from my brother?"

"Lord Immin bade me tell you that he will stay now with King Wulfhere, who has made safe all the land from Lincoln to the Humber. Even at the crossing at Barton, men loyal to Mercia now keep watch on the ferry and all the men from here to there have sworn oaths to him."

Still awestruck by the sign sent from God, Ethelred gave the order to move. "There is no need to wait for my brother, it seems. Let's go home." As they rode off, he turned and took another look at the open ground where the light had shone. It was a fine spot for an abbey. He would come back this way one day and see it built. From now on, his life would be one of duty, to his land and to his God.

Merchelm brought his horse alongside. "You mean we came all this way and will not even have the fun of a fight?"

"I am sorry, my friend; it looks like we have wasted our time, yes." In truth, he had wasted all his time since he came back from Wulf's campaign in the south, and that included his months in Wales. Sometimes it felt like his only purpose was to stay alive until Wulf had a male heir old enough to wear the king-helm, and that he'd been wrong to think or hope otherwise. He called out to Winta. "Ere we leave, I would beg one more boon. A message, if you will, to the abbot of the nearest house." He might not be back this way for some time, but there was no harm in finding out if local monks might wish to start a new community.

Merchelm touched his friend's arm. "See that?"

Ethelred looked to where he was pointing. A group of horsemen was coming towards them. "Who are they?"

Winta, who'd been preparing to leave with the message, shrugged. "I am not sure. I don't think I know them."

"Men from Wulf's army?" Merchelm offered the suggestion with little conviction.

They waited. Wulf's men would ride right up to Ethelred's group. This small band was not friendly, for the riders were now dismounting, and thus preparing to fight.

"Northumbrians," Winta said. "They seem not to wish to make it too easy for us."

"Helms on!" Ethelred slid out of his saddle and brought his shield round in front of him. He could hear that behind him, his men had done the same. In a surprise encounter like this there was no time to find somewhere to tether the horses. God grant they didn't roam too far.

The Northumbrians banged their shields with their weapons and began to run. Ethelred said, "Let them come. If they wish to tire themselves before they get here, so be it." He glanced to his left and right, nodding to Merchelm and Heaferth, and with no need for words, they formed a small shield wall to withstand the first impact of the charge.

The familiar shock shot up his left arm as the enemy hit the wall, but they could not break it. Slashing with their weapons, the Mercians held their ground and a number of Northumbrians soon lay in front of them, a threat only if the Mercians tripped on their corpses. Another clatter, another reverberation up through his arm, and then a release of pressure. Somewhere the line had been broken. Ethelred shoved his shield forward and managed to unbalance his immediate opponent. The snarl was still sounding in the air as the man fell, and Ethelred cut it off with a stab of his sword. Blood bubbled from the Northumbrian's throat, and Ethelred stepped over him, ready to take on the next assailant.

Their shields clattered together, and both lost their footing. Ethelred was the first to regain his balance. He shoved again and the man went down, holding his shield over his body to protect himself. Ethelred aimed at his legs, slicing across his knee and the man lowered the shield just long enough to expose his neck. It was his last voluntary action.

Behind him, a noise and flutter of movement just detectable in the corner of his eye told Ethelred that someone was about to jump at his back. He swung round, only to find that Merchelm had engaged and was doing his best to get his axe over and beyond the man's shield. The man parried every blow and Ethelred feared the axe would become embedded in the linden wood and Merchelm would be disarmed, but the power of Merchelm's next blow meant that the Northumbrian, shorter in stature, had to hold his shield up almost above his head and at that moment, Merchelm's axe went sideways and cut into his neck. It was over.

Gasping, Ethelred looked about him. Not all of his men were on their feet but those who weren't were sitting on the ground, panting, or on their knees, winded. Ethelred took off his helm, snatched off the linen arming cap and wiped the sweat off his brow with it. He looked up at the sky. There would not be enough daylight to bury the men, let alone to dig separate graves. Luckily there had been no hard frost and the ground would be malleable, but they would still have to wait until the morning.

Heaferth was all for leaving them where they lay. "It will only delay us. And these were foes who tried to kill us."

"Christians, nonetheless." Ethelred looked back at the site which had glowed under the godly light. "We should bury them over there, away from the open space." God had indeed blessed the place, granting him an easy victory. When he came back to build his abbey, he wanted no dead Northumbrians underneath it.

Winta said, "I will send to the steading over by the river. They will send men and spades on the morrow. Meanwhile I will set a watch here until these men are under the ground. You should find somewhere to overnight."

Ethelred opened his mouth to reply but let the words die unspoken as a lone rider approached.

The man brought his horse up sharp and said, "Lord Ethelred?"

"I am he."

"I come with word from the king. He has tents pitched a short ride from here. He bade me find you and bring you to him."

Ethelred tucked his helm under his arm, grinned and raised his voice so that all his men could hear. "You've fought well. When your breathing is calm let us go to my brother and we can overnight with him. He is never known to be without food and good ale."

They followed Wulf's man a few miles to the king's camp and Heaferth went off straight away to the forge to arrange the mending and sharpening of their weapons. Merchelm remained with the rest of the men and Ethelred sought out Wulf in his tent.

The king of Mercia was sitting on a folding leather-seated stool. He had a cup of ale in his hand, and he looked up and smiled broadly when Ethelred came in.

"Noni!" If his smile hadn't betrayed his exuberance, then the use of the childhood name certainly did. "I hear that you had a little trouble?"

Ethelred accepted the proffered drink from one of Wulf's hearth-thegns and took a long draught before replying. "I had to finish the task, since you could not."

Wulf laughed and sat forward. "In truth, Brother, I found it hard to believe there were any more of the scum left out

137

there. Oswii only sent a token army against us. Either he cares little for this land, or he has other business that takes him elsewhere. Who cares which? Lindsey is no longer under his yoke." He raised his cup and made a toast. "Mercia!"

Ethelred copied him. He was glad enough to have survived the day, pleased for his brother and for the folk of Lindsey, but now, aside from increasing his daily prayers, what would occupy his days, and his thoughts?

On the Dùn Èideann road, Northumbria.

"May we ride on now?" Alfrid's impatience and disapproval were obvious; he'd turned his horse around before he'd finished speaking.

Ecgfrith was still adjusting his clothing and wasn't sure he was ready to get back into the saddle, but his half-brother had been bleating enough before they'd stopped and would be whining like an annoying fly for the rest of the day if they didn't get going again.

Out on the road once more, Alfrid made it clear that he was not prepared to drop the matter. "I trust that will keep you sated for a while?"

Ecgfrith saw no harm; the girl had been willing. After they had stopped for a meal, a swift tumble in the hay barn had eased his body. He'd have preferred a bed, but needs must. If his old boot of a wife would part her legs from time to time, he'd not need to plough every herdsman's daughter who made cow eyes at him. He'd lived eighteen summers. Alfrid was older, much older; perhaps he had no more use for his cock than pissing, but Ecgfrith was not ready for the life of an old man.

The scenery had changed little and yet they were several days into their journey. Odd to think that the land they were passing through once belonged not to Northumbria but to the British Gododdin. The low hills and the vast tracts of woodland were so familiar that it was hard to believe it had not always been part of his kin's lands. He began wondering idly about the kingdom of the Picts and whether it would differ. Ignoring Alfrid's remark and changing the subject, he said, "This man, Drest, he will do as we bid?"

"Threats and promises worked with the last Pictish king and Drest is his brother, so, if one was loyal to our father, then the other should be. Did Oswii not speak to you of this?"

Go with Alfrid, Boy. It will be good training for you, and you can be my eyes. I do not know how trustworthy Alfrid is these days; he wished to go to Rome and I stopped him, and he's too thick with Wilfrid. Be my ears, also. "He told me to listen to what you had to say."

Alfrid grunted. "If you had heeded my words, we would have pressed on instead of stopping for..."

He'd needled him long enough. "I get what I can where I must. With my wife as cold as a winter sea and the priest Wilfrid urging her to stay that way... Kings do not wed for love, you know." Ecgfrith smiled, but if Alfrid noticed the double insult, to his own love match and his lower status as under-king, he showed no sign.

Instead, his half-brother waved an arm in the general direction of the men riding behind them. "It is they who grow restless." Then it came. "And you are not yet a king you know, nor even your father's only son." Was that a threat? Ecgfrith had no time to respond, for Alfrid was still talking. "Wilfrid brings balm to Northumbrian souls. It is good that he is back. Much blood has been spilled of late, and many men have turned on their own kin. We need to heal, and Wilfrid is the man to guide us."

That was a thinly disguised barb. It was true that Oswii had Efa's kinsman murdered and then threatened the new

139

king of Deira, his own nephew, who ran away to join Penda's forces, but why should Alfrid complain? That was the reason, lest he forget, that Alfrid got Deira in the first place. He should be grateful.

They rode on in silence.

As the sun began to sink in the western sky, they stopped by a river to make camp. Alfrid barely spoke during the meal of griddled flatbreads and dried smoked fish, except to thank the man who brought the food, an unnecessary indulgence, Ecgfrith thought. "How long…"

"Weeks. Then you will begin to see mountains that dwarf the hills of home, that make the Bamburgh outcrop look like a pile of pebbles."

It wasn't what Ecgfrith had meant to ask, but since Alfrid was seemingly less reluctant to talk now, he pressed on. "And when we get there?" *Don't let me down Boy.*

"It should be no more than a matter of ensuring that Drest is named king in place of his dead brother, and reminding the Picts of Oswii's strength should they consider naysaying it. Not like last time."

Last time, many years ago, he meant. Ecgfrith knew the story, of how Alfrid rode north to find their cousin, Talorgen, and persuade him that he was to be king of Pictland. The reigning king was about to die, they said, and Elwyn, always reliable, had ensured that it came to pass. Oswii had trusted Alfrid with the mission then, but clearly was not so sure of his loyalty this time. Talorgen was also dead now and so too was his replacement. Was Oswii losing his grip, on the Pictish lands, and on his own son? Ecgfrith picked his nails and then stared into the flames that were licking the sides of the brazier. There was much to think about.

Alfrid continued. "Last time, I rode with hopes of showing our father my worth. Your mother warned me that he would always be indifferent to me as a son, but would

140

use my hopes to make me act in his interests."

Ecgfrith swallowed his contempt, with difficulty. "Why ride as far north as Bamburgh in the first place? Why not bide with the Mercians, since you seem to love them so much?"

Alfrid looked up in surprise. "Why should I not love my wife? Such things are possible, you know. And you, surely, have naught but good recollections of your time in Mercia. Lady Derwena would not – did not, for look at you now – harm a hair on a child's head."

Memories swirled like mist and Ecgfrith's arm twitched as if putting his hand out would help him to catch them, but the pictures would not form, beyond a woman's soft voice, calling him to join her children for a meal. *While you are here, you shall be as one of my own.* He slapped an imaginary spark from his breeches. "And yet here you are, in Northumbria, with the Deiran king-helm snugly on your head. Like a barn cat, you fell on your feet."

The older man looked at him as if without comprehension and then said, "It is as you say. For my actions, I was rewarded with a kingdom."

There was some hidden meaning in his words, but Ecgfrith had not the energy to find it. "So, a matter of some weeks, then, until we get there?"

"If the weather is kind to us, yes. And let us hope that giving Drest the kingship of the Picts is as swift a matter as it should be, for I would like to get home before the first snowfall."

Alfrid had not lied about the landscape in the north, nor, it transpired, had there been any need to worry. Drest was installed upon the throne having sworn allegiance to Oswii, Alfrid left a small number of Northumbrian men in the north as a safeguard, and he and Ecgfrith travelled home. Alfrid's mood did not improve and Ecgfrith made no

141

attempt to lift him out of his dolefulness. Without talking, and with reduced numbers, they would make better progress and now all Ecgfrith really wanted was to get home. That was not completely true. He had no desire to see his father again, really, but at least Alfrid would go back to Deira and he'd not have to see his miserable elder half-brother for some time. Irritatingly, he was proved wrong. Alfrid did not take the road to York but stayed with Ecgfrith and they arrived back in Bamburgh together.

Something was amiss. There were few men at arms, and the smithy's forge was cold. Ecgfrith stood in the yard, shouting for his mother, for Elwyn, or for anyone who might tell him what had happened.

It was his wife who heeded his shouting and came walking, deliberately without urgency, from the direction of the chapel. Wilfrid was by her side; that interfering priest who spent far too much time at Bamburgh when he should be at Ripon. If the two of them weren't so in love with God, he'd swear they were cuckolding him. "Where is my father?"

Audrey bowed her head, ignoring his rudeness and lack of greeting. Good, she was learning at least. "He is not here."

"Do not irk me Woman; I can see he is not here."

Wilfrid took a step forward and Ecgfrith had to resist the urge to recoil, so great was his loathing for the man who had effectively cut his balls off. "There has been some trouble, Lord. In Lindsey, with the Mercians."

"There has been trouble in Lindsey for over a year. There is naught new there. The Mercians are meddlesome. We know this. What has happened that my father must now ride out?"

"Wulfhere of Mercia was a thorn, as you say, Lord, but we had word that his brother had brought more men into Lindsey, a number of battles were fought, and Lindsey is now under Mercian protection. Your father is on his way home, but he will be…"

Ecgfrith held up a hand. His father would be wroth. With the Deirans and half the Bernician men away in the north, Oswii had been caught out with limited forces to take south. And he, Ecgfrith, had missed an opportunity to battle the Mercians. "I swear..."

"Yes, Lord?"

He closed his hand into a fist and walked away to find a drink, and then maybe the cook-house girl who'd been so accommodating before he'd ridden north. Wilfrid called after him, but he saw no need to make his promise out loud. His oath was simple: he would never be in the wrong place at the wrong time again.

His mother was in the hall, Ositha was sitting nearby, and the boy Elfwin was walking round the room, holding the edges of the stools when he needed a little extra balance. The two-year-old had a large head as, Ecgfrith conceded, most walking-babes still did, but he had little in the way of a neck, even when he should be growing out of his baby shape. He would take after Oswii, and not their mother. Ecgfrith was indeed not his father's only son, but Oswii had taken little interest in Elfwin when he was born, so Ecgfrith had naught to fear. Or, was Alfrid right; was the king of Northumbria indifferent to all his children except where they could be of use to him? No, surely it was more a case of riches, for Oswii had never had difficulty finding wives who were prepared to open their legs for him and spawn sons.

Ecgfrith had felt little certainty in his life thus far. Sent away as a young child to enemy Mercia, he had been scared but, despite his father's breaking of the truce, he had been treated gently there. His mother's welcome upon his return had been hypocritical. Ecgfrith knew it had been Efa's idea to send him away, and she must have been aware that his life was in danger; aware, surely, that Oswii would not keep his word. Women were contrary creatures. His father might

143

not always seem to care, he was blunt to the point of almost perpetual rudeness, but at least he did not attempt to woo with false kindness.

Even so, he had his faults, faults which Ecgfrith was determined would not affect his own judgement. He was not his father's son, nor his mother's; he was his own man. He watched as Alfrid came into the hall, flanked by Audrey and Wilfrid. His elder half-brother had done Oswii's bidding at every turn, and it had brought him a kingdom but not, apparently, happiness. It was better, Ecgfrith decided, not to do anyone else's bidding, but to clear one's own path through the forest of life.

He stepped forward to receive a too-long embrace from his mother, who brushed his cheek with her lips before breaking away and scooping up little Elfwin. "We are glad to see you home safe," she said, but immediately turned and spoke to his sister. "Ositha my love, will you take him?" She handed the child to his sister and went over to embrace Alfrid. Why? She wasn't even related to him. Ecgfrith watched as she spoke a few brief words, touched Audrey's sleeve, and then stood back as the younger woman nodded and walked back to the hearth with her mother-by-law. Efa said, "Your brother and Wilfrid have much to talk about. I told them that the chapel would be a better place."

"He's not my…What does he need to talk to the priest for?"

"He has things on his mind. His soul is troubled. I told him I would have word sent to Carena in York that he is back, but that it will be some time yet before he can greet her there." She drummed her fingers on the table. "Or perhaps this rift with Ava can be mended in a shorter time."

Ecgfrith squinted when she mentioned his half-sister. Was the wraith here, in the hall? He looked into each of the dark corners, but could see nothing. His mother, as if hearing his unspoken question, said, "She is in the chapel. That's partly

144

why I sent her brother and Wilfrid there. They may be able to give her comfort in a way that I seem unable to do."

He scratched his head, doubting that her hopes were justified. Ava had murdered her husband. No matter that she was Alfrid's sister; Pieter had been Alfrid's greatest friend. Alfrid had never before been inclined to forgive and why would he? On the other hand, her actions meant that there was one more dead Mercian, a son of Penda's at that. Why was anyone upset about it? Ecgfrith had seen him once, that husband of Ava's, not long after he had arrived as a hostage in Mercia. All he could remember was a tall man, but then weren't all men tall, to a child of not quite ten summers? Ecgfrith recalled the tall man's words. *Another stray, Mother? Fear not, little Lief, my mother feeds boys like you and makes them big and strong. You'll be well cared-for here.* Stray? Shame that the tall man had not lived; shame that he would not see that little 'stray' take the Mercian throne one day.

Ositha loved her little brother. He was a boy, which meant she did not have to be envious of another sister, but in looking after him so much she had also proved useful to her mother. Efa doted on the little boy and so, by extension, began to notice Ositha more too. Ositha would have preferred to be loved for herself but being helpful was the next best thing. There was one thing, though, that had always made her feel special, and that was her name.

She had always been proud of, if a little puzzled by, the fact that of all his offspring, she was the only one whom Oswii named after himself. This gave her a special link to his royal line, and to her sainted uncle, Oswald, who had died before she was born. For this, she felt somehow more Northumbrian than even her full siblings. The half-brothers and sisters didn't count, for Ositha's mother was the only one who was a queen. The news that Lindsey, on their very border, was now back under Mercian control made her feel insecure. She'd never had her father's love, but she'd always thought he would keep them all safe. Perhaps she ought to pray to her uncle in Heaven? It was certainly beginning to look like Oswii and Ecgfrith could not protect her. Taking little Elfwin to his nurse, she made her way to the chapel, there to offer up a prayer. And if, at the same time, she happened to overhear the conversation between Ava and Alfrid, well, that couldn't be helped, could it?

Uncle Oswald's legend loomed large in the lives of Northumbrians. Oswii felt overshadowed by him, Ositha knew. Ositha was too young yet for marriage, but not for love. And she decided that she would devote all that love to the memory of her dead uncle. She would pray to him, and all her passion would be directed into that prayer.

The chapel was dark, with plenty of places to sit in the shadows. Ositha knew they would hear the door open, see the light that came in with her, but she was only a small child as far as they were concerned, and they'd take little notice. Besides, Wilfrid would be pleased to see her head bent in prayer. She fought the urge to sneeze, something that afflicted her almost every time she stepped inside the dusty building. The cold stone walls chilled her, and she was tempted to hurry her prayers and get back to the warmth of the wooden hall, but she made her way slowly to a bench and slid along it until she was close to, but not touching, the chilly wall. Clasping her hands together, she lifted her inner voice to God and the spirit of her uncle and asked them both to watch over her, and Northumbria. She also offered another silent prayer, suggesting that if it should be in God's interest, He could find a way to let her hear something that might prove beneficial to her father.

Was God listening? He must be. Through the gloom she could scarcely make out the figures near the altar, save for the tall outline of her half-brother Alfrid, but Wilfrid's voice rang out as if he either knew, or did not care, that she might overhear.

"He is out of step, with Rome and with Frankia. Your father must see the sense of taking up the Roman way."

"You doubt his love for God and the Church?" This from Alfrid, quieter.

"I do not doubt it as such. I fear for his immortal soul but that is another matter. Away from high lords and laden tables though, it makes no sense to have Easter marked at separate times. It confuses the ordinary folk, when some are feasting and some fasting for Lent, but this is not my only worry."

Ositha leaned forward but Wilfrid's voice had dropped to barely a whisper, and she could no longer hear what he was saying. He spoke for a while like that and then she heard, "And now I must leave you two alone. I will wait, dear Alfrid, and we can ride south together. Take as long as you must; I think there is much that needs to be said in order that both your hearts can heal. Ava, my child, you have asked the Lord for forgiveness, and He has heard you. Now, try to heal this rift twixt you and your brother."

He walked down the central aisle and paused at Ositha's bench, nodding to acknowledge her presence. She opened her mouth, ready with an excuse for listening, but he walked on, opening the door and forming a shadow in the light before closing it quietly behind him. He had known she was there, but did Alfrid and Ava? And did it matter? Ositha wondered if she should make some noise, but it was awkward now, for too much time had elapsed since she'd first entered the chapel. She would sit, quietly, and if need be pretend that she hadn't realised she was not alone.

In a small and wavering voice, Ava said, "It cannot be healed. It cannot be mended. Do not look at me Brother, for I know you hate me."

"How can I hate you? I see that you are hurting, and I

147

know that you loved Pieter. This is why I cannot understand, even now, why you did it."

"I… I am afraid to say it."

"You've naught to fear from God. You will be shriven, Wilfrid is sure. And we both believe that there was another hand in it. This was too foul a deed for you alone."

The scraping of a bench on the stone floor set Ositha's teeth on edge. The wood complained with a squeak as they sat down and then brother and sister were silent for a few heartbeats. Ositha wondered if her very breath was too loud, but trying to silence it only made her want to gasp for air.

"He sent word of what he wished me to do."

"Who did?"

A whisper in reply.

"I understand why you do not speak his name, for sometimes it sticks in my own throat. I thought I wished to know our father, but I know now that I should have heeded Lady Efa when she said he would be my undoing. It seems that he was assuredly yours." Alfrid sounded as if his wish for quiet was vying with his urge to give voice to his anger, for there was a rasp now in his tone.

Ava sniffed. "No one believed me and they never will, but it was not me who gave him the hemlock. Elwyn came…"

Ositha sat up at the mention of the name. Her father's oldest servant. His oldest, perhaps only, friend.

"He said he had word from Fath…from Oswii. I was to make sure that Pieter and I did not go to the hall that night, but that we must eat in our bower with only him, Elwyn that is, for he had words to share that must not be heard by anyone else."

"And what were these words?"

"Naught. It was only a ruse to keep us away from the hall so there was none to witness. Pieter fell ill and Elwyn was nowhere to be seen after that night. He came back only to get me out and bring me here before, well, I think you can guess what they would have done to me." There was another noise, of shifting on the seat, and then she said, "I had to do it, don't you see? Elwyn told me you would be killed if I did not, so I had to choose between harming my husband or letting you die. At that time, Northumbria was mightier than Mercia, I had no kin near me... How else could I keep you safe?"

Her sobs echoed around the chapel and then were muffled as if Alfrid was hugging her to him. He mumbled, indiscernible words, presumably to soothe her. The bench creaked again. He said, "You have held this inside for so long. I hope you can now let go of the weight and walk with a less heavy heart."

Her sniff was prolonged as if she'd wiped her nose with the back of her hand. "I know not, Brother. I only know that with gentle patience and understanding, Wilfrid has loosened the words from me. Whether there is any peace now to be found remains to be seen."

Another, shorter, scraping noise made Ositha realise that her half-brother and his sister were about to leave the chapel, meaning that they would walk past her. She could not leave ahead of them, for the light of the door opening would give her away. Instead, she sank down as far as she could in her seat and hoped that they, caught up in their own sorrow, would walk past without noticing her.

God did not disapprove of her that day, for not only did they pass by without looking to left or right, but she caught their words as they did so.

Ava said, "You must also wrestle with the demons that plague you, you know."

"That I rode out to battle against my wife's father? That I was given Deira after Oswii frightened the life from his own nephew? Perhaps he will see reason about Wilfrid and the Church. If not, there might be only one way to rid myself of the demon that is our father."

Ositha waited for some several heartbeats before emerging into the daylight and reacting swiftly to the first words that greeted her. "Look out!"

She shrank back against the chapel wall as the yard began filling up with horses and men. Carts trundled in behind them, carrying broken weapons, bodies, and severely depleted cooking supplies. Father was home.

Ositha took one look at his face and made herself scarce. The king was in a foul mood and servants were finding anything to do which took them in the other direction. Ositha spotted Elfwin's nurse and went to spend time with her little brother until the dust floating around the yard had settled. As she walked back towards the bread ovens, one of the bakers hurried past her. "Let the queen calm him," he muttered. "She is the only one who can."

Ositha took another look over her shoulder at her father, who was now taking out his temper on one of the lower-ranking thegns by thrashing him on the back and shoulders with his leather riding gloves. She wondered if even her mother could soothe him this time.

She waited, something that she was learning how to do with consummate patience, until much later when she spotted Oswii walking over to the wall, as was his wont when he wished to spend time with his thoughts after his temper had blown itself out.

Ositha settled quietly by his side, and said, "Are you rested now, Father?"

As if talking to his hearth-troops and not his thirteen-year-old daughter, he said, "At least neither the queen nor I are still in Lent, or Easter, or anything that meant we could not..." At this point he seemed to realise that he was speaking to his own child and he finished with, "You know. Things."

She said, "It does not irk me as much as some, for I simply obey my lady mother and feast and fast, as she does but, Father?" He had not noticed her reference, that she was no longer a child, and was old enough to fast.

He was staring out across the rocks to the sea. "Hmm?"

"Should you not settle it once and for all, the matter of Easter? Before Wilfrid and his followers spread any more unrest?"

Oswii looked down at her. "Daughter," he said, and the slight pause after the word made it sound like he'd only just noticed that she was, indeed, his progeny, "I should, indeed. I will not let that troublesome priest get the better of me. Yes, it is time we settled this. And I shall be the one to do it."

He took off towards the hall and Ositha called out after him. "Father? Did I not do well? There was more that I heard." But Oswii was not listening.

She stared at his back and then wandered off in search of Elfwin and his nurse. Her baby brother would have a hug and a smile for her, not caring whether she was useful or not.

Chapter Seven

Bamburgh, AD664: Summer

Efa would not attend. However much she would enjoy seeing her daughter Alfleyda and dear Hild again, it was a seven-day journey if undertaken in any relative comfort and she had no wish to travel with her bad-tempered husband only to watch him have yet more arguments with people such as Wilfrid whom he should really treat with more respect. He could ride faster without her.

The synod had been called to try to reconcile the differences between the Roman and Ionan Churches, one of which was the dating of Easter, and Efa envisioned long days of learned argument which her chaplain Romanus was better equipped to deal with than she. Ositha was sulking and Efa assumed it was because she would miss the chance to see her younger sister but really the two hardly knew each other. Having decided that they would not go, Efa's most pressing concern now was how to stop Carena from attending.

Her knees were stiff from kneeling on the cold floor for so long, but this was no time to stint on prayers. She had ensured that every candle in every sconce was lit but lighting the chapel did not heat it and the cold had seeped into her bones. She was not elderly, she was only thirty-eight, but to have another child at her age would not be without risk. And she must make Carena believe it. With one more plea to God to forgive the lie she must tell, Efa used the edge of the nearest bench as a prop while she rose to her feet.

Waiting for her at the chapel door, causing her mother to

wonder when she had begun to lurk behind doors and in corners, was Ositha, keeping a watchful eye on Elfwin who was spinning round and giggling as he then staggered, dizzy, across the doorway.

"'Gain, again!" He shouted.

Ositha reached for his hand. "No, little dearling, that is enough, or you will be sick. Look, Mother is here now."

Efa no longer had to bend her neck to look upon her daughter, for they were a match in height these days, though perhaps not in looks, for Ositha's hair was lighter than hers with a hint of the red which tinged Oswii's. "You are so good with him. May I ask a boon? Would you look after him for a while longer? I must have a message sent to York."

Ositha said, "I will be glad to. You send word to Alfrid?"

How odd that she should assume that. "No, I need Carena to ride here instead of going with him to Whitby."

"Why?"

The girl was nothing if not direct. Efa replied, "I will, er, I have need of her help." She rushed away. It was one thing to send a message, begging company and a promise of explanation upon arrival, but it was quite another to lie to her daughter face to face. Even now, the message might not arrive before Alfrid set off and he had no reason to stop Carena accompanying him.

Once the rider had left, with instructions to go with all haste, Efa gathered her courage and went to find her youngest children. They were sitting on a bench in the hall, and she stood silently for a moment, smiling at the tender scene as Ositha sang a little song whilst stroking Elfwin's gossamer-fine hair. The boy was three now, and was able to chatter coherently, more like a child than a baby, but right at this moment he looked like a bairn, eyes half-closed and long lashes blinking, thumb in mouth and fingers stroking his own cheek.

153

Ositha stopped singing and looked up. She shifted slightly and let the sleepy child slide fully onto the bench beside her. Efa sat down so that his slumbering form was between them. She took a deep breath, gave a silent apology again to God her witness, and said, "What would you say if I told you that you were to have another little brother or sister?"

Her daughter looked at her face, then at her stomach. "I did not know. Does Father know? May I look after the bairn when it comes?"

Efa paused before answering, certain that she was about to be struck down by a vengeful God. When all remained calm, she said, "No, Father does not know. He is busy making plans for the ride to Whitby and has enough to think about. This is why I sent for Carena." The lies which had been forming a blockage in her throat now came tumbling freely. "I have been feeling sick, nay, more than a feeling. I have been spewing at least three times a day. I've need of someone nearer my own age to look after me. And no, before you ask, it could not be you, my dear daughter. You already do so much, looking after Elfwin for me."

"It is no chore. Now I know why you do not wish to go to Whitby. I was sad not to go, but I understand. What will it be like, do you think?"

Efa sat back, remembering just in time to slide a hand across her belly as if her womb really had quickened. At all times now she must act as if with child, and all the lies and pretence would be worth it if she could just keep Carena away from Whitby. "The synod you mean? It will be boring, I think. There will be much talk of religion, and there will be men speaking for the Roman ways, and men speaking for the Ionan habits too, and much talk of the moon patterns and such like. Wilfrid will be there, and he will be hoping to bring your father round to his way of thinking on such matters as the marking of Easter."

"Father hates Wilfrid. So does Ecgfrith." Ositha sat

forward, putting out a hand when Elfwin stirred. "Could not Audrey have looked after you? Then you need not have sent for Carena."

Efa looked heavenward. What could she say? That Audrey was childless and would not know how to help? Carena, too, was childless so that argument would fall on its nose. She ran her little finger across her sleeping son's brow. "He is a dear, is he not? You're right," she continued, deciding to step around the question, "There is no love lost between your father and Wilfrid, nor indeed between the abbot and Ecgfrith. And Alfrid and Wilfrid are great friends, which makes the waters murkier."

"It has to do with Ripon, does it not?"

The girl did not need to know all the details, so Efa summed it up as best she could. "In part, yes. Alfrid sent Wilfrid to be abbot at Ripon, but there was a little unpleasantness with the monks, for they were followers of the Ionan ways. Wilfrid did not see eye to eye with them and had them sent from the abbey." Oswii was, in truth, becoming increasingly irritated with Alfrid's bid to appoint his own men of the Church and his attempts to wield real power as king of Deira, instead of taking orders from Bamburgh. His friendship with Wilfrid was not helping and Efa was worried, not least because she knew that Alfrid was still fretting about his part in the battle at Winwæd. He was wroth with himself, and that made him dangerous.

Five days later, Oswii and Ecgfrith rode out to begin their long journey to Whitby. Others, including Efa's chaplain, Romanus, and several of the community from Holy Island, were travelling separately, although Efa thought it ridiculous that they could not all ride together. Meanwhile, riding fast, and changing horses often, Efa's messenger would have reached York by now, or perhaps tomorrow. Would he get there in time to stop Carena leaving for Whitby? All Efa could do was wait, and hope, and keep up the pretence.

155

Almost a fortnight had gone by and the settlement at Bamburgh had been quiet. It was as if the folk who lived and worked there heaved a collective sigh of relief whenever their lord and king was away. Life went at an ordered pace, and though there was less activity over on the island, the little fishing boats still went out, from there and a little further down the coast. The fishermen brought their catches of mackerel up to the fortress, meanwhile the herdsmen drove the beasts out to the fields and the cooks and bakers went about their daily work, but all walked with heads a little higher, shoulders a little less hunched. Mealtimes were calmer, with less ale consumed, and those men who had remained to guard the settlement enjoyed games of Merels and told stories while the women were able to talk without shouting over the usual noise.

Audrey, always devout and rarely smiling, opened up like a flower in the sunshine now that Ecgfrith was away once more. Efa loved all her children, those living, those mourned, and those far away, but she knew their faults. Ecgfrith was far too like his father and had not the contrasting easy side to his nature that Oswii possessed, and Efa knew this was because his bed was cold. She was glad that in latter times she and her husband had at least rekindled that part of their life.

Sitting with Elfwin on her lap, Efa toyed with her wine cup, her thoughts turning from beds to births, or false ones at any rate. For her deception to be complete, she must strike a balance between eating and drinking too much for a supposedly pregnant woman plagued by sickness, and eating too little for sustenance. A noise at the door distracted them all, and Efa took the opportunity to drain her cup. She looked up a few heartbeats after the others and was late to realise that Carena was standing in the open doorway, dusty from the road, and frowning with worry. Efa loosened her grip on the cup. It would be all right. Her ruse would work.

In a way, Carena was Efa's daughter-by-law, but she was only four years younger and Efa, married to an older man, whose company out of the bed chamber had at times bordered on insufferable, genuinely rejoiced in spending time with Alfrid's wife, which made the dishonesty all the more bitter. She stood up and walked to greet Carena, meeting her in the middle of the hall and folding her into an embrace. "Thank you for coming. Bless your heart."

"I could not think of riding with Alfrid knowing that I was needed here." She cast about, as if looking for somewhere to put her cloak.

Efa took the garment from her and handed it to a nearby servant. "Come, sit with me and tell me what has been going on in your life since last we met."

Carena followed Efa to the table on the dais. As she took her seat she said, "Rather it is you who should be telling me."

And so, Efa explained, holding her belly the whole time, for emphasis, wretched to witness the concern on the other woman's face.

"How awful to feel so sick. Is the bairn set fast do you think?"

"The midwives always like to say that spewing is a good thing and means the bairn is healthy but, this time, it feels, well, not the same, somehow." At least that last part was not a lie. How could it be the same, when it was not real? She turned her head to look directly at Carena. "And you, my dearling, do not look well. We must take care to look after you, too, whilst you are here."

Carena nodded her thanks as Ositha filled her cup. She took a sip but shook her head when offered food by Efa's steward. "It has been a worry, I will not lie. Alfrid has been chafing for a while against his father's will. He was aggrieved to be sent up to Pictland when he could have been in Rome, or even back in Deira safeguarding our borders. And now

157

this trouble with Wilfrid... I do not know who put the idea of a synod into Oswii's head but now, instead of the needling, there will be an outcome."

"Yet an outcome will be a good thing, surely? With no more mismatching of dates and everyone following the same rules?"

"But what if it goes Alfrid's way? I wish for the Roman ways to be acknowledged, but I fear Oswii's wrath."

Efa paused before answering. She was tempted to say that Oswii was a spent force, but that would be disloyal. She was already at risk of being caught in the sticky web of lies she had spun. Let her not add to the tally by speaking ill of the king. "There are many learned folk at the synod. They will listen to all the speakers and then the outcome will be based on careful thought and consideration. Oswii has sworn to listen to everyone and declare fairly. I am sure it will help to mend the rift."

"We can only hope. And pray." Carena sounded less than convinced but she relaxed her frown, smiled, and patted Efa's hand. "Besides, we have more pressing worries. And you shall be my main concern."

Efa swallowed. "Thank you. It means so much to me to have you here."

"Not at all. You have been a true, perhaps my only, friend since I came north."

If only being a friend had not meant indulging in deceit, but only in such ways could women counter the actions of men.

The king and his son were away, but life and work must go on as normal. The folk in and around Bamburgh made the most of the warm weather and used the sunshine to dry seaweed, which in its turn would be used to smoke the bacon flitches later in the year. Youngsters scrambled on the cliffs to catch seabirds and brought them to be baked in

158

clay, which, when cracked open, would peel the feathers off. The cooks brought their pots outside, dropping heated stones into the vessels to boil the water, and the dairy women, having drained off the buttermilk, gave the butter granules the first of the cold-water summer rinses.

Efa decided that her little herb garden at the side of the hall needed some attention. Keeping up her pregnancy sham, she declared herself unfit for tending the plants, but expressed the wish that Carena would do so, and that Audrey would help, while she, Efa, sat nearby.

"Should I snip these blossoms?" Carena looked up at Efa, blocking the sun's rays with her hand and smudging soil onto her forehead in the process.

Efa smiled. There was colour in the younger woman's cheeks now. Perhaps this lie was not so bad if it brought Carena outside and away from her sad thoughts. She had suffered so much loss in recent years and God had seen fit not to bless her with children of her own. "Yes," she answered, "they are horehound and can be hung to dry and then used as a salve for the children's coughs over the winter."

Audrey, pulling weeds from the herb bed, said, "What is this?"

"It is glasswort. It can be eaten without being cooked," Efa told her. "Does it not grow in East Anglia?"

"It might do, but I have not come across it before." She bent to sniff the plant and wrinkled her nose.

"Do you miss your life in the southeast?" Efa recalled how strange it all was to her when she came to the north from her home in Kent. Even the clothes that the Northumbrians wore were different. In those days, some of the women still favoured a peplos style of dress, with pairs of shoulder brooches and she, in her kirtle and single brooch, had looked and felt an obvious outsider. Perhaps Audrey wasn't a joyless woman; she might simply be

159

yearning for home.

Audrey sat back on her haunches. "I had a good life with my first husband, and I was bereft when he died, but where I found peace and purpose was at the abbey. I was ready to take my vows when this new match was mooted. And we do not have too much say in these matters, do we?"

Efa, a royal daughter of Kent and Deira, could only agree. "We bring the blood of our kin and all the status that it confers, but we have to leave our homes far away." She ducked her head as a wasp flew by. "We are all bound by what the men do, and we should not be. Friendship matters. The men have their hearth-troops, but we women should have that too. This is why I have always kept my own household, separate from Oswii's. You should do the same."

Audrey said, "Would that be allowed?"

"I will make sure it is. You know, it was to my household that Wilfrid first presented himself, looking for a patron."

"He is a good man. I am grateful to have him as my confessor."

Efa sat forward. "We should speak freely while we can. Is my son kind to you?"

The other woman hesitated. "He is not unkind. There are matters though on which we seem unable to see eye to eye. Wilfrid, as I said, is a great comfort to me, but he knows that what I crave most of all is to return to the religious life. Ecgfrith would rather I was more of a wife." She hung her head, but Efa could see the embarrassed flush on her cheeks.

There was little Efa could say to comfort her. She and Oswii had always fought, but they had left their disputes in the hall. In bed, they had always been man and wife. Only after Winwæd had her passion cooled, and then the Mercian uprising had dampened his desires, but neither decline had lasted.

160

Proof of their renewed physical love came running to her now. Elfwin was quick on his feet for such a solid little boy. Ositha was some distance behind him and Efa suspected that he had given her the slip at some point. Trundling along with his arms out for his mother, Elfwin was smiling broadly, displaying his two new teeth. In a heartbeat, he was on the ground. There was silence, and Efa waited; there was no point in making a fuss if he did not need to cry, for it was her experience that the sight of a worried face would in fact, sometimes make the child think they ought to sob. When Elfwin wailed, Carena, who was nearest, scooped him up onto her lap.

Ositha came up to them, out of breath. "I told him not to run off. The tanner made new shoes for him, for his old ones were too small."

Efa nodded and smiled. "Little Elf," she said, "You must listen to Ositha. We grown-ups know that children are wont to fall over when first they wear their new shoes."

The little boy wiped his face on Carena's shoulder, causing her to make a face of mock disgust, and then jumped to the ground. "Elfy better now." He beamed at his audience, picked up a stick and began stabbing the soil. "Wiggly worm!" He held the creature in his chubby hand, triumphant. Ositha lunged to take it away before he could put it in his mouth.

He was irrepressible. Efa thought of all her sons and daughters, and Oswii's too, and concluded that none had ever been so cheerful and endearing as Elfwin. She sat back, lifting her face to catch the sun's rays, thanking God for the joy of this moment.

Behind her closed eyes, all she could see was a warm golden-red light. She listened to the bees moving in and out of the flowers, the metallic squeaking of Carena's hand shears, and the gurgling laughter of her little boy as Ositha tickled his tummy. She'd no need to open her eyes to know

161

this, for Ositha was reciting her tickling game.

"Belly rises, belly falls, tickle Elfwin more and more!"

Efa chuckled. Then, over the noises of the garden and Elfwin's giggling, she detected the sound of hoofbeats, and she opened her eyes and sat up. A rider had come clattering into the yard. News, then, presumably, that the king was on his way home. The steward was hurrying across to meet the messenger, and Efa beckoned and mouthed, "Bring him to me."

The horseman hurried across the yard round to the colourful garden. He bowed low and said, "Lady Efa, I bring word from the king."

"The synod is over?"

"It is, Lady. The matter of marking Easter was settled. The king decreed..."

So, it was decided. The Roman ways would have no place here any more, and all must follow the Ionan practices. No doubt Wilfrid would be banished, and her own chaplain kept from her. "What?" She sat forward. Had she heard correctly?

"I said the king found in favour of the Roman ways, my lady."

How had Oswii been persuaded? He must have seen, or been shown, some political advantage, surely? "And what of Abbot Wilfrid?" How had he won the day, with Oswii, and Abbess Hild come to that, so hostile towards him?

The man wiped his brow. Efa waved for her steward to bring him a drink. "Forgive me, I should have seen to your needs before pressing you for word of the synod."

"My lady is too kind. You asked me about Abbot Wilfrid. Lord Alfrid mooted that he be made bishop of all Northumbria and King Oswii was not pleased."

Carena stood up and brushed the soil from the front of her dress. "May I ask, do you know if Lord Alfrid is coming here? Or did he set off to go back to York?"

The steward arrived with a cup of ale and the messenger took a long draught before answering. Twiddling the cup in his hands, he became overly interested in the patterns on the stoneware. Efa shivered, even though the sun was still blazing high.

"Lord Alfrid," Carena repeated, "Is he on his way here, or going back to York?"

"I cannot be sure, for I was told only to ride with news of the king's decision, but I heard, when I stopped the next night, that things had taken a turn for the worse. Tidings came that harsh words had been spoken between Lord Alfrid and his father."

Carena held out her hand without taking her gaze from the messenger's face, and Efa reached for her fingers. "Go on," she said.

"I must repeat, I cannot know for sure, but I was told that Lord Alfrid threatened the king, and the king ordered him to be shackled. I heard that all the Deirans were hunted down like…"

Efa stood up. "I thank you. I think we have heard enough. Please, go to the hall and ask for food. Some now, and some to be packed in a bag for your ride back south in the morning."

Carena let out a big sigh and rallied herself. "Oswii will bring him back here. I will wait. It must be a misunderstanding."

Efa hugged the younger woman to her. She knew only too well how precariously the king-helm of Deira sat on men's heads. Her kinsman was murdered, and Oswii's own nephew, given Deira to rule, was bullied, threatened, and briefly changed sides at Winwæd before running from the battle altogether. He was never heard of again. "You must leave here."

"No, I should wait. If they have Alfrid in irons, which is hard to believe, they will bring him here, not take him to

163

York." She turned to face Efa, her eyes wide in panic. "Won't they?"

How could she tell this poor woman it was unlikely that Alfrid would ever be seen alive again? "I really think it would be better, for now, if you were to make your way south. I will have men ride with you, but I think you will be safest at your brother's hall." She held her hand up, "No, do not gainsay me. I truly think this is the best thing to do."

Carena shook her head. "But I cannot leave you. You said it yourself, that you need me here until the bairn is born, or at least until the sickness has passed. Once the king is back, and I can see Alfrid, then I can go home. But whilst you are so unwell, I must stay."

Efa now realised the flaw in her plan and needed time to think. "Ositha, my love, will you take Elfwin back to the bower and see if he will agree to a nap?" She turned to Audrey and Carena. "Ladies, shall we?" With a sweep of her arm, she indicated that they should return to the hall. Once there, she feigned tiredness and went to her chamber at the far end of the building.

Sitting down on the bed, she looked about the room. Perhaps she should have gone instead to the chapel, to pray for guidance. What a wicked web she had woven. Could it be undone, without Carena discovering the lie? She'd not thought beyond the synod. Her only purpose in deceiving Carena was to keep her from Whitby, and once Oswii came home she could have simply sent the girl home to York. She'd not thought beyond that, nor that at some point folks would expect her belly to swell. And if she were not to be exposed as a liar, then…

Efa looked down. She was still holding the shears which had been put in her hand when the messenger came. Years of having small children place things in her hands meant that she had barely noticed the action, much less could she say how they came to be in her possession. Except that, surely, God was playing a part in this. With the shears in one hand, she stood up and lifted her kirtle and shift with the other. Hoisting the material and holding it out of the way by tucking it into the crook of her arm, she leaned over and, shaking, sliced the top of her leg with the shears, pressing deeply to make sure the blood would flow. As soon as she saw the crimson, she lowered her skirt and pressed the linen against her thigh so that a stain appeared. Blood trickled down her leg and she waited until some had reached the floor before she called for help.

Carena came running. "What is it? I heard you cry out. No!" She lunged forward and grabbed Efa by the elbow, helping her to sit down on the bed. "Lie still, I will fetch the midwife."

Efa stopped her. "There is no need. I knew something was not right with this one. It was God's plan and I know this cannot be saved. Let me sleep a while. Please will you send for some cloths?"

Carena nodded and left the room. Now Efa had but a short time to work out how to get her out of Northumbria and home to her kin.

Efa ate in her room that evening. When the food was brought to her, she asked that Carena and Audrey be sent for. Audrey, who'd thawed when they were talking together in the garden, had frozen her features again, as if she felt she had said too much earlier. Still, Efa needed her, for the plan would not work without her. Carena was red-eyed, either from concern for the queen or, more likely, through frantic worry for her husband. Not for the first time, Efa was saddened that Alfrid's and Carena's love for each other was still not enough to heal the blood feud between the Northumbrians and the Mercians.

She sat forward on the bed and Carena took a step towards her. Efa put up a hand. "Do not fret; I am weary, but I am well. The most pressing thing now is to get you away from here before Oswii comes home." Again, she pressed her hand to the air. "I know you wish to stay and see Alfrid but, my dear one, I do not think they will bring him. Not whole, anyway."

The younger woman's lips turned inwards as she clamped her mouth to stop them trembling. There, in that moment, she showed whose daughter she was. Penda and Derwena had made strong, brave children; that was clear. Carena's shoulders sank down from their hunch, and she straightened her back. "What must I do?"

"Leave, at dawn. Audrey, I wish you to make it known that you have had a message from my husband's kinswoman, the abbess of Coldingham, asking that you visit her and yes, I do want you to go there. I think the calmness of that abbey and the company of the brothers and sisters there will soothe your soul. We will put it about that Carena is going with you. Once you get to Berwick, the men will split up, mine to go with you to Coldingham, Carena's to turn south, go round the forest and thence to Mercia."

Carena said, "Might we not meet the king riding from Whitby?"

"I think not. The rider who came today will have been sent well ahead. By the time the king returns, you will be safe away and the lie will not matter. Tell only Aneurin, and not the rest of your Deiran escort. They will follow orders, but cannot betray what they do not know."

Audrey spoke at last. "I do not like the falsehoods, but I cannot deny that even the thought of spending time at Coldingham is a balm for my soul. I will do as you ask."

Efa exhaled deeply. "Then it is settled. Come, let us go out; I will find the rider and you two must gather the things you will need." She made to get up and only belatedly remembered to make her actions slow, as if painful.

As they went beyond the chamber, a shadow moved from

166

the wall. Ava. Efa silently cursed; she'd forgotten about her. She hoped that Ava would scurry away as she usually did, but the younger woman stood in front of the group, blocking their way. Efa caught sight of movement behind Ava and saw Ositha coming to stand behind her. Had they both been listening?

Ava said, "You are running away."

Carena replied without hesitation. "Yes."

"I could tell my father."

"You could, but what would you gain?"

"Last time I did his bidding things did not turn out the way he planned, for Mercia still rebelled. Perhaps this would win me back his love." Then, more quietly, she said, "I could have some kind of life then, at least."

Efa had to resist the urge to put her arms out in comfort. The poor girl had been so ill-used by her father. "I think it best if we all say naught of this. Who knows, your father might be wroth with you for letting her go. And, let us be clear, you will let her go." It was no idle threat. They all knew that this poor wraith was no match for any of them. "He does not like it when folk fail him. So I think that he should never learn of this."

Over Ava's shoulder Efa could see Ositha nodding her head as if noting every word, though Efa could not think why she should be so interested. Ositha had never been badly used by Oswii and if Efa had her way, she never would be.

There was a short silence. It was as if Ava had seen a glimmer of hope, one last chance to move out from the shadows, but all her remaining courage left her when Carena stepped close to her and said, "You will go to Hell for what you did to my brother, and you have to suffer that knowledge. Alfrid told me why you did it, but don't you see? It was for naught. You did not save your brother, after all. Do you really still wish to do Oswii's bidding?"

167

Ava's shoulders slumped, she bowed her head, and stepped aside to let them pass. Ositha followed suit, but Efa was sure that the girl twitched a smile, for no reason that Efa could fathom.

Chapter Eight

Tamworth AD664: Late Summer

The sun was as high as it would be that year and cast a white light over the earth. The hedgerows were a mass of green foliage and aromas drifted across the fields as the process of smoking the summer cheeses got underway. Ethelred put down his scythe and left the field in search of a drink. Many who knew they'd be working late in the fields had leather bags containing hard cooked eggs and ale, but he had forgotten to bring one.

The sounds of the harvest continued in the yard, where the grain storage barns were being swept and the drying kilns prepared, the domed clay roofs being checked and repaired while the weather was still warm and dry. Crossing the yard to the hall Ethelred nearly bumped into Ermenilda, walking alongside her reeve and deep in conversation with him about the replacement of some lead vessels, whilst balancing her bairn on her hip, her little daughter Werbyra run-skipping to keep up with her mother.

Ethelred mopped the sweat from his brow with his sleeve and tried to ignore the tugging feeling around his heart. Wulf had fulfilled his own prophesy that he would have a son, and here was the living proof. Little Cenred, born less than a twelve-month after they got home from Lindsey, was healthy and thriving, and a tonic for Ermenilda who had recently had word that her father, the king of Kent, had died. The boy's face registered a glimmer of recognition of his uncle, and his chubby fist opened and closed in a baby wave. Ethelred copied the gesture and the boy gurgled, then hid his face against his mother's shoulder, suddenly shy.

As Ermenilda and the reeve walked on, baby Cenred peeped over her shoulder at Ethelred and giggled. Ethelred continued to the hall, losing the fight against his bruised heart, which throbbed with the pain of knowing what bliss could be. King Wulfhere of Mercia had a son, hale and hearty. Ethelred might once have hoped to be a father himself by now, but the only woman he'd ever thought of as the possible mother of his children was the wife of Dyfrig, and most likely already mother to the Welshman's sons.

Brother Lyfing was in the hall. The monk's visits from the nearby abbey had become almost daily and Ethelred was grateful for the comfort he provided. No longer the only atheling, the love of his life lost to him, Ethelred felt sometimes as if he did not walk upon the earth so much as bob about on the sea in a boat with no oars.

"Lord Ethelred," Lyfing bowed his head, "Hot work this day, I see."

Perhaps more so for himself, who worked harder than most, as if the physical toil would still his thoughts. "I have worked up a small thirst, yes. You are leaving?"

"I shall be in the chapel for a short while first. I brought some honey from the abbey hives and my cart wheel snapped on the way here. The wood turner is seeing to it." He peered up at Ethelred. "Join me in prayer?"

Ethelred slaked his thirst while Lyfing waited and then they walked together to the chapel. Blinking to adjust to the gloom, Ethelred followed his confessor to the front of the building and sank down on his knees. Time spent conversing with God was never painful. Side by side and in silence, each man offered up prayers and then they joined their voices to speak the Lord's Prayer. Blinking again as he emerged into the bright afternoon sunshine, Ethelred shook his head, trying to free his sight of the weird vision moving hazily before his eyes.

A woman was standing in front of him and for a heartbeat

170

he thought it was... But it couldn't be. "Mother?" he said, though he knew he was in some kind of waking dream. The vision moved closer and he took a step back, reaching behind him for the comforting presence of Brother Lyfing. He blinked again, but the woman was still there.

The vision was frowning, as if also trying to comprehend. "Noni?"

He opened his mouth, but no sound came out.

"Carena! Can it really be? God and all the angels be praised!" Wulf came pelting across the yard and scooped the woman up in an embrace which took her feet off the ground. He twirled her round, kissed her on both cheeks and then set her down, clutching her to his chest as if he would never release her. Over her shoulder he said, "Noni, our sister is home."

Ethelred was still mute. Images of his mother, so long buried, had come flooding back in that moment. He had no memory of his eldest sister, who went away to live in the north when he was only six. Now it was as if his mother, not his sister, with the same coppery-brown hair, and eyes with flecks of green within the blue, was returned to him, for this was how Derwena looked the last time he saw her. The dead did not age.

He tried to reckon back, and realised that this woman, only fourteen summers older than him, was still of child-bearing age. He was twenty, she now around thirty-four, and the gap in their ages should have been much less noticeable and yet, somehow, she looked older still. Christ in Heaven, what they had all lived through. Were still living through; her tears when she'd spoken to him were not distilled from joy.

Wulf had noticed too. Holding her at arm's length he looked at her. "What is it? You have not come to us with glad tidings, and even a blind man could know that."

With Wulf's arm still round Carena's shoulders, the three

171

children of Penda made their way to the hall. Behind them, Brother Lyfing gave up loud thanks to God, which now rang harsh in Ethelred's ears, for Lyfing had not seen the sadness in Carena's eyes.

Just as he'd sat in Wulf's hall six years ago when he first came home, Ethelred took his place at the board as his elder brother talked through what had happened to the remaining Iclingas, only this time, the revelations included the details of their mother's violent death.

"I had thought as much, although they never told me." Tears fell unchecked and dripped from her cheeks, and they sat silently for a while until Carena asked Wulf to continue. She stayed quiet, nodding, until Wulf spoke of his hopes that the twins were still alive, and that Starling might have seen them on her journey south. She gasped and put a hand to her heart. "Alive? Oh, but Starling, I had so hoped to see her here. Is she...?"

If she had been about to ask if her sister had been happily wed, she did not get the chance, for Wulf cut her off. "Why are you here though, sweet Sister? Your eyes tell me that yours is a sad tale."

Ermenilda, back from her duties overseeing the work in the storage barns and cook house, smiled when Wulf introduced her to his sister. She poured drinks and took the moment when she filled Carena's cup to pat the other woman's hand. Carena took a tiny sip and then put her cup down on the table, keeping hold of it as if her hands might shake if she let go.

Most of Wulf's hearth-troop were on their own lands, helping to bring in the harvest, and the hall was empty save for those few bringing kindling or loaves, or those who, as Ethelred had earlier, had come for a drink before returning to the fields. Even so, those few who came in paused to look at the visitor. None at Tamworth except perhaps the oldest of the servants would remember her but as Ethelred

172

looked from her to Wulf and back again, he knew that they would see, as he did, the strong family resemblance.

Wulf said, "Is it Alfrid? What has happened?"

Carena looked down at her hand, still choking the cup, then sat up straight, took a deep breath, and began her tale. "Yes, he…"

Wulf thumped the table. "I knew it. He has put you aside, has a new woman in your place."

She said, "No. Alfrid was, is, a good and loving husband. We wed for love; do you not recall? Naught has altered that in all these years. We lived in peace in York, his folk loved him, and they welcomed me." She gestured towards the dark-haired man who had been hanging back since she arrived but was clearly determined not to let her out of his sight. "Aneurin here, loyal to Alfrid since boyhood, has been my rock and my shadow."

Wulf acknowledged the man, saying that he vaguely recollected him coming with Alfrid and Ava to Tamworth when they first left Rheged to find shelter at Penda's court.

Ethelred, though, wanted to know what had changed, what had torn Carena and Alfrid apart. "But?"

"There was a synod, at Whitby. Alfrid and his father were at odds over the timing of Easter, and much else besides. Alfrid, with Bishop Wilfrid on his side, won the day, and Alfrid wanted to give Wilfrid a higher place in the Church. We were told that he confronted Oswii and he has not been seen since. Queen Efa thought it best that I come south; she thought that I too might be in danger." She let go of her cup and her hands disappeared under the table to rest in her lap. "And so here I am." She looked at her brothers and managed a smile. "It lifts my heart to see you."

"Not as much as mine is lifted to see you, little Lady." Using a stick to aid his strides, Sikke walked towards their table. His pale blue eyes were moist with tears and his bottom lip was trembling.

173

Carena stood up. "Sikke? Can it really be you?"

He leaned his stick against the table and took her hands in his, kissing each one and squeezing them before releasing her. "That I lived to see this day, I am blessed beyond reckoning. You are the likeness of your dear mother." He turned away and wiped the back of his hand across his face. Ethelred got up and went to help his faithful hearth-man to a seat. Sikke gazed at Carena, shaking his head gently as if he could not believe his eyes, even now.

Wulf was not appeased, nor distracted by the reunion. "So Oswii has killed Alfrid, is that what you think? His own son?"

Carena lifted her hands, palms up, and shrugged. "He would find a way to get word to me, if he were alive. I have heard naught as yet."

"I'll march on Northumbria." Wulf looked at Ethelred. "We'll march on Northumbria. And when we get to his hall on the rocks, I'll pull his heart out."

His sister reached across the table and laid a steadying hand on his. "I know this is the way of kings, but I would rather..."

"Yes?"

"I would sooner see steps taken to put our kin group together again."

Ethelred lifted her hand away and patted it. "You need time to mourn. We will do naught, plan naught, until you have marked his passing. And we grieve with you. I did not know him, but you say he cared for you and that is good enough for me."

She smiled and slipped her hands away and into her lap once more. "I had time aplenty to mourn him as I came south. I am weary and would like to rest now." She said to Wulf, "I beg you, Brother, let me search for my sisters."

She rose to her feet, and they stood too. Ermenilda moved round to stand beside her. "Let me take you to our guest bower. It must feel odd to be a guest in what was once your home."

Carena nodded, but Ethelred thought that nowhere would feel like home again for his sister.

The morning sun streaming through the gaps in the shutters woke Ethelred, but he lay in bed for a while as the previous day's events filled his mind with images of Carena's face, bruised with sadness, and the talk of kin, and home. Sounds of carts rattling in, no doubt filled with produce from the fields which now needed to be stored or pickled in old wine barrels, wafted through the shutters and into his awareness, and he got up, washed and dressed, and went out into the yard.

Outside the guest bower where Carena had slept, probably fitfully, what looked at first like a bundle of rags moved ineffectually, like a giant stranded earth worm. Ethelred watched the shape for a moment and spotted a once-blond head emerging from the pile of blankets. Sikke had slept outside the bower, protecting his young mistress just as he had once watched over her mother, and Penda's cousin Carinna before that. Ethelred walked over to him and waited. When a hand emerged, he reached down and offered to help Sikke up. "Is that your bones I hear creaking?"

Sikke emitted an old man's oof-noise as he got to his feet. "I can still reach to knock some respect into your head. My lord," he added.

Ethelred grinned. "Did she know you were there? It will have been of great comfort to her. But you're still a silly old man, you know? You should be living out your twilight years on that land of yours and resting those bones, instead of watching over us all."

Sikke said, "I can still sleep through the night without needing to piss, so there is life in me yet but yes, maybe we should all be in our own halls now?" He glanced at Ethelred out of the corner of his eye. "Anyway, talking of pissing, I need to…"

Ethelred waved. "On you go. I will see you after." As he watched the faithful retainer shuffle off, he considered Sikke's words. Perhaps it was indeed time that he had a hall of his own. Wulf had a son, Ethelred could make his own life, up to a point, and it was a big point; he had no one to share it with.

Later that morning he saw Carena walking away from the bake house and he hop-skipped to catch up with her. "Are you rested now?"

She turned and looked at him. "Little Noni," she said, "I can still scarce believe it is you. We have much to catch up on."

He glanced out beyond the gates to the fields. "I should be helping with the harvest, but I think they might not miss me, given that my sister has come home."

They walked out of the enclosure and, since Carena appeared to know exactly where she was heading, he allowed her to lead the way. She took him into the woods, past the circle of trees that had been a temple to Thunor, to an old oak tree. "Mother loved it here," she told him.

They sat down, and though he had no cloak to spread on the ground, the earth was dry enough at this time of year. "Can you tell me something of her? I can hardly recall her face, although I see it now in your own."

She gazed at him, her brows drawn in a frown of sympathy. "You were the last to see her alive, were you not? That must be hard for you."

"It is all a blur. I dream of it still. A man raising his sword, and a scream, which I think now was my own. Men grabbed me and bundled me away, and I spent three years in Wales with Sikke."

"Ah yes, my new shadow, it seems, much to Aneurin's

176

dismay. I was overcome to see him still living." Her voice wavered and she stopped to take some deep breaths. Ethelred knew what it was to lose a love; Carena was hurting, too much to speak of it yet. She took another breath and said, "Now, what of your life since you came home?"

He looked down at his boots. "There is little to tell. Wulf and I went to the lands of the West Saxons and fought them, and then we went to Lindsey and freed it from the Northumbrians."

She nudged him playfully. "You do not say much, do you? What secrets do you hold inside?"

His cheeks prickled, warming. It was true enough; his tongue often tied in knots when he was speaking with someone he didn't know well. And with Arianwen, well, it was usually she who did all the talking. "Well, at Merwal's hall I met…"

Carena interrupted him and put a hand on his arm. "Merwal? He is well?"

"Yes." He smiled. "He has daughters now, too, and Merchelm fares well. We have become good friends."

"You and he would be of about the same age," she said. She sat back against the tree trunk and closed her eyes. "Merwal, bless his heart, my big half-brother. I should like to see him and Efi again. I only met her briefly."

"Domneva," he corrected. "And you must call me Ethelred. I had to put away the childish names when I came home."

She nodded, her eyes still closed against the sun. "Aye, it was the same with Alfrid's half-brother. When he was in his cradle his mother called him Lief. Now he goes by his given name of Ecgfrith, though I think his wife has other names for him." Her voice trailed off. Thoughts of Alfrid and the ill-fitting parts of his Northumbrian kin group must surely be scraping the scabs off her barely mended heart.

Ethelred wondered what kind of man Lief the boy had become, and whether he remembered his little playmate from Mercia, but now was not the time to ask. "A thought," he said. "Come with me to Hereford to see them all."

She opened her eyes and half-turned to face him. "Really? That would make my heart sing. And then could we…"

"Go to find the others? Aye, why not?"

She hugged him to her. "Ah little Noni, and yes, to me you shall always be so, you are a balm to soothe me."

They dawdled for the rest of the afternoon, revisiting Carena's favourite childhood places, wandering through the woods for a while and taking off their shoes to dip their feet in the river. It was easier, she said, for here there were few memories of Alfrid, only the ghosts of her parents and siblings. One day, Ethelred thought, he would ask her about Pieter and Ava, but it was too soon, too raw.

Returning to the settlement, they were approached by Wulf. He grabbed Carena by the hand and tugged her towards the hall. "Come, we have decked the hall for your homecoming." He danced around her and when a hearth-thegn shouted out that Wulf never showed his wife so much attention, he replied, "Ah, well that merely shows that you do not watch over my bedchamber!"

Ethelred felt himself fading, like a boot print blown away by a storm. If Immin or Heaferth had said something so brazen to him, he would have blushed and struggled for something witty to say.

"Unc Efred?"

He looked down. Wulf's little daughter, Werbyra, was staring up at him with her large brown eyes. She, too, was a serious little creature and he was sure that in years to come she would be overshadowed by her little brother, who had his father's mischievous grin and lively eyes. "Yes, Sweetling?"

The child did not answer except to put her arms up. He

178

bent his knees, picked her up and swung her onto his shoulders. She clamped her hands around his forehead, and they made their way into the hall.

"Bumpee!" she shouted as he ducked to enter through the doorway, revealing that she had not forgotten the time once before when he wasn't quick enough and clouted her little head on the doorframe.

Ermenilda, clutching baby Cenred, was in the hall already and looked on with a quick frown of concern, which melted when Ethelred deposited his niece on the nearest bench and was rewarded with a smile from the usually solemn little girl.

He stood up and made a play of massaging his back and managed to elicit a little giggle from the child. He looked up at the decorated rafters, wrapped in ribbons of coloured cloth and draped with summer foliage, and noted that Wulf was still dancing Carena down the hall towards the dais, attempting to coax laughter from her. Eventually, when he picked her up and twirled her in a circle with her feet completely off the ground, he succeeded. She laughed and thumped him half-heartedly on the chest to make him put her down.

When they were all settled in their seats, Wulf banged his cup on the table. "Eat, and heartily. Especially you, little Brother."

"Why?"

"I have sent word out to all the tribes of Mercia. Did I not say I would pull Oswii's heart out? We will ride out as soon as all are gathered."

Ethelred finished his mouthful of bread, chewing slowly, giving his thoughts time to turn into words which would not provoke his brother. "I have already said that I will ride to Hereford. We agreed?"

Wulf clapped his hands. "Good, good. You can bring Merwal, Merchelm and the rest of the Magonsæte too."

Ethelred swallowed even though his mouth was now

179

empty, and then reached for a drink. It felt like a morsel was stuck in his gullet. After a long draught of ale he told Wulfhere, "No. I am taking Carena to see Merwal and his kin and then we are going to ride south to find our sisters."

The king's head jerked back, as if the words had hit him in the face. "You are what?"

He jabbed his eating knife in Ethelred's direction as he spoke. "I have already said that the time is now. Oswii has wronged us more than enough. We must ride north and end what Father started."

"We spoke of this last night. There are other ways to mend what Oswii put asunder. We should gather our kin, not our army."

Wulf stabbed his blade into the table and let go of the handle. Ermenilda was startled and held her son closer. The blade quivered for a heartbeat. Wulf took a deep breath and laid a hand on Ermenilda's shoulder, as if by way of apology, but to Ethelred he said, "You were too young. You do not recall."

Ethelred could not take his eyes from the knife, embedded in the table. "I wonder if, in truth, that might not be a bad thing," he said.

While several of the others gasped, Wulf said nothing. His sword hand was on the table, resting in a fist, the knuckles lifting off the board slightly, as though he was fighting the urge to let fly with punches. Ethelred watched him, wondering if he would keep a rein on his temper.

Wulf pulled his hand knife from the table and put it back in the scabbard on his belt. After what seemed like an age, he spoke. "Then we are at odds, Brother. And how does that help with your mission to gather our kin back together?"

Ethelred glanced across at Carena, silently beseeching her to intervene. Whatever he decided would add to her sorrow. She did not wish to see her brothers at each other's throats,

180

but did she really want more bloodshed?

She responded. "Oswii did not put Alfrid in fetters because he was, is, my husband. Oswii turned on his own son because Alfrid stood up to him and from that time onwards, he was doomed, no matter who was his wife." She pushed her chair back and walked round the table to stand behind Wulf. Leaning forward, she put her arms around his chest and rested her head on his shoulder. "I beg you, my dear. It has been so long since I saw any of you. Let me know you for a little while longer ere you go off and try to get yourself killed."

Wulf reached up and patted her arm. "For now. And only for now. There are other scores to settle that have naught to do with Alfrid." He looked up at Ethelred. "And you, Brother, what of you, once you have found all our sisters?"

"I was thinking that I need a hall of my own."

Wulf opened his mouth immediately to answer, then closed it again. He looked up at the ceiling as if having decided to give the matter serious thought, and then said, "Have this one." To murmurs of surprise from the group, he said, "What? You all know that my wife prefers our home at Stone. Sikke likes it here, and he should bide in one place now, I think."

Ethelred was at once grateful and suffused with a sense of unworthiness. His moment of asserting himself had done him no good and only resulted in his feeling, once again, like the lesser brother. Wulf had not only the blood, but the wits of a king. He should not have questioned him. "Brother, I can do no more than thank you. If you wish me to ride north once I have found our sisters, I will do so."

Wulf shook his head. "No, I am not so taken with myself that I cannot listen to others. Oswii can stew a while in his own midden. My good lady wife and I will go back to Stone and then," he glanced at Ermenilda, who raised an eyebrow, "I think I might go south, too. I feel like poking Cynwal

181

with a stick, to see if he growls." With that, the king with moods as numerous and variable as March weather, called for more ale and tucked into a chunk of soft fresh cheese.

They stayed until the harvest was in, joined in the feast and gave thanks for a good crop and food to see them all through the winter, then Ethelred, Carena, and Aneurin, along with Immin and Heaferth, made the journey to Hereford. They stayed overnight at the small settlement of Stoche and were nearly at Worcester when they received word that Merwal's household was not at Hereford but Leominster, so they turned north again. Carena was in no rush to arrive, which Ethelred thought odd until he realised that, out on the road again, her thoughts had most likely turned to Alfrid, and she was continuing to mourn. Declining the offer to ride in a cart, she had ridden alongside her younger brother but engaged little in conversation, and Ethelred deemed it best to leave her with her memories. He let his thoughts drift, too.

He went back to a time earlier in one summer, when the daylight stretched almost endlessly and the only sounds he could summon were the industry of bees, flowing water, and a gentle laugh which only ever heralded kindness, never mockery, and resonated at a tone which plucked notes of happiness from deep within him. Through the haze of memory, he saw her dark eyes narrowing as she squinted against the sun's rays, and her delicate hand coming up to her brow to what, mop a bead of moisture, or bat away an insect? He tried to look closer to see, peering deep into the image lodged somewhere inside his head.

"It would not be so bad if I knew for sure."

He jerked upright in the saddle, the sudden utterance wrenching him uncomfortably from his daydream. "Knew what for sure?"

"Whether he is dead or shut away somewhere."

Ethelred did not answer. Wulf had a vast network of watchers, who sent word from all kingdoms. If word had come that was even slightly encouraging, he would have told her. There were no words of comfort that he could offer her and, when he glanced across, he could see that she was struggling with both the hope and the pain that came with not knowing. Until she saw Alfrid, whole or dead, she would have no peace.

When they arrived in the small settlement of Leominster there was no more time for quiet reflection. The air carried the smell of fresh timber, the sound of creaking pole-lathes, the graunching of two-handed saws, and the shouts of men working to finish Merwal's new church, concentrating on the gabled porch, which would no doubt be lime-washed when it was completed. One of the carpenters was holding a small t-shaped axe for dressing the timber. On the ground beside him, a plane made from antler, with a sole plate made most likely from copper and tin, was glinting in the sun.

Merwal himself was standing by the half-finished porch, waving his arms towards the roof, and pointing to a stack of ready-sawn tree limbs. A priest was standing next to him, nodding, and opening and closing his mouth, trying to slip a word between all of Merwal's. The king saw his visitors and came striding towards them. He called over his shoulder, "By Yuletide then."

Behind him the priest shouted out, "Christmas, my lord, yes."

Merwal beamed at his visitors and winked before replying, "Yes, that's what I said, Yule." He held his arms out to his sister and she dismounted, falling into his embrace. He hugged her tightly, saying over her shoulder to Ethelred, "Father Aldred is too easy to tease. He thinks I have forsaken God and returned to our old heathen ways. Smell that?" Ethelred nodded, recognising the stench of woad pulp fermenting in heated water and wood ash. "Dear

183

Domneva has them dyeing it over and over, to make black cloth for the priests. Not so heathen after all, huh?" He chuckled, then put his face down to rest his cheek against the top of Carena's head. "Ah, Sister, it is so good to see you. Wulf sent word; I wish it had been in happier times."

Carena said nothing, but her shoulders were shaking. No need for words with those two, the eldest of Derwena's surviving children. No moments needed to recognise each other, no life stories to tell. Handing his reins to a waiting stable-hand, Ethelred moved away, leaving the two of them to hold each other. Immin, Heaferth and Aneurin followed suit and continued to the hall.

It had been some time, too long, since Ethelred had seen Merchelm but here was someone with whom he was familiar and he felt no emptiness, no yearning for times past, when his friend came running over from the smithy to greet him. He was browned by the summer sun, and his hair had been recently shorn, none too tidily.

They were uncle and nephew, but it had never felt that way. Ethelred walked into Merchelm's outstretched arms, and they hugged each other amid much back slapping. Stepping back, Ethelred said, "You have been working in the fields, I see."

Merchelm laughed. "Have you seen yourself? The sun has painted your face and left no white marks where a helm would have been. Does your brother have no one left to fight?"

Ethelred sobered. "Your father did not tell you then? I am here with my eldest sister, your Aunt Carena, who has come home after her husband went missing, or perhaps was killed."

Merchelm sobered immediately. "I am even more glad, then, that I have had a summer filled with naught more strenuous than digging up food. When do we ride?" Merchelm rubbed a hand through his hair as he looked around for the rest of Ethelred's host.

Ethelred sensed his reluctance though and assured him, "I brought only a handful of men. Wulf wished to ride north straight away but it was not what Carena wanted. She craved only to see her brothers again and then find our sisters. I have brought her to spend some time with Merwal and then we are riding south. Wulf has gone to start a new fight with Cynwal of the West Saxons, though, if you really want to bloody your sword?"

Merchelm looked across at the new church. "I think not. You know," he said, "you should bide here for Christmas. We have a new church to bless, Lady Domneva's kin are coming, and my father is planning the biggest feast ever seen. We had a good harvest and life here is good. Stay?"

Ethelred looked closely into his friend's eyes. "And?"

"Ha! Is there naught I can hide from you? Well then, yes, they are also planning a wedding. For me. A Kentish bride. It would be good if…"

"I would not leave before then even if a wild boar was chasing me." He clapped Merchelm on the back and they walked arm in arm to the hall, Ethelred swallowing but a grain of unwarranted envy at his friend's good fortune.

Inside the hall, sitting by the open door, Merchelm's stepmother was almost hidden from view by her gaggle of daughters; all had their heads bent over a huge piece of embroidery. Ethelred smiled. All the girls had the exact shade of hair, the same lustrous brown as their mother's.

Domneva looked up, needle halfway through the fabric, and smiled at the two young men as they walked in. "Ah, now he will sleep well, knowing that his closest friend will be here for the wedding." She looked at Ethelred for confirmation. "You will be here that long?"

Merchelm chuckled. "He has said he will, but I wondered whether we could suffer his bad feet for so long!"

Domneva laughed, a light and breezy giggle that always

185

had a suggestion that it could turn more bawdy if she ever let it. "That is unkind. Besides, there is always room in the cow byre if it gets that bad."

Her eldest daughter, Mildrith, said, "Uncle Effred, do your feet smell bad?"

He made a show of trying to lift his boot up to his head, hopping to keep his balance. "I fear I shall never know unless I can learn to bend a little better."

The younger girls giggled and Mildrith said, "Yes, you shall have to!"

Domneva stowed her needle, pricking it into the cloth and out the other side to hold it firm. "Sweetlings, I think that is enough stitch-learning for today. Run and find Wynfleyda and ask her to help you wash before we eat." As the girls scurried away to their nurse, Domneva spread out an arm, inviting Ethelred to sit down next to her and waved at one of the servants, indicating that she would like drinks to be fetched.

Ethelred slid onto the bench beside her, a warm sensation inside him which owed nothing to the low glow of the hearth and everything to a sudden feeling that he had come home.

In the weeks that followed, Merwal and Carena spent much time deep in conversation. Ethelred kept his distance, sensing that there was much for them to discuss which did not concern him. They spoke, no doubt, of times past, of folk whom they'd known who were now dead, and he would have little to contribute, for even though he had been alive for some of it, his memories were misty at best. Instead, he spent his days with Merchelm, frequently accompanying him to Wenlock, where his nephew and his new bride would be making their home.

Wenlock was a place that Ethelred associated with Arianwen, and her shadow was everywhere, in the hall, and

186

especially down by the river, but if he had any notion of wallowing in remorse and self-pity, Merchelm had other ideas. Merwal's hall here was serviceable, but Merchelm had decided that his bride would want, nay expect, something to match the richness of the halls in Kent, so he had commissioned new wall-hangings which Domneva had helped to sew, and he and Ethelred escorted the carts carrying the new embroideries from Leominster, along with two new carved chairs. These were not as richly decorated as Merwal's king-seat, but with depictions of intertwined beasts, each biting the next one's tail, along the arm rests, and carved leaf motifs along the backs, they were elegant enough. On the occasions where they travelled on horseback with no carts to slow them down, the two men were able, if they left at daybreak, to spend most of the day at Wenlock, overnight there, and then do more work in the morning before returning to Leominster.

"Near enough to see kin and for them to ride here, but far enough away to have my own household," Merchelm said with a grin, and Ethelred knew that at the very least, he would feel the same once he had sole occupancy of Tamworth.

Now, he was standing on one end of a long bench, holding a huge piece of stitched fabric while Merchelm walked up and down the length of the hall, assessing it from every possible viewpoint. "Higher up?"

Ethelred, wondering why on earth they kept servants at all, inched along the bench and tried to reach a little higher with the heavy cloth. The bench wobbled, he felt the end beneath his feet dip down as the other end tipped up, and he leaped off onto the floor, twisting in an attempt not to rip the cloth as he did so. Merchelm dived forward and grabbed the hanging, leaving Ethelred to his fate.

Ethelred hopped around desperately trying to regain his balance, failed, and landed on his backside, narrowly avoiding hitting his head on the corner of the table on the way. Winded, he looked up to see the servants, who had all now materialised, making a point of looking anywhere but at him. Merchelm's mouth was contorted as he tried to keep his laughter in. Ethelred sat for a moment, contemplating whether it was possible to break one's arse bones, and wondered what the scops would sing of it if he had. "One day," he said, "you might be an under-king of mine. When the time comes for gift-giving, I shall recall the time you left me to fall on my arse, all so that you could impress a lady."

Merchelm wiped the tears from his eyes and laid the hanging across the table before extending an arm to help his uncle to his feet. "Do not fear. In battle you need never look behind you, for you can be sure that I'll be there, keeping your foes' swords and spears from your back, but this is..." Ethelred thought his last words had been 'something else altogether' but could not be sure, because Merchelm was now bent double, wheezing.

"I hope," Ethelred said, "that your bride turns out to be frog-eyed, duck-footed and has an arse the size of a horse." He walked over to the bench, righted it, and called for a drink, while Merchelm sat with his hands on his knees, still laughing soundlessly, tears rolling down his cheeks.

If she were to be likened to any beast at all, then the bride would surely be a deer, with her big brown eyes and shy demeanour. She was, quite simply, beautiful, and Ethelred felt no envy at all, but only pure happiness for his closest friend, as he witnessed their marriage two days after Michaelmas.

Despite the dying of the season the weather was benign. Much of the festivities took place outside, with friendly competition between the Kentish folk and the Magonsæte. There were archery contests, and warriors taking turns to throw axe heads into a circle of rope laid out on the ground.

The bride walked from the guest bower to the newly built church accompanied by glee-men singing and banging drums. Father Aldred was unimpressed by what he saw as pagan activities. After the solemn service inside the church many of the men took up a length of rope and began a show of strength, the men from Kent pulling one end and Merwal's hearth-men pulling the other. Ethelred was called upon to join them and he tugged with all his might on the rope as they edged slowly backwards to bring the centre, tied with a ribbon, past the point where the wedding couple was standing. A cheer went up, announcing that they had pulled past the winning point, followed by laughter when the visitors let go of the rope and sent the Magonsæte sprawling. They came to lend a hand to pull the winning team back to their feet and then all went to the hall for the wedding feast.

Merchelm's bride, Bertilda, was a distant relative of Domneva's and the kin group had come to witness the occasion. Domneva sat next to Merwal, and beside her were two young men whom Ethelred recognised as her brothers, Æthelred and Æthelberht. He'd met them only briefly, years ago at Wulf's wedding, and they had grown now to manhood, and both had full beards and broader shoulders then when he had seen them last. Domneva was casting frequent glances at her daughters sitting on another table and her smile conveyed her contentment that she had her children, her husband, and her brothers all close by. Wulf and Ermenilda were not in attendance and Ethelred assumed that his brother had indeed ridden south in search of Cynwal.

It was only after the meal, of roasted mutton, pork, goose, and boiled vegetables, that Ethelred was able to talk to Domneva and her brothers. After the death of Ermenilda's father the previous year, her younger brother Ecbert had become king, but in name only. It was Ermenilda's mother

189

who ruled Kent for her young son, and even Ethelred, with his self-confessed naïve grasp of statecraft, could see that these young adult cousins of Ecbert's could pose a threat. In theory. In reality, a childlike innocence in their eyes conveyed a lack of interest in kingship, something he himself was sure to recognise. They were keen for diversion and the pair of them went outside and organised a game in which the seasoned warriors lined up behind two small shield walls and invited all the youngsters, restless now the food was eaten, to see if they could break through the lines.

Gradually those still seated indoors stood up and went to watch the game and cheered when the children, somewhat implausibly, managed to break up the walls as if the shields were made of nothing more substantial than thin discs of ice. The brothers, and Ethelred was still not sure he could identify which was which, were play-acting, feigning injury and allowing the youngsters to clamber all over them.

Domneva, standing beside Ethelred, said, "Aren't they growing up to be fine young men?"

He turned to look at her. "And yet your gladness at seeing them seems edged with sorrow?" He looked back out at the game.

He felt the movement as she inhaled and exhaled heavily. "Ecbert is young and my aunt is, well, she is a woman. How long can she hold all those yearning for the king-seat at bay? And what will happen to my sweet brothers should someone raise a claim in either's name? There are still many who feel my father was the rightful king, not my uncle, and that therefore one of my brothers should be king now."

Ethelred wasn't sure how to answer. Should he give false comfort, or agree with her that the boys' lives might be in danger? He opted for a general note of hope. "Perhaps, with a woman holding the king-helm in safe-keeping, things will be calmer. We must pray that she can bring Ecbert up in such a way that means he and your brothers can work

190

alongside one another, and not come to blows."

"Perhaps," she echoed, but not with any conviction. She reached for his hand. "I am glad though, to have you all here. And I am so sorry that Arianwen is not."

He squeezed her hand in thanks, but did not reply, for he found suddenly that his throat was constricted.

One boy was now getting ready to charge a Kentish warrior. The Magonsæte cheered him on from the other wall, banging their spears on their shields and whooping words of encouragement. He ran, his legs carrying him forward at such a rate that he surely must topple right over his own feet, and then he took a running jump at the man who fell backwards and made a show of dropping his axe. The rest of the men banged their shields in appreciation and the lad was hailed as a champion. Ethelred, grateful for the distraction, yelled as loudly as the rest and stepped forward. He and Merchelm carried the boy on their shoulders back to the hall, where he was given a cup of ale and bravely drank it, immediately running outside to throw up.

Dancing followed, and storytelling, and the hour was late by the time Merchelm and his young bride stood up and made their way through the hall. Folks threw small, dried flower petals over them as they went and then, with much raucous encouragement, they made their way to their bower. The guests remained in the hall and most, including Ethelred, slept where they'd sat, slumped forward over the tables, or curled up on the floor. Ethelred stirred only once, when Domneva placed a blanket over his shoulders before making her way to her own bed.

The next day, Merchelm and Bertilda left for their new home in Wenlock. Ethelred sought out Carena and asked about her plans.

"It is not far off Yule now," she said, putting down the shears she was using to cut pieces of linen. "Do you think we should bide here until the worst of the winter is over? It would give me and you some time to get to know one another, too."

He sat down next to her. "I do not think there is much for me to tell of myself."

She smiled. "Why do you think yourself so much less a part of our kin group? You were the youngest, yes, but you were so loved by our mother and father. We all doted on you; you were such a sweet little bairn, and you hardly ever fussed."

He gave a sad laugh. "I was nearing my eleventh Yuletide when it, when we had to…when I was taken to Wales. I should remember more of what life was like ere that, but I do not."

She folded the fabric up and smoothed it unnecessarily a few times. "What you saw was, well, no child should have to see that. We all mourned our father, but he was a man who died in battle. We never dreamed for a moment that Oswii would do that to a woman, and it is as well that I knew naught of that when I was at Bamburgh, else I might have endangered my own life by attacking him. It is no surprise that you lost all memories of earlier, more carefree times." She patted his arm. "But that does not mean there is no more to tell. Do you plan to sit in Wulf's shadow all your life? You are blinded by him perhaps, but you have strengths that he lacks. How our mother and father bred such different children I have no idea!"

"When Sikke brought me home, Wulf was already king, and he had watchers in all the other kingdoms. He did not need to learn kingship; he was somehow born to it. I stood back, only waiting to see if I was needed."

"I have watched you, with the younglings. You make them laugh and they love you. When you are not worrying about measuring up to Wulf, we see another side to you. Carefree, and childlike. One day you will be a fine father."

He looked down and worried at a piece of skin on the side

of his finger. "One day. I had thought that it might be sooner rather than later, but the lady I'd hoped to wed is now another man's wife."

"Ah, I knew there was a tale of love lurking there somewhere."

He looked up at his sister. "Yet any heartache that gives me pales against your loss. Forgive me."

She kissed his cheek. "You are such a caring man. Never lose that. Now, are we agreed; we bide here for Yule?"

"Yes," he said, "agreed."

Merwal had been born amongst people who worshipped the old Gods. He had embraced the new religion, and so had his half-siblings. There were many in the land who had not, or who added the Christ god to the many other deities to whom they made offerings. As midwinter drew near, the king of the Magonsæte was careful to ensure that the old ways were observed, whilst no offence was caused to Father Aldred who was excited to welcome worshippers to the new church in Leominster. On Mother Night there was a feast to mark the traditional start of Yule, but little ritual. The huge Yule log was felled and brought into the hall, there to burn throughout the period of celebration, but with no special significance attached to it beyond the fact that at this time of year an ever-bright hearth was especially appreciated. On the shortest day of the year, the inhabitants of Leominster packed into the church for the Christ Mass, and then proceeded to the hall.

Ethelred had been part of the hunting party which had brought down the boar, and its roasted head was now carried in and placed on the table on the dais. Other cooked meats included goose and bacon, and there were hard cheeses, bread made from finely sifted wheat, apples soaked overnight in wine and honey, and plenty of hazelnuts. Bowls of hot barley pottage, flavoured with leeks and cabbage, filled and warmed bellies.

Merwal's scop played his lyre throughout the meal and then, when everyone had finished eating and the tables had been cleared, he told stories of brave warriors, formidable ladies, and terrifying monsters, before other musicians, with wooden flutes and skin drums, came into the hall followed by a group of dancers, who held ribbons in their hands which twirled and swirled as they danced up and down the hall, beckoning folk to join them. Some diners patted their rounded bellies as an excuse not to move, while others jumped up and joined in.

Domneva stood up and shook her head when one of the dancers tried to persuade her to accompany them. To Ethelred she said, "I will never make him hear me from here. Please tell my husband that I have gone to kiss the girls goodnight and then to the church to give thanks for our bounty."

Ethelred stood up and made his way towards Merwal, dodging stomping feet and flailing elbows, and shouted Domneva's message into his half-brother's ear. Merwal nodded and thanked him, but the noise in the hall was too loud now for intelligible conversation. Ethelred pushed his way through the throng again and made his way outside. The night air was crisp and cold and had an odd aroma, as if snow might be on the way. It was right that he and Carena had decided to stay until the end of winter. He sat down on the step and tucked his legs in tightly to avoid becoming a tripping hazard for the revellers weaving in and out of the hall. He realised he had not brought a drink with him and stood back up to fetch one. As he did so, he saw a flash of movement as someone very small moved round the corner of the building. He followed.

Putting a hand out gently, he caught the interloper and turned her round. "Mildrith, what are you doing out here? You must be chilled to the bone."

194

The small girl looked up at him with big eyes. "Please don't tell Mother. I wanted to see all the pretty ladies dancing."

He chucked her under the chin. "I will not tell her, but she might already know. She left the hall before I did; did you not see her? She was on her way to kiss you all goodnight."

Mildrith's bottom lip began to quiver.

"Don't cry, Sweetling. Come, let us go and find her and put this right." He scooped the child up in his arms and carried her across the yard. She must have felt the cold but to him she was a warm little bundle, and she tucked her head in against his chest, snuggling in with complete trust. He rested his chin for a moment on the top of her head and breathed in her warmth, considering how lovely a thing it must be to hold one's own child so closely.

Fortunately, Domneva was not cross with her daughter and Ethelred had no need for the excuse he'd prepared on the child's behalf. He watched as she settled the children and then walked her to the church. Many of the revellers were now outside, even though the night air was cold. At the chapel door Domneva said, "Will you come and pray with me?"

He'd opened his mouth to say yes when the hall door was flung open and one of her brothers – Æthelberht, he thought – hurtled down the steps and swung round, his hand still on the wooden rail. He vomited where he stood, and Ethelred said, "You go on. I will see to him, find his brother, and make sure they both pass the night with at least a pillow and a blanket."

Despite the rules broken by wide-eyed children and the drunken foolishness of older youths, Ethelred felt warmed by the sense of having a part to play in family life. One day, perhaps, he would be able to create such a kin group of his own.

As soon as the winter snow began to thaw and the first shoots and buds began to push their way into the light, Carena and Ethelred packed their bags and, with Heaferth and Immin, and the ever silent Aneurin, they headed south in search of their sisters. It took them over a week to get to Starling's and Frithuwald's hall at Chertsey, for much of the terrain was still frozen, causing rutted hazards for horses and carts alike. A tearful and joyous reunion followed, and they stayed for another fortnight before moving on. From Chertsey they travelled north again, for Starling had indeed found their twin sisters and accompanied Carena and Ethelred as they went first to the abbey at Aylesbury where they spent time with Eda, and then to Bicester where they were reunited with Edith. Both of the twins had only hazy memories of how they came to be in their respective abbeys after their mother fled Tamworth in the aftermath of Winwæd, with vague recollections of hands grabbing them and bundling them into carts.

Edith said, "All I can see when I think back to that night is a small light glowing through a hole in the blanket covering me. I feared I would spew, for the rocking of the cart made my belly swill around."

Ethelred, sitting quietly in the abbey chapel with her, reached for her hand. He said nothing, for no words would form, and the tears flowed freely down his face. Such evil had been wreaked that night, when Penda's children were scattered to the lands of the south and the west. Edith was as a stranger to him, yet they shared an experience that bound them, and he felt that a missing piece of himself had been found.

The calm and quiet of the religious life contrasted sharply with the Yuletide revelries. Conditions were not austere, and they feasted well on freshly-caught fish from the abbey ponds, and honey harvested from the hives the previous year, but there was no storytelling, and no drunkenness.

Ethelred was happy to join in with the daily devotions and was sorry to leave when the time came, and not just because it meant saying goodbye to his sisters.

Starling returned to her hall, and Eda, who had accompanied them to Bicester, decided she had neglected her own abbey for long enough. There was spring planting to be done and the plough-blessing would need to be performed. The abbey apple trees needed grafting, and there would be lambing to help with.

Carena finished her meal one evening, set down her eating knife, and addressed her brother. "We must leave in the morning. Where will you go now; back to Tamworth?"

He was surprised, for he had not thought of the future for many days, living only for the company of his sisters and for daily worship. "I had not really thought. Nor about where you will go now."

She smiled. "I have it in mind to go to Minna at Medeshamstede, but I cannot ask you to ride there with me, for it is not on the way home."

He chuckled at her understatement. "It is a little out of the way, I will agree. Nevertheless, I shall take you there. Immin will not mind."

Immin looked up from his ale cup and tried to suppress a belch. He looked stricken.

"What," said Ethelred, "Can you not bear to leave this well-laden board? There will be as much food at Medeshamstede, I am sure."

Immin's features relaxed. "Well, in that case Lord, it would be wrong of me to shirk my duty." He grinned and helped himself to another chunk of honeyed bread.

Heaferth said, "I will be glad to ride with you. And by the time we get there it will be Lent, so no bread for Immin, only fish, fruit and dried nuts."

Immin picked up a chunk of bread, made as if to throw it at Heaferth, caught Abbess Edith's glare, and put it down

197

again.

Heaferth, undeterred, continued. "Immin can ride back to Tamworth and tell them where we are going. Only the best hearth-thegns need ride on with the Lord and his sister."

This time, the bread left Immin's hand and found its mark.

Medeshamstede was indeed in the wrong direction from home, but nevertheless only three days' ride from Bicester. They overnighted at Bedford and again at Raunds and were welcomed at both settlements by lords loyal to King Wulfhere. At Medeshamstede Carena slipped off her horse and went running in a less than elegant manner in search of the sister to whom she was closest in age. The nuns stood in stunned silence as their abbess picked up her skirts and ran full tilt at the visitor, hugging her and crying with happiness. Ethelred, by now used to such scenes, smiled, and nodded a greeting to the holy sisters. It was no surprise to him when, a few days later, Carena sought him out and told him that she was going to stay permanently at the abbey and join their sister and their young niece in holy orders.

"I will miss you Noni," she said as he held her in his arms.

"And I you." His disappointment at losing her was tempered by the fact that, deep down, he had always known that the family would never be together properly again. Tamworth held too many reminders for Carena. Her place was here, with Minna and Minna's young daughter, and she would at least find some peace. First though, she had the heartbreak of releasing Aneurin from his oath to her. "Go," she said. "Ride home to Rheged, and tell them all what a fine man Lord Alfrid was."

Aneurin knelt at her feet, and as he stood up, a flutter of his arm betrayed the wiping away of tears.

Ethelred stayed a few more days, then he said farewells to his two eldest sisters, and his niece whom he'd barely got to know, and he and Heaferth returned to Tamworth just as the spring flowers were blossoming and the lambs and kids were being born in the fields.

Deira

The king's hall at York was a splendid building, with tall carved painted supports and a dais which was also painted around the plank that formed the front riser. Servants worked efficiently and quietly, and the stewards and reeves ensured that the king had little to bother with beyond his own personal concerns. And, at the moment, he had only one of those. True, that concern was turning out to be somewhat of a meaty chew, but the rest of his life was as blemish-free as a bairn's arse. Ecgfrith swirled his cup, staring for a while at the amber liquid within it curling up the sides but never managing to escape over the rim.

They had buried the last of the plague victims some time ago and he doubted that anyone would question the story that his half-brother Alfrid had been among them. He smiled at the memory. With divine timing, the pestilence had taken hold in Northumbria as the synod at Whitby came to an end. Anyone who witnessed the confrontation between Oswii and Alfrid had been silenced, either permanently or with coin, and even while he hunted Alfrid down, Ecgfrith had got closer than he'd have liked to sick folk dying in the fields and on the roads.

He'd followed Alfrid for some miles after his half-brother had threatened King Oswii. Alfrid had only a small force with him and should have been able to travel swiftly, but he seemed not to have considered the possibility that he might be chased. Sitting at a camp they'd made not far from the settlement at Goathland, he'd stood up and tentatively welcomed Ecgfrith when he arrived.

Something was said about their father and his temper, and some comments made about Wilfrid. Ecgfrith wondered now whether that was the tipping point for him, the mention of the irksome priest. He took the drink Alfrid offered to him, drank it slowly while waiting for his men to manoeuvre into position, and then he'd simply taken out his hand knife and stuck it between Alfrid's ribs. Moments later, his men had done the same to the Deiran guard. It had been almost disappointingly easy. One day, he hoped, he'd find a worthier foe.

Now, he was king of Deira and controlled all of the southern part of Northumbria. In time, he'd be king of the north too, with a base at Bamburgh and lands all the way north to the border with the Pictish kingdom and there, too, they would bow to him as their overlord. He presided over meetings and gave lands and rewards to his men, especially to his hearth-troops who'd coordinated the attack on Alfrid's men so efficiently. He was rich, he was young, and he was successful. The people who ran this big settlement at York ensured that he was not disturbed by consultation on trivial matters and his hall filled up night after night with boisterous men and willing women, the ale flowed, and the music played. He drained his cup.

The only problem he had now was his wife. Living at York meant that they were now within easy riding distance of Ripon and Wilfrid was either a frequent visitor or host, and Audrey spent even more time with him than she had when she and Ecgfrith resided at Bamburgh. For some reason, she had travelled north while he'd been away at the synod, and now also spoke with reverence and longing about the abbess at Coldingham, some distant aunt of Ecgfrith's. When she wasn't sighing over the memory of her time with the abbess, all he heard was 'Wilfrid this' and 'Wilfrid that' and other than at mealtimes, he rarely saw her because she was constantly on her knees in the chapel.

Ecgfrith was not devout, far from it, but he had no objection to those who were. No, what chafed was that Audrey was not so devoted a wife as she was a Christian. One day, and soon, he would be the king of all Northumbria and had no desire to sire a brood of children by different mothers who would then fight for his leavings. What he needed was an undisputed heir, and he would not get that from Audrey.

He tapped the side of his empty cup and a servant stepped forward and filled it for him, backing away into the shadows again immediately. Ecgfrith saw a tonsured figure moving across the hall and his thoughts turned back to Wilfrid. The interfering worm had all but destroyed Ecgfrith's chances of a happy marriage and of securing the succession. One day, he'd deal with him, too. He sat back, idly wondering what the penance might be for the killing of a bishop.

As if conjured by his thoughts, his wife appeared, hurrying through the hall, and moving her lips as if still in prayer even as she walked. It was only as she neared the dais that he realised she was not praying, but merely talking to herself, muttering something about riding and the state of the roads. She barely acknowledged his presence, giving a distracted nod and reminding him, not that he ever forgot, that she paid him scant notice and even less respect.

Sensing even as he spoke that he would regret asking, he said, "What is amiss?"

"Bishop Wilfrid is here."

He sighed. Did she think he hadn't noticed? "Yes. Again."

She shot him a look of surprise but continued with her tale. "He brought word from Bamburgh. Little Elfwin has taken sick. I should go to give what comfort I can to your lady mother but…"

"What?"

"The rain. It has not stopped these past weeks and the roads are flooded at many points. And the word has taken

201

so long to reach us that by now it could well be too late."

Ecgfrith sat forward. "Too late? You mean that you fear the child is already dead?"

She picked at the end of her sleeve, worrying at a loose thread, and did not look at him but merely nodded. "Mmm."

His little brother might be dead. Aside from some half-Irish by-blow, begat by Oswii years ago, Ecgfrith was now his father's only surviving son. Oswii himself was an old stag with fraying antlers. Perhaps it was time to remind the Bernician Northumbrians that there was an able and legitimate sole successor to Oswii's lands. "You should go," he said to his wife. "And I will ride with you. After all, if my sweet little brother has died, then I should pay my respects."

Audrey turned to look at him and her eyes were wide with disbelief. "Thank you, Husband." She scurried away.

He called out after her. "Where do you go now?"

She turned. "To tell Bishop Wilfrid that you are coming with us."

"He's coming too?"

She nodded. "Why would he not? Your lady mother will welcome it."

"Christ Almighty." Ecgfrith sat back and beckoned for another drink.

Ositha saw them arrive, their cloaks caked with dried mud. The horses were clean, and the weather here had not been bad, so she surmised that all she'd heard about the Vale of York, its frequent rain and tendency to flooding, must be true. Sometimes the things she heard by listening behind doors or round corners weren't valuable, merely interesting, and she wondered whether Deira was as windblown as this part of Northumbria. She wrapped her own cloak around her and moved nearer the chapel wall, out of the maw of the wind.

No doubt they had come because of Elfwin. They would not think to enquire whether she, too, had fallen prey to the sickness. What matter if she, the spare daughter, died? The spare son, well, he was altogether more special. Ositha dug her nails into her palm and made silent apology to God for the envious thoughts. Elfwin meant the world to her, too, and she should not let selfishness cloud her mind. Instead, she would derive some pleasure from their wasted efforts, for whatever had struck them all down here at Bamburgh, it was not the plague but something milder and all who'd been afflicted had made a full recovery. Father still coughed more than he had before, but not one life at Bamburgh had been lost. As soon as Elfwin had recovered and she herself was on the mend, Ositha had made herself useful by helping her mother tend her father. If Audrey and Wilfrid thought to help, they had better think again. They were not needed.

She watched as the visitors dismounted and thought she ought to let her mother know they'd arrived. She stepped out from the shelter of the chapel wall and straight into Elwyn. "Take care, little Lady," he said, steadying her by grabbing her shoulders, "Never come round a corner too swiftly. For who knows who might be lurking?"

She shook him off, gently, for she had never felt threatened by him, even though she knew the stories told of him. "I understand how corners work," she told him, meeting his gaze and noting with satisfaction that he turned away first, unaccustomed to such fearlessness. "And I glean many things of worth."

He trained his gaze back upon her and said, "How many summers have you seen; ten and seven? No sweetheart yet?"

She wasn't sure she liked the way he was looking at her, for he was certainly seeing her anew, and no longer as a child. His appraisal was discomfiting because it was the first; who else had noticed that she was no longer a greyhound-thin child, but a young woman with hips? So no, there was

203

no sweetheart. What would be the point, when it was her destiny to wed whoever her father thought would bring the best alliance? Ositha held out little hope for a happy union and wondered if falling in love was even wise. When she thought about Ava and Pieter, and of Carena and Alfrid, she thought it might be silly to feel so deeply for another person. And yet, hadn't she sobbed for days and prayed on her knees when she thought little Elfwin might die? Even so, perhaps a pragmatic marriage, such as that of her parents, might be the safer route and she was of marriageable age now. Her father, as soon as he was fully well, would be casting round for suitable husbands for her. She looked Elwyn in the eye and said, "I would not dream to sully myself before I am wed to one of my father's under-kings."

Elwyn pulled his head back as if he found her answer surprising, but all he said was, "No indeed, little Lady."

Chapter Nine

Whitby AD670: February

Every winter since his illness had been worse than the one before. Now, not yet sixty, he had breathed his last only a few nights after Candlemas. Schemer, strategist, murderer, he had also, upon occasion, been a loving husband, and their early years together had been notable for the fierce arguments and the intensity of their physical relationship. Efa wiped a tear from her cheek and moved away from the rest of the funeral party. Bishop Wilfrid was still intoning, and the prayers were a comfort to her. Oswii, king of Northumbria, overlord of the Picts and scourge of Mercia, Wales, and Lindsey, was dead.

The old rogue had died in his bed, and she was not sure how he felt about that as he drew his last breaths. Did it please him, to know that he had outlived his foes and had the luxury of a warm blanket at the end? The journey to Whitby had been slow, and foolhardy at that time of year, really. The roads were uneven, bumpy with clumps of frozen earth, and the wind had cut holes through their bones. At least, as Elwyn pointed out, the cold had kept the body fresh. He'd made light but Efa knew that Elwyn was lost without his lord, with whom he'd been friends since they had both been children in exile.

Abbess Hild came to stand beside Efa and took her hand. Hild and Oswii had never seen eye to eye, but the abbess was kindness itself to his widow and children. And what a motley collection of children he'd had: a half-Irish son whose whereabouts were unknown; the Rhegedians Ava, so broken, and Alfrid, who'd hated his father and with just cause; Alfleyda, dedicated to the church, and Ositha, on the cusp of womanhood who was devastated by the loss of her father; Ecgfrith, who was determined to succeed his father in all things, including cruelty, and perhaps treachery where necessary, and Elfwin, whose sunny nature captivated all who knew him. Had all these really sprung from those loins?

Hild took her hand. "I did not think he would wish to be buried here."

Efa sniffed. "Nor I. May God forgive me, but I think I talked my husband into saying yes. He was too weak to disagree, truth be told. I have it in mind to rebury my father here, too, one day."

"It would please God, I think. Edwin was a good, devout man." Hild gave Efa's hand a gentle squeeze, then let it slip free.

Efa hugged herself under her cloak and shuffled her feet in an attempt to thaw them. She looked over at the assembled mourners. Among Oswii's offspring, were they all, in fact, mourning? Ecgfrith looked emotionless, but his face was twitching. Efa imagined that he would be fighting to keep secret his happiness at becoming king of the whole of Northumbria. Elfwin, though, was weeping openly. He had not known his father that well, for Oswii had paid him little attention, but Elfwin's heart was big, even though he was not yet as tall as his mother. Alfleyda's head was bowed in reverence, albeit for a father she had never really known. Ava stood tall, seemingly oblivious of the cold which was causing everyone else to hunch, and it was clear that her father's death had lifted a great weight from her soul. Ositha was staring blankly, as if she could see nothing. Anyone would think that her father's death had dealt her a physical blow, for she looked stunned and disbelieving. Efa would need to speak to her. "His daughters are reeling, one way or another," she said. "Ava and Ositha especially."

Hild said, "He was a big man, in build, and words. There is a hole now, where he once was. Whether they welcome or dread it, it is there."

Efa looked again at Ositha and Ava. "I will see Ositha later. Now though," she indicated with her arm, "I will speak to her."

What must it be like, to have loved a Mercian and then see him dead? And worse, then to live amongst those who were his enemies?

Hild had offered them a little room near her own sleeping chamber. They would be free to talk in peace here, she'd said, where the rest of the gathered kin would not hear them. Now Efa looked at the other woman and saw again how grief had really aged her. "Oswii is dead."

"Yes." The eyes were sunken in a pool of shadow.

"So now we both are widows."

A shrug. "I have mourned for longer than you. And yet I think my sadness will outlive yours. I loved my husband."

Efa gave a little nod in concession. "I was not wed for love, that is true. We found an understanding, but it was not a love like yours, I grant you."

"Still, now we are both free of him. This eases my heart."

"I can see that. You will walk taller now. And you should go."

There was a pause. A frown, perhaps of disbelief. "You mean it?"

Efa stood up. "Yes. Go. We should not have waited so long, but there it is. I have made up my mind. One woman to another. Men make the laws, they fight the wars, but it is we who bear the children, bear the losses when our men and boys do not come home. My son will be named king but for now, I am still queen here. And I say you must go."

Efa stood up and walked out of the little room, leaving the door open behind her. When she was called upon to stand in front of her creator, she would answer for her sins. But not for this.

The sun was high, and the crops were ripening. Easter was a distant memory, and the folk of Tamworth were enjoying the benign weather. The beasts were milked three times a day in the month where the May blossom began to form. Despite one sadness, an illness of someone dear, that cast a pall over the gathering, the year was full of promise. The king was in good cheer, recently home from another successful fight with the West Saxons, although Cynwal still evaded Wulf's grasp.

Every year since the Iclingas had been reunited by Carena's return, the children of Penda had met at Tamworth and Ethelred's settlement thrummed not only with the noise of work activity, but the sound of sibling chatter and children's laughter. Repairs to the hall roof were being carried out while the sky was set fair, and little Cenred was doing his best to help, attempting to drag bundles of thatching material across the yard.

Each holding an end of the two-man saw, Ethelred and Merchelm were cutting timber for a new storage hut, which they'd told Cenred could be his own little house until the autumn when it would be used for storing dried vegetables, although he'd not listened when they said it would be very dark, since the light must be kept off the produce. The little boy offered them one of the thatch bundles, but Ethelred shook his head. "Let us get the walls up first, and then you can help with the roof."

Cenred dropped the bundle and tried to reach his tongue across his cheek. Earlier, the cooks had brought out bowls of fruit and bread pudding, and told him that once the apples were picked, they would make little apple dumplings for him. He'd eaten the pudding, but there was a sticky smear on his face. Ethelred beckoned the boy, released his hold on the saw, and wiped the lad's cheek with his sleeve.

208

"There, all clean now."

Starling, on her yearly visit from Chertsey, was sitting with her sisters by the herb beds, playing with her baby daughter. Minna and Carena, along with Minna's daughter, had come from Medeshamstede and, although the twins rarely ventured from their abbeys, the kinship group was as whole as any of them could expect. Cenred ran over to his Aunt Starling, and it was clear from his arm movements that he wished to hold the little girl. Starling glanced over at Ethelred, and he nodded his assurance that the girl would be safe with the sturdy and dependable little boy. The three women helped Cenred to pick the baby up and showed him how to support her on his hip, but she proved too heavy for him and the arch of her back suggested that she was exerting the kind of force only a young child possessed, pushing and squirming in order to be released back to her mother.

Another child might have taken it to heart, but Cenred merely shrugged and sat down beside the girl, picking up a stick and drawing pictures for her in the soil of the herb beds, and gently restraining her whenever she put a chubby hand out to pick the plants.

Merchelm had stood up while they watched, to ease his back, and now he and Ethelred continued the push-pull motion with the saw. The action was satisfying for Ethelred; a rhythmic motion that reminded him he was active and in useful occupation. The sweet smell released from the inside of the tree trunk was a bonus, and he breathed in deeply. He began to hum.

Merchelm took up the refrain. "I know this one," he said after a few phrases. I think it was one that…"

"It was." Ethelred was sharper than he meant to be, but he had belatedly realised that it was one of the tunes Arianwen had sung, when they were all young folk together at Wenlock. He straightened up and wiped his brow, and was grateful for the distraction of his brother, who was striding towards them.

But Wulf was not happy. His mouth was set in a thin line and he was frowning. In his hand, a piece of vellum flashed its dark ink letters as he made his way towards his brother and nephew. "Oswii is dead."

Ethelred and Merchelm exchanged glances. Unsure why Wulf should be unhappy, Ethelred said, "This is a good thing. The man has gone to Hell, where he will answer for his sins. I should pray for his soul, but I will not. It is over, Brother. Be glad."

Wulf curled the vellum into his fist. "Bishop Chad sent this with one of his monks from Lichfield. He told me what it says. Oswii died in his bed. Of old age. This was denied to our kin, and that bastard should have died by my sword. Now his whelp will do so in his stead."

Ethelred nodded to Merchelm and they laid the saw gently on the ground. "Brother," he put his arm round Wulf's shoulder, "the son you speak of is the one who lived his childhood years with us. Mother cared for him as one of her own. He is Oswii's son, yes, but I feel sure he is carved from another tree. Let us put this feud in the ground with Oswii." He gave Wulf a gentle shake. "See, here are our sisters, our brother, their children. Let not the passing of that foul man spoil our gathering, hmm?"

Wulf scuffed the ground with his boot. "Perhaps you are right. I will give Ecgfrith some time to show me that he is more like his mother than his father. But if he should cross me…" He flashed Ethelred a dazzling smile. "Besides, I still have Cynwal to chase down."

He dashed away with a much lighter step and Ethelred shook his head. How could he be so wroth and then, in a heartbeat, be so blissful? He glanced at Merchelm to see that he, too, was grinning.

Wulf broke into a trot and leaped onto the second rung of

210

a ladder propped up against the bake house wall. He shouted to the men on the roof that he was there to assist them and began singing at the top of his voice. Ethelred laughed. "My brother is glad to be alive, but never more so when he thinks about an upcoming fight."

Merchelm chuckled. "I'd sooner have him beside me in a shield wall than face his axe, that is true!"

They resumed their work, still laughing, when a cry from the gate house stilled them. "You cannot merely go and speak to the king!"

A stranger had ridden in, evidently demanding to see Wulf, and the man at arms was hurrying after them, because the visitor had ridden through the gate without stopping. The hooded figure rode up to an astonished stable-hand and slid slowly from the saddle, handing the reins to the groom. Ethelred watched as the new arrival moved their head as if searching the yard for the king, who at that moment had nothing on display except his back, standing as he was on the ladder. The figure then looked directly at Ethelred and began shuffling towards him. As they approached, the hood fell back, and he could see now that it was a woman.

Something shimmered in his memory. He dismissed it; he'd been caught this way so many times before. Yet the woman was walking straight to him, squinting as if her eyesight was not what it once had been. When she arrived before him, she had to raise her chin, for he was a head or more taller than her. She stood there as if rooted, staring at him, taking in every detail of his face. He shifted uneasily and glanced at Merchelm, who was looking puzzled. Finally, the woman took another step forward and laid a bobble-veined hand on Ethelred's chest. His heart was beating furiously, and she must have felt it. She nodded, as if satisfied, and then spoke one word. "Noni."

He scratched about in every corner of his mind, searching for a recollection which would help him. This woman knew

211

him, that much was clear, but he did not recall any aunt who would now be this old. Had he had a nurse when he was a child? He did not think so, but then so much of his childhood was little more than a blur. Who was she? He tried to signal with his eyes that he wanted Merchelm to fetch Wulf or any of the sisters who might remember this woman and what part she'd played in his earlier life.

The elderly woman smiled, and tears slid down her face, tracking past her trembling lips. "Noni," she said again, as if she could not believe what her eyes were telling her. She tried to step into his embrace but instinctively he took a step backwards. "You do not know me? Well, why should you. I am…"

By now some of the others had come over, beckoned by Merchelm. Carena had arrived first. She was shaking her head and her face had drained to a shade too pale for winter, never mind late spring. "No," she mouthed.

Merwal was here. Ethelred let out a sigh. Merwal was the eldest of all of them. If anyone knew who this person was, it would be him. Perhaps she was kin to Merwal's father and had visited Tamworth when they were all little. Merwal would know.

But Merwal was crying too. Wet lines showed on his dust-covered cheeks as he pushed past the others. He took the woman gently by the shoulders and turned her towards him. As he did so, Ethelred had a view of both her and Carena. Carena, who had arrived after many years away and made him think of… He looked from one face to the other. No, it was impossible.

Merwal and the woman were in each other's arms and Merwal was whispering one word, over and over again. "Mother."

Baffled, emotions washing over him like a river in spate, Ethelred watched as his older brothers and sisters crowded round and hugged her until he thought the poor woman might break. Eventually, amid much chatter and crying, she eased herself from them and approached him once more. "My little bairn, you do not know me at all, and here I am back from the dead. Breathe, little one. It is too much for you all, I see that. I am glad to see you taking such good care of your father's old hall. Bring me to a bench and let me tell you all how I have come to be here."

They walked into the hall with her, and Carena helped her to a seat. Drinks were brought, Wulf took Derwena's cloak from her, and Merwal settled a cushion behind her back. Starling's baby daughter patted Derwena's lap, and her grandmother opened her arms and let the child sit there, stroking her downy hair. "There are more children? Are they here? Is that little Merchelm? Come into the light and let me see you. Oh, you were so small when I left."

Merwal put a hand on hers. "Mother, we all thought you dead. It has been fourteen summers and a few months besides. Where have you been; why did you not come home ere now?"

Ethelred looked at her face, willing the memories to surface. "You were dead. I saw it. Oswii raised his sword. As soon as you had given him back his son, he struck you down."

Derwena smiled sadly at him. "It breaks my heart that you thought you saw that. Have you lived with such sorrow every day since? He raised his sword, yes, but he fettered me. They, my beloved hearth-men, they got you away. Safely, I had hoped, but I never knew for sure."

Wulf said, "Did that bastard hurt you?" His hands were curled into fists, but he kept his arms by his side.

She shook her head. "Bodily, no. My heart was already shattered. Your father was dead, my kin scattered to the winds, dead or living, I knew not. They fed me, watered me, kept me alive. His queen let me go after he was dead. It has been a slow ride home." She sank back against the cushion

213

and closed her eyes, still stroking the small child who was sitting easily in her arms.

"Mother," Carena sat down beside her, "where did they keep you all this time?"

Without opening her eyes, Derwena said, "At Hild's abbey. At Whitby."

Carena took such a sharp intake of breath that it became a gasp. "I should have been there, six summers past, at the synod. Queen Efa told me not to go. Afterward, I thought it had been because she knew Alfrid's life was in danger." She stopped, as if wondering whether to tell her mother that part of the tale, but pressed on. "I would have been so near to you. Lady Efa was sparing me the pain of seeing you as a prisoner. How could Oswii have been so cruel?" Her hand went to her mouth, and she sobbed.

Derwena sat forward and reached past the child to put a comforting hand on her daughter's arm. "Dearest Carena, Sweetling, hush now. I am home. Naught else matters."

Wulf disagreed. "No. One more reason why we should ride north and nail his son's heart to a tree."

"Little Lief? No, he was such a sweet bairn."

"Perhaps when he was still wetting the bed. Now he is a man grown and his father's debts are due. Mother, is this not what Father would have done; ridden thither and hunted him down?"

"Yes, he would. If he thought it was warranted. Let us wait and see, shall we? Meanwhile I need to get to know my bairns again, and their bairns."

As they began to chatter once more, all speaking across one another, Ethelred tried to take in all that he'd heard. No wonder he could never actually recall the moment his mother lost her life, no wonder that he always woke from his dreams when the sword was raised and never saw it strike. *My beloved hearth-men got you away.* "Mother," he cut through the thrum of conversation. The word sounded odd to his ears, so he repeated it. "Mother, come; there is someone here whom you should see, sooner rather than later."

As they walked across the yard, Ethelred had to shorten his stride considerably to match his mother's slower steps.

"So, my daughters are all abbesses bar one?"

"Yes. Starling makes the best of being wed to a man whom she did not choose..." He caught himself, too late. Let Wulf explain the details of that one. "And we found the twins. They do not often come here, but word has already been sent that you have been given back to us."

"So, it is only you who is neither kneeling forever in prayer, nor wed." She gave him a sideways glance. "We will speak at length later. Ah, thanks be to Woden, it makes me want to skip, simply knowing that there will be a later."

Not for some, though. He opened the bower door and stood back to let her go ahead of him. She stepped into the gloomy room and sniffed the air. Ethelred knew that she could smell it too, the nearness of death. Gesina, who had been at the bedside day and night, now bobbed in reverence, and left the bower.

His throat aching, Ethelred watched as his mother went to the bed and sat down on the edge of it. She leaned forward and took the sick man's hand in hers. "Sikke, beloved man, I am here. Derwena is home."

Sikke's eyes fluttered open and he made a small sound. He lifted his forearm and made an attempt to kiss her fingers, but his arm fell back upon the bed. She didn't let go. "Sweet Lady," he croaked, "Is it really you?"

"Yes, dear man, it is I. Did you think to pass without my knowing? To die without my leave?" Her chuckle was more of a sob, and Ethelred's chest tightened as he witnessed her hurt.

"I would not dare, Lady. I kept the lordling safe for you. I kept my oath."

She grasped his hand tightly to her chest. "There was never, never," she repeated fiercely, "a more steadfast man than you. If we both lived to see one hundred summers, I could not pay the debt."

Sikke tried to speak again, but the noise came out as no more than a sigh. Ethelred, his vision washed with tears, backed away and left them alone together.

They buried Sikke three days later. Wulf and Derwena had differing views about the kind of burial it should be, but Derwena, bowing to her son's wishes, allowed the Christians their way.

That night they drank to the memory of a proud and fierce warrior, and the older ones told tales of Sikke and his brother, Sjeord, who had been the personal guard of Penda's cousin, Carinna, serving her loyally until her death, and then attaching themselves to Derwena. The scop sang songs of bravery, and whenever he paused to lubricate his throat with ale, one of the kinship group would tell another story.

Carena said, "Do you recall the day Sikke found me taking apples from the grove and stood there until I came down from the tree?"

"He tried to teach me how to carve with my hand knife, but I never could do it." Ethelred sat back, drank, and hoped fervently that if Sikke was now in Heaven, he would not be too cross with the idea that the Christians were right all along.

Wulf abandoned his plans for a summer campaign in the south. Merwal sent word that he would not be returning to Leominster for another turn of the moon at least, and messages were despatched to Chertsey and to Medeshamstede too. Penda's wife and children would not be parted again so soon.

The summer was a long one, and they were blessed to see

216

the crops ripen and the beasts grow fat. Bilberry fruits appeared, buttercups spotted the meadows with vibrant yellow and those up with the dawn were witness to the wood sorrel leaves opening to the sun. Ethelred oversaw the settlement at Tamworth with a renewed sense of purpose, proud that his mother approved of the way he was running things. He could not show or tell her that he was a worthy warrior like his father, but their home had been important to them, he not only knew this, but now found himself actively remembering it, and it gladdened his heart that he could show his mother something of the man he had become.

The coopers were hard at work making casks that would be needed for dry goods come harvest time. Older barrels that had been used already, some for storing butter packed with layers of salt, and then repurposed for wine and pickling, were now being broken up and used for lining the well. Shed antlers had been collected earlier in the year and now the bone carvers were busy taking orders for new combs and needles. They had already sawn off the tines and had them soaking in water, to make them easier to work, and then they would decorate them using a sharp knife.

Everyone who could was working outside in the sunshine, and those who sat on the ground instinctively pulled their legs in when their lord's mother, unsteady even with her stick, walked by, nodding at their industry and kindness. The only time she had stopped and stared was when she passed a wooden frame with a calf skin pegged out on it. "What is this?" She went up to the frame and touched the tightening pegs. "This hide is too thin to be of any use for shoes or belts."

Ethelred smiled. "This hide has not been treated the same as others. It has been soaked in lime to remove all the fat."

She grabbed the edge and stroked it with her thumb and forefinger. "Not worked with fats and egg whites to make it strong?"

217

"No, no fats. Otherwise the ink will not take."

She let go. "Ink?"

"It will be made into a book, Mother. I will show you one, after."

Eyes wide, she backed away. "Whatever next?"

Laughing, he had resolved to have a book written and stitched for her.

Derwena had been told of Pieter's death, not long after it happened. She cried her tears in her tiny cell at Whitby Abbey, and they had dried long ago, she said. Ethelred suspected that this was all his mother would ever say about her years in captivity, even though they must have been harsh, and indeed solitary, if she had not once seen a book there. He had learned quickly that she was an advocate of leaving the past in its place so as not to disturb the present. She did not believe, as he did, in an afterlife, so she looked neither forward, nor backward, especially now that the man responsible for her pain was dead. Derwena knew that their family was as whole as it ever could be, with all those missing accounted for, and was at peace.

In those long hot days, as Ethelred walked from hall to chapel, from bake house to gate house, ate his meals with his kin, and practised his weapon craft with his brothers and Merchelm, he occasionally looked up at the sky, grateful that there was naught to spoil the blue. God, though, was brewing a dark cloud.

As the preparations began to get underway for the midsummer celebrations, little Cenred fell ill, burning with a fever which Ermenilda feared would take him from her. Werbyra was poorly too, and then Starling's daughter succumbed. Priests were summoned, leechworts applied, and vigils kept in the chapel all night. Derwena, determined that she would not lose any of her grandchildren, left her own offerings to her gods.

They had all done what they could and now they waited,

218

gathering in the hall to gain comfort from company, but barely speaking. Ethelred's thoughts pressed him like a headache, for there was one person whose healing skills were legendary, but she was beyond his reach. Even were she not, even if a message could be sent, she would not be able to get to them in time.

On the third day, Ermenilda, hair loose from her veil and dark shadows under her eyes, came to find Wulf in the hall. She'd no need for words, for her face told them all. "The fever has passed. All the bairns are well. They will live." She stepped into her husband's embrace and the others hugged whoever was next to them. Ethelred, having kissed his sisters and Ermenilda, and patted Wulf on the back, made his way outside, intending to go to the chapel to give thanks.

As he walked across the yard, a young woman, a thegn's daughter whom he'd noticed from time to time and thought about getting to know better, turned and smiled at him. Little Cenred's brush with death had made him consider that it was perhaps time he gave some thought to the getting of his own sons but, while he returned the woman's smile, her eyes were the wrong colour, not dark like Arianwen's. They were beautiful, but they were not the eyes he loved.

Once again, his heart lurched as if trying to push him across the border to Wales. He made a slow and deliberate turn in the opposite direction, out of the settlement towards the woods, past hedgerows thick with bindweed blossom, and through the trees where nettles were in flower on the ground between the trunks. He thought of the day she teased him for getting stung, and he remembered how reluctant he had been to leave Llywarch's lands, feeling that with Arianwen, he was complete and there was naught else to know about him but that he loved her. Who was she now; was she the woman he recalled, or had she never been that person? Even though she had hurt him he could do naught but wish her well. Surely she must have bairns of her

219

own by now and, if she did, they would be her whole world. A fresh wave of relief made him shudder as he thought of how close they had come to losing his nieces and nephew, and his chest ached for a child of his own.

Chapter Ten

Northumbria AD671: Summer

"Will you stop that? It feels like the smith has burrowed into my head and set to with hammer and anvil."

The boy stopped knocking his wooden sword against the table and looked up. "Sorry." With no sulking and no resentment, Elfwin simply picked up the toy weapon and left the hall.

Ecgfrith watched him go. The lad was noisy and often annoying and yet how could anyone stay wroth with him? "And what are you looking at?"

Ositha gathered up her drop spindle and prepared to follow her little brother outdoors. "Naught. It makes me smile, that is all, to see you pretend to be cross with him." She went on her way, nodding to Elwyn as he came in.

Elwyn looked troubled but then again, the frown lines were etched deep now on his brow, for he was an old man. Ecgfrith occasionally wondered whether he shouldn't let his father's most trusted friend and advisor go and live out his days quietly on his own lands, but the man was still useful.

Easing himself into a chair, Elwyn looked at his king. "It is not good tidings."

"It never is with you. Why did my father put up with you for so long?"

Elwyn puffed out an amused sigh. "When God makes your plans go awry, it is always good to have a dog to kick." He settled in his chair and snapped his fingers for a drink. Once his cup was filled, he took a deep swig and placed the cup on the table, holding the base as if to anchor it. Staring intently at his hand, he said "The Picts are looking for trouble. It seems that now your father's iron fist is no longer holding them..."

"Bastards!" He'd thought his father to be a spent force, a king once strong but grown weaker in old age. The Picts evidently thought otherwise. Now he would have to ride at the head of an army to show the Picts that he was every bit as good, nay, better, than Oswii. This would severely delay his plans for destroying the Mercians.

"And your wife is making preparations to leave you." Elwyn spoke this last hurriedly and then put his cup to his lips.

"What did you say?" Ecgfrith leaned forward, resting his elbows on the table while considering whether he really should kick Elwyn. "Leave, how?"

The great oak door banged, and they both looked up to see Ositha back in the room. "You've told him then?"

Ecgfrith stood up. "How did you know?"

She smiled. "I not only know, but I can tell you what her plans are."

Elwyn chuckled and took another mouthful of his ale. "Listening round corners again, Lady? If only your father had realised how like him you really are."

Ositha ignored him and Ecgfrith cuffed the back of his head on his way to stand nearer his sister. "Tell me then." But she didn't speak. Was the girl addled? "Oh, I see. You want payment. Name your price."

"A husband. Elfwin has seen nearly ten summers, and he does not need me to look after him. He should be spending his days out in the yard honing his weapon skills. Mother is away to the abbey and Audrey is lady in this hall. I wish to have a hall of my own."

She was right. Ten was old enough that no boy still needed mothering; Ecgfrith certainly hadn't, although Elfwin's growing up would cause another headache in time. Still, their father should have arranged a wedding for her long ago and had not, so it was only meet that Ecgfrith should do so. Elwyn could find someone suitable. "I will find you a husband if by Lammas I still have my wife. Tell me what you know." She nodded and sat down. Ecgfrith looked about the hall and said, "Out! All of you, get out now." Thegns, waiting-women, and servants left hurriedly.

When only Ecgfrith, his sister, and Elwyn were left inside, Ositha began her tale. "You know how deeply Audrey cares for your kinswoman, the abbess at Coldingham? Did you also know it was that same abbess who helped Carena to flee before you and Father got back from Whitby?"

How she had gleaned so much information was a mystery to him, and he began to think that he had underestimated his sister. As she spoke, he wondered if she would be an adequate replacement for the elderly Elwyn, but surely she would have no stomach for killing. Then again, if their father's blood flowed through her veins…

She continued. "Audrey is there now, this we know. But she intends not to come back here and instead will make her way back to her dower lands in East Anglia."

He could not tolerate this. Audrey was a sour-faced woman who, in all their years of being man and wife, had never once willingly spread her legs for him, but he'd not let her be the one to walk away. His father had not been an easy man to live with, but Oswii had at least managed to keep hold of his wife, even after slaying her kinsman.

Ositha was peering across the table at him. "Brother, you are lost in your thoughts. May I speak mine?"

He nodded.

She took a deep breath, as he'd seen folk do many a time before speaking to his irascible father. "You do not live in anything like wedded bliss. Would it not be better for all if you let her go?"

How dare she? He opened his mouth to shout her down but then stopped to consider that there might be some merit

223

in what she was saying. "Yes. You are right. The old cow has served me badly. She should go, but at a time of my choosing, and on my word, not hers."

Ositha had witnessed many of her father's fits of temper. She had thought Ecgfrith to be woven from the same pattern of cloth, but this was different. A small group of hearth-thegns had been sent to intercept Audrey and the abbess as they made their way south from Coldingham. They'd been unable to apprehend the women immediately due to inclement weather which had caused the roads to flood, and the religious women had taken refuge on higher ground. Thus began a stand-off, which eventually resulted in the men climbing up the hill and talking the women into coming down, and Ositha would always wonder about the nature of that 'persuasion'. The sisters from Coldingham had been sent back north, and Audrey had been escorted home to Bamburgh. She looked furious, but Ecgfrith was calm, sitting back in his father's stone king-seat, with one foot resting on the other knee.

Audrey was a thin-lipped woman who no doubt would always have looked severe, but Ositha knew that the woman had been unhappy for a long time and that Ecgfrith was almost wholly responsible for that. Whilst she had been instrumental in foiling Audrey's plans, Ositha deemed it unnecessarily cruel that Ecgfrith had dragged his wife back, only to tell her what he had decided.

"Leave. Aye, and take that wretched creature with you." He gestured, but there was no need to look. Everyone in the room knew he was referring to Wilfrid, who had also been summoned to hear the king's declaration. "Let it be known that I, Ecgfrith, king of all Northumbria, release you from your wedding oaths. And let the bishop not set foot in my lands again."

Now, Ositha did turn to look at Wilfrid. He was red in the

face and looked as if he would burst with outrage. In the short time it had taken to glance in the bishop's direction, Audrey had evidently taken her leave of the king; she brushed past Ositha and walked towards the hall door. As she drew level with Wilfrid she nodded once and quickly, and he moved to join her. The two of them walked outside without a backward glance.

Moments later, Ecgfrith himself went past, calling for Elwyn. "Now to deal with these wearisome Picts. And Elwyn, find me another wife!"

Ositha put out a hand. "Brother? A word before you go?"

He paused. "Mmm?"

"Could Elwyn send out for a husband for me now? You did say that if you got your…"

"Elwyn will be busy finding me a woman who can bear my sons and we have a fight to plan." Ecgfrith was on the move again, talking as he walked. "Can you not find yourself a willing thegn if you itch and must be scratched?" He stopped, half-turned, looked her up and down, and then said, "On the other hand, no. You are a woman. Best not."

With that, he left her standing alone in the hall.

They called it the battle of Two Rivers and tales were already being told of those two water courses being dammed by the bodies of dead Picts.

"And then our lord king ordered the chase, and his men used the dead to ford the rivers. Many were slaughtered who ran, and all in the Pictish kingdom must now send tribute to King Ecgfrith."

The scop was still working on his song and would no doubt continue to refine it throughout the day, adding more detail with each telling, gauging the reaction of his smaller audiences, before performing the finished work at the feast that evening. Ositha, bored, stood up and tapped Elfwin on the shoulder in a bid for him to join her outside. Elfwin was enraptured though, staring at the scop as if he would physically catch the words with his hands and keep them there if he could. Dear God, let him not become like them. He was too sweet, too loving.

She left them to it, and went out to stare over towards the holy island. She recalled standing there with her father, describing to him the activity of the monks when his sight had begun to fail. Being useful. Today, she could not see much, for her own eyes were watering in the vicious wind.

Now there was a tap on her shoulder, and Elfwin moved to stand beside her. "I came away," he said. "I wish to hear the whole song at the feast, even though I know how the tale ends." He nudged her and grinned when she turned. "You will serve the drinks as lady of the hall. But..."

His grin was more catching than the plague and she couldn't help smiling at his dimpled face. "But what?"

"I heard that Elwyn is back."

Elwyn, too old now, had not been at the battle in the north. Where he'd been was of little concern to Ositha, who'd assumed he'd been tending his own lands. Sooner or later, he would leave to live there permanently. These days he walked unsteadily and with the aid of a stick. She raised an eyebrow in response to Elfwin's comment but said nothing.

"Back with tidings."

His smile must surely split his face if it widened any further. With mock exasperation she sighed dramatically and said, "Well, since you must tell me or burst, what is it?"

"There is to be a wedding."

She had thought Ecgfrith too busy with his fighting and proving that he was a better war leader than their father to remember his oath, but he had not forgotten after all. Yes, she would serve at the feast tonight as Lady of Bamburgh, but it would be the first and last time. Who would be her husband, she wondered? Perhaps someone from Kent, from

226

her mother's house; that would be most fitting.

"Ositha? I have to do my weapon training in a while, but can we go and look for shells on the beach now?"

He was still half a head shorter than her, and she paused for a moment to consider how firmly he was wedged between two worlds. He was keen to learn his fighting skills and stay up to hear the scop, but he also still wanted to play children's games. She ruffled his hair and said, "Sadly, no. I must go and open my chests, and find the best kirtle I can. I must look like a real lady this eventide." A real lady who would soon be a bride.

Elfwin's smile drooped a little, but he said, "You always look like a real lady."

She put a hand up to her face, wondering if she should gainsay him. The love of a brother was less discerning than that of a husband, but it gave her a rare confidence, so she merely said, "Thank you, Sweetling."

"If I live to be as old as Methuselah, I will never understand women."

Ositha turned away so that her brother would not see the tears forming. She never thought that she would miss her father's ranting, but Ecgfrith had none of the range of emotions that Oswii had displayed, being only ever calm, cold, and cruel.

He continued. "Our mother sent me away, you know, when I was younger than Elfwin is now. You'd think she'd wish to show her love by riding here, but no. She sits at Whitby with our sister, and with the creature Ava. You are the only woman left here of Oswii's kin, and you wander round looking like you've had your arse slapped."

No, she thought, she hadn't, not at first. At the feast last year after the battle of Two Rivers, she had smiled and worn her finest kirtle, the one dyed deep red, with embroidery round the neck and sleeves, that was so delicate and fine he'd assumed she'd taken it from one of their mother's chests. She'd behaved as she should, had been the perfect lady of the hall, and done the same at Yule, but with far less enthusiasm. Perhaps she hadn't hidden her disappointment as well as she'd thought, but wasn't she here, in the hall, dressed in that same fine kirtle and waiting to welcome his new bride? If only his heart was warm enough to allow that she might be upset because, despite his promises, she had not been able to dress as a bride herself. Elfwin, sitting next to her, squeezed her arm, and the kindness of the gesture released her tears.

The hall was cold, and not simply because the hearth had not been attended to. Elwyn had left to live out his years on his own lands, to be replaced by Colmán, who was far younger but was a stranger. Ositha had not taken to him, with his sallow skin that seemed barely to cover his skull, so that his eye sockets were sunken and his temple bones almost visible. As Ecgfrith had so petulantly pointed out, their mother and sisters were not here, and only the presence of Elfwin, and the spirit of her uncle, Oswald, kept her world from freezing over entirely.

"You know where he's gone, do you? That little shit Wilfrid?"

Ositha shrugged, neither knowing nor caring.

"Mercia, that's where. Colmán has brought me word that the bastard Wulfhere has given him land there. They do it to make me wroth, and they have succeeded."

She thought it unlikely that they would have naught better to do than think of ways to annoy him, but she kept her counsel.

"You know, I once swore never to be wrong-footed by our foes. Our father was beset by uprisings, but I shall not be. The Picts have felt the heat of my wrath, and now the Mercians shall too."

Ositha wiped her eyes with the back of her hand. By the

228

time he had met and bedded his new wife, and then taken the fight to Mercia, he would once again have forgotten all about her. She forced her lips into a smile and prepared to meet the woman who would replace her as Lady of Bamburgh.

Tamworth, AD674: Summer

Slaves as they were to the seasons, and to the weather especially, was it any wonder that their mood was lighter in the long summer months? Ethelred knew that he was not the only one whose heart lifted when the days grew longer and the crops ripened. These days, he had additional reasons to be glad. Defying her age, Derwena rode regularly between Stone and Tamworth. Messengers were sent every time she set out to see her youngest son, and Carena would ride to meet her there.

Sitting on a bench, waiting for his sister to arrive, Ethelred pressed a package into his mother's hand. Derwena unfolded the material wrapping and stared at the object. It was hardly bigger than her hand and was covered with two boards, lined with embossed leather. She turned it this way and that, bemused, until Ethelred laughed and took it from her.

"It opens thus, see?" He opened the decorated metal clasp on the gospel book and then turned some of the pages, showing her the neat uncial script and the illumination, worked with gold and vermillion. "They used the very vellum skin that you saw being dried." He pointed to the edges of the pages. "And see here, how it has been stitched, with waxed thread." He handed it back to her.

"How do they make these marks?"

"The ink is made from oak galls. See how they mark the lines out, finely with a knife?"

She ran her forefinger over the words. "And what does it say?"

He took it back from her. "Ah well, it is Christian Gospel, since the monks would write no other words." She made a face as if in disapproval. "If you do not wish to keep it, I thought what a fine gift it would make for Carena?"

She made an old lady harumphing noise and snatched it back. "She has plenty, I am sure. I might keep this one; the workmanship is fine enough."

Chuckling, he kissed the top of her head. She leaned against his shoulder, holding the book in her lap and stroking the leather.

A noise at the gate house alerted him. Riders. They were expecting a group from Medeshamstede, but Carena and whoever of the holy sisters accompanied her always rode in quietly. Ethelred sat up, and saw that it was Edbert. If he was here, then the tidings were not glad.

Edbert slipped from his horse and, spying Ethelred, made his way to him.

"Mother." Ethelred gave her a little shake, thinking that she might have fallen asleep.

She did not move, but said, "Here comes trouble. Do not worry, no one has died."

He sat up, cradling her head for as long as possible so that she didn't bump it when his shoulder moved. "How can you know?"

She brought her head up, moving it slowly right and left as if to ease her neck. "Believe me, I have heard enough men ride into Tamworth with tidings of death and that," she gestured at Edbert, "is not a man who is frightened to speak to his lord." She stood up, stick in one hand and book in the other, and shuffled off.

Edbert approached and bowed. Ethelred said, "Is it too much to hope that you have come merely to share my ale, tell me a tale and let me beat you at Merels?"

230

His visitor shook his head slowly. "Tempting as that would be, I have to say no. Penwal has ridden to Leominster with the same message. Ecgfrith has claimed Lindsey yet again, and the king is riding to free it from the bastard's grip."

A strange feeling moved through Ethelred. It was as though his heart was sinking, but into a belly churning with excitement: a fight, which always got the blood pumping, a chance to return to Lindsey where he'd met good people and felt a sign from God, but also a distraction, for the company of his dear mother and sister kept his loneliness at bay only during the day.

In the morning, the men gathered in the yard, waiting while supplies were loaded into the carts and the smith packed what he would need into his chests. His young lad would remain to see to the needs of the settlement, but the smith must ride north, for no one was in any doubt that this would be a hard campaign, with many weapons requiring swift repair.

Derwena waited by the hall door while Ethelred took his leave of Carena, who'd only arrived the previous evening. Immin did a check of the men, making sure outriders were sent out with messages for others to join them on the road. Heaferth had gone to gather men from his own heartlands and would catch up with them further north.

Ethelred walked over to his mother and kissed her on the cheek. "You will be glad to know it will all be settled soon, one way or the other."

She looked up at him with watery eyes. Not tears, but simply the malfunctioning of age which made her eyes leak. "You would think so, but I hold a corner of my heart open for that small boy who lived with us all those years ago. I know that he has grown up to be as much of a bastard as his father was, but nevertheless my heart aches a little for him, that he could see no other way."

He felt similarly torn, for he and Ecgfrith had been playmates once. He had to ask. "What would Father have done?"

Derwena smiled and gave a little sigh. "He'd have done all he could to put a bairn in my belly the night before and then he'd have ridden off to do what was right." She put her hands on his shoulders, standing on tiptoe to do so. "Go, with my blessing. Never think for one heartbeat that your father would not have been proud of you."

As he rode away, he wondered if this would, in fact, be the distraction he hoped for, because his mother's words echoed in his head, reminding him that he was alone, and could not leave a child in anyone's belly. It was also more of a wrench than he'd thought it would be, to leave his mother and sister.

All thoughts of home, and homeliness, were banished though when they arrived at the mustering point at Northworthy, the settlement by the River Derwent, and he saw the numbers of men, mounted and on foot, who had massed there.

Under flapping banners of various colours and designs, from scarlet and gold, to crosses, boars and ravens, hosts had come from the Thames Valley and from the island beyond the land of the Meonwara. King Athelwal had brought his South Saxons, and there were groups too from the East Saxons, and from Surrey, led by Starling's husband Frithuwald. To Wulf's annoyance, because he'd not had a hand in it, Cynwal was dead; his widow had but a tentative grip on his lands, and so the West Saxons were too busy with infighting to be a hindrance, while the rest of the south had come in support of Wulfhere of Mercia. Ethelred found himself slack-jawed as he looked at the massed warriors. Wulf's swift, decisive action against the southern kingdoms and his skill in forging alliances had certainly paid off.

Did it come naturally to some men, to lead? Surely Wulf

had not been old enough to learn by watching their father and yet here he was, riding at the head of a vast army, ready to take on the bully of Northumbria. He must have used his time in exile wisely, and it had served him well. Swallowing down any doubts about his own ability to lead should the need ever arise, and the knowledge that Penda, too, had led out a great army against Northumbria but had lost, Ethelred instead tried to remember that if naught else, he was a competent swordsman. He'd feel happier though once he had located Merchelm. He had never fought without him by his side or at his back.

As soon as he was able to pass through the throng, where the smell of leather and sweat and horse mingled with something else which was perhaps the odour of fear, Ethelred found his brother inspecting his horse's bridle, his face etched with lines of concern. Wulf was stroking the beast's nose and murmuring words of comfort. He stepped back when he saw his younger brother, and in an instant the frown was gone, replaced with a smile that would make a good substitute if the sun disappeared, for it matched its radiance. "Noni! Is it not a wonderful day?"

Ethelred was about to ask after the horse's welfare, but Wulf's beaming face brought thoughts of the upcoming fight to the fore and he said, "You have gathered enough men, for sure."

For a heartbeat, the smiled slipped, before Wulf wrapped his arm round his brother and led him over to a grassy bank, saying as they walked, "And right glad I am of it. Ecgfrith has not even talked the Picts into riding with him, and my watchers tell me that we have two men for every one of his." He laughed. "I had hoped to annoy him when I gave shelter to Wilfrid, but I never thought he would ride out so angry and ill-prepared. What a boon!"

One of Wulf's thegns brought them each a drink, and Ethelred drank thirstily. Who knew how long they would be riding before they met the Northumbrians?

As if hearing his thoughts, Wulf said, "He is waiting for us south of Lincoln. Some of the men of Lindsey have already taken the fight to him but have been pushed back. They have been watching him, but they cannot beat him without our help." He drained his cup, shaking the dregs onto the grass. "So let us finish this. Let the son pay the father's dues, let our father's death be avenged and let Mercia and Lindsey be free now and for ever."

Usually, he welcomed the warmth of the sun but now it was his enemy. It glinted off the rims, decorations and bosses of the linden shields, its rays hit the metal of the helms and shot back into his eyes, and only the familiar solidarity of the shield wall kept him from total bewilderment. The Northumbrians had chosen their position well, and the Mercians were fighting with the morning sun directly in their eyes.

The earth under their feet was dry, and loose. Whilst they'd been waiting for Wulf's forces, the devious northern king must have ordered the ground churned up by horses. Now, with the ever-present easterly wind, the dried mud flew up into their faces, reducing their vision still further. Stabbing wildly over the wall with his sword, Ethelred was blinded. Sometimes he made contact, sometimes his blade cut through naught more substantial than air. Merchelm was by his side; he knew this because he could feel him and hear his voice. His sister's husband, Frithuwald, was on his other side. Merchelm was surely swinging his axe, else he would not be moving the way he was, but was he able to see any better?

Guided by sensation, Ethelred waited for the moment when the shield walls came together again, or for a sudden release of pressure. If this happened and he lurched forward, then they had broken the enemy wall. If it happened and he fell backwards, then the Northumbrians had broken theirs. An ear-bursting clatter, a shudder along his arm, and he was being shoved, holding firm with his feet, pushing against the force. All around him the intense heat of sweating straining bodies made the work hotter, and with his vision hampered his ears were keener than usual, bringing him grunts and screams, while his nose found the iron smell of blood.

Awareness sharpened, he heard the ringing song of blade upon blade, the duller sound of weapon upon helm, and now he could smell more than spilled blood: the stench of innards with half-digested meals opened to the air. The ground grew slippery underfoot, it became harder to keep one's balance, yet still they pressed with their shields. Fighting here was confined and difficult but Ethelred knew that their forces outnumbered Ecgfrith's. All they had to do was hold their line for long enough so that the rest of the combined army could flank the Northumbrians. Even after Ecgfrith's trick with the dusty ground, they could beat him.

A pain, a white light, then temporary blackness. A whistling sound in his ears, an odd noise that came both from without and within. A sudden memory, of a childhood swim in the river, and an older brother, it wasn't clear which one, calling to him from the bank. All the voices around him were muffled, as though he was once again underwater.

An ache, dull, then sharp. A wound, deep in his belly? He was on the ground, the grass oddly wet and cold under his back. Heels catching in the churned earth, making tracks no doubt. Someone pulling him. A high-pitched whining in his head as if a gnat had flown in behind his eyes. A clearer voice now, someone saying, "Should have drawn them off the ridge."

Merchelm. It sounded like Merchelm. Was his friend dragging him along the ground? The sunlight, beating down like another foe, now disappearing. Everything dimming, sounds fading, light retreating. Feet running, men shouting far off in the distance. Was it night time already? He was cold. It was dark. The footsteps had gone away. His heart beating loudly, then silence.

The burning wood was crackling, and smoke was blowing towards him. He lay, eyes closed, trying to recollect. The battle had been fought, he remembered that, but little else, other than a pain in his stomach. He wiggled his fingers. No fetters on his wrists, so he was not a prisoner. He lifted one hand and ran it over his belly, expecting to feel stickiness, but his clothing was dry, and there was no binding around his midriff. Had he merely been winded after all? His other hand went to his head, and there he felt a wet patch and the edge of a wrapping. A head wound then; perhaps the winding had floored him, and he'd been kicked or trampled as he lay there. He opened his eyes, careful not to move his head, and tried to see who was with him. From that angle he could not make out much, just the shape of men sitting around the fire. No one was talking, so he had no way of identifying them.

He tried to prop himself up on one elbow, but the motion brought on a sickening swimming sensation in his head, and he grunted as he put his head back down. The sound alerted the man sitting nearest him.

"Ah, you have come back to us then."

Merchelm put down his ale cup and got down on one knee, arm resting on his thigh. He peered down at Ethelred and put his other hand out to feel the head wrapping.

"I'm not dead then."

"No, you are not. And there is no fresh blood either. There might be some scrapes and bruises on your, erm, underneath."

"How so?"

Merchelm stood up, snapped his fingers for a cup, and

236

brought it to Ethelred's lips, letting him drink. When Ethelred put his head back, he withdrew the cup and sat down beside him. "We had to drag you a long way. It was a sea of madness and all I could do was run, pulling you with me. When we got far enough away, Heaferth helped me carry you but it was not a gentle ride."

Merchelm had run with him. The men were sitting in subdued silence. Ethelred said, "We lost."

It had not been a question, but Merchelm answered anyway. "We did. Ecgfrith had fewer men but he chose his ground wisely, and roughened ours. We were throwing up dust and mud, pushing uphill and into the sun and we could not get them off the ridge. Not only that, but he sent men far away to come up behind us. We were fighting to the fore and to the back, when we should have been able to close around him."

Ethelred swallowed several times, fighting the urge to spew and unsure whether it was the head wound or the news that was making him feel ill. If Wulf's forces had been surrounded, and they had not been able to shift the Northumbrians from their position, then… "Who did we lose?"

Merchelm rubbed his face and pushed his hair back from his forehead. "Too many to name all but I know that Frithuwald fell."

"My poor sister. Widowed a second time. Frithuwald was not a man she'd chosen, but he was steadfast, and we will mourn. The king?"

"He lives, thank God, but he has had to swear never to bring an army into, or even set foot in, Lindsey again and Mercia must send tribute to Northumbria."

Ethelred sighed and shut his eyes, exhausted with the effort of even this small amount of talking. It had all been for naught. Men were dead, Lindsey was not free, and now Mercia was back under the yoke.

Sometimes he opened his eyes and knew it was night time, and sometimes he was not sure and thought that his eyesight had failed. Occasionally he felt the jarring of movement, but then he would open his eyes and see that he was still in the same place. More than once he heard Arianwen's voice, telling him that it was better to remove the scabs to reduce the scarring, but then he would wake and know that he had been hearing a memory, either in sleep or madness.

He could not detect whether it was summer or whether the leaves had fallen, or even if winter had arrived to cover the earth in white blankets, for he was in turns too hot, and then too cold and, in those times of extremes, soft but pressing hands would lay poultices that smelled of the lady's mantle plant on his forehead and, he thought, somewhere else, for he had the sensation of being turned, but he did not know whose hands they were, only that he was sure they were not Arianwen's. Then he felt scared, and muttered, "She is the most skilled healer. She should be here." But whoever was tending him only told him to hush and save his strength.

Then he began to discern night from day and felt the sun's warmth as it pushed through the shutters. He knew that it was late in the year, for the yellow light was soft and came from low in the sky. He was more often awake now. He knew that the gentle hands belonged to Carena, and he understood that one or more of the wounds from the battle had festered at some point. He began to sleep untroubled by dreams, and to feel hunger before his bowls of broth were brought to his bed. As if stepping from a fog into brilliant light, he left the world of fever-madness and came back to the sights, sounds, and smells of the world of the healthy.

Strong enough to sit up and feed himself now, he was blessed with frequent visits from Heaferth and Immin, who encouraged him to build up his strength by arm-wrestling with them. Gradually, with their help, he was able to stand up and begin to move around the bower. Immin pronounced him hideous enough to frighten the children, and Heaferth made recurrent references to all the Northumbrians who would one day pay for what they'd done to his lord, and Ethelred realised that, although he felt markedly better, he was still little more than rattling bones, with a limp that might never leave him.

"We did not see it at first," Heaferth had told him as they sat with him one morning, "But the erm, scuffs where Lord Merchelm dragged you, well they, they turned into open sores and went bad."

Immin said, "Not that your arse was overly pretty before. Shame the elf-shot spread down your leg though."

"I have one good leg still to kick you with." Ethelred smiled and laid his head back on the pillow. It was not so much his backside, he now knew, but his hip and outer thigh which had been scraped raw, but that did not stop the playful remarks. At least he was still alive. Now to get to the practice yard and build up his strength properly.

With that in mind, he asked Heaferth to go and prepare some sacks for him to hack with his sword, and his faithful hearth-thegn nodded and left the bower. In moments he was back, twisting his tunic hem in his hands. "My lord, your mother. Lady Derwena..."

Ethelred sat up, eased his legs over the side of the bed and reached for his breeches. Immin, thinking swiftly, already had them in his hands and gave them to him, fetching his tunic while he dragged them on. He waited with Ethelred's belt while he pulled the tunic on, and had his boots ready for him before the belt was buckled, though it needed tightening more than it used to.

Ethelred hobbled out, ignoring the faint throbbing in his head and willing his legs to work properly. He'd made stupidly slow progress towards Derwena's bower when

Heaferth came to walk alongside him, hand cupping his elbow. "No, my lord, she is down by her tree."

Not ill in bed then. So why was Heaferth so concerned? As he approached the woods on the other side of the fields beyond the settlement, he saw immediately that his mother was in distress.

Derwena was sitting on the ground, her back against the tree trunk. She was as still as a corpse, the only movement that proved she was alive being the tears trickling down her face. She seemed not to be aware of them and made no attempt to dry her cheeks or wipe her nose.

"How long has she been like this?"

Heaferth, standing behind him, said, "She was seen by the shepherd when he came out of his hut at dawn, but it was a while ere anyone thought aught was amiss. Your mother has often-times sat here while you have been unwell."

Ethelred nodded, and Heaferth left them alone. Derwena had not acknowledged his presence but Ethelred bent his good leg, reached and cleared a patch among the fallen acorns, then eased himself down beside her. He took her cold hand in his.

She did not turn to look at him, but after a while, she spoke. "I came to this old oak with your father, when I had to tell him that Carena and Alfrid wished to wed, and he hit the tree with his fists. Did you know he'd first met me when I was sitting under such an oak? No? Anyway, this time he was wroth, and I told him they loved one another. Then he let her go away, and it nearly broke us apart."

He looked across the glade and saw the plump berries on the bittersweet now covered with bush crickets in a feeding frenzy. Years as well as seasons had moved on since Arianwen spotted the bittersweet blossoms in Wenlock and spoke of returning to them in the autumn. Stroking Derwena's hand, he said, "It is too late in the year for you to be out here. Why do you think of these things now?"

"It took so many years to build. Our love, our children, his kingship. Penda did not seek to be an overlord; they came to him. Men you will not recall, like Lothar, and Berengar, and Elidyr of Elmet: all were united in their rage against the Northumbrians, though your father had his own scores to settle, for those northern kings hurt his kin. And they still do."

"That is why Wulf has fought on."

She turned to look at him then, and he was shocked by the deep grief he saw on her face. "But do you not see? It is happening all over again. I thought it would all be gone now, buried alongside those who began it. Penda marched with all the southern kingdoms under his banner, and he was killed. Wulf gathered all the smaller kingdoms under his own banner, yet he lost. You were hurt and we did not know if you would live. I do not want to have been freed from that tiny room in Whitby, with the foul salt air and the ugly bird calls, only to see my sons die ere I do. Every mother knows her sons might fall in battle, but I never thought it would be that same feud, the one that took your father from me, that lost me my sons years later. I did not weep while you were sick but now, I cannot help it."

He put his free hand up and gathered her to him, allowing her to rest her head upon his shoulder. "We have failed you."

She took in a long, ragged breath. "No. Pay me no heed. These are merely the tears I should have wept when they first brought you home on the bier. You have none of you failed me."

"How can you say that? Oswii died in his bed, Ecgfrith has taken Lindsey once more, and Cynwal died but not by Wulf's hand."

"Ah, my sweet son. You have all done me proud and your father's name lives on, for do not the scops still sing of him? Oswii died in his bed, aye, but not before Wulf had

241

overthrown him, and Cynwal spent his whole life on the run after he put your aunt Audra aside. He might have thought himself safe when your father died but Wulf saw to it that he never again slept with both eyes shut. That is enough."

"But we are still not free."

"Hmmph. Hide the tribute; that is what I did." She sat up and looked him in the eye once more. "First, though, you must rest. Do not anger the elves further by not taking care of yourself. Eat well, do not drink too much. Build your strength back up or the elves will fire more arrows at you." He tried to dismiss her concerns, but she took his face in her hands. "You must get strong again but swear to me. Swear that if and when you become king, you will only ride out and fight if it is to right a wrong."

He covered her hands with his own, and gently took them from his cheeks. "I cannot speak of being king, for that would mean wishing my brother harm." He leaned back against the tree, willing his head to stop pounding and wondering what had truly upset his mother. "Besides, why are you speaking of such things? What has been happening while I have been abed all this time?"

In the winter silence, snow fell, none but the most essential work was done, and folk huddled in their huts and halls. Hearth fires had called the weary and the excited, as both old and young sheltered from the weather and more snow came, falling on the thick blanket and reminding the world to remain hushed. Never was the sense of belonging, and security within the hall, so acute as in midwinter. Children were given watered ale, for the animals were dry over winter and there was no milk, and they drank it as they peered through the gaps in the shutters, clamouring to go out to find badger tracks, or to spot the tail tips of otherwise white stoats.

The Iclingas celebrated Yule at Tamworth, having

gathered there before the land turned white. Wulf wished to speak to Ethelred who was still, according to the leeches, too unwell to ride. The king of Mercia paced the hall, stretching his long legs and flexing his arms. Ethelred watched him, thinking that should they ever capture a wolf, this would be exactly how the trapped animal would behave. Wulf was angry; he had no bodily wounds to lick, but his pride was bruised, his status was damaged, and in the stillness of the white winter he had no way of releasing his body, or his mind.

With the snowmelt, the settlement came back to life, as did the world at large, and the screeching calls of mating foxes echoed from the woodland. Folk fetching onions and garlic from the stores no longer needed to don their fur cloaks to cross the yard. Wulf stared out at the diminishing snow, watching it recede and proclaiming his wish that it go as swiftly as the tide went out at the end of the lands of the Meonwara.

Ethelred should have known. Derwena had sensed it, and that was why she had been so upset. She knew Wulf much better than his younger brother did, perhaps because it was Wulf who was so much more like their father. Wulf needed to gather his strength, rein the smaller kingdoms in, fetch them back under his banner. He wanted the men of Tamworth, wished to have Heaferth ride with him, and as soon as he was able, he called Merwal and Merchelm too, for another march into the lands of the West Saxons. Derwena watched the men ride out through the gate with a sad, strange look in her eyes, one which her youngest son had thought a mixture of pride and terror.

They all came home, but it had been another defeat. Mercia's grip on both north and south had been loosened, and this time it was Wulf who was brought home on a bier. The lifelong anger that refused to be quenched had led him beyond the shield wall, a moment of blind courage that had

243

left the West Saxon warlord dead but his deputies bent on swift retribution. For sixty days Wulf wandered the worlds, sometimes on earth, sometimes speaking to God, but not in words that anyone else could fully understand. His wound, a deep gash running from shoulder to hip, was bathed and bound, dried red nettle made into poultices, and dried parsley was pounded into butter, mixed with holy water, and applied to the wound.

On the sixty-first day, the hearth-troops and tribe leaders of Mercia bowed before their king and gave thanks for his life. And as they hailed King Ethelred, Derwena's howls echoed from the forest.

Chapter Eleven

Tamworth AD676: Spring

The sunshine took the edge off the cool breeze, but summer was still a long way off. Ethelred's wedding attire was warm; even though the hawthorns were blossoming, bumble bees were making their first forays for nesting sites and the fields were full of bleating lambs, the sun still dipped out of the sky in early evening at this time of year. As soon as they moved from sun to shadow, he would be glad of his coat of blue wool, crossed over at the contrasting edges of grey that were themselves lined with a colourful embroidered band, and of his madder-dyed cloak, held at his throat by a gold and garnet clasp. He wore new leg bindings, the same red as his cloak, and his hand knife hung from his belt in a new leather scabbard.

His bride was similarly warmly dressed, with a paler red crossover coat over her sage green kirtle. Two bands of coloured glass beads at her throat were of differing lengths and, sitting between them, was her brooch of white enamel and blue glass. Her hair was covered with a simple veil. She looked uncomfortable wearing clothes more Mercian in style than those of the land of her birth, and he noticed that her hands were shaking.

Merchelm was beside him, dressed in a dark red tunic. His beard was neatly trimmed, but a curl of hair which had been wetted down kept springing up. In all the solemnity, the painful absence of so many friends and kin, amid all the doubts that he was doing the right thing, Ethelred couldn't help twitching a smile every time Bertilda motioned from the other side of the yard and Merchelm's hand went up to

245

his head to stick the offending curl back down again.

Derwena, her head uncovered as always, stood with wisps of grey hair blowing in the breeze. She made no attempt to hide the tears and Ethelred tried to keep his gaze elsewhere rather than look upon her. Even so, their recent exchange of words bounced round his head.

This will not end well. It should not have been agreed.

Why not? Because she is not Mercian? You are not Mercian either and that did not matter to my father. He was happy to let Carena marry Alfrid. And for Pieter to marry Ava.

And look how that turned out. I argued with him, because I did not want my daughter going so far away. Even though they loved each other I was worried. It was the only thing he and I ever fought about, and it brought me no gladness to be proved right. You do not even love this girl.

I do not even know her, so you are right about that. I was given no say in this, none at all. You know I barely remember Father, don't you? I can hardly recall anything that happened before the night I thought I saw Oswii kill you. And all I have seen since then is bloodshed, blood feud, blood... He had stopped when he thought of what he had seen in the south. *Father went up against the Northumbrians and lost. Wulf went up against them and lost. What makes you think that I can win? Perhaps this might be the better way, at least for now?*

For whom? Carinna, Audra, Carena, Ava: all suffered heartbreak after leaving their homes, but they had their love to keep them strong. This young woman does not even have that.

Then I will make sure that she is treated with kindness at the very least. And in his heart, he knew that was the most he could offer, for there was one in that group whose fate had not been quite the same, and his mother's last comment was heavy with double meaning.

Derwena remained outside the chapel, not too proud to accept the chair which had been fetched from the hall. She'd seen sixty-seven summers and earned the right to bow to no one, yet still Ethelred was relieved to enter the chapel and be out of her disapproving presence for a while.

He had not lied when he said he'd been given no choice, for the alternative was another battle and neither he, nor Mercia, had the strength. The wedding had been forced upon him but he was not worried for himself; after all, love had not been kind to him thus far in his life anyway but, like his own sister Starling, this bride had been sent to her husband as no more than a symbol of her brother's authority, and she would be frightened and upset, especially since none of her kin had made the journey with her. He turned to her and said, "I am truly sorry that the matters of men have brought you here against your wishes."

Lady Ositha looked up at him and stared for a moment, as if taking in every detail of his face. "Oh no, I welcomed the betrothal. I am here of my own free will."

The chapel here was made of wood, not stone, and the interior was warmer and brighter, with larger window openings which must, she thought, make the place colder in winter. Sweet smelling herbs had been strewn on the floor, and the sign of the cross was everywhere, from wooden replicas on the altar, to paintings on the walls. At least these folk were now mostly god-fearing. Ecgfrith would be surprised.

You'll go willingly? Good God, Elfwin said you would not like the thought.

Of a husband? I have been asking you long enough for one. Granted, it had not been the offer from the young Kentish king, but it was a king, nevertheless, and at least not of the Picts. If she had to be a peace-weaver, at least she would be warm.

Yes, but those heathen Mercians… Well, no matter. It is agreed, Penda's whelp will take you, not that I gave him any choice. I have

247

*weakened the bastards, and I shall stamp them further into the
ground, but first I shall have a little fun with them, and you will put
your skills to use.*

She'd not said yes or no to that part, only thinking that at
last, for better or worse, she would have something,
someone, of her own. At least to begin with, for Ositha was
no fool and she knew that she was being sent as weaver of a
peace that Ecgfrith had no intention of honouring. This was
merely his way of keeping the Mercians down, not a
promise to leave them alone. She was pleased to go, curious
to see what would unfold, the only wrench being that of
having to leave Elfwin behind.

As the priest intoned in Latin, she took the opportunity to
look again upon her new husband's face. She gazed for
longer than was perhaps decent, but she was still taken
aback by his beauty. Standing beside him she could not quite
see the soft hazel eyes, but she could see the line of his long
nose, his cheek framed by the curls of light brown hair, and
the side of his mouth raised in an expression of what looked
to be a genuinely kind smile. Ecgfrith made no secret of his
wish that her story would be the same as Ava's, but Ava had
wed for love, whereas Ositha was being bundled off to wed
a stranger, which should make the killing easier. Yet now
that she was here and looking up at her husband, she could
only wonder why God had chosen to bestow such richness
upon her. This man might make a fine husband indeed.
Time spent garnering information to send back before – if –
she took her knife to him, would be rather pleasant.

Walking from the chapel to the hall, she thought once
more about her new surroundings. Much was familiar, with
cooking done outside now the weather was warmer, and the
quern stones outside the bake house were the same as the
ones used at home to grind grain into flour. Many of the
sounds were the same, with the clanging of metal from the
forge and the scrunch and squeaks from the basket-weavers,

248

who wove osier rods onto wooden bases in exactly the same way. Much, though, was not like home. She could not hear the sea, only the running of the river where the water all went in the same direction, so there was no whooshing of the ebb and flow of waves. The birds were small, and mainly of hues of brown, not the white and black she was used to seeing circling the rocks at Bamburgh. The air smelled wrong.

Something else was odd, too. Granted, it was a wedding day, but even so, all the folk were smiling and happy, as if they loved, rather than feared, their lord. Since her father's day, folk at all the royal Northumbrian residences had walked with heads bowed and shoulders hunched, and approached the king with trepidation. She caught herself then, realising that she also rarely lifted her mouth. She must remember always to smile, else the Mercians would think her a sour-faced hag.

Her husband led her to the dais in the hall, a building decorated much the same way as her brother's, with depictions of beasts with curling tails, plant motifs, and spiralling patterns on the upright timbers and on the chairs. Before they took their seats, they stood in front of the table, and she expected his household and hearth-troops to present themselves. She could never hope to learn who they all were, and prepared to listen intently and repeat their names back to them.

Apart from Lady Tette who, she'd been told the previous day, was to be her waiting-woman now that she no longer served Lady Ermenilda, none but her husband's kin came formally to the dais. Ositha thought it must be an insult, their way of showing that she was a hated Northumbrian, but Ethelred said softly, "It would be too much for you." It was no slight, but a kindness to her, a nervous stranger.

She endeavoured then to familiarise herself with his close kin and their names, and she focused her attention on them.

249

His sisters, she knew, were in holy orders, and all looked like Carena, but with varying degrees of darker or lighter hair and eye colouring and their mother must once have looked the same; perhaps Ethelred's other brothers had been similar. All the siblings had shared the same mother, and all but one the same father. Was that why they seemed so close-knit, unlike her own father's brood?

The food – roasted kid, soft cheeses and pottage flavoured with fresh spring herbs – was brought in and was tasty enough. They cooked in the same way, although the lack of saltwater fish reminded her once again how far she was from the sea. She had to ask what they were and, in her view, this eel and perch were far less superior to herring or sturgeon. The ale had a slightly different flavour but was still recognisable as ale. The riddles from the scop were much as she would hear back home, though far less lewd, but here there was dancing, too.

No, she realised, this kin group was not tightly bonded because of shared parentage, because also present were cousins and nieces and nephews, and they were genuinely happy in each other's company. Loyalty to the lord, sense of community, coming together to share happiness: all these were lacking in her homeland, where feasts were rare and not as homely. Here, they didn't even seem to adhere to the social rules, but leaders of various tribes sat with their men on lower tables instead of all the noblemen sitting together nearer the dais. No one was shouting, except to make themselves heard.

The royal kin and their closest companions were all laughing and smiling, nudging one another, and passing jugs of ale across the tables and taking turns to ensure that Lady Derwena was comfortable, plumping the cushion at her back and ensuring that her plate and cup were always filled. Ositha wanted to be part of it all, at the same time wishing she could shrink back against the wall and remain where she felt safest, in the shadows.

She drank too much. All her life she had wanted to be noticed, but now she found that the constant glances in her direction, the unexpected smiles of and shouts of "Be hale!" made her cheeks hot. She hid as much of her face as she could behind her ale cup and accepted every offered refill.

They discussed recent news from King Wulfhere's widow, Lady Ermenilda, who had retired to a monastery in the kingdom of her birth, but then the talk turned to reminiscing about Ermenilda's wedding, and how her Kentish kin had come to witness the occasion. Attention then turned to the lady called Domneva, who spoke wistfully of her brothers, and Ethelred said, "Dear Domneva, were I to live until I'd seen one hundred summers, I would still not be able to tell your brothers one from the other!"

They laughed then, and began recalling other visits from friends and family, and Ositha wondered whether she would have felt less like a duck in a dairy had any of her own kin attended her wedding. She dismissed the idea immediately; it was clear that they bore her, an innocent woman, no ill will, but she doubted that Ecgfrith would have been a welcome guest at their table.

Colmán, Elwyn's replacement, had accompanied her to her new home and was seated on another table, not engaging, nor being engaged, in conversation. As she thought of Ecgfrith and his instructions to her before she left, she looked again at the people with whom she must now live. They were mourning the death of their king, the Northumbrians had taken almost everything from them, and yet they accepted her into their midst. She had embraced this union, considering it her birthright to leave home and wed a king, but surely Ethelred hadn't?

It couldn't have been easy for him to accept a bride foisted on him by his foe. Had these people no pride? Were

251

they stupid? One of the sisters caught her staring and smiled at her with such warmth that Ositha looked away, confused. Was it guilt, on her part? She knew what she had been sent to do, but they had no idea. Perhaps the welcome was genuine after all; she had never come across such open-heartedness. Only one person, the thegn she thought was named Heaferth, glowered at her whenever she glanced his way and, though it was not pleasant, it was less difficult to understand. Besides, scowls did not bother her; she'd grown up knowing little else.

Mercifully, the merriment died down, the children were put to bed, and the trestle tables, moved to allow the dancing, were now being folded and placed against the walls, and folk were laying claim to the benches and spaces on the floor nearest the hearth to bed down for the night. Ositha felt light-headed and hoped that she would not have to step out into the night air, for it would surely cause her to spew. She prayed that all she had to do was move with her husband to the curtained chamber at the back of the hall and then... Well, and then she would become his wife in bed as well as in life. She laid a hand on his arm to get his attention and nodded towards the curtain. "Is that...?"

He turned and smiled at her. "My father made the hall bigger and I used to sleep in one of the bowers, but there is space enough here, so I have had wall hangings put up and a bed built behind the farthest one. Shall we?"

An oozing sensation slid down from her heart into her belly, as if she had swallowed a spoonful of honey. It made her warm inside but also left her tingling. They were in the short passageway separating the main hall from the sleeping chamber when someone called out the word "Noni." Strange, for she had the feeling this person was addressing her husband, but that was not his name.

Sure enough though he turned, and she carried on for a few more steps, reaching her hand up to draw back the second curtain, intending to go into the room to make herself ready for what was about to happen, wondering if she would now have to wait for some time while folk continued to offer their warm wishes to the Lord Ethelred. She half-turned and saw that it was just one man standing there, the one she thought was his nephew, Merchelm of the Magonsæte. He made a few remarks, as expected, about the wedding and offered his thoughts on the day's festivities. She stroked the embroidered curtain, feeling the small, smooth stitches and wondering how that particular shade of green dye had been produced. It was pale, so perhaps they used gale leaves here, too.

"And the bride's kirtle was lovely, Bertilda bade me be sure to say that again."

Ethelred's response was a low, rumbling chuckle. "And you wish to return home with both balls still attached, so would not dare forget!"

Both men laughed and Ositha, still staring at the embroidery, smiled. Perhaps these Mercians were every bit as crude as those in her homeland after all. Their mirth subsided, and the shuffling of soft leather on the floor indicated that Merchelm had moved off. Ositha moved into the chamber, but now there was another voice, female. Carena.

"Brother, I know I have said it ere now, but it must be said again. She has not had a loving childhood. It will be hard for her and we must..."

The words fell away to a whisper and Ositha turned and pressed her cheek against the material to listen without being seen. It did no good; Ethelred's answer came through to her as naught but a soft mumble, and it struck her that he, in fact, had a quiet way of speaking generally and this would not help if she were to succeed in her task of hearing Mercian secrets. For now though, the tears stung her eyes. Carena had made it clear that the welcome for Oswii's

253

unloved daughter had been driven by little more than pity. The warm feeling that had slid down like honey now came back up to burn her throat.

There was a knock on the timber, Ositha lifted the hanging, and her bones jumped inside her skin as she found herself face to face with Tette, her waiting-woman. Ositha's eyes might be wet but her mouth was dry, and no lie came forth to explain why she was loitering right by the curtain.

"Is there aught I can help you with, Lady Ositha?" Tette was smiling, hands clasped in front of her belly. "Would you like me to comb your hair?"

Her heart was still hammering, but Ositha managed to remember to smile and then, determined that she must not make them think she was deserving of their pity or in need of any aid, she said, "No, thank you."

Tette's expression was unreadable, but as she retreated, Ethelred appeared and the two exchanged glances. Ositha suspected that the unspoken message was not complimentary.

The sun was pushing daylight through the shutters and she could see the warm orange glow through her closed lids. Ositha could sense even without opening her eyes that she was alone and, for the time being, she did not mind. She could also tell without moving that when she did, her head would begin to throb, for she was not used to drinking ale in such large amounts. Still, her drunkenness had helped her get through the night and now, alone, she had time to recall how she had become a wife and was no longer a maiden. None of it had hurt, all of it was gentle, and he had snuffed all the candles to spare her blushes. She let the tears fall down the outside of her cheeks and felt them wet her hair as they trickled round to the back of her neck, for she knew it was a mixture of kindness and pity that had driven such consideration. Had she expected a love match, such as

Alfrid and Carena had made? No, but nor had she expected to find her husband so lovely to gaze upon.

And if you get the chance, here is a little knife. Colmán will get you away swiftly, after. Could she do her brother's bidding? Oh, she could listen round corners and from behind curtains, but murder? She was not sure she even wished to; she'd seen what had become of Ava. Ositha could see no advantage for herself. In fact, she could have a life here, free from the demands of others. She sat up and wiped her face. She might have arrived as a mere token of peace between Mercia and Northumbria, but she would not be pitied. Whether or not she was capable of killing, she could not do it immediately and so she had to find a way to make life bearable, and that meant transforming pity, and kindness, into genuine friendship and, perhaps, love. She was the daughter of the most wily king who ever ruled. She could make people love her, surely?

Dressing quickly, used to doing so by herself, she walked through the hall scarred with evidence of the previous night's celebration. The floor had been swept and all plates, pitchers and cups taken away, but on more than one of the benches, snoring figures remained, and the stench of fart and spilled ale was overpowering. At the doorway, she took a gulp of air, found it disappointing for there was no fresh sea breeze, and strode out into the yard where, for a heartbeat or two, she had difficulty locating her husband, for there were men, women, horses, and carts blocking the view from the hall to the stables. Folk were chattering, the horses nickered as the stable-hands attended to them, and servants loading up the carts talked cheerfully amongst themselves.

The sisters who were abbesses and were impossible to tell apart, were already seated on the front of the carts, and Lady Derwena was holding the hand of one of them, as if she did not want them to leave. Merchelm was also ready to depart

255

and was helping his wife up into the saddle. When she was settled, he mounted his own horse and, once comfortably astride, turned the beast and called out to Ethelred, who came bounding over from the huddle of folk who'd been fighting for his embrace.

If she stepped forward to thank them all for coming, would they appreciate it, or would they ignore her? If she went to stand meekly next to her husband, would he stand with his arm around her, or would he carry on making his farewells on his own? While Ositha was rooted to the spot, unable to make up her mind, Lady Derwena shuffled towards her, leaning heavily on her stick. The older woman came to stand beside her and said, "It always breaks my heart to see them go. Will your mother miss you?"

Ositha heard no warmth in the other woman's tone, but it was no real surprise. How could they ever speak freely knowing what Oswii had done? She thought it best to answer lightly. "No, when I came south she had already left to take holy orders at Whitb…" Her hand went to her mouth in a tardy and futile attempt to stop the word slipping out.

Derwena did not turn, but stared straight ahead. "That place always stinks. Of fish," she added, as if another insult had been lurking in between somewhere.

Ositha stood silently, wishing she could catch her words and stuff them back into her mouth.

The older woman shifted position, using her stick to help her pivot so that she was able to look Ositha in the eye. "I shall speak plainly, if I may? Your father killed my husband, by treachery, and for that I hoped the crows would pick his bones while he still lived. He kept me locked up in an abbey, knowing that I have no belief in the Christ god, and he let my children think I was dead."

Ositha nodded, mute.

Derwena continued, with a softer tone. "Does this mean

that I hate you? You might think so. I knew your brother when he was small, and I cared for him like one of my own. He was a sweet child, but my guess is that he is not a sweet man. All that said, I will treat you as I would treat any woman wed to one of my sons and I would only hate you if you gave me reason."

Ositha blinked back tears, her resolve melting. Derwena had no idea that as far as Ecgfrith was concerned, she was here to do as much harm as she could. The Mercians might not blame her for what her father had done, but they none of them knew what it was like to be his daughter, to be Ecgfrith's sister, always seeking approval. They thought her innocent, but she could not escape her lineage. She would always be Oswii's daughter and she would need to do more than simply not murder their king to make them forget that. She glanced across at the little wooden chapel and reminded herself that she was also Oswald's niece. Later, she would pray to him and ask for guidance.

As Derwena left her side to say farewell to another group, Ositha stood and looked at her new husband. The love that all his folk felt for him was plain to see. Men slapped him on the back, women hugged him, and the children wrapped their arms round his legs. She continued to watch as one young girl – Ositha had not worked out whose child she was – clung fast to his legs while he let her stand on his feet. He walked with her, perched thus, over to the next party of well-wishers. Ositha let the tears fall unchecked; she'd done that with Elfwin.

She knew what she had to do, knew exactly what to say to persuade them all that she was not the enemy, but was exactly like them. Wiping briskly at her face, she marched up to Ethelred and said, "I have another brother."

He turned, peeled the child from his legs gently, and handed her back to her mother. Flashing what looked like a silent apology at his guests, he said with questioning tone,

"We should have been welcoming, had any of your kin sent word that they wished to witness the wedding."

Oh, God in Heaven, he thought she was complaining that her brother had not attended. Would she make such mistakes every time she opened her mouth? She had only sought to remind them that Ecgfrith was not the only Northumbrian man. "Yes, I know, I mean to say, that is not... He is a sweet boy. I wonder if you would allow him to ride here, bide a while? It would be a comfort for me to have a friendly..."

"Friendly?" Now he was looking at her sharply. "Have you not been made to feel at home? That saddens me. Yes, speak to Heaferth and we will send word for your brother to come."

He moved off towards the hall and she stayed in the yard, listening to the sound of the carts moving off, and the fading chatter, and wondering whether she had won or lost the day.

Ethelred rubbed the space at the bridge of his nose with his middle finger, attempting to massage the headache away. Who had gone against his orders to treat his new wife with kindness, and to welcome her to the fold? He had said for many years that it was not his fight, not his blood feud, but he had still paid a high price for it. He had not wanted to be king; he would have stood as regent for Cenred but his counsellors would hear naught of it, wanting a proven warrior at the head of Mercia in such challenging times. Heaferth had perhaps been the most vociferous, arguing against the wedding and pushing for a rebellion. *Immin, Edbert and I did it for your brother, and Immin and I can do it for you. There is no need to bring this woman here, no need to bend the way Ecgfrith tells us to.* The mention of Edbert had kicked Ethelred anew, for he'd died protecting his beloved lord, Wulf.

258

He sat on the new bed, its ash laths and leather webbing creaking under his weight, where only hours before he had committed an act of faith and also betrayal. He'd lain with his love outside in daylight so many times that, last night, he had blown out the candles to make the scene as different as possible for him, but the darkness had served only to hide his true feelings from his bride. He'd been a fool to think he could forget. He looked at Ositha's wedding garments lying on the floor, and immediately thought how Arianwen would have picked them up, quietly and without fuss. Clearly his wife was used to servants attending her, day and night.

His life had changed, and there was no going back. If the feud was not his, then surely it was not Ositha's either, and he must do what he could to be fair to her. His mother's words rang in his head again. *They had their love to keep them strong. This young woman does not even have that.* Indeed, she was not a bride in love, and she was far from her home, but if Ava could be talked into killing a man she loved, what would a woman do who had no feelings for her husband? Ethelred remained convinced, like Derwena, that Ecgfrith was not as evil as his father had been, but even so, he had promised he would take steps. *She has not had a loving childhood. It will be hard for her and we must treat her kindly but Brother, never forget that she is Ecgfrith's sister, Oswii's daughter. Keep a man always at your back.* Carena had spoken thus before he'd gone to his chamber last night. Caution would ever be the watchword, but they must never condemn for suspicion alone.

A cough on the other side of the curtain made him turn, and Immin's voice came softly, "Lord?"

Ethelred stood up, making a half-hearted attempt to smooth the bedcovers as he did so. "Yes?"

Immin drew back the curtain but did not step forward. It was unspoken, but it was there. This was no ordinary new chamber; it was the room where the king and his queen now slept. "Penwal, Heaferth, and Osric of the Hwicce have not yet ridden out, and they would gather for a moot."

Nodding, Ethelred said loudly, "Where? The hall is a little, er, ragged, this morning."

Immin winked and said clearly, "At the old tump, where your father used to hold the moot."

They walked through the hall together, and Ethelred acknowledged his wife, who was sitting with his mother. It was not a situation that any of them would have wished for, but he knew that Derwena, if anyone, would open her heart to yet another Northumbrian stray. She, perhaps more than any of them, had refused to blame Oswii's children for his wrongdoing. Still, there was no harm in taking precautions and the deceptions were sweetened by the fact that Ositha seemed pleased.

She thought the new sleeping chamber had been made especially for her, and did not need to know that it had been done deliberately so that there was no room in the hall for moots, which could be conducted at the tump again, away from listening ears. She'd been relieved when he told her so few names, but he'd merely been ensuring that she had no idea how many of the tribes and sub-kingdoms of the Mercian federation had gathered for the wedding.

Out beyond the grove of Thunor's temple, the ground was soft from recent rain, though the dampness could not smother the strong smell of fox. A fledgling mistle thrush was perched on an old tree stump and behind it, the cheerful blooms of red campion swayed in the gentle breeze. Penwal, Heaferth and Osric, each with a handful of their own thegns and hearth-troops, were waiting for them, and whilst their expressions were not stony, neither were they smiling.

Penwal, his shoulder against a tree, nodded in reverence. "You know we are steadfast. I serve you as I once served your brother. But we have worries; worries that cannot be washed away with bride ale." He gestured towards Osric of the Hwicce, who stepped forward to stand with his own men behind him. Ethelred did not know this successor to King Enfrith especially well, but the man had pledged loyalty and that was enough.

Osric said, "Lord, the rain has been too heavy this year, and has come too often."

Crops and cattle; the tribute owed to Northumbria. Ethelred offered the only comfort that he could. "Most of the tribute will go from Tamworth and other Iclinga settlements. I will ask for less from each of the tribes and smaller kingdoms. For the time being, there is little else that can be done."

Penwal peeled away from the tree trunk. "Perhaps it is not for us to speak of it, but we know that the cost of peace was your wedding and that it was a high price. We would not press you, but we do not see how this Northumbrian bride will put grain in our barns or food in the bellies of our folk."

Now Heaferth spoke. "We should fight the bastard. There'll be no freedom for Mercia until the Northumbrian turd is dead."

Ethelred sighed. The headache was back. "We are not strong enough. Wulf had the whole of the southern kingdoms under his yoke, willing or not, but it was not enough. We also lost many men in Lindsey last year, as well as those who fell with my brother." What could they do? It came to him, then, in a heartbeat. *Hide the tribute. That's what I did.* "So, meanwhile we must do what we can, and not dwell on that which we cannot. Penwal, you have brothers with sons, yes? And Osric, you have many monks already at your abbey at Gloucester. Let all who ride under the Mercian banner know what must be done. Weapons must be forged; boys must be taught. Any man who thinks to send his sons to the abbeys to be monks or priests, must

261

not, but teach them instead to wield a sword, an axe, a spear. I know we cannot fight on empty bellies, but we must do what we can. Our women will find a way to eke the food out. Not all of the tribute will reach the north. We will find ourselves prey to cattle thieves, or so Ecgfrith will hear, anyway. We will build our strength back up, and I will forge new links with the rest of the southern kingdoms." Not with the bloodshed that defined Wulf's reign. There was no need for that, he was sure. "What do you think?" He took a deep breath, and then closed his mouth. He had never spoken so much, even at a moot.

They were silent and he was not surprised. He was asking them to train boys to fight, and to do it whilst going hungry. *What do you think?* Damn, he should not be so weak as to ask them. Wulf would not have done such a thing.

Heaferth was the first to speak. "It is as you say, Lord. It is all that can be done, and we have done it before, so we will do it well."

He smiled with relief. "There is one more thing we can do."

"Yes, Lord?"

"We can pray. Heaferth, if anyone wishes to know where I am, tell them I will be in the chapel."

As he made his way back to the hall, wondering what he would say to his wife, he noticed a rider rushing back in through the gate even while more guests were leaving. "Merchelm?" Suddenly his heart was leaping, beating furiously. "Why are you back?" He ran to his nephew who, at the same time, dismounted and strode to meet him.

"It's Father," he gasped. "On the road, only a short while after we left. He fell from his steed, but Lady Domneva said he clutched at his chest before he slipped from the saddle." He bent down, with his hands on his thighs, and breathed quickly through an open mouth.

The men from the hastily convened moot were strolling

262

back up from the woods. Ethelred called to them. "Penwal! Find an empty cart and follow me as soon as you can. Along the Leominster road." He shouted to his reeve, who was in conversation with Ositha. The outlining of duties would have to wait. "A drink for Lord Merchelm." He ran to the stables and ordered his horse saddled, and waited impatiently, curbing the urge to curse when the horse-thegn fumbled with the buckles on the saddle straps.

After what felt like too long a time, he and Merchelm arrived at the point on the road where Merwal had fallen. Domneva had arranged for him to be placed on a blanket, and was seated with her legs curled under her, cradling his head in her lap. She was calm, but her cheeks, darkened with dirt from the road, showed two clean lines where tears had streaked down. "He has gone," she said.

Ethelred and Merchelm dismounted and knelt on the ground beside her. Merchelm began to sob, and Ethelred's throat closed so tightly that the pain burned.

"He was an old man," Domneva said. "God has called him." She looked at Ethelred. "Is it a sin that I wished for more time, even though I have been blessed to live so many years with him?"

He shook his head. He could not speak, and would not try. He looked up at the girls, her beautiful daughters, all sitting at the front of the cart they'd been riding in, faces pale, hands in their laps. They were not weeping, but their lips were trembling, and his heart broke to see them trying to be strong for their mother's sake. The greenish flowers of the black bryony were bobbing in the hedgerow. How fitting that he should notice this poisonous plant on this darkest of days.

Penwal came with the empty cart and he, Ethelred and Merchelm lifted Merwal's body onto it, Domneva slipping the blanket onto the wooden boards just before they placed him down.

Ethelred touched a hand to Penwal's shoulder. "I know you are keen to be home with your wife and daughter, but I have one more boon to beg. Please ride back to Tamworth and tell Heaferth I will not be home for a while and that he must look to Lady Ositha and ensure she has all she needs. And…" he paused, waiting for the threatened sob to subside, "Please bring my mother back with you."

How much more could she endure? He might have expected his mother's heart to shatter but, somehow, she stayed whole. He worried though, that she might decide to end it all; in her belief system there would be no Hell after such a death. She had greeted him upon her arrival at Leominster with the words, "I have lived too long," and he understood that it was not right for mothers to bury sons, when those sons died not of childhood illness or battle wounds, but of old age. Again, she stood outside the chapel while they said prayers for Merwal's soul and when they emerged into the daylight, Ethelred took her hand and helped her walk down to the woods where she could perform her own rites, while he stood at a respectful distance. Father Aldred was disapproving, but Ethelred could not see that God would begrudge this noble old woman a final farewell to her eldest son.

In the hall, Domneva sat in silence as men of the Magonsæte came forward with memories of their lord, praising his battle skills, his wisdom, and his fair hand in all disputes. Ethelred looked at the girls, all of them still wide-eyed and stunned, and wondered what Domneva would do now. After Wulf's death, Ermenilda had taken Werbyra and gone back to Kent, to live the holy life. There was little doubt that Domneva would follow her cousin's example, but it was too soon to ask her of her plans. He was also reminded that he had not yet spoken to his new wife about Cenred, but that would have to wait. The first task was to help Domneva settle things here at Leominster. Would Merchelm make this his main residence, or was he content at Wenlock? There was much to consider, much to discuss, and Ethelred told himself that he would need to bide here for a while. He pushed his boots into the floor as if to root himself to this hall, to this place. He had no desire to go back to Tamworth.

Derwena ate little, pushing the slices of kid meat around her plate and shredding the bread, rolling it into little balls, then lining them up on her plate. Her daughter-by-law had the finest decorated earthenware and Derwena placed the bread balls with precision so that they followed the lines of the patterns. She spoke, softly, but even so it startled him. "You will sink if you do not take the weight off your shoulders."

Even now, in the midst of unspeakable grief, she was thinking of him. He had no response.

"Have you ever thought," she continued, that you argue against your own words? You say it is not your fight, not your feud, that you were too young to remember, yet you seem also to think that it is your duty and yours alone to hold us all together." She stopped playing with her food and put her mottled hand on his. "Go amongst the trees and scream," she said. "It's what I do."

But he did not move. He kept pressing his boots upon the floorboards until he was sure that his feet would not send him running away from the kingship, for he feared that if he fled, he would never come back.

The sound was not a scream. It was more a howl, an animal cry; not one of anger, but pain. It was raw, and it had the power to shred the heart of anyone listening. Ethelred's tunic was wet with the tears, but still he clung on. Holding her, swaddling her, knowing that if he let go, she would shatter into pieces. Domneva had accepted the death of her husband with a forbearance that was to be admired, but this was too much. Ecbert, her young cousin, had reached his maturity. His first act as full king of Kent had been to murder her brothers.

"And Merwal is not here now to avenge it." Derwena had her arms round the two younger girls and, nodding to the eldest, Mildrith, led them all from the hall.

Ethelred watched her go, back bent but gait still strong and even, and he recalled her words to him shortly before Wulf's death. *Swear to me that you will only ride out and fight if it is to right a wrong.* Still holding Domneva in his arms, he spoke over her shoulder to a passing thegn. "Call the moot." Merchelm was on his way from Wenlock and would be here by nightfall. The others would take longer to get to Leominster, but Ethelred needed to act. This killing could not go unpunished.

Penwal, Immin and a few others trickled in over the coming days. Heaferth would not attend for he was guarding Tamworth and the Lady Ositha. Other leaders came, all wanting to pay their respects to Lady Domneva. Ethelred was almost envious to see that she inspired so much love in others, for he had come to think of her as his own. Many of these men had gathered in a matter of days and yet there was still no sign of Merchelm. Ethelred had begun to worry that yet another disaster had befallen them, when news came that he had arrived. Ethelred ran to the gate to greet him and stopped in the yard, stunned as if hit by a rock.

Merchelm had indeed arrived, and had already jumped down from his horse. He had ridden in at the head of a great number of men, and when Ethelred saw who was with him, he understood why it had taken longer than expected for Merchelm to get to Leominster.

Llywarch dismounted and left no time for awkwardness to cloud their reunion, stepping forward to embrace Ethelred.

"It is good to see you, my friend. I am sorry though that it is at such a sad time. I could not stay away, but had to come to pay my respects. I heard only that Merwal had died; Merchelm here rode to meet me and on the way, he told me about the murders."

Over Llywarch's shoulder, Ethelred saw a hooded figure slip from one of the carts and head to the kitchens, but he thought no more of it, for Merchelm had placed a hand on his arm. "My mother is within?"

Ethelred nodded his reply and only belatedly realised that Merchelm considered Domneva to be his true mother now.

Giving Domneva and Merchelm a brief time for embrace, Ethelred waited before entering the hall, and then took what had been Merwal's chair. It would be Merchelm's now, but he needed a moment. He sat for a while, stroking the carvings on the arm rests, recollecting what he could of his half-brother. He'd really only ever known him once he himself had become a man grown, and mostly what came to his mind now was Merwal's wisdom, his calm response to aught that was put in his path, and his deep and abiding love for his wife and children.

The men who represented the various tribes and smaller kingdoms of the Mercian federation were seated on benches, all with drinks either in their hands or on the boards in front of them, but few were drinking. Penwal spoke first. "We had thought to have worries enough, with the Northumbrians sending for our food and cattle. This evil deed in the south has shocked us all. Lady Ermenilda must be distraught that her little brother has slain his own cousins."

There were hushed murmurs of agreement, but no one added anything. Ethelred knew what they were all thinking and that it was beholden to him to speak it aloud. "We do not have the strength to ride into Kent and teach Ecbert a lesson." He looked round the room. All of them were leaders; battle-hardened, proven warriors and men of sound judgement. Yet they looked defeated, staring at their cups, their hands, the floor. "What should we do, do you think?"

They glanced at each other. A few shook their heads but almost more in disbelief than in helplessness.

"What is it? Have I misspoken?"

Merchelm, seated closest to him, took it upon himself to answer. "Not at all, Uncle. It is, well, it is simply that, King Wulfhere did not ever really ask us what we thought. The moots were more the time for him to tell us what we were going to do. Naught wrong in that, but we welcome the chance to give counsel."

Ethelred sat back as if shot by an arrow. Like the sun rising after a long dark night, new light flooded into his world and his eyes saw anew. Years ago, Merwal had assured him that being unlike Wulf did not make him any the less his father's son. He looked across the room to where his mother was sitting, quietly stitching, even though her eyes surely were no longer up to the task. She did not look up, but he knew she sensed his gaze, for she nodded, slowly.

He said, "What then, must we do? We are weakened and I have seen too many grieving widows to ask any of you to send what few men we have. I know that every man who went to Lindsey with us and to the kingdom of the West Saxons with my brother fought fearlessly. I was not well enough to witness the gift-giving afterwards, but I know there were too few who came back to be rewarded thus. Our plan was to build up our strength again, before riding north, if we needed to. We had not thought, as you so rightly say, to have to deal with something so treacherous in the south."

Merchelm coughed and glanced at Llywarch. He said, "Lady Domneva has been a mother to me since I was a small child. There is naught that I would not do for her and her kin. I am not the only one." He looked directly at

Ethelred. "Llywarch here has also always spoken highly of you, Lord King."

Spoken highly? How? He pondered this as Llywarch stood up and said, "Lord Merwal and Lady Domneva were kindness itself to my sister, and I came to pay my respects as soon as word reached us of Lord Merwal's death. But since I am here, and since I now know what other sadness has befallen this great lady and her kin, let me say this: Mercia is weakened, but not for the first time. Nor would it be the first time that Welshmen rode out with Mercians, side by side to right a wrong."

Ethelred was rendered speechless, which mattered little, for the talk was then of strategy, gathering-places, numbers of men, and general preparation.

Llywarch informed them that others from Wales would be willing to ride out under his banner and when the main business of the moot was over, he came to sit by Ethelred and said, "You lived with us as one of our own. You helped get our cattle back, hunted with us, helped mend our roofs and fences. I know, from spending time with you and from what Rhiryd told me, that you are never false. This is why I never believed what we were told, all those years ago." He looked up. "I think you should go to the cook house when we are done here."

Derwena had come back in, holding her hand over the side of her jaw and muttering. "They cannot find me any henbane root," she said. "Not that I have toothache; I simply like to chew it." She sank down into a chair and let go of her cheek. "You know, your father was not young when first he led a warband. He waited while his brother was king, even though that brother was a useless waste of skin. When the time came, men rode under Penda's banner through love for him, because of the man he was. You doubt yourself, and that is truly endearing, but you are more than worthy of wearing the king-helm. See this?" She

269

pointed at her own hand. "Gnarled on one side, smooth on the other. Two sides of the same hand. Your father had two sides and Wulf was like one of them, you the other." It was the same thing that Merwal had told him. Perhaps he should start to believe it. She patted his arm and sat back. "Now find me some henbane ere I shock you with some highly unchristian words."

Chuckling, Ethelred stood up. Were it anyone else, he might have sent a servant out for the plant, but when Derwena issued an order, it was wise to see to it personally. He thought the first place to look, as Llywarch had suggested, would be the cook house. No doubt Domneva had herb stores in a locked box somewhere, but he did not wish to disturb her. He opened the cook house door, lowering his head to step into the room, blinking at the loss of bright light.

There was, oddly, only one person in there, head bent over the bench. He turned to leave.

"Ethelred?"

He stopped in the doorway. The noise from the hall as folk left the moot had made him mishear. He stood for a heartbeat or two, and then stepped outside.

"Noni?"

He turned round. No, it could not be. He closed his eyes, waited, and opened them again. The apparition was still there. "Arianwen." The urge to step forward and hold her in his arms was so strong that he had to tuck his thumbs through his belt and curl his fingers round it. He clung onto the soft leather as if it were a rope thrown to him in a roiling river. If he let go, he would be swept away. He tried to think only of his feet grounded upon the earth and the feel of the embossing under his fingertips.

He'd no need to dredge the depths of his memories to find her. He had never forgotten her face, her smile, those dark eyes, and he did not need to take a step closer to know exactly how her hair, rinsed with a mix of mint and other herbs that he'd never fully identified, would smell. On any given day, he could stop whatever he was doing, close his eyes, and summon her image. Of late, he had been doing so less often, but he had not lost the ability. The vision accompanied him always, wanting only his attention in order to appear before him. The sight of Llywarch had invoked it, of course it had, but he had not expected this. She was here. Not a figment, but here in flesh and spirit, real and touchable. And he did not know what to do.

The room moved a little, his vision disturbed by the tears in his eyes. He was still staring mutely at his lost love, and she was smiling at him in that way she had, that made him feel as if he were made of naught stronger than tallow, that could melt on her command.

"Forgive me," she said, "but I could not stay away at such a time."

If his heart hammered any harder it would leave his chest altogether, and it was taking up so much room that he had to breathe in shallow bursts. He moved his arms and clamped them by his sides, so much did they ache to hold her.

"When my brother heard about Lord Merwal, I had to come, too. He and Lady Domneva were like a mother and father to me. And then to hear whilst we were on the road what had befallen her brothers..."

He nodded. What was there to say?

She said, "It is good that you are here. It is a time for kin to be together."

He made a show of looking past her shoulder. "You have not brought yours with you. Only you and Llywarch rode here?"

She lowered her head and spoke softly. "My sister died last winter. She never fully regained her strength. Bleddyn was beside himself and has gone on pilgrimage."

"I am sorry for the loss of Heledd. She did not have an easy life. But for your care, it would have been worse."

"She was a great comfort to me, too. When you left, I…"

"Where is Dyfrig? Is he with the horses?" The words had rushed from him, anger slipping out in this unguarded moment.

She stepped forward and grasped his hand, setting it tingling. "My love," she said, "I fear that a great wrong has been done, to both of us. Please, will you hear me?"

No, he would not hear her, this woman who broke his heart and left the sharp pieces there to stab his insides whenever he thought of her. She had made him believe that she loved him and then wed another. It was beyond cruel, and he could not forgive. Yes, of course he would hear her. He had never stopped loving her. Those pieces had spilled the love so that it moved around his body, invading his thoughts, clouding his every action. Near him or miles away, she would always be a part of him. "Speak then," he said.

Arianwen crossed to the table and lifted a chair, rather than dragging it, so that it would not scrape loudly on the floor. Even now, he thought, her every action was gentle. She sat, and he leaned against the table, arms folded across his chest, waiting for her to speak.

"I wish I had come ere now. When you left…"

"You keep saying that as if you do not know why I went."

She looked at him with eyes so sad that he wanted only to hold her. "But I did not know. Not at first."

Now he was utterly confused. He'd left because she was promised to Dyfrig. How could she not have known? "Dyfrig told me. About your plans to wed him."

"Ah yes. But he told me something else." She looked down. "I did not wed him, not when you left, not then." She continued to stare at her shoes. "The day you left, I searched. I went to our nest in the woods, I asked Llywarch if he had asked you to ride out somewhere for him. Then

272

Dyfrig came to me and told me that you had gone because, because..." Her voice was quivering now, battle joined, between the sobs and her determination not to cry. "He said a rider had come, bearing news that a woman in Hereford had borne your son. I did not believe it, but word came in roundabout whispers from steading to steading that an atheling had indeed been born. Even so, I did not wish to wed Dyfrig."

He reached forward to pat her arm, but his hand hovered in the air, and he put it back by his side. "There is more to the tale."

She sniffed. "It was not enough, you see. He'd thought that, broken-hearted, I would wed him instead. And when I would not..." She lifted her head and gazed at him. "Do you recall that evening, when there was fighting in the hall and I had to get Heledd out?"

"Yes. Not long after I had witnessed you arguing with him."

"Dyfrig started the brawl. A few weeks later, there was a fire in the barn next to Heledd's bower. A short time after that, when she and I were out in the woods foraging for antlers, an arrow missed her by a hair's breadth."

He could hardly bear to say the words. "You wed him to keep her from harm." He was at once hot and cold, the anger at Dyfrig boiling his blood while his heart froze with the realisation that Arianwen had not been lost to him then, but was now, even while she sat so near.

"The threat was always there; I could not take the risk that he would not hurt her, so I did his bidding."

For a brief, unforgiveable moment, he had the urge to say that it was all for naught, because Heledd had died anyway, despite it all. He shut the cruel thought from his mind and stared at the woman whom he had never stopped loving. He dared the question. "And now?"

"I am still wed to him. I wish it were otherwise, for now

he cannot hurt her and I would be free. Our laws are not the same as yours but even so, I have no right to leave him." She cast her gaze back down. "You know, I always clung to a tiny, foolish hope that you would think of a way to untangle it all."

The front of his neck was hurting so much that he thought this must be how hanging men felt. He could not speak, but all he could think was that it would not matter anyway, for he was no longer free either. What had he ever done, that God played with their lives thus? After two attempts to clear his throat, he managed to say, "There was no son. It was a lie."

Again, she looked up at him, staring into his eyes until he felt that she could see his very soul. "But there is a wife."

There was nothing else to say. However angry he was, however much he wanted to shout, to reproach God, he could not undo the wedding. He moved closer to her, and she rested her head on his arm.

How long they stayed like that, he did not know. It was long enough for him to relive all their moments together, and to think of all that they had missed. No doubt she was doing the same, but neither spoke. What would be the point?

At length, she shuddered and, shaking off the sadness, at least on the surface, she stood up. "I must not forget why I am here, and must go to Lady Domneva."

He slapped his forehead. "Henbane!"

She tilted her head in query.

"I was sent to fetch henbane for my mother, even though she insists that she does not have toothache."

Arianwen smiled and somehow his legs were no longer full of bones, only soft marrow. "I have some dried in my herb chest. Come." As they stepped out into the daylight, she said, "Life will go on, no matter if we accept it, or rail against it. Elderly ladies will always have toothache."

She was not wrong. But how much sweeter his life would have been if he'd had this sensible, calm, and loving woman to walk through it with him. It was an ache that he feared would never dull.

They met the rest of the Welsh south of Hereford, and the massed troops made their way south, taking rest at Bicester and at Chertsey. After that, the welcome would not be so assured, and they took what they could from the land, skirting round the settlements, all the while waiting for news that Ecbert of Kent had heard of their presence. Would he come? Would they have time to ready themselves before battle? If Ethelred had learned only one thing from watching Wulf for all those years, it was that he must send eyes far beyond the immediate landscape. Riders were sent out day and night, to scour the area and keep a lookout for approaching foes. They did not come.

"What do you think holds him back?" Penwal was in Ethelred's tent, polishing his sword with a soft cloth.

Ethelred thought back to the occasions where, years ago, he had met the young king of Kent. He batted away an annoying insect that was intent on feasting on his blood. "I think he is so sure of himself that he does not feel the need to ride out and meet us. He will choose his own place for the fight, and we will be the weaker for it, unless we find another way." He had to be careful to keep his wrath flowing in the right direction. On the ride south, all he had thought of was Arianwen, and the more miles he travelled, the more his inner voice told him that this was Wulf's fault. Wulf's fault for taking on the might of Northumbria, Wulf's fault for dying, Wulf's fault that Ositha was now Lady of Mercia. His nights were filled not with sleep, but of thinking about all the lost nights, the kisses never given or received, the children never born.

The insect had made another attempt to get at his flesh,

and he tried to catch it and enclose it in his palm. He opened his fist, but it was not there, and soon he saw it again, drawn to the flickering candle light. "I know what we must do," he said.

They set off as soon as dawn broke the night sky, at some point moving into the kingdom of Kent, and hardly a word was spoken, even by the leaders. All were tight-jawed, sitting tall but tense in the saddle, alert for any movement through the trees, any sound of horses coming towards them. Yet they saw no one, other than in the few steadings they passed along the way. Ethelred had ordered that those settlements remain unmolested. If his plan worked, they would have little need to divest these folk of their food stocks, much less of their lives.

Not long after the sun had reached its highest point, they arrived at a river. On the other side was a major settlement. Ethelred and Merchelm rode ahead and watched from a distance as the folk went about their daily business. They had approached from the west, marching along the Watling street, and now the only way into the settlement was via a bridge that spanned the river by means of nine stone supports. At the other end was a gate house but the men at arms were relaxed, leaning against the palisade and engaged in idle chatter. Men and women carried baskets of spun wool, loaves of bread, and the first crop of peas from the fields, the guards waving them in with naught but a cursory glance. An old man working the field outside looked up at the two strangers on horseback but did not react to their presence.

"They behave as if naught is amiss." Merchelm wiped sweat from his brow with his sleeve.

Ethelred said, "That is because for them, there truly is naught wrong. Their king has done murder, but it was longer ago than we think, and word came late to us. Ecbert has not ridden out to meet us because no one has told him we are here. He keeps no watchers on the boundaries of his kingdom, and he did not think that the small matter of two killings would bring anyone forth to punish him." Having counted how long it took folk to walk over the bridge, he now peered beyond the open gate, assessing the numbers of huts and houses. He looked to the north, then over his shoulder, then back to the gate. "Let's go back."

They turned their horses around, and as they made their way back down the road, Ethelred told Merchelm of his plan.

When the animals had been brought into the huts, and the bell for evensong had rung out, a portion of the combined Welsh and Mercian forces came at speed, charging over the bridge and through the gate. They carried lit torches, and as they ran through the settlement, they set buildings on fire. Men and women came running outside, cowering as if expecting instant death. The attackers ignored them, and many began to run towards the church. Ethelred, leading the men of Tamworth, and Merchelm, leading his own hearth-troops, continued until they came to where the river began to bend, flowing round the other side of the settlement. Now, having set the place alight, they must run back through it, and get out the same way they came in. The evening sky itself appeared to glow red, and the crackle of burning timbers grew louder. The smoke made Ethelred's eyes stream, and flakes of ash were blowing on the breeze. He dared not speak, for he didn't want a mouthful of embers, and instead used a series of arm movements to signal that it was time to turn round.

Now, it was a race to get through while they still could, before the flames reached up from one side of the path to the other and trapped them in the centre. He looked at Merchelm, whose face was covered in soot, and nodded. They pelted back towards the gate and Ethelred thought that somewhere in the process his lungs had caught fire, so much was his chest burning with the effort. He could feel the heat at his back and on his cheeks, and as they neared the bridge, he could see that they would have to dodge streams of water, as the locals were now desperately filling pails from the river and passing them back to those nearest the burning buildings. A huge cracking sound reverberated over the roar of the flames, and Ethelred was suddenly on the ground, the wind knocked from him. He scrambled to his feet as swiftly as he could. There was no time to thank Merchelm, but the younger man had saved his life by pushing him clear of the falling roof support which now lay, still aflame, on the ground. They ran on.

It had all happened so swiftly, and the folk within were so intent on saving their homes and barns, that the aggressors faced no armed opposition. As they streamed across the bridge and ran to the trees where others were waiting with the horses, Ethelred tried to thank Merchelm, who shook his head and waved away the gratitude.

One of Merchelm's men pointed to the crops in the fields. "No," Ethelred said, his throat stinging. "They can rebuild, but they will not be able to sow more seed on scorched ground and hope to harvest it. I will see none harmed, and none starve."

Merchelm, hands on his thighs, coughed and then spat on the ground. "Where now?"

Ethelred said, "That, I am told, was Rochester. We will ride on until we find another settlement of similar importance and do the same again. And again, and again until Ecbert comes out of hiding."

Chapter Twelve

Tamworth AD676: Summer

Ositha wondered if it were possible to spew up one's insides. The mutton she had eaten last night had come back up almost straight away, and the ale had done the same. She had asked for some buttermilk this morning to see if it would settle her belly, but that had come back up too. Now she sat outside the hall, fanning herself with a piece of linen and thinking how she could fill the hours until Elfwin came back. He'd been out since dawn with young Cenred, and she was beginning to resent how much he left her on her own, seeming to prefer the company of the Mercian boy.

Ethelred had not told her about his nephew, although when she thought about it, she realised she should not have been surprised that Cenred would bide here in Mercia rather than following his widowed mother back to Kent. It was unkind of God, though, she thought, that having given her a husband to call her own, He had taken him away from her the day after her wedding and now, even though Elfwin was her brother and she was the one he'd come to see, Cenred kept getting in the way. Would it be so terrible for God to grant her one thing that she could keep for herself? Another wave of sickness swirled in her belly and she looked to the sky. Of course, God had granted her this bairn. She had prayed, and promised that if it was a boy, he would be named Oswald.

Harvest month would soon be upon them. Ositha would not be able to help to bring in the barley if she still felt so ill. She began to wonder who would, in fact, be helping to bring the harvest in, if the men did not come home. The sheep and goat herds were bent old men, which again, was nothing out of the everyday, but the younglings had been of little help with lifting heavy ewes who fell into ditches, or to pull on the hooves when the lambs got stuck during birthing. The memory made her shudder, for it was not only beasts who had troublesome births.

She could not sit on this bench all day. Any kind of work made her feel sick, but the last thing she wanted to do was make the folk of Tamworth think she was idle. No matter how hard she tried to please them, they seemed not to wish to know her. She'd thought to show them that her homeland was not merely full of loathsome warriors, and tried to entertain them, arranging for Colmán to play his applewood Northumbrian whistle. She had chattered, pleasantly she thought, about what life was like in Bamburgh, explaining that they ate food from the sea and tasty weeds that washed up on the shore. "Women in the north wear their hair thus," she had told one of Derwena's ladies, hoping that she might be interested, but the woman had scowled at her and walked off.

The ever-present and none too friendly shadow that was Heaferth muttered, "It sounds like you think Mercia is not as good."

She tried again. Overhearing a discussion about the campaign in Kent, she had tried to express her gratitude that she had not, after all, been wed to the murderous Ecbert, but somehow that had come out wrong too. "I had thought at one time to be wed to him", she'd said, leaving them with the idea that she would have preferred to be Ecbert's wife. Before she could say, "No, I meant that I am glad I was not wed to him but am wife to a better man," they had turned their backs and continued their conversation in low whispers.

Still, she must try to get up and busy herself. She would not be welcome in the weaving shed, as she was not strong

280

enough to help with the heavy looms, and the smells in the cook house made her heave. She was ashamed to feel tears burning her eyes, but she was at her wits' end. She did not know how to make folk love her by any other way than being of use to them, and if she could not work, she could do naught until her husband returned.

The lilt of conversation peppered with laughter lifted her head and she looked out across the yard. Elfwin and Cenred were back from their morning's fishing and were walking towards the hall, each with an arm round the other's shoulders. Ositha stood up to greet them, a smile fixed to her face as if nailed there.

"Brother," she said in greeting. "I am glad to see you. I thought that today we might go to the…"

Elfwin was not even listening but still chuckling over something Cenred had said and repeating the odd word before dissolving again into giggles. "Trout," he spluttered, as if it were the wittiest word ever thought of.

Ositha's jaw began to ache. How could she even show the folk here that she cared so well for Elfwin when he ignored her almost daily? She decided she would go and lie down, and if any of them dared to say a word about it, let them. They would soon know that she was carrying the king's child and then they would treat her with a little more care.

"Wait!" Elfwin called.

She went back to them. "What?"

The boys looked at each other, still grinning, and it was Cenred who answered her. "We have tidings."

Her smile was slipping and she was becoming increasingly irritated, as anyone would, surely, not knowing what it was they found so funny. "Tell me then, or not. But do not keep me waiting," she snapped.

Cenred said, "You should sit down, Lady, you look wan."

Finding it hard to hold onto her ire when faced with such concern, she did as she was bidden.

281

"Uncle Ethelred is coming home. We heard it from a rider who came in as we were setting out this morning."

Her heart beat more swiftly at the mere mention of his name. "When?"

"In a day or two, no more." Elfwin skipped a little dance and then flung himself down beside his sister on the bench. "I have heard such tales… They burned their way through Kent, you know, and then when the king agreed at last to meet them, you will never guess!"

Nor did she want to. Why could they not spit it out?

Cenred picked up the story again. "Uncle told him that he would not stoop as low as the Kentish king and had therefore not harmed anyone. But now the king of Kent must bow before him and pay the wergild for the Lady Domneva's brothers."

"So the man price for the killings was paid. What of it?" It was hardly a tale worthy of harps and flutes.

"Ah, but the Lady had sent word that she wished for the payment to be made in land, not silver. The story goes that she asked for as much land as a hind could run round in a day, and that she would have that much for an abbey. Is she not wonderful?"

Ositha was growing a little tired of hearing about women going off to live in abbeys, for it made women like her, who stayed to do their duty at home, look somehow less. Her mother had done it, and taken Ava with her, leaving Ositha to try to keep order at Bamburgh. Then Audrey had done it too and, as soon as Ecgfrith remarried, Ositha had been sent off to this unfamiliar kingdom, a far greater challenge. "She could have done none of this without Ethelred," she said.

The boys shrugged. "True enough," Elfwin said. He leaned in and rested his head on her shoulder. "Cenred is right, you know, you do not look well."

And so she forgave him for abandoning her. Elfwin need

only smile, or say a kind word, and folk around him melted like candles left out in the sun. She closed her eyes and reflected on what had been said. She would not be convinced otherwise; Ethelred was the man who had been Domneva's salvation. He had cared so much for her that he had avenged the slaying of her brothers. Ositha ruffled Elfwin's hair. Ethelred would come home, he would love her brother as much as she did and she knew that, if ever the need arose, God forbid, he would avenge Elfwin in the same way, to show how much he cared for his wife.

"They are alike, are they not? Had I not known otherwise, I would think them brothers." Ethelred had come into the bedchamber late. Elfwin, with Cenred as always by his side, had been presented to the king before the meal. Their evening had carried on, but Ositha had left the hall early.

She was a little out of breath, having leaped away from the curtain only just in time to pretend that she had been lying down on the bed the whole time. "Yes, and there is already a strong bond between them." Was there a touch too much bitterness in her tone? Although, she thought with pride, Elfwin, at fifteen summers, already had the bulked-up body of a young man, whereas Cenred at only twelve was still scrawny like a child.

She kept her back to her husband and could hear him undressing, pulling off his boots, the hopping on one foot as he took off his breeches, and then the jangling clunk as his belt hit the floor. She put a hand out to brace herself as he lay down and the bed sagged. Even that small motion made her insides flutter again, and she swallowed a few times, hoping she would not have to throw up in front of him. He said nothing more and she soon detected from his steady breathing that he was asleep. She lay still, hoping not to disturb him, but the urge to be sick grew too strong.

She sat up and, as she did so, felt something warm

283

between her legs, much like the signal that her monthly bleed had begun. Except, she was with child, so her monthly bleed should not be happening. She shuffled to the edge of the bed, sitting as much as possible on one buttock, in an attempt to keep the blood from soiling the bed coverings. She half-stood and propelled herself into a crouch in front of her chest, searching for her monthly cloths. After that, she had no idea what to do, whom to tell. Tette had recently been in childbirth herself, but Ositha would not call on her anyway, for the woman did not like her. Could she shame herself before the Lady Derwena? How could she admit that she had failed to do what should come so naturally to every woman? Besides, the old woman had only that day arrived back from the lands of the Magonsæte and was no doubt as tetchy as Oswii used to be after a long journey.

She was aware of movement behind her. "What is wrong?" Ethelred asked.

"I think all is not well with the…" She sat back on her heels, with the cloth lying useless in her lap. She had not even had the chance to tell him that she was with child, and now it was too late.

She looked truly pitiful, lying pale and frightened in his bed. He had not taken to her, this Northumbrian king's daughter, who was covered in invisible thorns that pricked anyone who attempted to get close to her, anyone who showed her kindness. And so, folk had already begun to leave her alone. His homecoming had been a muted affair. He was tired and he was grieving, not only for Merwal but for Domneva, her losses and, indeed, his loss of her. She and her daughters would be content in the new abbey, but it was in a far corner of Kent and he doubted he would see her again. He'd ridden into Tamworth weary to his bones, still tender from his brush with Arianwen. After so many recent deaths and losses, he needed her calm presence, needed to be with someone who understood, not a stranger, and he'd sensed that his new wife had not endeared herself while he'd been away.

Comments had come with little barbs attached to them; subtle emphasis when food was served, "For you, Lord King," with the stress on 'you', and remarks about the affable Elfwin. "Who would have thought that there would, after all, be a likeable Northumbrian?" Naught that he could take them to task over, but it was there, nonetheless.

He hoped that his own sister, Starling, had not been made to feel similarly unwelcome when wed to Frithuwald against her wishes. Ethelred had expressed misgivings about Starling's nuptials, but had anyone spoken out in Northumbria on Ositha's behalf? Had any of her folk begged Ecgfrith not to ill-use her thus?

He had not called a moot when he returned home, but Heaferth had made sure that no one could hear them when he'd asked Ethelred to tell him the details of the campaign in Kent. Ethelred recounted in brief that the southern kingdoms were not settled, and disputes over kingship were rife. Ethelred had sent word that he would not force any to ride with him; he asked only that they stay out of any fight between Mercia and Northumbria. He had assured them all that he was not looking to make his own kingdom larger, but was merely looking to make safe his borders. Heaferth nodded, though Ethelred knew it was not enough for him. He counselled patience. "We are not strong enough yet." Heaferth had grunted and walked off.

Whatever Oswii and Ecgfrith had done, the least Ethelred could do now was to give his wife the best possible care, but his knowledge of such things was poor. He could not ask his mother to nurse her, and he doubted that any of the other women would be able to disguise their dislike. Lady Tette had just been delivered of her own bairn, so was not able to help. There was one, though, who was full of naught but selfless love. She had already tended one such grieving young mother-to-be, but she could not be here; if she were, then there would be no need for Ositha's presence, and that turned the small knife in his innards a few more twists.

He sat down, taking care not to rock the bed too much. He took Ositha's hand and said, "I am going to send for someone who knows how to, well, who knows you." He patted her hand and let go.

She arrived four days later, not in a rush, but calmly asking for her bags and boxes to be unloaded, and immediately waylaying one which was being taken to her bower in error. "No, not that one, if you do not mind. It holds the dried worts and I shall have need of those." She looked at Ethelred, smiled, gestured toward the hall and said, "She is in there?"

He nodded, and she moved to walk past him. He caught at her hand to stop her. When she turned, he simply said, "Thank you."

"Do not thank me yet, Brother. I've borne no children of my own, and it has already been days since she fell ill. Prayer is better than hope, I fear."

He hugged her. "Prayer has already brought you here." He busied himself then with overseeing arrangements for the gift-giving, delayed because of Ositha's condition. Penwal was chafing to be with his wife and new child, a son this time, Immin was itching to be with his new woman, and Merchelm was keen to be on his way home, but Ethelred had gold arm rings for them all, rewards for their deeds in Kent, but also, especially in the case of his nephew, a token of love and friendship.

Crossing the yard to the chapel, Ethelred saw Ositha's man Colmán, leaning against a wall, one foot lifted against the daub. Ethelred considered asking him to ride north with a message for Ecgfrith that his sister was ill, then decided against it. The man was looking at him and had acknowledged him with a brief nod, but there was no respect in his eyes. In fact, he was staring as if with hatred, eyes narrowed, and lips pinched together.

Ethelred remembered how Wulf had eyes everywhere, men whose task it was to get close to the enemy and send tidings back to their lord. Ecbert of Kent had no such watchers, but Wulf could not have been the only one, and now Ethelred looked afresh with his own eyes at this man whom Ositha had brought with her. No, he would say naught to him of Ositha's health. He sought out Heaferth, and asked if he would find Merchelm, and then the three of them would go riding, he told him. Heaferth raised an eyebrow in query but went off without hesitation to do his lord's bidding.

The next evening, Carena came from the curtained chamber and sought him out in the hall. The feasting over, he was preparing to sleep, once again, in the hall with his men. He made room for her on the bench, and she sat down beside him, hands in her lap. "She will not lose the bairn," she said. "It is set fast. Once the sickness passes she should start to feel better. I have asked for knapweed to be brewed in honey and given to her daily."

He threw up a silent prayer of thanks. "I do not understand though," he said. "The bleeding?"

"It happens sometimes. It does not always work but lying still can help to keep the bairn inside. I think this time all will be well."

He reached for her hand and took it in his own. "Thank you. It cannot be easy, caring for one whose kin were so unkind to you."

"She did not ask to be Oswii's daughter. Her mother was good to me, in fact it was her wish to protect me that brought me to her side and had me learning what can go amiss in child-bearing, and let us not forget, my own dear Alfrid was Oswii's son, so the blood is not wholly bad."

287

He looked at their entwined hands, but had no answer for her.

"Stop it," she said softly. "Do not blame yourself. If I found myself with my back to the wall and a bear who swore not to eat me if I lay down and became its plaything, I would be on the ground faster than you could blink." She leaned against his arm. "You had no say in any of it. I understand. The Northumbrian bear has a strong arm and sharp teeth."

"God forgive me, but I blamed Wulf. For weakening us. I could not say no to the wedding. Mother was not pleased."

"Mother was not the least bit glad when I wed Alfrid and no doubt she told you she was right all along to argue against it? Yes, I thought so. My heart breaks anew every dawn when I wake and recall that he is not with me, but I would not have forgone those years we had together. Ositha was not so much a mistreated child as simply one not noticed. Be kind to her and who knows? Perhaps love will grow."

Not if Ositha ever learned what he and his men had been discussing earlier. "I must beg another boon, and you must say no if your heart cannot bear it."

She turned so that she could look fully at him. "Ask."

Ositha stretched her hands out and ran them over the coverings, feeling the embroidery stitches and smiling at the thought that, even now, she was being given the best that Mercia had to offer. The pillow under her head was stuffed with the finest goose down, the cart lined with straw, then layers of blankets and furs. There was a beaker of water for her thirst and a bowl in case she should spew on the journey.

For days she had been in despair, praying for the bleeding to stop, and thanking God for the angel he had sent. For surely that was what Carena was, feeding her broth with beans, peas, and bone marrow, and sleeping drafts of radish, hemlock, and wormwood, taking her bloody cloths away, cleaning her gently, and soothing her with a sweet song, the words of which she could not comprehend. Ethelred's sister was no longer a minnow in a vast Northumbrian river, but an abbess of Mercia. Her appearance must be a sign of how much Ethelred valued his wife. Ositha did not fool herself; she was precious to him more as the mother of his child than as the keeper of his heart, but that was changing. Now they knew that the bairn was not lost, his care for her was more than kindness, surely? Her husband was falling in love with her.

Now, he was so concerned for her well-being that he was sending her away to gather her strength somewhere less busy, and the angel was going with her. Elfwin had not been allowed to see her while she had been ill, but he had come to her that morning to wish her well, tell her that he was going home, but that he would ride to see her soon, perhaps once the bairn had been born. So far, apart from the brief worry of losing the child, and the unfriendliness of the folk of Tamworth after the initial welcome, her life in Mercia was going better than she had feared or even dared to hope.

The cart slowed almost to a stop, and she realised that they must be passing through the gateway. She heard voices but did not attempt to make out the words. Her days of listening round corners and from behind curtains were a thing of the past. She yawned; the potions Carena was giving her to make her sleep at nights were leaving her drowsy by day, and sometimes her head felt like it was full of dense mist. She settled down, holding one hand protectively on her belly, and above the noise of the cart wheels she was only vaguely aware of the guard calling out, "Fare you well, Lady Carena." Ositha closed her eyes, wondering briefly why they had not called her name, too.

At Medeshamstede, she was greeted by another of her

husband's sisters, the one whom they called Minna. As she was helped down from the cart, Ositha knew it was not the sun warming her, but the knowledge that she had been delivered into the care of not one, but two royal sisters. How much more proof was needed that Ethelred was safeguarding her as closely as a hoard of gold?

The summer was stepping aside for autumn, but even so, the land here was bleak. "Where is this place?" Ositha asked, of no one in particular.

Minna sucked her cheek for a moment. "Hmm, how best to say it? East of Tamworth, still a long way south of your homeland." She paused again. "This is the land of the Gyrwe. No? Let me see… Oh yes, the Lady Audrey was once wed to a leader of the South Gyrwe, before she wed your brother."

The woman looked pleased with her explanation. To Ositha, all was now clear concerning Audrey's constant grim mood. Who could live in a flat, wet place like this and still smile? She drew her cloak about her to shut out the wind. Growing up by the sea, she was used to the onshore breeze but this carried no smell of salt, no freshness, and was like little cold knives piercing her clothing.

After being shown to her bower and taking a nap, that evening she approached Carena as they made their way to the chapel for evensong. "My lady, you have been kindness itself, but am I to bide here until the child is born? For if the sickness goes, I should go back ere winter sets in." Odd, really, but now she thought on it, she'd begun to feel better before they'd left Tamworth, so this move to Medeshamstede was perhaps over-cautious.

Carena caught the folds of her skirt and lifted them from a threatening tendril of bramble from the wort beds. "I must have the hayward see to that," she mumbled. "Er, yes, my dear, I think my broth… King Ethelred will come here on his way back from…"

"From where?" Ositha was beginning to feel that all was not well and that something was being kept from her.

"He is riding across his lands while the skies are still bright, and the days are long enough. He has not had the time since becoming king. There is much to do, and Lady Tette was busy with her own bairns, which is why we brought you here, for we would not have you on your own and our mother is too... Now my dear, you should be back abed. Ah, Minna, wait for me." She hurried to catch her sister up. Ositha watched them go. What was Lady Derwena; too elderly? Or too full of hatred, despite what she'd said, for anyone related to Oswii?

The pains came much like her monthly cramps, but more severe and spreading out so that her back hurt too. Outside the world was quiet, the light coming through the shutters was tinged with blue, and she knew that snow was falling, muting the sounds of industry. Occasionally she would hear voices, but they faded into muffled noises as the cramping turned into a succession of tightening spasms across her belly, during which she could hardly breathe. In between each bout, all she wanted to do was curl into a ball but, for the moment, that was impossible.

Gradually, the immediate world began to fade away altogether and all that was left was her, and her body, doing what it must. She was only vaguely aware of exhortations for her to take sips of a drink, and could only barely hear what was being said. Her elbows were on the bed and, behind her, someone was telling her to bear down, and then her stomach moved like the waves in the sea, and she had the sensation of needing to empty her bowels. She was wrenched by an intense pain, stinging but more so, and she thought she might die from the agony. Mercifully it eased, and then she heard an unfamiliar sound and only belatedly realised that what she was hearing was the crying of her child. Someone helped her onto the bed, and another person handed her a bundle, and she fell into darkness.

She awoke and knew, somehow, that she had been slipping between sleeping and waking for some while. Hazy memories surfaced, of the room being light, or dark, and at all times someone being there with drinks and to bring the child to her. Now, she half-opened her eyes and saw a man standing near the cradle. He bent forward and scooped the bairn into his arms, and then sat down gently on the bed beside her. She smiled and opened her eyes fully, taking in the heavenly sight of her husband, cradling his new-born. All her life, Ositha had craved only to have purpose, and a place in someone's heart. Now, this beautiful man, with tears in his lovely brown eyes, was sitting beside her, overwhelmed with love and happiness.

A knock on the door frame: designed to be loud enough for him to hear, but soft enough that it would not disturb Ositha. Ethelred stood up, and placed the infant back in the crib, taking care to tuck the blanket around the tiny form. He went to the doorway and spoke in low whispers to whoever had knocked. Ositha was content, she had no need to listen, but her sense of hearing was keen, and she could not help herself.

"You will be a wonderful father. I have seen you with all the other children and they love their uncle. This bairn will love you more. What, are those tears?"

A sniff. "They might be. I cannot help it. To have my own child is a gift from God. It is also a comfort now that so many have gone."

"You miss them. We all do."

"To be the last of the brothers... Merwal was older, calmer. Wulf, well, there is a silence now. He was so loud, so full of life. I think that Mother saw our father every time she looked upon Wulf and the sun is not as bright now that he has gone. I never really knew Pieter. With you and Minna here, Domneva and Ermenilda back in Kent, Starling and the others…"

"You still have Mother."

"Aye, but for how much longer? And for her, I am no…"

"No Wulf? You are more of our father than you think. And you are your own man, too, never forget that."

Ositha thought her heart was so full that it might overflow and spill blood onto the blankets. Ethelred was lonely. If she could get him away from here, and deal with his mother, then she would have him all to herself. Her son would bind him to her, and she and the bairn would be all the kin he needed. He would speak in a moment of his love for her.

There was a long pause, then Carena spoke again. "It is not only that. I understand that the birth of a son would bring thoughts of brothers long gone, but there is more to your sadness."

Ositha was puzzled. Sadness?

Her husband said, "How can there not be? I craved a son, it's true, but… There are heavy weights to bear. I was never at peace with the lie we had to tell in order to bring Ositha here. None of this is her fault, after all."

"And?"

"I could not be like Oswii, with children by different women. Yet this bairn's birth makes me think again of all the things that could have been. I worried for Ositha because I know what stillbirth can do to a woman. It brought it all back. I cannot help thinking of Arianwen."

Ositha suppressed a gasp. She tried fervently to breathe silently, so that the faint rustling of the bedclothes with each inhalation would not drown out the soft speech. Her heart was thumping, and she struggled to hear over it. The talk continued.

"Ah, my sweet Noni. I did not know her, but I know what she meant to you. As to the lie, you did what you must. And I do not see it as an untruth, merely that you have done

293

things which you have not spoken of."

Another sniff, and then the sound of two sets of footsteps, as they both went outside. Ositha sat up, heart still pounding and her hands in fists but with nothing to punch except the bedding. The room was a haze until she blinked to free the tears. Who was Arianwen? Carena spoke of her as if she were a dead woman, apparently not surviving childbirth, and that was fortunate; otherwise, when she was fully better, Ositha would have hunted her down and stuck a knife in her back. That was the way her kin ended every argument, removed every foe.

Could she do that to Ethelred, though, as Ecgfrith had ordered? Ositha felt as if her head would split in two, one half full of murderous thoughts, the other completely bewildered by this display of selfless love. *None of this is her fault, after all.* No one in Northumbria ever spoke like that. He had said he would never be like her father, littering the land with bastards. So, what was the lie?

Colmán, sent north months ago with news of the birth of her child, would not be back for some while but Ositha hoped that when he returned, he would bring Elfwin with him. She was not happy with the name chosen for her son. Baby Cærlred had been named for a long dead king of Mercia, who had sheltered King Edwin when her own grandfather had forced Edwin to flee from Deira. The naming of her boy for the last king who'd never been subject to Northumbria and who'd even been strong enough to shelter the enemies of Bamburgh, was distasteful. She sensed Derwena's influence in the choice.

He was asleep in his crib, a rare settled moment for the fretful bairn who'd been denied the name Oswald, his little puckered mouth moving every now and again, making her think that he was dreaming about suckling. She moved nearer to the hearth, feeling the draught from the hall door which was constantly opening and closing as folk went about their daily business. The crops were growing well and it would be a good harvest, for which Ositha had given thanks. Winter was always harsh, as folk in the settlements tried to keep warm and fed through the hunger gap until the earth thawed and woke up again in the spring, but now it was more important that she kept well-fed, for she had a little life totally dependent on her.

Ethelred had visited Medeshamstede frequently when the weather allowed, and it warmed her heart that he could not stay away. She looked over at him. His head was bent over his work, and the little knife flashed every so often as he flicked it back and forth. With him leaning forward thus, the skin on the back of his neck, normally hidden by his hair, was exposed. She longed to reach over and place a kiss there, to smell his skin. She began to wonder when he would share her bed again, for she'd long since recovered from the birthing ordeal. Indeed, he had been, in her view, over-solicitous, for she recalled that her father took her mother to bed much sooner after childbirth and even when she was round with child. Ethelred, she mused once more, was not like the men she'd known in Northumbria. Even Alfrid, perhaps the most honourable among them, had been passionate and moody. This man of hers was calm, thoughtful and, above all, kind.

The knife slipped. "Woden's arse."

She assumed this was a saying learned from his resolutely pagan mother and was both amused and shocked. Briefly she thought of Wilfrid and wondered what had become of him. He most certainly would not have tolerated such pagan cursing. Ecgfrith would be surprised to learn that here, in supposedly heathen Mercia, they suffered far less torment from their priests.

Ethelred put down the object and sat back in his chair. "It is not a skill which I have kept from my youth, as you can see."

Ositha reached over and picked it up. She knew it was meant to resemble a horse, but the small piece of wood looked naught more than a lump, with one side rather thinner than the other. She sucked her bottom lip.

"Oh, do please laugh. It is not my finest effort. Sikke taught me how to carve when I was a youngling, but I have lost the knowhow, if indeed I ever had it." He pushed his chair back and put his feet up on the edge of the bench nearby. "Ah well, no doubt I shall be better at teaching him weapon craft when he is older." He looked at her for a moment. "I would like to give him what..."

He did not finish, but she knew. He wanted to give his son what Penda had not been able to give him, and he had stopped because he knew it would be hurtful to her. Would this man of hers ever stop thrilling her with his constant consideration of her feelings?

Ositha loved to hear him speak thus about the future. Was it possible that he had already forgotten about the dead woman who had at one time claimed his heart? She would never reveal what she'd heard; she wanted no reminders, for herself, and certainly not for him. Like a cow pat, she thought. If you walked round it instead of stepping in it, you could not spread the muck any further. She could not stop him thinking of the woman, but she could make sure she did not help him to do so. "You will bide a while longer here, before you go off again? Or perhaps I could ride with you?"

He put his feet back on the floor and sat forward. "I need to go to Wenl... I think it likely that your brother will be here before the harvest. You should wait here for him. Them. Wait here for them to come back. Yes, that would be best."

He wandered over to the crib, checked that the bairn was well swaddled, and then called for Carena's reeve. She watched him go, knowing that he would always be on the move, always busy, for any lord of any settlement was ever thus, and kings more so. She had seen it with her father and brother, although they had been content to let others do the overseeing for them, and it occurred to her that for anyone who did not know how much Ethelred loved his wife, he would seem in a hurry to get away from her.

She had no time to dwell on it though, for the harvest was not even gathered when a messenger rode into the abbey, bearing news from the north. Ositha did not know the man, but she could see that he was careworn. "What? Has something befallen my brother?" She ran alongside the man as he ignored her, instead touching passing folk on the arm and asking where he might find the king.

Ositha hurried to follow him out of the abbey gates and down to the smithy, where Ethelred was checking progress on a new blade. Ositha thought it odd that he should be concerned with blades here at the abbey, but she was too intent on the tidings to muse on it.

The man bowed before Ethelred and said, "My lord, we were riding south, Colmán, Heaferth and I, when we were set upon by robbers, on the Lindsey border."

Ethelred said, "What of Lord Elfwin? He is not with you."

Ositha could see that he was deeply concerned for the safety of her brother, and she was touched. Elfwin had the ability to make all fall in love with him and she was pleased that his charms had worked on her husband too. Or was there more to the tale? Ethelred was not only frowning but urging the man to give him more detail.

"My lord, we were not riding with Elfwin."

Ethelred's features relaxed and she knew he was relieved. Ositha, though, could not understand why Elfwin would not come to see her. "Why was he not with you?"

"He has been sent by King Ecgfrith to York, Lady, there to be under-king of Deira. He had already left Bamburgh when we arrived, but we sent the tidings of the birth by another rider."

Ethelred wanted to be clear. "So only you, Heaferth and Colmán rode back from Bamburgh?"

"Yes, and no, Lord. Heaferth waited for us in Lindsey, for he would not ride into Northumbria. He has returned to Tamworth. Colmán did not survive."

"You saw him die?"

"I did, Lord. And saw to his burial."

The king placed a hand on the rider's shoulder. "You have my heartfelt thanks."

The rider nodded and they all made their way back to the hall. Ositha was not distraught by the news of Colmán's death for she had never liked him. Ethelred was concerned though, which made her warm to him all the more, and he was indebted to his man for making sure Colmán had a Christian burial. Perhaps she should have been worried that there were thieves and outlaws on the roads, perhaps she should have been upset at the loss of Colmán, but all she could think about was the perilous kingship of Deira. No one survived that, not while there was another king in Bamburgh.

"It is an honour for Elfwin," Ethelred said to her. "It shows that Ecgfrith has great faith in him, more so given that he is young still. He has seen what, sixteen summers? It is not many."

"He is too young." But old enough to be a threat.

He said, "My brother was not much older when he became full king of the Mercians. Elfwin, from what little I saw of him, is a fine young man and will make a good king of Deira."

She said nothing more, miserably aware that her father and Ecgfrith thought the only good king of Deira was a dead one.

Later that day, after she had fed Cærlred and he was

sleeping, for once contentedly, in her arms, she said to Ethelred, "I wish my brother had come south one more time."

He, busy honing his hand knife, did not look up but simply said, "I am sure he will come again, when he has had time to settle into his kingship."

"I wish he had not been sent there."

This time, he put down his whetstone and looked at her. "You speak as if it is a bad thing. Does it not show that Ecgfrith sees promise in him? Elfwin is likeable, and young, but his elder brother must see that he is ready for leadership. And the day's tidings mean that we can go back to Tamworth." He went back to work on his blade.

"Why does it?"

He looked up again briefly. "Mmm?"

"Why does it mean we can go back to Tamworth?"

"Oh, I simply meant that we no longer have to wait for Elfwin to come here, so we can pack up and ride west without having to leave word for him."

Ositha shifted the bairn to her other arm; who knew they could be so heavy whilst still so small? She stared at her husband. In Bamburgh, there was no way of knowing whether folk spoke the truth, so easily did lies fall from their mouths. Here, it was different, and she knew that Ethelred was not being completely honest with her.

The journey to Tamworth was not arduous, as she found that the rocking motion of the cart kept the bairn asleep for most of the time and she had to wake him up to feed him. He was swiftly settled again, and she thought with a smile that perhaps now he had got over the shock of being born, he would be more soothed and grow to be as even-tempered as Elfwin. Perhaps her softly-spoken husband had been a likewise child.

She sat back in the cart and wished the landscape would

change. Even once they left the boggy flatlands of Medeshamstede, they travelled through only fields and woodland and the sky was never far beyond. She could stand by the wall at Bamburgh, stare out at the sea and watch it change from day to day, from morning to night. Here, all was calm and even the clouds kept their shape. Perhaps this was why the Mercians were so calm too? Her father's and Ecgfrith's moods certainly rose and fell as frequently as the waves. The smell was all wrong away from the sea, with the air full of sweet blossom and warm wood, with no trace of salt in the air. The birds sang but it was a garbled trill, nothing like the shriek and cry of the seabirds. After a while though, she found that the birdsong was soothing and could be ignored, and did not startle like the circling gulls screeching overhead. It was, indeed, much harder to be wroth when all around was so peaceful.

Ethelred brought his horse alongside her cart. "Is all well?"

He did not often ride with the cart, but when he did, he was considerate of her needs. She knew that once they got back to Tamworth, and yet more distance had been placed between him and his sisters, his feelings for her could only grow. She tried some honesty. "I was thinking how I miss the sea, that is all."

He was looking ahead, but she thought she detected a twitch of his mouth. A smile? "My mother hated the sound of it when she was at Whitby. And the harsh sea birds. I saw it once myself, when away fighting. I cannot say I care for it much, and those were not happy times. Firm earth under my feet feels safer."

She cursed herself. Would she ever be able to speak and not say the wrong thing? The bairn made a snuffling noise and she reached over to lift him into her arms. He smelled of warmth, and milk, and softness. As she cradled him she realised that, though he was fractious, she would die for

300

him, even kill for him, as she would for Elfwin, and she began to think again about these Mercians.

It wasn't that they thought they had been wronged; they really had been. Sons lost, husbands dead, daughters hurt. And her own kin; how had they been hurt by the Mercians? Penda slew her uncle, the sainted Oswald, but she conceded that it was in battle and Oswald would have killed Penda if he could. Penda killed Edwin, too, but Edwin had misused Penda's kinswoman. All done on the battlefield. Not like Pieter's death, not like Alfrid's. No one locked away for years. Ositha did not care much for the old woman and her sharp tongue, but surely Derwena had not deserved to be kept away from her kin for all that time? She even spoke fondly of Ecgfrith, something which few folk did.

The cart struggled over the rutted track and lurched, throwing her forward. She clung tightly to little Cærlred and her thoughts veered again, taking her on a flight of fancy in which Ethelred came avenging her and their son after they had been taken hostage by a hostile warband. She watched him, with her mind's eye, slaying them all to save her. She had never been so loved in Northumbria. All she needed to do was discover the nature of Ethelred's lie, and she certainly had the skills to do that, and then her life would be perfect. She now had a mission of her own, and Ecgfrith would have to wait. Besides, with Colmán dead, there was no one to send north with any tidings for her brother.

Tamworth was busier than she recalled. Or was it simply that all had been so still and silent at Medeshamstede? As the cart trundled through the gate the first thing she noticed was the smell. There were many more horses than normal, too many to be stabled, and they were tethered to the rails and fences and there were several piles of dung steaming in the midday sunshine. The chatter of voices assaulted her ears, and it was not only odd because of the volume, but also the tone. Almost all of the folk wandering to and fro were men, and older boys. Medeshamstede had been populated by nuns and monks but beyond the abbey apart from the elderly steward, she remembered mainly seeing only women.

She placed little Cærlred on his bed in the cart, slid down to the ground, and then scooped him back into her arms. Another sound rang out across the yard and again, she realised that she had not heard it in many a long month: the clack of wooden practice weapons, and the singing clash of metal blades. Medeshamstede, being a settlement mainly for worship, had no need of such things. It was the only answer her muddled brain could come up with.

Ositha stood for a moment, shy about walking into the hall, but also distracted by her husband. He had leaped from his horse and had run to embrace King Merchelm. The two men had jumped up and down, still holding each other, and then moved out of the hug and thrown a few make-believe punches. He was a quiet, pensive man usually, but when Ethelred laughed his head tilted back, and she stared at his exposed throat. She almost stepped forward, compelled by a strong urge to touch that spot with her lips. He was squinting in the sunshine, and he reached up to push his hair from his forehead. Her fingers twitched with the urge to do that for him. She wondered if he would ever be so carefree when in her company.

No one had come forward to greet her, or to offer to take the bairn, and the yard was full of folk going about their business. She had to move aside for a man wheeling a barrow full of axe blades and spear heads and decided that she'd be no more and no less welcome, but probably safer, indoors. Ositha set off towards the hall and saw a familiar face. Heaferth was talking to Ethelred's reeve, and she chanced a smile. "Good day. You all seem busier than bees in clover here." Even as she spoke, she had to step aside as a man rushed across the yard carrying three shields. "I had

302

not thought to see so many men honing their weapon craft."

Heaferth, scowling at the interruption, muttered, "And you think that was by chance."

Sometimes, when she was a child, Ositha had gone out in the early morning to watch the sea fret as it curled its cold tendrils across the shoreline at Bamburgh. She'd enjoyed the thrill of watching as the sun rose and burned off the mist, forcing it to recede and revealing the frothy sea stretching out to meet the sky far off in the distance. Now, with Heaferth glaring at her, she felt that the same thing was happening with her mind. The journey to Medeshamstede, even while she was already recovered, the prolonged stay after the birth, her husband's mysterious trips, now all became clear. They were preparing for war, and she had not been told. "There is to be a fight. I did not know."

"Did you really think my lord would trust you not to send word back to your brother?"

She felt the heat rising in her cheeks. What a fool she had been. Now she knew what the lie was, knew why she had been kept at Medeshamstede for so many long months. Well, let them try to stop her doing what she was sent here to do. This would go straight to Ecgfrith's ears. She looked around for Colmán and remembered that he was not there, and the image in her mind became even clearer as the last of the mist rolled away.

Determined not to shed tears in front of this brute of a Mercian, she pushed past him and made her way straight through the hall and into the curtained chamber beyond. There she placed the sleeping bairn in his crib, then she sat down on the bed and wept.

It had all been a lie. He had not cared about her welfare, nor that of the bairn. He had simply wanted her out of the way so that she could not tell Ecgfrith that Mercia was raising a host against him. Ethelred should have trusted her;

303

at least got to know her before making up his mind that she was as much his foe as Ecgfrith was. And what had really befallen Colmán? Did she dare to stride up to Ethelred and ask him outright? If Colmán was dead, had Ethelred ordered it done? That would make him no better than her father and brother. She still had her own little knife, and perhaps she should use it.

Cærlred made a small noise, and his mouth worked as if suckling, but he remained asleep. She stroked his cheek with her forefinger and thought what a precious gift he was. She was blessed, in a way that Ava had not been. Forced into killing her husband, Ava had not even had the succour of having her own child. Ositha would not be like Ava, even had she not found Ethelred to be so pleasing to her eye, for she saw that following Oswii's orders had broken her half-sister. What sort of life, to be sent back to Bamburgh there to live forever in shadows?

She sat back and ran her hands over the bed cover, her fingers following first the warp and then the weft of the woven threads, and cast her mind back to that first, and only, night with her husband. She did not want to be sent back. What was on offer for her at her brother's house? Elfwin had gone to York, and Ecgfrith's new wife made Audrey look like a giddy happy child, so sour was she. What would be her fate, though, if she stayed in Mercia? She knew the women had not taken to her, but that Ethelred's closest friends and advisors also mistrusted her was a bitter blow, and unfair, considering she had already decided not to betray them.

The child snuffled again and Ositha made up her mind. It hadn't all been a lie. Carena had taken care of her, tending her unselfishly when she, Ositha, was the enemy. Derwena had told her she was not to blame. It was only the women, like Tette, who disliked her, and they mattered not. Whatever had happened to Colmán, it was Heaferth's doing, and his alone. The Mercian thegns were not browbeaten like her father's and brother's men were, so they acted without orders. Ethelred really loved her. Let the rest be envious, she did not care. It was time to make her mark.

Chapter Thirteen

Tamworth AD678: Spring

Ethelred put down his sword and shield and massaged his lower back. Was he too old for this? He had only seen thirty-four summers, so he should not be out of breath after sparring with his nephew, but the lad was big for his age and though he was not yet fourteen, he had a man's broad shoulders, and he matched his uncle for height. Wulf had always been the skinnier brother, lithe and swift of foot, so Ethelred imagined that Cenred took after his mother's male kin. He was certainly no cuckoo from that nest, though, for as soon as his face cracked into a smile, it was the same look of his father, from the slightly protruding tooth to the boyish exuberance. "You have me worn out already Youngling," he shouted across the yard, and Cenred made a flamboyant bow. In return, Ethelred made a rude gesture and, laughing, left the younger ones to their bouts. He only wished that there would be more food for them when they had finished their practice. He was no lord at all if he could not provide enough for his folk to eat.

Outside the hall, he found his mother, sitting enjoying the first rays of the new season's sun. Someone had brought a blanket for her and tucked it over her legs. She was pretending to embroider, but he knew that her eyesight was no longer sharp enough. Ethelred sat down on the grass beside her. "Don't stay out too long. The sun will not be high much longer and then a chill will creep into your bones."

She reached down and pretended to cuff his head. "That is the sort of thing I should have said to you when you were small."

"Should have? Did you not?"

"You were my ninth child. I did not have time to spare to look out for you."

"Mother! I am wounded." He clutched his chest and then half-stood, planting a kiss on her brow. He winced and sat down again.

She stabbed the needle into the piece of cloth to hold it safe, and then put the mending down on her lap. Staring down at him she said, "All teasing aside, you do look to be in pain. What is wrong?"

"Naught," he lied. "A slight twinge in my back, that is all. I am getting old."

She made a noise, the sort that only elderly folk seemed capable of making. "I'll tell you what old feels like."

He lay back on the grass with his hands behind his head and breathed in deeply. The sun was warm enough today as the breeze had stilled, and the bleats of lambs and kids in the fields and the song of wrens, dunnocks, and finches overhead, gave a proclamation that winter had gone. For a few heartbeats, Ethelred was thoroughly at peace. Only for a few, though, because the sun which he had always loved to feel on his face and his back had been his enemy for the last two summers, keeping away the rain and spoiling the harvest. If there was drought again this coming summer...

"Your father used to lie like that."

He opened his eyes and turned towards her, though from here he could only see her shoes. "Really?"

"Yes, with his feet one over the other at the ankle thus. And always with his hands cradling his head."

He smiled. It wasn't much, but at least there was a piece of him that reminded her of Penda.

He sat up and hugged his legs, resting his chin on his knees.

"He did that, too."

"Mother, I sense you wish to speak of him?" He was

307

worried, though he would not tell her, that she was once again thinking of her own impending death. Much as he wished to reassure her that she was, despite her creaky joints, in good health for a woman of her years, he also did not wish to prevent her from talking about his father.

"He was like a whirlwind; a force rushing through life. At least, that is what most folk saw. He never kept still, much like Wulf, and his ire when stoked…Well, you know. But he was unsure, hidebound by a sense of right and wrong that fired him but also held him back." She paused and cleared her throat.

He noticed that she did that a lot these days, especially after eating. He was in no doubt that the coarse bread, bulked out with peas now the grain stores were nearly empty, was not helping.

She continued. "I thought he should have slit his brother Eowa's throat, but he would not. He stood back and let Eowa be king. He gave Cynwal of the West Saxons a chance to prove himself, for he and your Aunt Audra had declared their love for one another. Penda only hunted Cynwal down when he put Audra aside and broke her heart." She peered down at him. "And I see that in you, that you will not make a move unless you have good reason and that it sits right with you and your God."

Ositha walked by, holding tightly to her son's hand. He was still not stable on his feet and often she would lean over, catching him when he decided to stop trying or when she thought he might stumble. She nodded in acknowledgement, but Ethelred was disheartened to note that she had once more been in the chapel. She'd insisted on the placement of a shrine there to her late uncle, Oswald, which had not been received well. Tette had told him that Ositha had been making her presence felt in the cook house and weaving sheds, too, and that such interference was not always welcomed. *She will settle in time, I am sure. I will keep*

308

trying to befriend her, Lord, but I cannot pray to Oswald.

Derwena cleared her throat again and waved her hand in the direction of Ositha. "And you are like me, for there you have your own little Northumbrian stray."

He watched his wife and son as they went into the bake house, no doubt looking for some soft bread for Cærlred to chew with his four teeth. "But it is not the same, Mother, for you were able to give back your Northumbrian stray."

"Maybe you can, if one day you win against them?"

He shifted slightly. "But does it not feel wrong to you? She was sent as a peace weaver. By rising up, I would be going against my word."

"Huh. Oswii cared naught for that. He marched to fight your father even knowing that we held his son. I would not have harmed the boy, but that bastard did not know that."

"Yet Ecgfrith gives me no reason to fight him." None that he could feel, in his heart. He could never rid himself of the feeling that the feud should have died with Oswii and Wulf. "And if I moved first, then I most surely would not be like my father."

She looked him in the eye. "There is still the matter of Lindsey." She cleared her throat once more. "There is no part of me that believes he will hold the peace. Sooner or later Ecgfrith will come for Mercia, maybe sooner now that he will no longer get tidings from Colmán. One of you must end it; only the timing is in doubt. Wait too long, and everyone will be weakened by famine."

He wriggled again, uncomfortable to be reminded of Colmán's removal and the lie told to Ositha. Colmán had been persuaded, with bags of silver and jewels, to return not to Mercia but his homeland of Ireland, and Heaferth had escorted him to the boat to ensure his departure. Ethelred had not enjoyed deceiving Ositha and was still saying daily prayers for it. "Aye, and that is the other thing which troubles me. Timing."

She gave a slight shake of the head. "Cenred is old enough now to rule Mercia if need be."

He reached round and massaged his back again. "I know that, and it is as well that he is. My son is barely walking and anyway…" He kept the rest of his thought to himself, stood up and kissed the top of her head. "Come in now, the sun will be sinking soon."

She nodded her agreement and handed her embroidery and the blanket to him to hold. He offered his free arm for support as she eased herself out of the chair, again making a sound that only the elderly emitted when standing up. "You are right. It is not the same."

She had lost him. "What is not the same?"

"About the Northumbrian strays. For, at the time, I had a fondness for mine. I am not so keen on yours."

As he helped her to the hall, he said, "Is this about the cheese again?"

She grunted. "Might be."

It had been hard to keep the peace, with Ositha insisting that all the cheese be eaten up before Lent, and Derwena saying it was a waste and that they should keep all stocks of food for leaner times. More recently there had been an argument about whether or not it was better to use plant rennet in cheese-making. Ositha claimed that boiled nettle and the flower of the teasel should be used, but Derwena had told her that her methods would produce a soft, weak, and useless curd. Ethelred had detected that Ositha was attempting to fit in, but it was as though the Mercians were cats, all being stroked the wrong way. He found this an added burden, for he felt even more guilty, then, for not being able to love her.

He made sure that Derwena was comfortable by the hearth, attempting to put the blanket once more over her knees and then leaving it next to her on the bench when she batted him away. He moved through to the curtained chamber and began searching in one of the chests.

"What do you seek?" Ositha had come in behind him, so quietly he had not heard.

"Clean breeches. These are stained green. I had not thought that the grass might still be so wet."

She knelt beside him and searched the other side of the chest, pulling out what he was looking for. "Why do you need to be clean?"

He spoke at the same time. "Where is the child?"

They both smiled awkwardly and he gestured for her to speak on.

"He is with your mother, though I think he will tire her out. I asked where you are going?"

"I need to ride out to see Immin."

For the briefest moment, her bottom lip came forward, much like their son's often did. "And you rode out with Penwal to his lands only the other day."

He sat back on his heels, the new breeches on his lap. "What of it? I am the king and this is what I do."

"My brother does not ride out. His men come to him."

Would she ever learn, he wondered, not to bring her brother and the Northumbrians into every conversation, as if the northern way was the best way? "That is not how we do things here. Each of my men is head of his own folk and therefore it is not my place to summon them here. Besides…"

"What?"

He stood up, pulled off his grass-stained breeches and started dressing again, winding his leg bindings slowly as he considered how much to tell her. "I go to see how the younglings are faring with their weapon craft. I have not seen some of them since…"

"Since you went when I was at Medeshamstede, heavy with your child." Her tone was almost triumphant. "You were not merely riding through the lands as your sister told

311

me. You were already planning for war, even that long ago."

Ethelred could not deny it, but it was not the whole truth. She was aware that the other settlements would be short of food, but he would not remind her of it, for she was worried enough about the child. She must know that he did not trust her brother, but he did not wish to offend by speaking it out loud. "In such times, only a fool king would think he had no need of men who knew how to fight." God help him, sometimes he was more sharp with her than he meant to be. She was looking at him now with tears ready to fall, and he knew they would spill when he told her the rest. "And I need to see that everything is in order, for I will soon need to ride to Wales."

She stood up and lifted her chin. "Wales? Why? You will be gone for months."

Could he risk telling her of the offer of help from a distant cousin of Llywarch's in the north? The men of Gwynedd were tired of sending their tribute to the northern king; they were only waiting on Ethelred's word and they would ride with him against Ecgfrith. He decided against revealing his plans and he left her then, knowing without turning back that she was weeping. It tore at his insides to know that he was the cause of any woman's tears. He never spoke of it, but he knew that she was in love with him. If he had been less kind, less keen to make her feel at home, would that have been better? He rode off as soon as he could, driven by the urge to distance himself from her, but all the while knowing that no matter how far he rode, he could not escape himself. Damn Ecgfrith. Damn Wulf. Damn this never-ending feud which saw such innocents swept along and battered by its force.

She stood for some time after he'd gone, staring at the curtain which was still shuddering back into stillness. She steadied her breathing, wiped her nose with the back of her hand, and asked herself why she cared so much that he'd gone again. It was the impending loneliness for, despite her efforts, the women had not welcomed her and whenever she tried to join in their conversations, adding details from her life in the north, they stopped talking and returned to their work. They came to pray with her but showed little enthusiasm for her new shrine, so perhaps they weren't so godly after all.

She sat down on the bed and stared at the open chest, its contents unfolded and lying over the sides. Ethelred's discarded breeches were still in a heap on the floor. She picked them up and held the fabric against her cheek. Ositha inhaled sharply. It was not the women's coldness that made her sad to see him go. Like a sharp blow from her father's hand, the truth hit her. She had fallen in love with her husband.

The curtain swung to the side and she looked up, heart fluttering, hoping that he had changed his mind and come back to her.

"May I help you tidy all this away, Lady?"

Ositha put down the breeches and glared at Tette. Why did the woman think that she needed her aid? Had Tette not already had two bairns of Penwal's and another on the way, Ositha might have needed to think of a way to get rid of the woman, for she knew that Tette took reports to Ethelred about her. Indeed, only Tette's clear devotion to Penwal stopped Ositha viewing her as a love rival. "No. I will deal with it." She did not move though and continued staring at the other woman until Tette bowed her head and left.

Waiting until the curtain stopped twitching again, Ositha slid off the bed and onto her knees in front of the chest. She began pulling the garments loose from the grip of the pile underneath, lifting them out completely to refold and replace them. She was rough with them to begin with, taking out her temper on the clothing. Ethelred's leaving had upset her, Tette's refusal to leave had angered her, and now she was reminded that Heaferth would soon appear, for he shadowed her whenever his lord was away and, now she thought on it, when Ethelred was at home, too. The care of the elderly Derwena would also fall to her again now. Her frustration was no friend to the clothing and, as one tunic snagged on a belt below it, she had to dig deeper to free the clothes and smooth them all. As she reached down to unhook the belt from the tunic sleeve, her fingers found something hard, wrapped in fabric. Retrieving the item, she placed it in the palm of her hand, marvelling at the delicate striations in the amethyst beads.

Her hand was shaking. Was this a gift for her? In which case, why was the necklace at the bottom of the chest? And what was the meaning of the cloth that had been wrapped around it? Ositha rubbed her thumb over one of the beads until it was no longer cool, having absorbed the heat from her skin. She was the daughter of Oswii and Efa, and one thing she had inherited from her parents was the ability to think. Of course this was not a gift for her, for it had been stowed away under clothing, out of sight and, she hoped, out of mind. This had belonged to the long dead Arianwen.

She wondered what the woman had looked like. Ositha had no idea if she herself was a beauty, for no one had ever said, but if memories of this dead woman were buried at the base of a chest, then there was hope yet. Ethelred and she had argued, but he loved her now, and she him. All she needed to do was bind him to her a little more. What would her kinsmen do in this situation? Surely they would fall back on their known and tested skills? And they would stop at naught to get what they craved. There must only be one queen in any hive.

Out in the hall, Derwena was sitting with Cærlred on her knee. The child was playing with his grandmother's hair, twirling it round the fingers of one hand, whilst in the other he held the remains of a flat cake. Ositha called to Tette. "Would you take the child? Perhaps he would like to play with Pega and Guthlac?"

Lady Tette looked surprised but delighted that Ositha had chosen to ask for her help, and she scooped the little atheling out of Derwena's lap and took him outside to play with her daughter and baby son.

Ositha sat down beside her mother-by-law. The older woman's belly rumbled and Ositha realised that she'd given her food to Cærlred. "Lady Derwena, you look tired. Let me help you to your bower?"

Derwena made the familiar and by now irritating noise, clearing her throat. She gazed briefly at Ositha and then said, "Hmm. Well, why not?" She stood and let Ositha guide her.

Within moments Heaferth was beside them. "Lady Derwena, lean on me. Better still, what may I fetch for you?"

This time, Ositha was ready for him. "I am taking the Lady to her bower to rest." The one place he could not follow.

When they reached the bower, Derwena sat on the bed, and patted the space next to her. Ositha considered for a moment. She did not want to get too close to the woman but on the other hand, it would make the deed easier. She tried not to think about the little knife at her belt. She must be clever; if they knew it was her, they'd send her home. It had to look like a natural passing. Doing as she was bidden, she sat down on the bed, looking past the old lady to see if the pillow was in easy reach.

Derwena said, "You are not happy here, and that makes me sad."

The words jolted her and she sat straight-backed, unsure how to respond. "Y...your kin has been kind to me."

"I hope so. I would like to think that my Carena was cared

315

for in the same way. I believe that your mother is a gentle and loving woman."

Ositha felt the warm wetness of tears, brewed from resentment. Oh yes, Efa had cared deeply for Carena, indeed she had shown more concern for her than for her own daughter. "She left me and went away," she said, the last word coming out on a sob.

The old woman shifted on the bed and lifted her arm, dropping it over Ositha's shoulders and drawing her nearer. Ositha could not respond, much as it felt natural to put her head down and lean against Derwena, for the gesture had left her feeling even more confused. Why did this woman refuse to hate her? She'd change her mind in a moment when the pillow began to steal her breath. But even Oswii's daughter found it difficult to contemplate smothering someone who was holding them close. She broke from the embrace and stood up. "I must go and er, the child will be... Have a pleasant nap."

Hate, envy, and self-pity washing around inside her, she felt sick. Naught would settle in her gut and it was as if the fat had dripped off a roasting deer into a pail of water and lay in globs, unable to mix. She stumbled out into the daylight of the yard and bowled into Heaferth. Had he been outside the bower the whole time?

"Lady Derwena," he called out, "is aught amiss?" From within, the reply came that all was well. "Lady Ositha, let me walk you back to the hall." It was not a request.

She went with him, wondering what he would have done had she refused. He did not trust her, and rightly so. If Colmán were still here, she would have told him to get rid of this irksome Mercian, but she was neither strong enough nor clever enough to manage the deed herself. She knew that now. "You do not like me."

He did not break stride. "I do not need to like you. I need only keep all safe here whilst my lord is away." He glanced

316

sideways at her. "And when he is here."

The day had been difficult and now, overwrought like a child too tired to sleep, she let go of caution. "The king will be home soon, and you can be sure that I will have his ear then, not you."

His response was a splutter of derision. He said, "I am never too far away to speak into the king's ear."

It was true. He was always lurking nearby and if he couldn't be, then Tette would be hovering like an irritating fly. Between them they gave her little peace. She stopped walking and grabbed his arm, making him spin round to face her. "You have wished me gone since the day I arrived, but my husband loves me and I am here to stay." It sounded braver than she felt, for she was beginning to wonder if she could truly snuff out memories of a dead woman. He had buried the necklace though, had he not? Arianwen was no more than a wraith, gone from Ethelred's thoughts. He had hidden it away so as not to hurt her feelings and where kindness existed, deeper feelings could grow. All she had to do was feed and water them.

"He does not love you, Lady, be in no doubt about that. His heart lies elsewhere, in Wales, and always has."

How dare this man speak to her thus? "I am your king's wife; do not think to insult me. He would not dare put me aside, or risk pulling the wrath of my brother upon his head. I am the mother of his child and…" He was looking at her, his lips pulled into a smile that infuriated her beyond reason. "He does love me." Her voice was becoming shrill. She took a deep breath. "Let us speak plainly: his past love is a dead woman whereas I, as you can see, am alive, hale and hearty."

To her fury, he began to laugh. "Dead? She is not dead. She is lost to him, that is true, but she lives." He stepped closer to her, so close that she could feel his breath on her face, and it made her want to turn her head. "She is one of the finest women I've ever known, worth ten of any Northumbrian whore." He walked off and left her standing in the yard, alone, ridiculous.

Arriving in Immin's lands, Ethelred had seen once more the result of the prolonged drought. The barley had not grown but stood withered and shrivelled in the fields. Pasture was no longer green, but patchy brown. The children were gaunt, and nursing mothers sat with sad expressions, unable fully to sate their infants' hunger. There were periods when sometimes the winter stores had been used up before spring brought new life to the fields, and food back to the table. This gap did not happen every year, but had for the last two, and this year it had come earlier. No one had been left untouched by the shortages, for it affected rich and poor, old and young. Even the abbeys were suffering.

Immin was in the practice yard, overseeing the weapon training. He put a hand up in greeting when he saw Ethelred. "Lord! Come, I would like your thoughts on this."

Ethelred stepped past piles of shields, lined with ox-hide and of various sizes, given up by youths who'd outgrown them and were passing them on to younger boys. As he approached, Immin exchanged words with a young man and the youth handed over his sword for Ethelred to inspect.

The weapon was an expensive one, its delicate bluey shimmer showing its pattern and displaying the way it had been made, by twisting lengths of iron together to forge a tough blade. Ethelred hefted it and felt the balance twixt blade and hilt. "A fine piece. Yours?"

The youth nodded and beamed with pride, but Immin made the reply for him. "Heahbert here is our smith. Aye, you'd have thought him to be a rich man to wield such a blade. The truth is that he made this himself."

"But if our smiths are to fight…"

"Lord," Immin interrupted, lowering his voice in

seriousness where once he would have made a crude comment about young men not knowing how to make their swords rise when needed. "If we are to do this thing and do it right, then it must be once and forever. Heahbert has not only learned to wield this sword like one born to it, but he has taught his young brother all he needs to know about smelting, firing, twisting, and hammering. When he goes to fight, his brother will keep the smithy lit. All the younglings here have become men, more swiftly than we would have liked."

Ethelred looked at them all, thin when they should be strapping, and worried again about how they would keep up their strength. Fighting was usually left to those born to wield weapons and fight for the lands they owned. Men who tilled the fields and kept the forges lit were rarely called upon to kill. He gazed at the bright blue sky, devoid of even the wispiest cloud and holding no promise of rain.

Conscience was a weight on his shoulders. It was time to stop blaming Wulf, for any of it. Yes, the loss against Northumbria meant that Ethelred was now yoked to a wife whom he did not love, but even had Wulf won, Arianwen would still not be free, and the harvests would still have failed. Now the king of Mercia needed to assess the situation, with a clear head and a focused eye. Immin, Penwal, Heaferth and the others were ready to fight if needed, but if the peace held, if they could manage to keep sending the tribute without starving, then they must. It helped that they did not send as much as they should and for this, he thanked his mother's ingenuity. Word had also come from Osric of the Hwicce that all was calm in the southern kingdoms. They would not rise up against either Mercia nor Northumbria, but nor would they side with either kingdom. It was as much as he could hope for.

They had done all they could, they were as ready as possible should Ecgfrith choose to strike, and Ethelred had no reason not to return home before setting out for Wales later in the summer. He had left his wife in tears, and that was not honourable. He could not bring himself to love her, but he must try to make amends. He also knew that he should spend time with his son, the little boy who made the pain of a loveless marriage more bearable but whose existence added weight to the guilt pressing on him. He glanced heavenward and asked his brothers' spirits for forgiveness. They had been better fathers, because their children were forged from love.

He found her down at the retting pits where it had been a struggle in recent times to keep them filled. Once, years ago, at Wenlock, he had watched Arianwen as she worked to take off the outer layers of the plant stems. Her shoes were off, and every now and again she'd wiggled her toes in the cooling grass. Her skirts were hitched up, and she had flung her veil off in an attempt to cool down while she worked. Ositha was neatly dressed, with only her sleeves pulled back. She stood tidily while she worked and if she was hot, it did not show. Her veil was in place, and she swung the mallet with precision, but little force or even enjoyment. Her actions were rhythmic, but joyless, and no one was singing. She had not seen him, so he stepped forward and coughed.

She looked up and put down her mallet. A brief smile lit her face but was swiftly replaced with a frown. Evidently she was not ready to forgive him yet awhile, although he could not help noting that her reaction was stronger than their mild argument warranted. "Back so soon? I had not thought to see you for weeks." Her tone was so cool that her breath, even in this heat, might have iced over the water in the pit. Had something happened in his absence?

He decided that they should find somewhere less crowded. "Walk with me?"

She cast a glance over her shoulder. "Cærlred will wake soon."

His heart ached to see his little son, but he needed to mend things with his wife first. It would do no good to enflame the situation by appearing to care more for the boy than he did for his son's mother, even though it was true. "Is he with Tette? He will be well cared for."

"Mmm." She frowned again. "I do not like to leave him for long."

"A stroll down to the river and back then? I came back to say that I am sorry. I should not have spoken thus."

Her face changed as relief washed over it and she smiled. "You came back to see me? That was the only reason?"

She fell into step beside him and from the corner of his eye he could see that she was hugging herself as she walked. Perhaps an apology was all that had been needed.

In the silence, he wondered what the birds had to be so cheerful about, but the blackbirds were singing, and occasionally the females would chirp angrily, suggesting that they already had nests close by. The usual scent of blossom was missing from the air, and the blackthorn had yet to flower. Dust rose up from his feet as he walked along the path. Was it the unseasonably dry conditions that were alerting him to every sound and making him aware that the smells were missing? Or was it that when he walked with Arianwen, or even his sisters, he was too content to notice his surroundings?

Down by the river the water fowl were pecking without success for worms on the hard bank and the water level was low. Still, the occasional damsel fly flitted its brilliance across the surface.

Ositha's voice, breaking into the quiet, startled him. "Have you been to the hall yet?"

He shook his head. "I came straight away to see you."

She blushed and smiled. Clearly she had taken so much more from his words than he had meant to give. "Then you will see when you go how hard I have been working while

321

you have been away. I have ordered the old chests cleared and moved." She looked at him, almost as though she expected a reaction. "There are new hangings on the wall by the bed, and I have put a new blanket on the bed."

He had not been away long enough for her to have sewn new hangings or woven new blankets. Therefore, these were things which she had brought with her from Bamburgh. Northumbrian things. "They will remind you of your old home," he said, trying to convey that he hoped it would be of comfort.

Ositha turned to look fully at him, her expression that of a small child being informed that they could not play in the snow. Her lip trembled and she said, "No, these are things which I have been working on for some months. I had thought to surprise you with them."

Ethelred felt as though he had just kicked a puppy into the river. "I am sure they are fine indeed." Why was it that whenever they tried to mend fences either he or she knocked them down again? "I shall have time to see them ere I ride out again. Let us go now, shall we, and you can show me?"

She nodded and they turned to walk back to the yard. As they went, she placed a hand on his arm and said, "It pleases me when we can share time alone."

He knew that she was trying hard, and he must do so too, but it would be cruel to keep the truth from her. "I shall do what I can to make that happen more often, but I will not lie; I am going to be busy before I ride to Wales."

He felt the lightness as she removed her hand. "You still mean to go? To Wales?" Her words had come out cracked, brittle as vellum stretched too thin in the sunlight.

"I have to go to Gwynedd; I told you of this and naught has changed. My father had friends there but I know not whether they will be mine too. He glanced at her and added, "If it came to it that I had to fight your brother."

322

She stopped on the path and he was forced to take two steps back. "You are lying. My brother has always been too busy with the Picts to trouble Mercia, yet you would have me believe that you are riding to a place where you are not even sure of a welcome? I know full well where you are going and meanwhile you leave me here." Her voice was high now, screeching. "And if you are speaking truly, then you might get killed and what would become of me, a widow in a strange land? Like my sister?"

He clenched his jaw and took a deep breath. It would not do to argue; she was distraught, and he sensed it went deeper than the mention of his riding to Gwynedd. "The thought of my riding off might frighten you, but it is not the same. Your sister became a widow because she murdered her husband, my brother."

Her eyes were wet, but they were tears of anger. "Ah, you seek to calm me with clever words, but what, then, of your sister?"

"What has Carena to do with it? She was glad to be wherever Alfrid was. She came home only when…when she had to." He walked on. Would she really continue to fuss that he was riding to the northern part of Wales and leaving her? Weren't these Northumbrians meant to be made of tougher bones than that? And perhaps he would not go, for he had not missed what she said; that Ecgfrith was always busy with his northern neighbours. Had she spoken true, or was she deliberately misleading him about her brother's plans? If they could just have a good summer, a plentiful harvest, perhaps it could all be avoided.

She ran to catch him up. "I would not ever wish to displease you, my lord. You are right; Ava was a killer, and I cannot deny it. I…"

Ethelred stopped again, for her pause was a long one. It was almost as if she was listening to an earlier conversation again in her head. Her eyes were dull and he wondered if she had lost her wits. "Yes?"

"I am not a killer; you may be sure of that. And so could anyone else who might ask." She gave a little laugh, and her cheeks flushed red. "And you are right, of course, about Carena, too. She was in love and happy to be living in York. Had it not been for Alfrid's death she…"

He whipped round and grabbed her arm. "What do you mean? We never learned what happened to him. We heard there had been plague in those parts but we never knew for sure."

Ositha's eyes were wide in horror, and her hand was over her mouth, as if to stop any more words from escaping.

Ethelred leaned towards her and belatedly softened his grip on her arm. "If you know something, aught at all, you should tell me. It would ease my sister's heart beyond reckoning if she could know what befell her beloved." Still she did not speak, although she lowered her hand from her mouth. He tried again. "I would be grateful, too."

She looked up into his eyes. "Would it be useful for you to know, my lord?"

He nodded. "Aye, it would be." He wondered at her choice of word but yes, useful would do, he supposed. "If you really do know."

She tilted her chin and settled her shoulders. "Folk think little enough of me, but I hear things, I know things. No one you know in Wales would be as useful to you. My brother is wily. He will attack soon, while he thinks Mercia is still weak." She was speaking swiftly, and he thought she was now so addled that she had forgotten not only what she'd just said about Ecgfrith being preoccupied in the north, but also his question. Then she gathered herself. "Alfrid displeased our father and rode away from him. My brother found him and put a knife in his ribs."

The birds were still chirruping, the pounding from the retting pits continued, carried on the breeze. Those still

324

working there had begun to sing and their voices were faint but discernible. The clanging from the forge rang out, as it did every day. Ethelred was sure that the ground was still solid beneath his feet, but something had shifted, and his world was not the same. He felt sick, like he had been thrown around in a moving cart whilst sleeping. Ecgfrith had made a widow of Carena, not on the battlefield but by the most cowardly of actions, the most treacherous. He had murdered his own brother.

Ethelred backed away from Ositha, leaving her standing on the path with a puzzled frown creasing her brow, then he turned and ran, calling for Heaferth.

Heaferth came rushing from the stables. "My lord?"

"Killers, all of them," Ethelred said. "The Bamburgh kin. The sister, the brother. Murderers."

His friend reached up to place a hand on his shoulder. "No, she could not. I always watch her and anyway, I could not be sure, had no proof…" He stopped, looked at his king and then said, "Lord, who has been killed?"

Ethelred paused. Would saying it out loud make it hurt less, or more? "It runs in their blood. Ava killed Pieter, now I know that Ecgfrith killed Alfrid. His own brother. But more than that…"

"Yes Lord?"

He must send a rider to her. "He made my sister suffer. Sent her back here with her heart broken." And his message would break it anew. The weakness in his limbs subsided as shock hardened into resolve.

Heaferth's mouth lifted into a grim smile. "And so?"

"So, it is time. Send the word. Let us finish this." He strode off towards the hall, and only belatedly spied his mother, leaning on her stick by the well. He started to change direction but she met his gaze, held up her free hand to stay him, and simply nodded.

Chapter Fourteen

Lindsey AD679: Summer

He'd not always had the same number of watchers as Wulf had employed, but he had watched. He did not always agree with his brother's actions, but he had learned from them. Wulf had gathered the southern kingdoms, as had their father. A lumbering, noisy beast of an army which had gone bellowing to the north, where cunning kings heard the call in time to pick their defence positions. By peaceful agreement, the youngest son of Penda had ensured that the southern kingdoms stayed away.

Ethelred sent the Middle Angles first, urging Penwal to ensure they arrived under cover of darkness, leading their horses for the last mile or so, in order that the sound would not cause too much disturbance as they entered the settlements. Next went the Wreconsæte, doing the same but positioning themselves a few miles to the east. It took more than the turning of the moon to get them all into place but now Ethelred and his Mercians from Tamworth and from the Trent Valley, Heaferth with his men of the Arosæte, and Merchelm with the Magonsæte, were in place too. The Chilternsæte had melded with a settlement further west, and Llywarch, his men, and the allies from Gwynedd had sent word that they were on the border of Northeast Mercia, awaiting the signal. All would fail if just one of the Northumbrian watch sounded the alarm, but the Mercian federation had kept a lookout, the watchers were watched, and so far no one had realised that Lindsey was now full of enough men to overthrow Ecgfrith. Cenred had been left behind, and had accepted the decision with disappointment, but demonstrated his understanding of his duty. Told that he must remain to take over the kingship if necessary, he had simply said, "I will, Uncle."

The boys of Mercia were men now, young, admittedly, but well trained and many in number. They had brought what food they could, for the folk of Lindsey had suffered with poor harvests too, and that meant Ecgfrith would not be receiving his tribute this autumn, but if this plan went well, that would not matter.

On one of his rides through the settlements, Ethelred came near to a place he remembered, an area of flat land beyond a grove of trees. He had won a small skirmish here when he and Wulf first came to Lindsey, and at the time he was sure God had spoken to him, calling for a church or abbey on this site. Now he spoke to the Lord. He did not offer a bargain, a win in exchange for an abbey, but hoped God would understand that he could not build in praise of Him if he lay dead on a battlefield.

Wherever the fight was to be, it would not be here, for this was not a good place for a large battle. Last time, Wulf had responded to Ecgfrith's advance, which meant that the Northumbrian had the choice of battle site. This time, it would be different. Instead of the regular tribute, a message would be sent. The Mercians and the men of Lindsey would be waiting.

His hair blew back in the biting wind, a feature of this area that he recalled from last time. He turned his face against it and after a few more moments of thought, did not head back to the settlement where he was camping with Heaferth, but made a slight detour. At the first steading beyond the open ground, he was delighted to find that Winta, the man who'd been his guide all those years ago, was still alive, and was happy to ride out with him. On the way, Ethelred explained.

"I need high ground, near a river, but one which Ecgfrith will have to cross to reach us."

Winta cleared his throat, which took some time as a coughing fit ensued. "I know of such a spot. Follow me."

Ethelred did as he was bidden, until they came to a place on the east bank of the River Trent.

Winta waved his arm. "Yonder, Alkborough is three miles or so to the north. Go much further, and you'll meet the Humber."

They would need to draw Ecgfrith across that great river. Here, they were not so deep in the heart of Lindsey, where Wulf had been engaged the year before he died. Then, they'd been chased too far across open ground. This time they would still have open ground behind them, but if they could get Ecgfrith's forces on the run, then the Northumbrians would have to cross the Trent and the Humber to get home.

Ethelred, blinking watery eyes against the incessant wind, looked at the river. Here, the Trent was wide and on its east bank, they were on high ground. "Where is the nearest crossing for the Humber?"

"A morning's ride east of Alkborough, at Barton."

"No good then. He could trap us with our backs to the Trent, if he crosses there."

Winta said, "You need a boat to cross there. And, Lord, there are enough of us who could block it, make sure there are no boats on that side of the water."

Wondering if the old man would accept a hug, Ethelred allowed himself to smile, to hope. "And if we did so, where could they cross instead?"

The old man squinted and pointed across the river. They'd have to ride west, take their horses through the low water near Ousefleet. Which means…"

"Yes?"

"It would mean that they'd end up on the wrong side of

the Trent, and they'd have to cross here, too, to reach you."

"And to get away from me." He scuffed the earth beneath his feet and it came up in clouds, reminding him of the last time he'd faced Ecgfrith's forces. At least there was no danger of rain, the element which had been his father's undoing at Winwæd.

Slowly, day by day, they had slipped out of the settlements and come to make camp on the flat land beyond the ridge of the eastern bank. Men of the Chilternsæte had made instead for the ferry crossing at Barton, there to ensure that the Northumbrians were herded west before they could cross into Lindsey. Then, they waited. Watchers were set on the rise, looking out for any sign of the approaching enemy.

When they came, they drew to a halt on the far bank, and sent three riders across the river. In the middle, the horses could keep their hooves on the river bed, but foot soldiers would have to swim. They made it to the eastern side and their riders stood, dripping, looking. They could see naught, and waved to say they were returning.

Beyond the ridge, lying flat on his belly, Ethelred didn't dare hope that they would not come nearer, until he saw them turning back. The Mercian force was ready to fight, but it would be to their better advantage to draw the Northumbrians across in the morning.

The harsh dry weather, so long a threat to life itself, was now his friend. Ethelred woke from a restless sleep to feel the warmth of the sun as it woke from its own slumber. It would be another bright day, and the Mercians had their backs to the sun. They began to form a line a short way back from the top of the ridge, with the river bank in front of and below them. Merchelm was, as ever, by Ethelred's side. Further down the shield wall, Immin was with his men, while behind them, Penwal and Heaferth, with the Middle Angles and the Arosæte, stood ready in the second wall.

Llywarch had ridden to see Ethelred the previous evening, with confirmation that his forces, along with the men of Gwynedd, had moved closer and were camped in the woodland behind the battle ground. He'd also brought news that Rhiryd had died a year ago, and Ethelred was denied the chance of meeting his boyhood friend, but God worked in wonderful ways; had it not been for that brief friendship, these men of North Wales would not be here now. Odd, he thought, how men's actions could stir events, for good as well as bad, even if they did not know it at the time.

Merchelm scanned the far bank and said, "Do they know we are here? Should we poke them?"

"No. I do not wish to be the one having to cross that river. They will come." There was no need to tell Merchelm how worried he was that they would not. That was a private conversation, one which he'd had only with God.

One of Merchelm's hearth-thegns said, "You do not think they might keep moving south, try to take Mercia while we are all here?"

For so many years, he had wished only to be like Wulf, swift of foot and keen to fight. Now, he was glad to be his own man, slow to wrath. After his wife had told him of her brother's murderous act, Ethelred had thought long about all the successes and failures, all the possible mistakes he might make, now that he was the one in whose hands the fate of Mercia lay. "Look about you," he said. "Who is missing?"

The thegn looked up and down the line and turned to scrutinise the men gathered in the second wall. In a low voice, he spoke their names as he counted them. "King Osric. He and the Hwicce have not come. Nor do I see the Pecsæte or the men of Elmet."

Ethelred smiled. "Have no fear, they have not abandoned us. We once wrested this place from Oswii because he'd sent nearly all his men north to the land of the Picts." A lesson learned, for Ethelred, at least. "If Ecgfrith chooses this day not to cross the river, but carries on riding south, he will meet the men of Elmet and the Pecsæte, who are ready to fight. If that happens, a rider will be sent to Osric, and he will bring the men of the Hwicce north into Mercia."

Merchelm said, "It is a good plan."

"I hope it will come to naught. I want to fight him here, and I think he will cross that river soon."

"How can you know?"

"I learned from him. And I remembered that a foe has a back, as well as a front."

The urge to creep forward was strong, but he had to keep them out of sight. He wished the sounds away, of men shifting in their mail coats, of shield edges scraping against each other, of coughs and murmuring, so that he could hear the signal. Then, a slight wave to the air, a haze that would be missed if not sought. He flared his nostrils, trying to pick up the scent, but it had not reached them for the wind, calmer today anyway, always blew from the east here. Then, it came. Faint, but someone had shouted, "Fire!"

Merchelm heard it too. "You have set a fire? Like Rochester?"

"Behind them. Old Winta sent some younglings out to cross further down, to make hearths of their supply carts and then run like the wind. Now, let them come."

As soon as they heard the Northumbrians shouting, scrambling to dress and arm themselves, Ethelred raised his hand and the Mercians stepped forward, to show themselves along the top of the ridge. The men across the water began to notice them, yelling and pointing. The voices conveyed that anger was misting their vision, and they charged across the river, running easily at first but then becoming bogged down as the water sucked at them. If their leaders had urged caution, none had heard. Holding shields aloft, struggling to keep their footing, they then had to wait until enough were

331

on dry land, so that they could work their way up to the Mercian shield wall as one unit.

They advanced but were hampered by the rising sun shining directly in their faces, and were impeded by their wet clothing. Finally at the top of the rise, they smashed into the Mercian wall. Most had managed to keep their shields dry and the impact was so fierce that splinters flew from the linden boards as they struck. Ethelred pushed and stabbed, jabbing then retracting his arm, feet planted on the dry earth, weight forward. The Northumbrians could get no purchase, could not shift the solid wall of shields and men, and after the initial sally they retreated, to gather once more on the bank below.

Ethelred gave the order to move back. When the walls broke, he wanted flat ground to fight on. The Northumbrians regrouped, bolstered by more men as they continued to cross the river. They made their way back up the rise, into the glare of the sun, and lost momentum when they reached the top of the ridge to find that the Mercians had shifted their position. The clash of shield on shield was less jarring, but still powerful. Ethelred was momentarily off-balanced and leaned into Merchelm until both feet were steady and grounded.

The heat was intense and all around was the smell of moving, sweating bodies. A call from behind alerted Ethelred and Merchelm and they opened a gap between their shields as a spearman from the Arosæte thrust his weapon forward. The Northumbrian he'd targeted fell back, and Ethelred and Merchelm closed the wall. The smash of shield wood against shield boss got louder, men grunted as they hefted their weapons, the leaders shouted orders, and Ethelred tasted blood, splattered into his open mouth from the face of a Northumbrian split open by his sword.

There was a point, a subtle shift in the pressure, that presaged the breaking of the wall. As soon as he felt it,

332

Ethelred braced himself, ready to step back so as not to be wrong-footed. As the shield wall split apart, the noise barely changed. Men were now fighting one-on-one, shoving, slashing, swinging. Ethelred pushed his shield boss into an assailant, knocking him off his feet. A step forward, a downward thrust of his sword, and the man's eyes stared vacantly.

"Noni!"

The cry made him pivot, but his knee did not quite follow, and a wrenching pain burned around the joint. A Northumbrian had been at his back, but Merchelm had brought his axe down across the man's neck, hacked deep into his body, and was now retrieving the blade. Ethelred, voice hoarse, said, "Again, and always at my back. God save you!" He swivelled to face another foe, thrusting his shield upwards to parry an axe blow, and reaching low with his sword to hamstring the man before he could regain his balance. Next to him, a giant of a northerner stepped forward, axe swinging wildly, but before Ethelred could ready himself, Heaferth leaped at the tall man, smashing his shield into his face and landing on top of him as they both hit the ground.

Ethelred did not have time to see if Heaferth was unhurt, for another burly attacker was attempting to off-balance him by hitting him with his shield boss. Ethelred defended himself with his own shield, trying again and again to reach round with his sword to strike a blow. After several attempts he managed to hold the man's shield with his own and they pushed against each other for a while, in a one-on-one imitation of a shield wall. Ethelred relaxed the pressure for a heartbeat and the man stumbled forward. As he toppled, Ethelred brought his sword down on his shoulder, slicing at an angle and driving deeply.

Gasping for breath, he looked around. It was hard to tell friend from foe in the melee, but it looked like there were now more men facing the river than coming away from it. All the Northumbrians were now on the eastern side of the Trent, caught between the Mercians and the water. Casting a glance in the direction of the woodland, he saw the Welsh beginning to emerge. Soon, it would be over.

The Welsh advanced slowly, conserving energy, and fanned out so that they could outflank any Northerners who thought to manoeuvre around the main Mercian force. Spying Llywarch at the head of his Teulu, Ethelred made his way to meet them, then stopped. Coming towards him was a man he'd never thought to see again.

Dark hair hidden under his helm, and his fingers bare, there was nothing immediately to mark him out, but the look was there; the eyes blazing with hatred even after so many years. Dyfrig moved forward and then he, too, stood still.

Ethelred could think of naught to say, yet in no more than a blink he had asked himself why Dyfrig was even here. Could he be such a loyal member of Llywarch's hearth while still being so evil-hearted? Did he think they might meet here?

Their gazes locked, the two men remained motionless. Then Dyfrig flew sideways, rammed by the shield of a Northumbrian running full tilt at the Welsh. Ethelred turned his head to follow the movement but by the time he'd fully comprehended what had happened, Dyfrig was on the ground, the other man on top of him. Ethelred threw his shield and sword to one side and leaped to haul the man away, grabbing the back of his mail shirt and attempting to drag him off the Welshman. With a final heave, he succeeded, tumbling onto his backside as he lifted the assailant and freed Dyfrig. Scrambling forward, and unable to wield his sword, he threw punches until the Northumbrian was unconscious. As the northerner fell back, his arm went out, his fingers still curled round the

334

hand knife. Ethelred shuffled on his knees over to Dyfrig, but it was too late. The Welshman's neck was an open gash, that had already ceased to pump blood.

Ethelred had no time to react, for another Northumbrian was hurtling towards him, sword high, ready to slash it down on Ethelred as he knelt on the ground. Ethelred rolled to the side, making a desperate grab for his sword, but it was just beyond reach. He snatched the knife from the dead man's hand and turned in time to thrust it into his attacker's calf. In the few heartbeats of time that this bought him, he was able to retrieve his sword, get to his feet, and bring his blade down on the Northumbrian's lowered shoulder. The force took his balance too, and he slumped down beside the body.

Trying to restore his breathing, he stayed on his backside on the grass. He contemplated taking a moment to consider Dyfrig's death, what he felt and what it meant, but all that would have to wait. The Welsh continued to run past him, heading towards the river, and he picked up his sword and stood up, groaning as his injured knee complained and threatened to stall his progress. Half-running, half-limping, he kept moving until the pain subsided enough to be ignored, and caught up with the Welsh as they collided with the main ranks of combatants, but the surge pushed them onwards to the river, and only a few were still engaged in hand-to-hand fighting.

Most of the enemy had turned and were now trying to get back to the river bank, pursued by the men of the Mercian federation, and the Welsh from Llywarch's Teulu and from Gwynedd. Outnumbered, exhausted, chased by men fresher and better prepared, their only hope was to get back across the water. Still moving forward but slowing his pace, Ethelred looked up and saw that he was now at the back of his own army. It was over.

His eyes were stinging from sweat, which had run on

down his cheeks, soaking his lips and chin. The back of his neck was wet, and his muscles and chest were burning. With his shield hand, he reached up to remove his helm, grateful that it was not badly dented and came off his head easily enough. Every breath hurt, but the breeze on his damp skin was welcome relief. His legs at once felt like iron and soft mud, heavy and solid but with no sense that they would hold him upright if he tried to lift his feet one in front of the other. The smell of blood was so sharp in his nostrils that he wondered if he had a bleed, and he wiped his nose with the back of his hand. Naught there but sweat, so the cloying, tangy smell of iron was from other wounds, other men. The rank stench of stale sweat was fully his though.

He took ragged breaths past a throat that was burning, and surveyed the area. Moans of the wounded and dying came on the breeze but they were soft now, and all the time diminishing. The roar that had accompanied the chase was but a murmur in the far-off distance. Ethelred sheathed his sword, got carefully onto one knee, put his hands together, and gave thanks to God for the victory. He knew he would weep yet for the fallen but for now, he finished his prayer with a promise to build the abbey, and an added plea: let this be the last of it.

"My lord?"

Wincing, Ethelred put a hand on his thigh and eased himself to his feet. His muscles and the wrenched knee would scream for days. Once fully upright, he turned and answered Heaferth. "You fought well. I saw you fell that man with the…"

"Lord, you need to come with me. Now."

His head buzzed with an urgency that his body could not match, but he followed Heaferth as swiftly as he could, stepping over the bodies of the fallen, and in the end giving up making the sign of the cross each time, for they were too many. Heaferth led him across the flat land below the ridge, onwards in the direction of the river. Just beyond a line of small scrubby trees, he saw a man lying on the ground, his head under a rolled-up tunic. As Heaferth stepped to one side, Ethelred came to a halt, sucking in his lips to stop them trembling. Then, despite the pain, he ran the last few steps, hurling himself down on his knees beside the prone figure of Merchelm.

His nephew's clothes were a devastating mess of mud and blood, and one hand lay across his stomach, the source of his pain. He turned his head and managed a weak smile. "Uncle. Friend."

Ethelred let the tears fall. There was no use in pretence. In a moment, Merchelm's eyes would close for the last time, and Ethelred did not think the searing pain that would follow would ever let him breathe freely again. "Do not speak. Rest," was all he could say.

Merchelm took a few shallow breaths, and reached with his free hand for Ethelred's. "I am sorry, Lord. I did not mean to let you down."

He shook his head emphatically. "No. Never. You were ever at my back; you gave me my life this day."

Merchelm tried to lift his head. "We won, yes?"

The sobs, held in check, had formed a mass that threatened to choke him. He took some deep breaths and managed to force out a hoarse response. "We did. It is over."

A small sigh escaped from Merchelm's mouth. "I am glad. Tell Bertilda…"

Ethelred squeezed his hand. "I will."

"Forgive me, I think I shall slip away now."

The tears were blinding Ethelred. He wiped furiously and when his vision cleared, Merchelm's own eyes were now unseeing, open to the sky.

Moments of their carefree younger days in the sun danced across Ethelred's mind. The re-modelling of

Wenlock, running down to the river there, drunken evenings, the two of them laughing with Arianwen. All the days when Merchelm had saved his life. "Go swiftly, friend," he said. He reached and shut Merchelm's eyes, whispering, "It will not be long ere you can open them in Heaven, and I will see you there one day."

He would not stand. Could not stand. How could he bear it, to get up and walk away, leaving his dearest friend behind, alone, cold? He bent his head and wept without shame and wondered if the sun would ever feel quite so warm again now that Merchelm could not share the summers.

A gentle hand touched his shoulder. He wanted no pity, no sympathy. Let him stay here on his knees, praying for Merchelm's soul and for forgiveness that he had brought about his death. No matter the justness of the fight, no matter that Merchelm was fully behind the decision, Ethelred would always bear the burden of this and all the other lost lives. He did not want the pain to end. He should carry it forever, a reminder that he lived when others did not. And he would always be cold now that Merchelm was no longer there to warm his life. As if to concur with his thoughts, God now sent rain, splashing chilly on the back of Ethelred's neck.

The hand pressed again. "Lord? I am sorry, but you should see this."

No. He did not need to see any more. "Tell me."

"It is... I think you should come. The men have found a body and the dead man's hearth-men say he was their king."

God was vengeful. Just as Penda had lain dead in the rain-soaked mud on the bank of the Winwæd, Ecgfrith too had been killed and now lay in the rain by a river. Ethelred stood up slowly, his aching muscles becoming tighter and stiffer as each moment passed. "Do not leave him," he said to one of the men. "King Merchelm must not be left alone. Stay on

338

watch with him until a bier can be fetched." He and Heaferth followed the messenger, Ethelred curious to know if Ecgfrith, whom he'd not seen since boyhood, would bear enough similarity to Ositha for them to identify his body. He would of course let the Northumbrians take the body back for burial, and he hoped that it was reasonably whole. As they walked, he asked, "Does anyone know how he died?"

"It seems it was a spear wound through the body, Lord."

At least then his face would be recognisable to his loved ones. God was merciful.

They went further towards the river, and Ethelred wondered how any one man could have been singled out, for here by the crossing there were so many bodies, many on top of fallen men, who had been crushed in the frenzy to make it safely to the far bank.

The messenger led them to a group of captured Northumbrians who were standing with their arms tied in front of them. On the ground at their feet was the body of their lord. Ethelred stepped forward, looking at the group. "This was your king?" Two of them nodded but the group remained mute. As well they might, for their shame at not protecting their lord would be immense.

He tried to control his breathing, unable still to quite believe that this was the moment; that he was about to see his foe lying dead on the ground, the most solid proof that this feud was indeed over. After what seemed an appropriate pause, he looked down at the body. "Christ in Heaven!"

Heaferth stepped forward. "What is it?"

"Not what. Who." Once again, Ethelred was on his knees, reaching down to close dead eyes. The eyes of the king. Not of Bamburgh, but of Deira. Aye, it was like Winwæd, for once again the wrong king lay dead by a river. Elfwin, the young brother who was Ositha's world, was dead.

They could not leave immediately for home, and Ethelred was not sorry for that. Clearing the battle site took time, with the bodies of the Northumbrians having to be carried over the river, there to be gathered by their own. Dead men of Lindsey were taken off either on biers or on sundry beasts; some on horses, some on oxen sent from the nearby steadings. As soon as Mercians were identified, they were hoisted onto the carts and sent off as soon as possible. The summer was hot, despite the recent rain showers, and they must be moved swiftly or buried where they fell. Ethelred oversaw this himself, reluctant to leave, and spent several nights to the east of the ridge, sleeping under the trees, his heart ripped open anew after seeing the body of Immin loaded onto a cart. He doubted the scalding pain of loss would ever cease to burn. Heaferth never left his side but Ethelred, already shredded by grief and guilt, began to worry for the older man's bones, for the ground was hard and the blankets thin.

Just as they were preparing to leave the site, a prisoner was brought to Ethelred who, he was told, had been found near Elfwin's body, assumed to be dead, and left with the other fallen warriors awaiting burial or retrieval. "What shall we do with him, Lord?"

Ethelred sighed. "High born?"

"Aye, he says he was in the Lady Audrey's household. He wishes to go to her at Ely."

There had been enough bloodshed and, in any case, cold-blooded killing of prisoners was not to be countenanced. A ransom could be paid though. "Let him go. But, Heanric, isn't it? Ride with him to make sure he swears true, and bring back the payment." Ethelred was not convinced he would see Heanric again, much less the coin, but he cared little.

He spent a few more days riding to the settlements, presiding over gift-giving ceremonies, leaving men who'd volunteered to bide for a while to ensure that the Northumbrians would not come back as soon as Mercian backs were turned, and electing men of Lindsey prepared to act as watchers, to send word immediately should any trouble arise. Ecgfrith might have eluded him, but he would not worry Lindsey again. He went then to Bardney, the site of his promised abbey, leaving instructions for building to begin, and for the local lord to send out the word that a new community of monks was required. Then, he knew he could put it off no longer and, gathering what was left of his hearth-troop, he set out for home.

If he'd felt torn before, he was now fully rent in two, unable to decide whether to ride first to tell Lady Bertilda about Merchelm, or to see his wife and break her heart with the tidings about Elfwin. He had never especially craved to wear the king-helm, and this was one of the times when he wished he could cast it off. The urge to ride away was almost overwhelming, to keep going west until he crossed the border to tell another woman that she was now a widow, but he knew if he did that, he would never come back. And that was the cringing coward's way.

Alerted by the foreriders, Ositha was waiting near the gate, and he noticed her frown melt away to be replaced by a smile of relief to see him not only alive, but able to sit astride a horse. Those not so fortunate were taken by their women, or the leeches, to be made comfortable and to have their wounds tended. Ositha stood with hands clasped neatly in front of her, watching but not attempting to direct the activity. Ethelred issued a few instructions, trying not to think how different his homecoming might have been had another been waiting there for him. There was no sign of his mother, so his wife was standing alone.

When he had run out of reasons not to, he walked over to Ositha and gave her a formal embrace, feeling her body stiffen within his arms as she realised he would be no more

341

demonstrably loving than that. "Come," he said, "There are things I must tell you."

Any attempt to mend or improve their marriage was futile from that time on. Ethelred had lost Merchelm, who was more friend than nephew, and was nursing his own broken heart when he shattered Ositha's with the tidings of her brother's death. She wept, she wailed, and then she blamed him. How could she not? He had not thrust the spear into the young man's body, but he might as well have done. It was not lost on him, the fact that Elfwin was so well-liked, loved even, in both kingdoms, that he might well have one day healed the rift, but his death would rip their peace-token marriage apart.

As was her wont, she poked and prodded him with sharp words until he fought back. He was playing with his son, the one true innocent among them all, hiding an old loom weight in his hands and prompting the boy to tap the fist he thought contained it, while Ositha was pulling weeds from Derwena's herb garden. "I used to do this with Elfwin and now thanks to you I shall never be able to do so again. I feared for him when he took the king-helm of Deira, but I never thought it would be you who brought about his death."

It was but a fresh wound, he knew, but he wondered what it was about folk that made them pick at scabs until they bled again. "It was you who told me that Ecgfrith would not keep the peace, you who told me he had killed Alfrid. What did you think I would do, but ride to fight him?"

"I did not care about the peace. I knew it would not hold, and Ecgfrith never meant to keep it. I wished only to be wed. I tried so hard to be a good wife. I only ever craved to be wanted, to be first in someone's thoughts and heart. I left my home and everything I knew to be with you."

Like a sullen child he told her, "No one asked you to."

She went quiet, put down her trowel, looked at him through her tears and said, "No. I was not asked. I was told. I did my best to make it work for me." Then, almost inaudible, "And I came willingly."

He had naught to say, and wondered if he should go and find a duckling to drown, for that would seem a less cruel pastime. He had not wed willingly. The threat from Ecgfrith and the weakened state of Mercia were the only reasons he had agreed.

Ositha had more to say, more to beat him with. "Elfwin played no part in it, the silly feud. He was guiltless. He barely even knew our father, and grew up surrounded by love, not hate. He was the only good thing in my life, until..." She did not finish speaking her thought.

He opened his mouth to protest. To tell her that he, too, only dimly recalled his father and had spent many years railing against the blood feud, not sensing its relevance to his own life story, but it was ridiculous to start a contest for who was hurt the most. He also knew that she meant he, Ethelred, was the only other good thing. Or had been. Her pain was every bit as sharp as Domneva's had been when her brothers had been killed. Ethelred had razed Rochester in retaliation for that, but for his own wife's loss, all he could offer was the sulky replies of a child caught stealing honey.

"So much for peace," she said. "You turned out to be no better than the rest of them."

That stung, for it was the truth. He did not need reminding though, of his failings. "What would you know? Of loyalty, of love amongst kin?" He was being cruel and he knew it, but guilt was driving his words. "Christ, do you think I walked away carefree? Merchelm is gone. Merchelm who saved my life more times than I can reckon. And I will fulfil my oath to build an abbey on the spot where first he did that."

Cærlred had wandered to the far end of the little garden, and just as well, for Ethelred knew his last words had been spat out too loudly. It was not good for a child to hear his parents wroth with each other, even though the boy seemed not to mind, and was busy poking at worms with a stick.

Ositha had no such misgivings. With anger raising her voice, or perhaps, he thought, it was fear, she said, "And now, no doubt you will put me aside. As I said, you are no better than the others."

Another low blow, that also hit its mark. It had indeed crossed his mind that he could set her aside, but in doing so he really would be no different from the rest of them. Edwin, Oswii, Ecgfrith, Cynwal; all had got rid of wives who either no longer pleased them or who were of no more use to them, but Penda had not, and neither would his son. He stood up, dusted the soil from his breeches, and walked away from Ositha. He had fulfilled his promise to keep Derwena's little herb plot tidy, and took some comfort from knowing that the one person he had not let down was his mother.

They had lost her less than a month after the fight at the Trent. It was as if she had been waiting, determined not to release her hold on life until she had word of the battle. Confined to her bed, she had not been there to welcome him home and after breaking the news to Ositha he had spent the rest of the day with his mother, stroking her hand. During his absence in Lindsey, his sisters had visited, and Derwena was content to have said her goodbyes. A woman who had seen some seventy or so summers, she was able to smile and credit her years at Whitby. "Nuns eat well, you know." Again, he marvelled at how little detail she ever divulged about her years of incarceration, but she was ready to let go of grudges, as well as of mortal life. "You won the fight?"

"We did." He did not tell her of the loss of Merchelm, nor

of Immin. She was at peace, and he saw no need to disturb that.

She reached for his hand and patted it. "So, like your father, you avenged a sister. And Ecgfrith, little Lief?"

"He lives. He is thoroughly beaten and will trouble us no more, but he lives."

"Good. He tried to be as bad as his father and failed. That is a good thing."

With tears in his eyes, he could barely believe what he was hearing. In return for giving Ecgfrith back to his father, Derwena had endured fifteen years of being locked away, her kin believing her dead. Oswii had killed Penda, winning the battle with bribes, threats, and treachery, and behaved murderously to members of his own kin, too. Ecgfrith had shown himself to be little better, killing Alfrid and trying to impose his authority both to the north and the south of his own kingdom. How could she wish him well?

"When your father died, so did I. You Christians speak of rebirth; mine was when Queen Efa released me and I was able to come home to my children. I have lived long enough to see how the tale ends and know that the Iclingas are free. That is all I need because, unless you can bring your father back to me, there is no other reason to bide here in this body."

To live for love, and for it to bind two souls so completely, must have been a wondrous thing. Weeping now, not only for his mother but for his own lost love, he had kissed Derwena's brow and left her to sleep.

As the last of the leaves blew from the trees and when the songbirds of the summer had all gone, he had presided over her burial, away from the church grounds, to the outrage of his wife, of the priests, and Brother Lyfing from the abbey. His mother had lived a long life full of love but had suffered too. He would not besmirch her memory by burying her as a Christian. Perhaps God would forgive him, perhaps not.

345

On the day of reckoning, he would find out. But for now, he knew that it was right for him to bury her under her favourite oak tree. He knew she would not mind that, as he stood back from putting the last handful of soil over her, he said a prayer. Not for her soul, for she would not want that, but an offering of thanks to God for bringing her back to him.

Chapter Fifteen

Tamworth AD679: Autumn

Ositha watched her husband as he walked back up from the woods where he'd gone to pay his respects at his mother's graveside, now a daily ritual. Though the sight of him still made her heart beat more swiftly, she could see that he was weighed down by his sorrow and part of her was glad. She had her own ritual and had just come back from the chapel where she prayed thrice daily to Oswald, cut down as a martyr on the field of battle exactly as her brother Elfwin had been. One day, perhaps, she would be able to forgive Ethelred, since she knew, if she looked deep enough inside herself, that he was not to blame. And now here they were, the two of them. She without her dearest brother, and he without Merchelm, and now his mother was gone too. Ethelred had no one left but her. Once, that would have thrilled her and in a way it still did, but for different reasons.

She waited until he was through the gate, and then she stepped forward to meet him. "The abbey that is being built. I wish to help."

He turned to look at her, his already careworn face furrowed now by a deep frown. "How?"

On the way to the hall, she explained. "The site means much to you, but should it not be seen as a symbol of penitence too?"

He said nothing, but she took a slight nod of the head as an invitation to continue.

"What if we were to found it together? If it were not simply in memory of Merchelm, but a sign of repentance for what befell Elfwin. My father…"

"Your father was made by your mother to found a church after he'd murdered her kinsman. You think we tread in their footsteps?"

This was not going as well as she'd hoped. She would never seek to compare her parents' marriage with her own. Efa and Oswii had never done more than tolerate each other while she, Ositha, had loved her husband. Why could he not see it? She stumbled on. "And what if the bones of a saint could be housed there?"

Again, there was no response.

"Folk assume that I was named for my father, but I have always felt a bond with the uncle for whom I could as easily have been named. With his bones there, this would be not your abbey, not mine, but ours. We could show all throughout the kingdoms that we stand as one."

"You mean Oswald? My father's foe, slain by him after he marched to take Mercia?"

When he worded it thus, it sounded a far from ideal plan, but she was not going to give in so easily. "He was much more than that. He lives on in the hearts of all Northumbrians for his Godly ways and the miracles wrought after his death."

"I know he had the sense not to trust your father, so that's one good thing. But you forget two others, not so good."

She had thought of everything, going over the plan again and again, until she could see in her mind's eye the very reliquary which would house Oswald's bones. So what did he think she had missed? "What things?"

"Firstly, the folk of Lindsey. They will not suffer to have a Northumbrian, dead or alive, in the abbey. Oswald was no friend to them."

He had increased his pace and she skipped to keep up with him. "Then all the more reason. It will mend rifts."

"Secondly, as I understand it, most of Oswald's remains were taken to Holy Island. If you mean to ride there to fetch

348

them, you will do so without me at your side." He stopped on the path. "Come inside. Let us speak where none can hear."

In their chamber he sat on the bed and waited while she talked through it all once more, how the spirit of Oswald spoke through her, but still she could see from his expression that he was not in agreement. In fact, he was looking past her and before she'd finished speaking, he stood up and looked out of the window space.

"Cærlred. Stop that!"

She joined him and looked out to see her son, poking one of the polecats that moused for them in the barns. He had a stick in his hand and kept hold of it as he stood up to see where the cross voice had come from. The polecat went into the barn, moving like flowing liquid through the gap left by the partly open door. Cærlred stared first at his father, then his mother, and then walked away, still with the stick in his hand.

"That child has the devil in him."

She protested. "All children have to learn right from wrong. It takes time."

"I never saw any of my nieces or nephews behave thus. Perhaps it was because their mothers and fathers were kinder to each other."

Ositha thought, but did not say, that she had seen her brother, Ecgfrith, do what her own son was doing, and worse. Nor that Cærlred was not the sweet boy Elfwin had been and so brought her no comfort. With the mention of his nieces and nephews it occurred to her that she and Ethelred had both loved children but, in a bitter twist, their own child brought them no happiness at all. She turned back to the matter of Bardney and the new abbey. "I wish to help you. We two are alone now, and we must find something on which we both agree. And all to the glory of God." It would also raise her husband in Northumbrian

349

eyes, and he would be grateful because she had been of use to him.

He sat back down on the bed, elbows on his knees. "Truly?"

She busied herself folding Cærlred's clothes. "I will not lie. I am born of folk who have murder in their hearts. Ava killed your brother on orders from Oswii. Oswii murdered my mother's kinsman. Ecgfrith killed Alfrid. And I was sent here and told to kill you if I could. I even…" She paused, wondering if she should mention that she had graciously spared his mother. She wished beyond all else for him to realise how much she had once loved him and how beholden he now was to her. And how important it was to venerate Oswald and for Ethelred to be cleansed. "I even thought I might kill her, Arianwen, when I found out what you had meant to each other."

She turned, thinking she had heard a noise beyond their chamber. Perhaps it was Cærlred, seeking his parents. No one knocked on the post or came in, but Ethelred had heard it too, for he had sat up straight to listen.

After all had gone quiet again, she turned back to see him staring at her, the truth piercing his mind like an arrow. When he spoke, it was one word, but the threatening tone made her cringe. "What?"

She was more flustered than any hens would be in the barn now that the polecat was inside it. "Someone was here. Why did they not show themselves?"

He shrugged. "It will have been naught. Someone seeking me who heard us talking and went away again, not wishing to burst in."

Ositha felt cold. She had hidden round enough corners, behind enough curtains, to know that someone had been intent on listening. And that someone, whoever it was, had heard her say how she was sent to kill Ethelred, and then wished to stick a knife in Arianwen. They'd not stayed long enough to hear the rest: that she had come to love her husband, that when it came to it she could not bring herself to harm his mother, that having a home and a husband had proved to be more precious than she'd dreamed, and she'd vowed never to hurt any of them. That it was only Elfwin's death that stopped theirs being the union all others would want to emulate. The moment had passed, and Ethelred would not hear it either. She ran from the chamber, back to the chapel, and threw herself on the floor beneath the shrine.

Spring AD680

Birds were back, buds were sprouting, but there were still some hungry bellies, for the harvest had not been good and it was a relief that at least they'd not had to send any tribute north last year. Ethelred was sitting outside with Cenred and the two of them were sharpening their blades. The young man had lost some of his love for life, his keenness for laughter as dull as the blades they were now working on. The death of Elfwin had hurt him too, for the young men had been friends. Between them they might have brought the two kin groups together, lifted the pall of hatred, but it was not to be. It was on the youth's mind though, for he said, "I am glad we do not have to send anything north any more. It will take time to build up our strength and God willing, we will have boards laden with food again soon."

Ethelred said nothing, but kept moving his hand knife against the whetstone.

Cenred continued. "I understand, Uncle, and I hold no hatred in my heart. I am only glad that you came home whole, for I did not feel ready to wear the king-helm."

"Was that the only reason you were glad to have me back?"

351

The young man looked stricken, until Ethelred laughed.

"Do not tease, Uncle. Of course I was pleased to see you home again. I miss cousin Merchelm though, as I know you do, too."

Ethelred blinked rapidly and concentrated on the rhythmic scraping song of the blade on the stone for a moment before answering. "I am sorry to place such a burden on you, but you are still the atheling. Cærlred is young and..." As always, he did not finish his thought. Indeed, he had not spoken to anyone about the boy, not really.

There was a commotion at the gate. Ethelred stood up. He'd not had word from the foreriders but assumed that Ositha was on her way home. After her admission that she'd been sent to kill him, they had skirted round each other. Both angry, they couldn't say anything for fear of being reproached by the other. Even so, what had possessed her to take off to Bardney so soon, he still could not fathom, but at least Heaferth had opted to go with her, persuading Ethelred that he need not accompany them for this first visit, although in truth the persuasion was unnecessary. Word had come that the monks at the abbey had refused to take in the bones of her uncle, but after that, he'd heard no more and assumed that she had gone back to her homeland to overwinter there. He doubted that Heaferth would have set one foot in Northumbria, so perhaps he'd spent the colder months at Bardney, waiting for her return.

Shielding his eyes from the sun, he looked out beyond the gate but could see no cart, no guard, only a single rider. "Lady Ositha is on her way home?" he called out.

The rider dismounted, left his horse with the stable-boy who'd come running, and made his way to Ethelred, bowing his head. "My lord, I bring awful tidings."

Cenred had come to stand by Ethelred. "Tell the king what you know," he invited. Ethelred was grateful for his presence, and noted the authority in his voice.

The man's Adam's apple bobbled as if he had swallowed hard before speaking. "Lord, Lady Ositha was killed, some months ago. It has taken this long to…"

For a while, even though the man kept talking, giving him the details, Ethelred heard little. His eyes showed him images of a woman who, despite having a sharp tongue and little ability to see others' points of view, had tried hard to settle in a strange land and, at the last, had not done her brother's evil bidding. What cruel fate that she should have had her unhappy life cut short by a riding accident. He would shoulder the guilt, even though sense told him it was not his fault. Little Cærlred would be distraught, as Ethelred himself had been when he thought his mother was lost to him. At least the child would have the comfort of knowing that his mother's death was not at the hands of her foes.

The man's words came through to him clearly now, and hit him with such a force that he thought his heart might stop beating. "Say that again," he said slowly, "and keep in mind that it is your king to whom you speak."

"Y-yes, Lord, I am highly aware." He looked then at Cenred, perhaps hoping that the young man would protect him if the king decided to lunge at him. "They were riding back from Bardney. The monks had refused to take the saint's, I mean Oswald's, bones and left them outside the gate. In the morning they took them in, and the Lady and her riders made for home. On the way, Heaferth ordered her off her horse and he…he…"

"Slit her throat, yes." Ethelred did not make him say that part again. That was the bit which had brought him back to the present with a thump. His fingers worked in a flexing motion, ready to curl into fists. "And where is Heaferth now?"

"Gone, my lord. He told us that he sought to spare you, and these are his words, 'death at the hand of Ecgfrith's evil sister'. He said she was planning to kill you, or the Lady Arianwen, or both. He wished Mercia to be fully free, and if his deeds put him outside the law, he was willing to pay that high price. With that, he and his men rode off. All I can tell you is that by my reckoning, they were heading east."

Fully free. Heaferth had only ever craved a free Mercia, and after the battle had sought to remove the one last northern thorn in their side, knowing that Ethelred would never have put her aside, and seeing her always as a potential pawn of Ecgfrith's.

He had never had the chance to ask her how she knew of Arianwen; he'd thought it his best kept secret. How long had she known? How long had she carried that burden, of knowing he loved another? Sometimes he thought the guilt was a shroud, wrapped tighter with every new event. "And the Lady's…"

"Taken back to Bardney for burial, Lord."

Cenred patted the man on the shoulder. "You have done well to bring us these sad tidings. Go to the hall and find a drink. You will be in sore need of one." He turned to Ethelred. "Uncle?"

Ethelred shook his head, as if such a gesture could really empty it. "I shall be in the chapel." There was naught else to do, until he could ride to Lindsey and pray by her tomb.

When he'd had time to think on it, it was apt that Ositha was buried neither in Mercia nor Northumbria, but somewhere in between. Had she lived, she might have settled into Mercian ways. They had not liked her, but they might have warmed to her given time. She could not help her nature, being one more person who had been moulded by, and suffered from, the hatred between the two kingdoms.

Ethelred rode to Leominster, for it was time to put the king-helm of the Magonsæte on someone's worthy head.

Lady Bertilda attended the moot, speaking about her late husband and his love for his overlord. The men of the Magonsæte then stepped forward one by one and knelt before Ethelred, swearing a hold oath and asking that their folk come under his direct authority. "There is none left," Lady Bertilda told him, "and we believe Merwal and Merchelm would agree that you are the best one to lead us."

Humbled, he accepted, staying for a while to celebrate Lammas with them. He used to sit at kin gatherings feeling sad that he could not bring memories up from his childhood. Here at this hall, memories were all he had, and every time something moved in the corner of his vision he turned his head, expecting to see Merchelm there, laughing, throwing light-hearted insults at the hearth-thegns, challenging him to a game. Merwal was gone, too. There were no longer small children running around, no round-eyed daughters of Domneva peeping at him from behind curtains. There was a gap, everywhere, where Domneva should be.

"You miss your kin, my lord," said Bertilda.

He nodded and took a sip of his ale. "I heard that Ermenilda has lately moved from her abbey in Kent to Ely. I have sent word asking if Werbyra would like to come back to Mercia and run an abbey here. It would be good to have some kin living here once more."

She squeezed his free hand. "A wonderful plan. I should like to enter such a house, for I feel it is time for me to take holy vows."

Ethelred left Leominster feeling hopeful for the future, and rode on to Heaferth's tribal base at Arrow, overnighting in Worcester, where he was told a messenger had been looking for him. He left details of where he was going, and hoped the message was that Werbyra was indeed coming back.

At Arrow, the men of the Arosæte greeted him cautiously,

with one of the leading thegns reminding him that reparations for the killing of Ositha had already been paid. "We sent the wergild to her brother in Northumbria, Lord. Should we have sent it to you instead?"

He waved away their concerns. "No, all is as it should be. I am here to find out who will now lead the men of the Arosæte. Before he...before what happened, Heaferth was the most loyal thegn and his boots were big, should any seek to fill them."

In the dark hall, not as ornately decorated as some, he was offered a seat and a drink. It took a while to gather the hearth-thegns, and it would take longer still for those who had their own halls to ride in once they heard that their over-king had arrived.

"It matters little," his host told him. "When we heard the sad tale of Lady Ositha, we all agreed that Bertwald would lead us. It was always the plan, in truth."

While he'd been speaking, the man had nodded in the direction of the doorway where a young man was now standing, having walked in not far behind Ethelred and his host, and been stopped by a steward who needed to ask him something. Ethelred watched as the two engaged in conversation, and he frowned. Perhaps it was the darkness of the hall, and the fact that the young man was in the doorway, the light behind him, but there was something about his face, his teeth in particular, and the way one of them stood proud of the others.

"Lord King?"

"It is naught." He was seeing ghosts in every shadow these days. "You will all swear oaths to this Bertwald? I am afraid I do not know him; I should have come more often to Heaferth's lands, but I trusted him to..."

The other man coughed. "Indeed. Yes, it was ever King Wulfhere's wish that Bertwald would one day have a..."

Ethelred put his hand up to stop the man's speech. "King

Wulfhere?"

The man looked surprised. "Yes, Lord. Bertwald is King Wulfhere's son, born some years ago. He would be a few summers older than Lady Werbyra."

Word came in roundabout whispers from steading to steading that an atheling had indeed been born. Arianwen's words from years ago rattled round his head, and gradually they began to make sense.

For so many years, Ethelred had lived his life by walking in a straight line carefully laid out for him by others. Even his bride had been selected for him and that wife now lay in Bardney Abbey, slain by her husband's own man. Oswii and Ecgfrith had stooped low enough to kiss the devil in his underground world, but they had never gone so far as to kill a woman. Now, here in this hall, was a bastard son of Mercia. Little wonder then, that Wulf was never worried about his ability to father a son. He knew, even ere Cenred was born, that he could.

Could Ethelred say before God that the Mercians were any better than their foes? Was all of what he'd achieved in life a bundle of useless gestures born of lies? He pushed past his host. "I need air," he said, and rushed for the doorway. As he passed him, Bertwald smiled, and Ethelred was all at once a youngling again, seeing Wulf grinning at him, only this time he could see his brother through a grown man's eyes, too, saw the bastard son, the dead men on the fields in the south and in Lindsey, the ravages that the burning anger, on both sides, had wreaked on them all.

He mounted his horse and saw another rider approaching. The man raised his arm in greeting. Ethelred squinted, trawling his memory. "Heanric?"

"The same. Greetings, Lord. You are hard to find, but I come with word from Ely."

"Lady Werbyra is coming?"

"Aye, Lord. The rider you sent will bring you more on

those tidings. I was there myself, though, and thought to ride back and find you. I went with the Northumbrian prisoner, but we got to Ely to find Lady Audrey had died, only weeks before. We parted ways, he to Kent, I to come home. Lord, he told me something, about the battle. I can scarce believe it, but he said that his lord, King Elfwin, well, that his wound was in his back. It bothered me and I know not what it means, if aught, but I thought you would want to know, what with him having been the Lady Ositha's brother."

The suspicion came swiftly to Ethelred's mind and did not surprise him. Kings of Deira never ruled for long and seldom died in a fair fight or in their beds. The likelihood that Ecgfrith had ordered his own brother's death should have lifted any residual guilt, but somehow did not. He'd been right to take the fight to the Northumbrians, to a man who killed without conscience, born of a father who'd done likewise. He looked back at Bertwald, content all this time to lead a tribe, not plot to kill his half-brother Cenred. Perhaps the Mercians could still hold their heads high. Ositha, though, was still dead, and so were too many others. Far too many.

~~~~~ o ~~~~~

AD685

The scops would tell the tale. Perhaps they would embellish it, perhaps not. How he went against the advice of yet another bishop, this time Cuthbert. How, having once sworn never to be in the wrong place at the wrong time for a battle, he was fooled by his old foes. He, and his father before him, had sought always to be overlords of the Picts, forcing leaders upon them whom the Northumbrians had selected. But the Picts had risen up and had their revenge for the battle of Two Rivers and he, still reeling from the losses at the Trent, and wishing to prove himself better than his father, had ridden north to reassert his authority. They lured him into the mountains of the north, made him think that they were fleeing, and his forces were so depleted that the Northumbrian grip on the Pictish kingdom would forever be as weakened as its hold on the lands in the south.

Efa stared at the coffin, and offered up a prayer for the son she'd barely known. Ecgfrith had never truly forgiven her for giving him up as a hostage, never understood how it broke her heart to give his sister to the Church in thanks for the victory over Penda the moment she got her boy back from the Mercians. She'd never had all her children together in one place, and now had outlived them all but one. That daughter, bundled off to Hild whilst she was still a bairn in swaddling, now stood beside her, the two of them joint abbesses at Whitby since Hild's death. Oswii was here in the crypt, as was her father, Edwin, so too sweet Elfwin. Ositha was far away at Bardney and naught could be done about that now. So here, where Ecgfrith was shortly to be interred, the kin group was still not whole, even in death.

She had lived too long, buried too many children. *It is we who bear the children, bear the losses when our men and boys do not come home.* She had spoken those words to another, long ago, the woman who had cared for Ecgfrith in his childhood, the woman who had outlived too many of her own children. She'd heard from Ositha that Derwena had passed, and she'd said prayers, but was glad the pagan woman had lived to a good age. Efa felt a pat on her arm and turned to smile at her one surviving daughter. "What now?" she wondered aloud.

Alfleyda said, "I have spoken at length with dear Cuthbert, Mother. There is one who could be king."

Efa smiled, despite her sadness. She had often thought

359

about him over the years, wondering if and when he would come looking for his Northumbrian kin. Perhaps he'd heard what happened to Alfrid and Ava, and thought it best to keep away. "Will he come?"

"If he can be torn away from his books, then yes."

"It is fitting. All will be well." She patted her daughter's hand and went to offer up prayers in the chapel. One last child of Oswii's, the son of his Irish bride. A man known as a scholar, and one more likely to be found on his knees in prayer than with sword in hand.

The mist hung in the valleys, but would soon be in retreat, thinning visibly as the sun rose higher. The horses in the stables nickered softly, pleased to see him but aware that this was not their horse-thegn, and that though it was a new day, they would have to wait a while longer for food and attention. His own horse was restless in his stall, ready to go out. He fumbled with the saddle, his fingers numb with the early morning cold. Rumblings in his stomach made him question his decision to ride out without breaking fast, but now that his mind was made up, it had closed to all other possibilities. He had cheese and ale in his bag for later, and that would have to do.

Leading his horse out into the yard, he threw a rueful look at the other beasts, a silent apology that they could not come too. Mounting up, he took a last look around, at the chapel, the herb beds, the bake house where the smell of baking loaves was already wafting on the air, the weaving sheds, silent before the day's industry. The great hall, with its carved doorway and the floor which had taken the weight of so many feet, and been the scene of so many conversations and celebrations and children's games, where he himself had thrown pebbles along the length of the hall and where he'd watched his nieces and nephews and, latterly, his own son, do the same.

The guard at the gate was mid-yawn, and belatedly covered his mouth, nodding and stepping aside. The leek beds on either side of the path were full of promise, the vegetables were responding well to the welcome recent rains and would provide a good winter crop. A little way down the path, he passed an elderly couple and he waved in greeting. They were standing by the web-bedecked hedgerow, picking hips which would be pickled later in honey. Further along, the hazelnuts were almost ready for collecting, if the dormice did not get there first, and the elderberries and blackberries looked to be full and ripe. On the ground, there were nail galls on fallen beech leaves. The season was turning and over the last few days the wheatears, nightingales and cuckoos had been less noticeable. Ivy flowers were beginning to form and would soon provide food for wasps and brimstone butterflies.

He stopped when the sun was high, finding shelter under a tree by the river. He was a little way off a place that Wulf had built. Ulverley had been cleared for Wulf to build a hunting lodge but Ethelred had skirted round the little settlement. While the horse drank, he ate his cheese, drank a little of the ale, and saved the rest for later. After relieving himself, he remounted and continued on his way. The days were getting shorter, and the western sky was aglow with the red hues of the sinking sun when he arrived. The bell was being rung for Vespers, to call the sisters and brothers to Evensong. They moved with purpose but not urgency, spilling from the sheds and workshops and coming in from the fields, and the aroma of boiling fruit was released when the cook house door opened. The community was thriving, clearly, and all looked content.

Werbyra saw him before he could pick her out from the group, and she came to greet him. "My lord, welcome to Hanbury," she said and then, less formally, "Do you like it, Uncle?"

She had learned much from her time with her mother and at Ely, and Hanbury was a model of piety, order, and prosperity. "You have done better than I could have dreamed. I thank you again for coming here and founding such a wonderful abbey."

Werbyra tipped her chin in the semblance of a nod. "But it is not me you have come to see."

"Am I early? I wondered if I had left Tamworth too soon but…"

"But you could not wait, I know. No, you are not too early. Yesterday, you would have been. So all is well. I shall leave you now and go with my brothers and sisters to prayer."

He embraced her and watched her progress to the chapel, noting how others fell into step alongside her without saying a word. They all disappeared inside, and the large oak door swung shut. He stared at it for a moment, thinking how silent everything had become, and then he turned, and saw her.

He was not sure that he would be able to speak. He swallowed a few times but his mouth remained dry. It did not matter for, as always, she would have words enough for them both.

Arianwen stepped forward, her hands at her side, but she lifted them partway and then slapped them down by her hips. Was she, too, feeling awkward? She said, "You are here. I could not believe it when the rider came. I thought perhaps it was a cruel trick on someone's part."

She stepped forward into his open arms and he held her tight, his tears falling into her hair. He breathed in the scent of her, the mint herb water that always lingered, inhaling deeply as if he might hold it there inside his lungs forever. Not to store memories for the future, merely making up for lost time. There would be no farewells, not now, not tomorrow.

Her voice was muffled against his chest. "Walk with me."

"Where?"

"To the top of the knoll."

They climbed up and he took off his cloak, spreading it on the grass for her to sit on. He sat beside her, wincing at a faint twinge in his knee and all the other old war wounds, and she leaned her head on his shoulder. The clouds had moved away and it would be a clear night, with perhaps the first frost come morning. Below, he could see the last few remaining teasel flowers in the hedges and what was probably a field vole darting among the clover in the meadow. "The fall had just begun when I rode away from Wales, and here we are again, in autumn." He'd thought about bringing the amethyst necklace. "I had a gift for you. I never gave it to you, but I wrapped your gift to me around it." He and Arianwen were too old for such trinkets. Derwena would have said that the amethysts had kept him safe all those years, but he had no such belief in amulets, and needed none, not now that he had his love beside him.

"You have left all in order?"

"Cenred has been acknowledged as king. He will be a good leader and I foresee no trouble from the north. They say Aldfrith, Oswii's Irish son, is a lover of books and of God. Neither he nor my nephew have any reason to renew the fighting."

"And your own son?"

"He will be brought up as one of the hearth-thegns. What befalls him is up to Cenred, and whether he has sons of his own." In the end, he could not have done it. Even had Cærlred been old enough, Ethelred could not leave Mercia to be ruled by one who had Northumbrian blood. In this, he hoped he had done enough, played his part, not disgraced his father's legacy. To do that, he'd had to be a king, not a father, and name his nephew as heir. "It is over, for us, anyway."

She shifted position, took his face in her hands, and kissed him. He wanted to hold the kiss, not wishing ever to break away, but she let go and said, "Whenever we had to part, I always held onto one thought." She settled back against him, and they watched as the sun dipped lower and began to skim the land far in the west.

"What thought was that?"

"Daw eto haul ar fryn," she said.

They sat, looking across the land that was no longer his, to her homeland far away in the West. He repeated her words in his own tongue. "The sun will rise again. Better days will come."

Author's Notes

Northumbria never regained ascendancy and in the eighth century was so riven with internecine squabbles that its kings came looking to Mercia for marriage alliances and aid.

King Ethelred (Æthelred) of Mercia abdicated to become a monk in, we are told, the year 704 and was succeeded by his nephew, Cenred (sometimes Coenred). The *Anglo-Saxon Chronicle* also tells us that his wife (real name Osthryth), was killed by the Mercians in 697, eighteen years after the battle of the Trent. I altered both these dates for specific reasons. The first is simple: I wanted to give my character Ethelred a few years of happiness with his Welsh love first. I'll come back to Ositha's timeline and why I changed it in a moment.

It only occurred to me after I'd completed the first draft of the book that the two brothers, Wulfhere and Æthelred, as I'd written them, lived up to the translation of their historical names: Wolf Army and Noble Counsel.

Ethelred had a long and largely peaceful reign, punctuated by two moments of extreme violence – so I had to wonder why. The incursion into Kent makes little sense unless in the context of reprisal for the murder of Domneva's brothers and, to that end, I shortened the time lag between those two events. The final showdown with Northumbria came well into Ethelred's reign and is in stark contrast to Wulf's decision to campaign in the south so soon after being bested in the north, which cost him his life. Ethelred, to my mind, was not a man prone to making hasty decisions and it paid off for him. He was a remarkable leader who maintained his rule for a long time and only lost his temper twice – winning both times – and was able to retire to a monastery leaving the kingdom in capable hands.

People

Arianwen and all the other Welsh characters are fictional. It was inconceivable to me that Ethelred remained unmarried/unattached until at least 675 but there is no record, so I was free to use my imagination. Sikke and Gesina are also fictional, as is Winta of Lindsey. So too Elidyr of Elmet, Lothar, Berengar, and Aneurin, all mentioned briefly in *Cometh the Hour*. Frithuwald, the kings of the Hwicce, and the named West Saxons are real historical figures, as are all but one of the named royalty of Kent.

Edbert (Eadberht), Immin and Heaferth (Eafa) were named by Bede as the three thegns who rebelled and put Wulf on the Mercian throne. Penwal and Tette were the recorded parents of Pega, and her brother Guthlac the Hermit. Oswii's henchman Elwyn (Æthelwine) was named in the sources as a conspirator in the murder of Efa's kinsman.

Various children of Wulf's are recorded, and it is not clear who their mother/s was/were. For simplicity, I have assumed that Werbyra (Werburh/Werburgh) and Cenred were Ermenilda's children, that Bertwald (Berhtwald) was the result of an earlier liaison and have ignored the unlikely story of two other sons murdered by Wulf at Stone. He might have had another wife, Eadburh, but it's not clear whether she was his first or second wife, nor whether she was the mother of Bertwald. For ease, I left her out of the story. My erstwhile university tutor, Ann Williams, says that Bertwald had some authority in North Wiltshire and South Gloucestershire, but having chosen to make Heaferth represent the Arosæte, I realised that in my story, he was the most likely candidate for harbouring Wulf's secret child.

We have few details about Merwal (Merewalh) and his family, and we don't know when or how Merwal died. We know that Merchelm and his brother Mildfrith – not

366

mentioned in this story – were kings, possibly jointly, but it's clear that the line died out and, at some point, the Magonsæte came under direct Mercian authority. Most of what we know about this family comes from a collection of texts known as *The Mildrith Legend*, focusing on that lady's religious life. I chose not to name Mildrith's two sisters since their names – Mildburh and Mildgyth – were too confusingly similar! Merwal had a son Merfyn (Merefin) by his first wife, who did indeed die in infancy. I named him at the end of *Cometh the Hour*, but there are more than enough 'M' names in this cast list so, as he doesn't feature, except to be mentioned once, I chose not to name him and left him and his two unnamed sisters off the family tree at the beginning. Similarly, Minna's daughter was only an unnamed baby at the end of the last book, and she and Starling's daughter (both fictional) make only the briefest appearances here, so again they were left off the tree and remained unnamed.

Merchelm's wife, Bertilda, is a fictional creation. We don't know if Merchelm ever married, but Bertilda sounded a suitably Kentish name. Audra, Penda's sister, really existed and her repudiation by Cynwal (Cenwalh) of the West Saxons caused Penda to take up arms against Cynwal. She is not named in the sources, so I called her Audra. Her and Penda's brother was indeed called Eowa and featured heavily in *Cometh the Hour*.

I have no proof that Edith and Eda (Eadburh), were twins but, given the number of children accredited to 'Derwena', it seems not impossible that at least one of her pregnancies might have resulted in a multiple birth. There is some doubt as to whether they were the daughters of Derwena and Penda, so they haven't played a prominent part in the story. An interesting side-note about these two is that they are assumed to be daughters of Penda because they were, apparently, aunts to, and responsible for the upbringing of,

St Osgyth, who was the daughter of 'Starling' (Wilburh) and Frithuwald, and who ran away from an arranged marriage.

As usual, I have simplified personal names where I could. Domneva needs explanation. She appeared at the very end of *Cometh the Hour* and her real name was Domne Eafe, or Domneva. As she only briefly appeared, I called her Efi. Only when I began *The Sins of the Father* did I realise what an important part she must have played in Ethelred's life, and so she became Domneva, since Efi was too close to the name I'd given to Ecgfrith's mother, Efa (Eanflæd). Ecgfrith and Ethelred were small boys at the end of *Cometh the Hour* and had the nicknames Lief and Noni respectively.

Where possible, I've used modern versions of names. Audrey, Ecgfrith's first wife, was Æthelthryth, the saint and founder of Ely abbey. Her name was modernised to Audrey and it's where the word 'tawdry' comes from: inferior souvenirs were sold outside Ely on her feast day. According to Bede, she maintained her virginity throughout both her marriages, and we are told that Wilfrid encouraged her in this.

Other characters with name changes include:
Alfleyda – Ælfflæd
Alfrid – Alhfrith
Athelwal – Æthelwalh
Ava – Alhflæd
Carena – Cyneburh
Cærlred – Ceolred
Derwena - Cynewise
Elfwin – Ælfwine
Minna – Cyneswith
Pieter – Peada
Oswii – Oswiu/Oswy

The recorded date of Ositha's killing, eighteen years after the battle of the Trent, makes no sense to me. It might have been due to circumstances now lost to us, but it is possible that it was somehow linked to her attempts to inter Oswald's remains at Bardney, the foundation of Bardney being variously recorded as occurring in 679 or 697. Ositha was reportedly killed in 697. Could that date have been transposed? It would make more sense if she pushed hard for the translation of the remains shortly after the battle and was killed not long afterwards. It is recorded that the monks refused, at first, to accept the remains as they did not remember Oswald kindly.

It's assumed that Ethelred favoured Cenred as his successor over his own son because apparently Cærlred was a drunkard and a wastrel who came to a bad end, but the truth is we don't know when or where he was born; he may simply have been too young to rule. We don't even know when Ethelred and Ositha married. Some sources say the wedding took place before the battle of the Trent, and some as a consequence of the battle, and that Ethelred had to marry Ositha in recompense for the death of Elfwin. I think they must already have been married at that point, because we are told that Elfwin spent time at the Mercian court and, had his sister not already been living there, I see no reason why he would have travelled south into enemy territory.

The abbess at Coldingham was called Æbbe. She was thought to be a sister of Oswald and Oswii but might in fact only have been a half-sister. Since she did not appear in *Cometh the Hour*, I have kept the relationship vague.

The Meonwara of modern-day Hampshire were also known as the Meonsæte but that looks too similar on the page to Magonsæte so I used the alternative name. Likewise at this time the West Saxons should probably be referred to as the Gewisse but I felt that readers would be more familiar with the West Saxons, who ruled what would one day be called Wessex. Although Merwal ruled the territory of the Magonsæte in modern-day Herefordshire they might not have used the name for themselves during this period but again, for ease, I've used the name most associated with this area.

Places

As noted above, there is some uncertainty about when exactly the abbey at Bardney was built. It had definitely been founded by 697 but might have been around before that so I'm using licence, to fit in with my theory that Ositha, who was indeed buried there – as was Ethelred, eventually – was killed earlier than 697.

Ashdown, where the Mercians fought the West Saxons, is probably in modern-day Berkshire, and not the Ashdown in Kent. Cuthred was given land by Cynwal in this area and was killed in 661, so it's not unreasonable to suppose that when the *Anglo-Saxon Chronicle* tells us that Wulfhere 'harried on Ashdown' this was the outcome.

All of the places and settlements mentioned existed at the time. Ulverley does seem to have been a hunting lodge of Wulfhere's (it translates as Wulf's Clearing). This period, where people spoke a language that was not English as we know it, can feel inaccessible so I've once again taken the decision to use modern-day place names, with a few exceptions. Edinburgh was known as Dùn Èideann and since Alfrid is the one who talks about it, I kept the British name. The place of Stoche where Carena and Ethelred stayed became Stoke Prior. Medeshamstede Abbey was begun by Pieter and Oswii, and work continued under Wulf's reign. It became Peterborough Abbey. Northworthy was the Old English name for Derby, which is very much a 'Viking' name and since they hadn't arrived at this point, I used the Old English name.

We don't know where the battle of the Trent was actually fought, nor who was the aggressor, but Ethelred was the victor, and Elfwin was indeed killed. Bede tells us he was a youth of eighteen, and much loved in both kingdoms.

Events

After the synod of Whitby, Wilfrid left for Gaul, claiming that he had to go abroad to be consecrated as bishop of Northumbria, since no one in England had the necessary authority to perform the service. He had the habit of rubbing people up the wrong way and I have simplified his eventful career. Alfrid disappeared after Whitby; we can't know what happened, but he does seem to have issued a challenge to his father and conveniently vanished afterwards. A plague was indeed recorded for the year 664. There is a story that Alfrid was killed by Oswii's forces at Ebberston, but it is purely legend, and we don't know for sure what happened to him after the synod. (I happened upon this tale after I had made Ecgfrith his assassin, and decided to keep it so, as there is no documentary evidence that I can find for the battle at Ebberston.)

Audrey's escape from Northumbria was said, in one version of the story, to have been facilitated by the abbess of Coldingham, with the sisters praying for a flood which held back Ecgfrith's forces.

There is indeed a story that Domneva, after the murder of her brothers, tricked her cousin Ecbert (Ecgberht), the king of Kent, into giving her far more land than he'd expected to have to yield. She founded the abbey at Minster-in-Thanet which still thrives as a religious community. I did change the timeline here a little. Ethelred razed Rochester at the time depicted, but Ecbert was dead by then, and the murders happened a few years earlier than I've suggested here. We have few clues to explain Ethelred's uncharacteristic attack on Kent and the theory that best suited my story was that it was in retribution for the murders, so I altered the date to suit my narrative.

Eddius Stephanus, author of the *Life of St Wilfrid*, tells us that at the battle in 674, Ecgfrith was indeed outnumbered by Wulfhere's forces.

There was a recorded famine in 680 caused by three years of drought.

Bede tells a story of a nobleman, Imma, captured at the battle of the Trent who revealed himself to be an erstwhile member of Audrey's household. This is one of the reasons we know that the queens of Northumbria kept separate households. The secret that he tells Ermenilda, though, about Elfwin's death, is my – not implausible – invention.

According to Bede, Ecgfrith's decision to go to battle against the Picts in 685 was "much against the advice of his friends, and particularly of Cuthbert ... who had been lately ordained his bishop." Bede tells how Ecgfrith was drawn into "the straits of inaccessible mountains" after the enemy pretended to have fled.

Historical Detail

Seventh-century gaming pieces have been found, notably in the famous Taplow burial. There was a board game called Merels, so I have used the name to describe what the characters are playing.

An amethyst necklace as described here was found in a seventh-century grave. Those who've read *Cometh the Hour* might have spotted that Ethelred had a purse of garnets, which I like to think was kept back when his mother's servant buried the Staffordshire Hoard. Perhaps Derwena did not want to send her son off on his own without some 'money in his pocket'.

The Welsh refer to the English, but the Mercians, Northumbrians, West Saxons *et al* did not think of themselves thus, so the term English is anachronistic, but I used it for ease when referring to more than one of the 'Anglo-Saxon' kingdoms, or when the Welsh characters are talking about them.

I have occasionally used the term 'princess' which was not

a word known in this period, nor was it really a concept, but I have used it as there is no female equivalent of atheling, which technically didn't mean prince (son of a king) but one who was throne-worthy.

The lullaby which Arianwen sings is in Old Welsh, rather than modern Welsh and comes from *Y Gododdin*, written by a Welshman in honour of the Gododdin, a Brythonic people who fought at the battle of Catraeth (possibly Catterick, North Yorkshire) in 600. It is possible that it was an oral tradition before being written down and might well have been familiar to the British in the north. (Taken from https://www.gutenberg.org/files/9842/9842-h/9842-h.htm and free to use). As historian Alex Woolf recently pointed out, many babes would have been rocked in their cradles by women who spoke a different language, be they distant relatives, servants, or slaves. It is likely that people were able to communicate with those from other kingdoms. On the subject of communication, it is known that personal letters were sent in the early 700s, but they are unlikely to have been used much earlier, and certainly not in the vernacular. Therefore the Mercians see only Latin, written by scribes who were monks. It might well have been different in Wales, which is why I deemed it plausible that Llywarch might have received a letter written in Welsh.

A water mill was excavated at Tamworth in 1971. It dated from a later period but there is evidence which suggests that water mills existed in the seventh century, so it is possible that there was an earlier one on that site.

In the story, Merchelm marries Bertilda at Michaelmas. I've kept it vague, calling it the 'dying of the old season' but old Michaelmas was 11th October rather than 29th September. There has been some suggestion that Christmas was once observed at the time of the winter solstice.

Kings and courts at this time were itinerant and I have tried to give a flavour of this, but I have pared it down, rather than have my characters permanently on the road. Some may wonder about the lack of mention of the Witan (the king's council), but this was very early on in the conversion period and whilst the Witan undoubtedly met, it was not so formal or well-established, especially in Mercia, as later in the period. We have no extant charters of Oswii's, only one of Ecgfrith's, and in Mercia only one of Wulf's, and ten of Ethelred's. It must be remembered that literacy comes with Christianity, and Wulf was the first Christian king of Mercia, so we might assume that formal business was not being recorded on 'paper' as much during this period. It is likely that the Mercians, ironically, were converted not by 'Roman' but British priests and so actually had something in common with Oswii.

And speaking of religion, it might seem strange that I've portrayed Christians as being tolerant of paganism, but I assume that, given how newly converted the people were, and the numbers who apostatised, there was a certain amount of 'rubbing along' and that Ethelred would have respected his mother's views.

Acknowledgements

My thanks go to: Anne Phillips, for helping me with some aspects of Welsh period detail, to Cathy Helms of Avalon Graphics (www.avalongraphics.org) for designing the cover and producing the map of the ancient kingdoms, and to Lin White at Coinlea Services (www.coinlea.co.uk) for turning my – very – rough sketch into the family tree. Writing is a solitary occupation, but never lonely, and I am grateful to the 'Historical Fictioneers' Cryssa Bazos, Anna Belfrage, and Charlene Newcomb for their support and their willingness to become a sounding board during the dreaded blurb-writing process, and the inimitable Helen Hollick without whom etc. A cliché, but true!

Other Novels by Annie Whitehead

To Be A Queen The story of Æthelflæd, Lady of the Mercians, daughter of Alfred the Great, and the only female leader of an Anglo-Saxon kingdom. Born into the royal house of Wessex at the height of the Viking wars, she must fight to save her adopted Mercia from the Vikings and, ultimately, her own brother.

"Well-written and well-researched. A remarkable novel." ~ Historical Novel Society (HNS)

Alvar the Kingmaker A king's reign begins with scandal, and his young life is cut short. Can Earl Alvar keep the throne secure for his even younger successor? And when another king is murdered and civil war ensures, can he protect his loved ones whilst also ensuring the queen's safety?

"Ms Whitehead knows her stuff - A must-read for anyone interested in the early Anglo-Saxon period."
~ Helen Hollick, author of *The Pendragon Trilogy*, *Harold the King*, *A Hollow Crown*, & *The Sea Witch Series*

Cometh the Hour Four kings, connected by blood and marriage, vie for the mantle of overlord. Three affect to rule with divine assistance. The fourth, whose cousin and sister have been mistreated and whose friend has been slaughtered, watches, and waits. He is a pagan, he is a Mercian, and his name is Penda.

"With a careful hand and keen appreciation for the era's material culture, Annie Whitehead, the inaugural winner of the HWA Dorothy Dunnett Short Story Competition, depicts five tumultuous decades in early medieval Britain. A solid choice for fans of the period." ~ HNS

9 781803 022307